The peace settled into her soul ... soothing the restless need to run that had consumed her since she'd hit Nicholas with the whiskey bottle.

When she wandered back to the cabin, she expected Ryder to be in bed, but he was still in the tub, his knees drawn up, pale and knobby, his head resting on the rim.

She grabbed Beau by the scruff of his neck and shoved him outside closing the door with a sharp bang.

Ryder jerked upright, sloshing water over the sides.

"I'm sorry," she said. "I'll come back."

"No." He leaned back and closed his eyes. "I'm done. I just want to wash my hair."

"I can do it for you." Before the words were out of her mouth, she questioned what part of her brain they'd come from.

Maybe it was because Ryder was safe, and this was a chance to physically connect with a man on her own terms, without fear.

Maybe she needed to satisfy the curiosity that had taunted her all week, urging her to explore the body of this man she desired.

But maybe it was simply because he was Ryder MacKenzie, and in his own determined, unassuming way, he'd touched her heart and become her hero, and there would never again be a man she so ached to know.

Praise for *A TARNISHED KNIGHT*

Second Place Winner of
2013 Pennwriters Inc. Annual Writing Contest
Novel Beginnings Category

A
Tarnished Knight

by

Kathy Otten

Carole,
Enjoy your time
with Ryder & Victoria,
and Percy too.
Thanks! :)
Kathy Otten

A Tarnished Knight

Cover Art by *Debbie Taylor*

The Wild Rose Press, Inc.
PO Box 708
Adams Basin, NY 14410-0708
Visit us at www.thewildrosepress.com

Publishing History
First Cactus Rose Edition, 2013
Print ISBN 978-1-62830-057-4
Digital ISBN 978-1-62830-058-1

Published in the United States of America

Dedication

Kevin,
Never quit.
This one's for you.
Now you have to read it.
Love you.

Chapter One

Hidden in shadow, Victoria shifted in the wing chair, the black silk of her peignoir sliding easily against the velvet cushion.

Light from a small lamp spilled across the smooth surface of her husband's desk. Behind his leather chair, the glow from a pair of pewter sconces warmed the cherry patina of the paneled wall. The golden halo of their combined light cast the corners of Nicholas' study into darkness.

Focusing her gaze on the closed paneled door, she strained her ears for the faintest click of his heels against the polished marble floor. She held her breath for several seconds, listening. Tick-tock, tick-tock. The knot inside her chest loosened a bit.

She switched her gaze to the fireplace and to the Seth Thomas clock which stood on the mantel. Behind the clock's glass door, the minute hand crept toward the hour of three. On the lower half of the glass, a picture of rolling hills and a lake with a small sailboat had been painted to hide the swinging pendulum. The pastoral scene was as beautifully crafted as the mahogany timepiece, but she hated it, just as she loathed every knick-knack and item of furniture in this house.

Nicholas had given her the clock on her last birthday. Before she could lift it from the box, he'd snatched it from her hands. With an appreciative smile, he gazed at the timepiece. "This will look perfect on the mantel in my study." Of course, he'd been right; the clock did look nice there.

Nicholas always knew what looked good, and he cultivated his refined taste by selecting only the highest quality, from his French wines, to his tailored suits, to the art which hung from the walls of his lavishly decorated mansion. He'd even chosen his wife by those same high standards.

Victoria should have been pleased he thought her such a perfect example of womanhood, but instead she despised him for it.

She leaned back in the chair, allowing her aching spine the chance to sink into the padded comfort of the cushion behind her. Maybe Nicholas forgot. Maybe he wasn't coming. *Fool*, she chided herself. Nicholas never forgets. Nicholas always comes.

Once-upon-a-time her imagination flowed with fanciful notions of princes and princesses, evil dragons, and happily-ever-afters. No more. That naïve girl vanished soon after her wedding. In her place existed an empty shell, like a Meissen figurine, beautiful, hollow, and easily broken.

She shivered and wrapped her arms around herself, wishing Nicholas had ordered a fire to be lit. Though it wasn't usually cold in New York the first week of June, rain this evening had left the air damp and chilly. She longed for the warm flannel nightgowns and robe she'd worn when she was young, when her grandmother cuddled her close, passed her a lemon drop, and chased away her nightmares with tales of knights, and ogres, and faraway kingdoms.

Low voices rumbled in the hallway beyond the

paneled door. Her heartbeat quickened and she jerked upright, her spine six inches from the back of the chair, her hands folded in her lap.

Nicholas entered and strode straight to his desk. Apparently he didn't see her in the darkened corner, for he pulled open a drawer, dropped a thick packet inside, and pushed it closed. Lowering himself into his chair, he looked directly across the room to the threshold.

"Get in here, Palmer, and close the door." He gestured with a wave of his hand. Silent on well-oiled hinges, the door shut with a soft click.

Victoria shifted her gaze to the man standing just inside the study. His eye patch immediately caught her attention, a circle of leather over his left eye, with dark ribbons that reached around his head to tie at the back. Silver streaked his black hair and mutton chop sideburns. He wore a coarse black suit, the cuffs ragged where they brushed the heels of his scuffed shoes. He seemed the antithesis to Nicholas' immaculate clothing and blond, Adonis-like, good looks.

She squeezed her interlaced fingers together so tightly her bones hurt. Should she tell Nicholas she was here? He'd left her specific instructions to meet him in his study when he returned home. Her maid had awakened her twenty minutes ago on the word of the butler, Sullivan, that Nicholas had arrived.

However, her husband never permitted her to meet his business associates. Should she stay quiet? Would he punish her for not speaking up? Her heart thudded against her chest. Every muscle in her body tensed, poised to race for the door.

The leather chair creaked as Nicholas leaned back and fixed his ice-blue glare on Palmer's face. "Tell me precisely what Thorndyke said."

The man shifted uncomfortably. "I marked him waitin' at the bridge like ya said…" His baritone voice held an abrasive quality, like a pebble rolled against cobblestone beneath the ball of her shoe. "…but he had two young coves with him."

"Who were they?"

"Dunno, but they was dressed too fine to be Jack coves."

"Hmmm." Resting his elbows on the arms of his chair, Nicholas steepled his fingers and tapped the tips together. "They must have been his sons, Phillip and…."

Spencer, Victoria almost said aloud. She'd danced with both of them at one function or another. Handsome young men, but as pretentious as their father, a cold man she hated almost as much as her husband.

Nicholas snapped his fingers. "Spencer."

She knew he'd remember. He never forgot anything.

Palmer shrugged.

Nicholas inclined his head, and Palmer continued.

"Thorndyke, he give me the envelope with the blunt an' said 'twas his last payment. He's done payin' ex-tra…ex-tro-shun…"

"Extortion."

"That's it, sir. He said there'd be no payment next month an' if I give him any trouble, he'd have me hauled afore the local beak."

"Well, we can't have that now, can we? We'll have to send Mr. Ainsworth Thorndyke a little reminder that I am not a man to be toyed with. One of his sons will serve our purpose."

"Yes, sir. If ya want, I can kill the cove for a century."

Nicholas smiled.

Once upon a time, Victoria had imagined that wide smile to be a reflection of his kind heart. Now she recognized the calculating leer for what it was—an expression of his twisted nature.

"A hundred dollars?" Nicholas chuckled. "Is that what you charged Thorndyke all those years ago? I wasn't aware murder could be bought so cheaply. Fortunately for me, Thorndyke didn't think to purchase your silence as well."

Nicholas rose and gave the bell pull behind him a tug. Then he withdrew his billfold, stepped around his desk, and held out some money. "For completing your errand tonight."

Palmer reached forward and snatched the bills from Nicholas' fingers.

Nicholas chuckled. "There, you see, Palmer, how easily you've earned ten dollars. I will let you know when I want you to deliver my message. I only ask that you control your enthusiasm this time. I do not want Thorndyke's son found beaten to death in an alley like young Weston. This time motive could be easily traced back to me."

Victoria gasped. Immediately, she shoved the meaty part of her hand between her teeth and clamped down. Nicholas turned, his gaze riveted on her corner.

She sat paralyzed, afraid to breathe. To her astonishment, he returned his attention to Palmer. A surge of hope swelled inside her, grateful Nicholas had chosen the black negligee for her to wear tonight. Her muscles ached, and she longed to shrink back into the upholstery, but she held herself still, terrified the slightest movement would draw his attention.

Dear God, Nicholas had had Stephen Weston *killed*! Her stomach rolled, and she shoved her hand tighter against her mouth so she wouldn't be ill. Last week she'd been horrified to learn, along with everyone else, that Stephen had been found dead in an alley near Five Points, presumably the victim of a robbery gone wrong. She'd never imagined Nicholas had been behind it.

Had it been because Stephen had flirted with her during a dinner party two weeks ago? Had it been because his silly stories had made her laugh? She blinked against the burning in her eyes. He'd been so young, so energetic. How could Nicholas believe he had the right to end a man's life over some harmless teasing at dinner?

What about Stephen's parents, his sisters? And now Nicholas was blackmailing Ainsworth Thorndyke and threatening to have one of his sons beaten because he didn't want to pay. Who did Nicholas think he was?

A knock sounded against the door.

"Come in, Sullivan."

The butler entered. His black suit was immaculate even at this late hour.

She despised the balding, middle-aged man whose dour expression never changed. She hated him for spying on her and reporting her every move back to Nicholas. She hated him for being her husband's lackey, for turning a deaf ear to all that went on in this house, and for not being man enough to help her, on that first day and every day after.

And though he never looked her way, she was

certain he was aware of her presence. Nothing happened in this house Sullivan didn't know about. He knew Nicholas had been delayed, that she would arrive in this room first, and she would suffer the punishment. The toady was as depraved as her husband.

"Sullivan, please see my guest out."

Palmer turned and walked past the butler into the hall.

"And Sullivan, that will be all for tonight."

"Yes sir." He gave Nicholas a slight bow. "Thank you, sir." Backing out of the study, he pulled the door closed with a soft click. Her only chance was if Nicholas left the room. Instead he moved around the desk and stopped within a few feet of her wing chair.

Her body went numb. Her breath escaped in short rapid puffs.

"What are you doing here?" he demanded. "Spying?"

She shrank away from him, pressing her shoulders against the back of the chair. "I'm sorry. I thought I was to wait—"

Reaching out, he grabbed her arm and yanked her from her seat.

"I'm sorry." Her fingers tingled as his grip around her wrist tightened.

"You are *never* to be in this room when I'm conducting business." He drew back his hand and slapped her, snapping her head to the side. She stumbled, but with her arm held tight, she didn't fall.

Her free hand reached up to press against her burning cheek.

"My personal business matters are not your concern."

His next blow slammed against her temple. The force of its impact sent her reeling. Nicholas released his hold, and her shoulder slammed into the edge of the book shelf. Pain radiated through her body as she tumbled to the floor.

"Please, I'm sorry…" Tears slipped down her cheeks. She rolled to her knees and waited with her gaze lowered to the carpet the way he liked. Streaks of lamplight reflected in the tips of his polished shoes, and she braced for the impact of a kick.

"I dislike seeing you so cowed. Stand up."

Slowly, she obeyed. Her knees trembled so badly she had to lock them to keep them from buckling. Her stomach shivered the way it had last winter when he refused to allow her inside the house. What new game did he play tonight? Waiting was torture. At least when she knew what came next she could prepare.

"Look at me, Victoria."

She lifted her gaze to his face. Once upon a time a passing glimpse of his handsome features set her heart aflutter. With his blond hair and blue eyes, his broad forehead and high cheekbones, and his straight nose and strong jaw, she'd written in her diary he was perfect, as beautiful as Michelangelo's David. Now she knew better. His perfect face meant nothing, for his heart was evil.

"I'm feeling rather exhilarated tonight." A sneer pulled back the corner of his mouth. "I want you to look at me the way you used to."

He must know he'd killed her love for him years ago. Did he now have regrets? She was good at pretending, but she wasn't the actress her grandmother had been.

He grabbed her upper arms and gave her a quick shake. "Where's the fire, Victoria? I want to see that fire in your eyes again. I want you to fight me the way you did when we first married."

She blinked at him in disbelief.

"Go on, Victoria. Scream, scratch, kick, hit, throw things. Make me work for it. I don't want you to just lie down and spread your legs." He gave her another shake and shoved her away.

She stumbled back into the corner, catching herself with one hand on the back of the chair and the other on the bookcase. She'd lost the will to fight him years ago when she learned that doing so only brought more pain.

She would never win. There was no way out. Yet if she didn't force herself to give him what he wanted, her punishment would be worse than the bruises she'd receive during this twisted game.

Snatching a book from the shelf, she threw it at the center of his chest. It fell to the floor without touching him.

"Come on, Victoria, fight me." He stepped closer. She moved behind the chair. She glanced around for something else to throw, and her eyes fell on an onyx sculpture of a knight on a rearing destrier.

In one smooth motion, she whisked it from the shelf and threw it at his head. It grazed his temple and hit the carpet with a thump. She gasped.

Nicholas touched his fingers to his head, looked at them and then at her. Seeing the trickle of blood, she dashed across the room, behind his desk.

Frantic, she searched for something other than papers to throw. Her hand closed around the inkwell. She hurled it toward his head. He ducked, and the small bottle hit the carpet—his imported Persian carpet.

Her gaze shot to his face. His nostrils flared as he stared at the spreading stain. "Look at what you've done," he bit out.

She darted around the desk and dropped to her knees. With a shaking hand, she picked up the inkwell as she blotted the black stain with the hem of her nightgown.

"Get up! I don't want some cringing servant girl. Come on, Victoria, defy me." He drew back his foot.

Instead of rolling away as she usually did, this time she reached out, grabbed his foot with both hands, and shoved it above her head. He crashed to the floor as she jumped to her feet and ran for the door.

A hand clamped around her ankle. She shrieked as her hands and knees slammed against the floor. Twisting around, she kicked. Her heel smashed against his nose. Through the thin sole of her slipper, she felt the crunch of cartilage, and his hand loosed its grip.

He would punish her for hurting him. Terrified, she scrambled to her feet and dashed around the desk. Nicholas snapped out a vicious curse as he stood. His hand clamped over his nose; blood dripped through his fingers onto his snowy-white shirt. She yanked open each drawer, flinging aside the packet of blackmail money, as well as every pen and piece of paper.

"If you're looking for my gun, it's not in there."

She looked up.

He stood grinning at her from across the desk. Lamp light reflected in his ice-blue eyes, while the blood which smeared his face resembled the fire of an evil dragon.

She ducked down and dug through the bottom

drawer, but all she found was a long-necked bottle of something.

He lunged across the expanse and grabbed a hank of her hair. A squeal escaped her throat. As she felt herself being lifted up, her fingers wrapped around the neck of the bottle. Her other hand reached for his. Digging her fingernails into the thin skin above his knuckles, she scratched and clawed at his fist, trying to free herself.

He laughed and pulled, dragging her up over the edge of the desk. The roots of her hair tore from her scalp. His other arm stretched toward her. She tried to twist away, but he grabbed a fistful of her nightgown and pulled.

Swinging the weighted bottle like a club, she smashed it against the side of his head. The bottle didn't break, but Nicholas collapsed limp across the desk. His fingers lax, yet still woven through her hair, Victoria frantically pulled free, leaving strands of blonde tangled around the fingers of his bleeding hand.

She backed away, staring at him, terrified this was a ruse. Hefting the bottle, she waited for him to rise and come at her again.

Was he dead or pretending? While she stood frozen in place, her mind spun through a dozen scenarios. Should she call Sullivan? Hide in her room? But the thought that screamed the loudest was—Run!

While the servants slept and without taking a moment to change clothes, Victoria Anne Winters Van Der Beck snatched the packet of money, dashed across the room, flung open the door and fled the house, her slippers silent as she raced into the night.

****

From the refuge of shadow, Ryder MacKenzie leaned into the light. "I'll raise you two." He tossed two silver dollars in succession toward the center of the table. A soft chinking sound followed each coin as it hit the pile of, what was for most men, a month's wages.

Though only a few scattered lanterns illuminated the tiny log building, it was enough for Ryder to notice the bounty hunter, known as Flint, didn't fidget or lick his lips or look at his cards. He appeared calm, almost bored.

Ryder leaned back, retreating into the gloom, and mentally cursed. He should have called. Shifting slightly, feigning a confidence he did not feel, he braced the ball of his foot on the edge of the nearest chair. With only five dollars left to his name, if Flint raised the stakes again, Ryder would have to fold or sell his saddle. But damn, there was close to thirty dollars in that pot.

His pulse thrummed against his jaw as he waited for Flint to decide. The first time Ryder raised the stakes, he'd hoped Flint would fold, but the man had immediately raised the bet.

Ryder reached for his beer, forcing himself to maintain his façade of indifference. He lifted the glass and swallowed the warm brew. Without shifting his gaze, he studied Flint's deeply etched features from across the table.

Grabbing a nearly empty bottle of whiskey, Flint tipped it to his mouth, his lips all but hidden beneath a long drooping moustache. Wiping his mouth on the sleeve of his buckskin shirt, he called out, "Hey, barkeep, what time you got?"

"Quarter past three," the man replied from behind a

counter that was nothing more than a wide plank set across two oak barrels.

Flint downed the last of his whiskey and set the bottle on the table. "Well, MacKenzie." He sighed. "I reckon I got all the money from you I can get, so I'm packing it in for the night. I'm heading out at sun-up, and I got me a little red-headed gal waiting over to Miss Belle's." He tossed his money onto the pile. "Call."

Dread twisted Ryder's stomach like a wet rag. He spread his cards out on the scarred, wooden surface. A full house—jacks over sevens.

"Sorry, MacKenzie." Flint chuckled. With casual finesse, he tossed his cards across the table, where they landed face up and fanned out, right beside Ryder's losing hand.

Four nines. Ryder stared at them for several heart beats, foolishly hoping the next time he blinked they would have transformed into two nines and two sixes, or two eights and two threes, any combination that would bring the wonderful pile of money sliding across the table to fill his pockets instead of Flint's.

He swallowed his bitterness with the rest of his beer.

"Are you broke again, MacKenzie?" Flint taunted.

"None of your damn business."

The bounty hunter reached inside his shirt and withdrew a cigar along with a folded piece of paper. He tossed the paper across the table as he bit off the end of his cigar and spit the piece on the floor.

"I do hate seein' you down on your luck again, so I'll throw this little bone your way if your interested." He struck a Lucifer against the table top and held the flame to one end of the rolled tobacco while he puffed on the other.

Ryder unfolded a telegram for Arnold Pratt of the Pinkerton Agency. LOST LADY IN KEARNEY STOP BOARDED U.P. WESTBOUND STOP PLEASE INTERCEPT

"What is this?"

Flint leaned back in his chair and blew a cloud of gray straight across the table. "'Member Arnold Pratt? He was a railroad detective before he went to Pinkerton."

Ryder shook his head.

"It was years back when you met him. Well I seen him in Ogallala this afternoon. Played a little draw poker. He tells me some rich, fancy pants, New York city-boy had a fight with his spoiled, little wife, and she run away. So her husband, Nicholas Vandy Beck, hires Pinkerton to bring her back. Seems agents been watchin' westbound trains up and down the line, tryin' to catch her. Someone seen her and sent word to Pratt."

Ryder tossed the telegram on the table and leaned back in his chair. Van Der Beck was an old New York family with even older money. They hobnobbed with the Rockefellers and the Vanderbilts. A society to which Ryder's own family had only danced around the fringes. He lifted his gaze to the bounty hunter. "What's this got to do with me?"

Flint shrugged. "Pratt owed me. 'Sides, he already had a prisoner with him. Some con man stealin' money from old ladies. He's plannin' to tell Pinkerton the wife give him the slip. All's you got to do is take her home, unharmed and untouched, and collect five thousand dollars."

"Five thousand dollars? Why are you telling me?"

Exhaling a cloud of smoke, Flint said, "Reckon it ain't right those cattle thieves ambushin' you like they done and shootin' your horse."

Ryder frowned. "It wasn't, but again, why are you giving this to me?"

"'Cause I like you MacKenzie. 'Sides, I got plans. I don't reckon I got the time to traipse all the way to New York City with some female that don't want to go."

Ryder stared at the telegram until the edges blurred. He'd known Flint too long. The man was up to something. Blinking the paper back into focus, he met Flint's gaze. "You're putting together money for another one of those secret high stakes games. Seems odd, you not wanting the reward."

Flint shrugged. "I got what I need, and like I said, I ain't got the time, but sounds like you could use some cash."

Ryder eyed him skeptically. "Just take her back? You sure it's that simple? Van Der Beck isn't hiding something?"

Flint stood. Thick cigar smoke swirled around his head and hung like fog between the beams of the low ceiling.

"Don't know. I been following her since Ogallala. When she got off the train here, I sent a telegram to this Vandy Beck feller, letting him know she'd been spotted. Seems set on catching the stage south in the mornin'. Reckon she's trying to throw the Pinkertons off her trail. She's all yours iffin you want." He started toward the front of the saloon.

Ryder stood also, tossing his saddlebags and bedroll over his shoulder. He'd had his fill years ago of spoiled, rich princesses who looked down their noses at anyone less than perfect. He wasn't all that anxious to get involved with another one.

He collected his rifle in its scabbard from where it leaned against the wall behind his chair, picked up the telegram, and stuffed it in his vest pocket.

All he could picture was some beautiful, well-dressed, young woman with the façade of an angel and the temper of a shrew. His gut told him something was off kilter with this whole scheme, but five thousand dollars… "How am I supposed to find this spoiled little princess?"

"Go down to the rooming house near the tracks and wait for her to come out in the morning."

Ryder followed then stopped near the door where he'd dropped his saddle when he'd come inside. He leaned over and hooked his hand in the hole just behind the pommel then swung it over his shoulder.

Outside, Flint turned left toward Miss Belle's.

Ryder could grab the princess in the morning and take her to Ogallala. He could stash her someplace while he checked the area for his stolen cattle. The rustlers had been driving the herd east. It was his guess they had a buyer waiting. With the new loading chute and cattle pens being built, his herd could easily be sold and shipped to Chicago.

A week ago he'd been sitting on a rise, looking out across land dotted with his cattle, admiring his new crop of calves. In those fleeting moments, life had been good. He'd been on the verge of success, ready to retire from a life of chasing down outlaws, sleeping on the ground, and constantly watching his back. Finally he had value. He was no longer worthless.

Now it was gone. And come hell or high water, he was not going to let those two-bit cattle thieves take it all away, but just in case…

"Flint!" Ryder yelled into the darkness. "What does this princess look like?"

Laughter rolled down the street like a tumbleweed. "Last I seen her, she was big as a heifer, wearing black."

Ryder nodded and turned toward the livery where he planned to bed down. Maybe this wouldn't be so bad after all. At least she wasn't pretty.

Chapter Two

Victoria shifted her bulky, unwieldy body on the hard bench, trying to ease the kinks from her back. At least she had the extra padding her widow's costume provided. Resting against the log wall of this cabin which served as the stage station, she returned to her knitting.

Her new friend, Mary Donovan, sat beside her. Though Mary must have been just as uncomfortable, she sat reading her book as serenely as a nun absorbed in her Bible. A buxom widow, Mary had gravitated to Victoria on the train, more than likely assuming the loss of her husband would be understood by Victoria.

At first she felt guilty for deceiving Mary, but she came to realize it didn't matter. They just enjoyed each other's company, and Victoria had been lonely for a long time. Then yesterday when she suspected the man in the buckskin shirt was following her, Mary had inadvertently provided the perfect solution by inviting Victoria to spend some time with her at her brother's ranch. Victoria declined but agreed to accompany Mary to her destination then continue to Greeley and take the train to Denver from there.

So far the ploy seemed to have worked. The man had gotten off the train when she did but had made no move toward her.

Then in the early hours before sunup, Victoria and

Mary had walked to the livery. Mary had made arrangements the day before to have the livery owner drive them across the South Platte River, to the stage station which had once marked the town of Julesburg in the days before the railroad. Their hope was to catch the stage as it came through first thing in the morning.

Though she searched for him, Victoria saw no sign of the man from the train. Maybe she'd been wrong, and Nicholas hadn't hired him to find her. Though it was a possibility, she couldn't afford to take that chance. She hoped to lose herself in San Francisco before Nicholas found her.

With the thick envelope of Thorndyke's money and a carpetbag stuffed with old costumes from a shop in New York, Victoria began her round-about journey west. Taking this little-used stage route would be perfect.

A steady rain began shortly after they arrived at the small, single-story cabin. Cursing under his breath, the stationmaster set buckets out in various places to catch the scattered drips. Wind lashed against the windows, causing the rain to ping like sleet against the glass.

The door swung open. Rain blew in with a gust of cold air. Victoria looked up to see the silhouette of a man in the doorway.

"Shut the damn door!" the stationmaster yelled even as the man kicked it closed with his foot.

Water dripped off his black hat and black, gum rubber poncho. He stepped toward the corner where she and Mary had placed their bags and dropped a saddle and saddlebags onto the dirt floor. He leaned a rifle in its scabbard against the pile then pulled off his hat and poncho, shook them out, and draped them over his saddle.

He turned and met her gaze from across the room. Though lamplight only brightened small areas of the cabin, making it hard to discern his exact features, she was immediately struck by how handsome he was. His light brown hair, parted slightly off center, fell on either side of his forehead. Dark stubble covered the length of his jaw line and coated his upper lip. He had a straight nose and strong chin with a small indent. Oddly, she had the fleeting sense that she'd seen him before.

His brow tugged together briefly as he looked from her to Mary and back again.

The corners of her mouth quirked up at his confused expression. She and Mary must look like twins—two widows of identical size sitting side by side.

"Damn, MacKenzie," declared the stationmaster. "What happened to you? Where's your horse?"

Through the gloom Victoria noticed the deep red of a bad bruise running the width of his cheek bone, up into the hair line at his temple.

"Ran into a bit of trouble with some rustlers. They shot my horse."

At least he wasn't a man of violence, prone to bar room brawls and fits of temper.

"Damn, what's the world comin' to? Shootin' a man's horse. Sonsabitches ought'a be hung."

MacKenzie moved to the table and lowered his lean frame onto a three-legged stool. He leaned forward then stopped just short of resting his forearms on the greasy table top. Straightening, he crossed them over his chest instead.

The stationmaster lifted a blue enamelware mug off

a shelf. "Coffee?"

"Obliged."

The stationmaster reached for the pot on the back of the stove and filled the cup. Moving to the table, he set the mug down next to a glass cruet. The stopper lay beside the bottle; a dozen or more dead flies floated on top of what Victoria assumed was vinegar.

The stationmaster had offered them coffee earlier, and while Mary had accepted a cup, Victoria declined, reluctant to remove either her heavy veil or the cotton handkerchiefs stuffed between her cheeks and gums.

She was glad now that her disguise remained intact. From the way MacKenzie kept looking between her and Mary, he'd either never seen a widow before or he knew who she was.

He stood and stretched. Picking up his coffee mug, he dropped it into the same bucket Mary had placed her dirty cup earlier.

"How long before the stage gets here?"

The stationmaster shrugged. "An hour or so after sunup."

"You have any work needs doing?"

"Broke again, MacKenzie?"

MacKenzie stiffened and glanced her way. She switched her attention back to her knitting.

"I need a horse."

"Goin' after them rustlers?"

"No. I got word on Hiram Everett, and I need a good horse to go after him. Reckon I'd be grateful to hitch a ride out to Bud Parks place. I hear he's got quality mounts."

The stationmaster snorted. "Hear he charges pretty damn good for 'em, too." He spit a gob of brown into a dented Wells Fargo spittoon on the floor.

"Okay, MacKenzie." He wiped his mouth on his sleeve. "I'd just as soon stay dry today. Switch the teams along the way an' when Charlie gets here, I'll let ya ride inside to Parks' place."

"Obliged to you, Sid."

Victoria glanced up to see MacKenzie coming toward her. He lowered himself to the floor on her left. With a low groan, he crossed his ankles and arms, then leaned against the log wall and closed his eyes.

He remained motionless, less than an arm's length away as the gloom faded and morning light seeped through the tiny windows on either side of the door.

She had the oddest sensation he was guarding her, like some great English Mastiff, lying at her feet. She looped the yarn around the tip of her needle. She was being ridiculous. This MacKenzie was on his way to purchase a horse, nothing more.

He obviously had no interest in her.

Mary turned a page in her book.

Nicholas hadn't hired him to track Victoria down. She gave herself a mental shake and glanced at MacKenzie. His chin had dropped to his chest, and soft snores rumbled in his throat.

Bits of hay clung to the wool of his vest as if he'd spent the night in a barn. Unlike the many westerners she'd seen, he didn't wear his dark canvas pants tucked into his boots, and now the hems were wet and splattered with mud and pieces of chaff. The heels and soles of his scuffed brown boots were also coated with dried mud. But it was his spurs that captured her interest.

They were made of steel with medium sized

rowels, and the leather straps which buttoned over the arch of his boots were plain, without any fancy tooling or silver embellishments. But it was the buttons themselves that intrigued her, for they were fashioned in the shape of small hearts.

What kind of man wore spurs with little hearts? Someone gentle and kind, with a good heart and—*Stop it*, she admonished herself. When would she learn? Look where her girlhood fantasies had landed her. This man had probably killed the kind and gentle man and stolen those spurs. The romantic stories her grandmother had filled her head with were just that—stories.

She stuffed her needles and the sock she'd been working on into her small knitting bag, set it on the bench, then rose to stretch and move around a bit. The stationmaster, Sid, walked over and kicked the bottom of MacKenzie's boot.

He groaned and rolled to his feet.

"The horses for this run are in the first corral."

"Any of them green?"

"Nah. They'll take the harness without a bit of trouble." Sid followed MacKenzie across the room, waiting while he pulled on his poncho. "Tack's in the barn." Sid continued his instructions, telling MacKenzie which horses to pair together.

MacKenzie nodded, put on his hat, then stepped into the rain.

It wasn't coming down in buckets anymore. Still, Victoria felt a tiny bit sorry for him.

He returned a short while later, shaking off his hat and poncho. He gave her a brief nod when their gazes met, then he crossed the room to the coffee pot. She turned to stare through the window while MacKenzie and the stationmaster talked.

The wide rolling landscape of yesterday appeared bleak and desolate, and the vivid blue that had stretched in every direction was obscured by this oppressive dome of gray.

Cobwebs fluttered in the breeze where the window frame met the log wall. Raindrops trailed down the glass, taking her back to her girlhood and the window seat of the parlor where she sat with her dolls and books when it was too wet to play outdoors.

She would pretend one drop was a dragon, the other a handsome knight. Sometimes the knight caught the dragon, and sometimes the dragon caught the knight.

Lately she felt like one of the raindrops, wondering if the evil dragon would catch her. Maybe this stage trip would act like a bit of dust on the glass, diverting her in another direction, away from the man in the buckskin shirt and any of Nicholas' other minions.

The blast of a bugle sounded somewhere in the distance.

"All right, ladies."

She turned around.

Sid placed his coffee cup on the table. "Westbound stage is a mile out. Don't mean ta be blunt, but if ya got business ta attend to out back, now's the time. Once we get the teams hitched the stage ain't waitin'. If ya miss it, ya gotta wait fer the next one."

Mary and the two men stepped into the rain. Victoria waited by the window, glad she hadn't had any coffee. The stationmaster yelled to MacKenzie something about the chestnut in the lead and the black in swing.

The stage clattered to a stop. Mary emerged from around the side of the building and climbed inside the coach. The rain-soaked horses were led away, and the teams MacKenzie had harnessed were backed up to the traces. Sid grabbed their bags and MacKenzie's saddle then loaded them under the tarp at the rear of the stage as the driver stepped through the open door.

"Best get on board, ma'am." He pinched the brim of his dripping hat. "We'll be headin' out directly." He walked to the coffee pot and poured a cup.

Victoria turned back to the bright red coach and prayed she hadn't made a mistake by leaving the train.

Inside she took the rear facing seat next to Mary. Across from them sat two gentlemen. The taller one, dressed like a cattle rancher, sat closest to the window. Beside him sat a portly man in a checkered suit.

From above, the driver yelled, "Yah!" The stage lurched forward with a jangle of chain. At the last moment, MacKenzie swung inside.

He slammed the door and wedged himself between the window and the portly man in the suit. Victoria had the fleeting impression he deliberately positioned himself across from her so he could better watch her.

Pulling his hat brim over his eyes, he extended his legs as far as he could in the cramped space and crossed his arms. She breathed a sigh of relief.

To pass the time, she started knitting. With the leather curtains tied down, she stole covert glimpses of MacKenzie as she finished each row of the sock she'd started.

His tan complexion and brown hair were so different from her husband. Maybe that was the temptation, to believe because he was opposite in looks his character was also opposite.

She was so tired of traveling alone, of constantly watching, of wondering if she would ever feel safe. She shifted on the leather seat. Beneath her the springs squeaked. Her husband, a powerful man, had connections across the country. To evade him, she would have to rely on her wits and trust no one.

She'd met Nicholas Van Der Beck when she was seventeen. Her best friend from boarding school, Lydia Westerly, had invited Victoria to her home for a spring gala. When the handsomest man in the ballroom asked her to dance, her elation had floated her across the floor.

That evening she'd written in her journal, *I've met my Prince Charming and he is perfect.*

Nicholas quickly won her grandmother's heart as well, and just after her eighteenth birthday, Victoria Winters became Mrs. Nicholas Charles Peter Van Der Beck and moved into one of the largest homes on Park Avenue.

If at first she'd compared her life to that of a princess in a castle, she quickly realized she was nothing more than its prisoner. For five years she sought an opportunity to escape, but there'd been nothing she could do—until now.

Two hours later the stage stopped to change horses. MacKenzie jumped out to help, and in less than ten minutes, they were underway. The rain of early morning had stopped, and gradually the alkaline dust churned up by the horses and coach wheels drifted through the air space around the curtains. While no one complained, the salesman had begun coughing, and she noticed a thick coating of the light colored dust stuck to the pomade in his hair.

They continued throughout the day, stopping every twelve miles or so to change horses. After sixty-five miles they made a stop at what Mary called a home station. As he'd been doing, MacKenzie jumped out to help with the horses the moment the stage pulled to a stop.

Outside the coach, Victoria stood like a sailor who'd stepped from the deck of a ship, acclimating her body to being still. She leaned into her lower back and rolled her shoulders to ease the stiffness. Rather than join Mary and the other passengers inside the small sod building, she walked toward the corrals where the horses and mules stood sleepily absorbing the sun.

Late afternoon shadows stretched from the fence posts like long gray stripes across the grass. In the far distance, beyond the flat of the plains, rose sheer cliffs of brown rock, dusted with snow.

A couple of curious horses wandered close to the fence, and she reached out to pet them. A deep rumble rolled through her stomach. "I guess I'd better get something to eat," she said, giving the closest horse one more pat. "Before the stage leaves without me."

Turning back toward the station she froze.

Head down, MacKenzie's long stride brought him straight toward her. Almost upon her, he stopped abruptly. His head jerked up, and their gazes collided through her veil.

Highlights, deep green as the grass, were reflected in his widened hazel eyes. He moved back a step.

"Uh, sorry, ma'am," he mumbled.

Sunlight illuminated his face. What she'd thought

to be a bruise when she'd glimpsed his face that morning, she now recognized was a birth mark. The dark red splotch started in his hair at his left temple, curved around the top of his cheek bone to mid-way under his eye then dipped slightly and curved back to disappear in his hair near the top of his ear.

The tan he'd acquired had muted the redness so it did look more like a deep, purple-red bruise than the bright red wine stain she'd seen on a little girl once at boarding school. The other girls had teased her, and she only stayed one term.

Had MacKenzie been teased as well?

His body stiffened, and his lips pressed together.

Suppressing a twinge of guilt for staring, she murmured, "I'm sorry." There was nothing else to say without causing them both more embarrassment. "Please, excuse me." She stepped around him and hurried inside the adobe building. Though there was still something familiar about him, she never would have forgotten meeting him.

Lamplight spread toward the darkened corners from lanterns placed in the center of a long plank table. The aromas of strong coffee and braised beef started her mouth watering. As inconspicuously as possible, she took a silver dollar from her coin purse and gave it to the stationmaster.

He passed her a bowl and a cup of coffee, but rather than eat it at the table, she wanted to eat outside. The salesman stood near the door, his face florid as he sipped from a silver flask. While she didn't care for men who drank, he was polite and held the door for her as she stepped through into the sunshine.

To the left stood a long bench with a bucket of

water at one end. A bar of yellow soap lay beside the bucket, and a threadbare, blue towel hung from a nail above it. Adjusting her skirts she sat.

With no one around, she lifted her veil and removed the stuffing from her mouth. She ate quickly before someone came along, and while it wasn't the best fare she'd eaten since leaving New York, it wasn't the worst. After making final adjustments to her disguise, she went inside and scraped her plate, then told Mary she was going for a walk.

Pulling her shawl tight over her wide bosom, she walked along the front of the earthen structure breathing the clean air deep into her lungs. Her steps fell silent against the patches of grass and sandy soil. At the corner of the building, she turned right and followed the short length of the left wall toward the back of the station.

Long legs caught her attention, crossed at the ankle, extending from where he sat on the ground against the back wall of the building. The heart-shaped, spur buttons gleamed in the lowering sun. She didn't want to intrude on his privacy, for she guarded her own, but she did wonder why he hadn't eaten. She was about to return to the front of the building when the black head of a kitten popped up from the other side of MacKenzie's crossed ankles.

A long stem of grass appeared then, the seed tassel sliding backward from his ankle to mid-calf. Victoria smiled as the kitten's eyes widened, and he raised himself to pounce. But before he could make his move, a little tuxedo kitten vaulted onto MacKenzie's legs and swiped at the tassel of grass, knocking the first kitten to the ground.

A soft chuckle rumbled from the throat of the man she couldn't see. Her heart skipped a beat. While it didn't sound as if MacKenzie laughed much, genuine amusement resonated in his chuckles.

Nicholas' occasional snickers had always been so calculated and insincere. Victoria wished she'd noticed that before they'd married.

Not wanting to disturb MacKenzie, she returned to the front of the station and waited on the bench. Pulling a small journal and a pencil from her pocket she wrote—

I am intrigued by this man, who hides in shadow and is slow to laugh. He wears spurs with hearts and plays with kittens. Is he a true and valiant knight or a shape-shifting minion of the evil lord?

Ten minutes later they were underway with a new driver and guard in the box. As he'd done before, MacKenzie pulled his hat over his face and went to sleep. The salesman, Mr. Puglisi, continued his drinking. Eventually, he slumped onto MacKenzie's shoulder and began to softly snore. Mary and the second gentleman struck up a conversation about ranching and traded amusing stories of childhoods surrounded by horses and cattle. Content to listen, Victoria pulled out her knitting.

Two hours later, the stage rolled to a stop at the next station.

"Ruth," Mary addressed Victoria by the false name she'd given her. "Are you sure you don't want to visit with me at my brother's ranch?"

Victoria shook her head. "I wish I could. I've enjoyed our time together, but I need to get to Denver. My grandaunt is expecting me."

"At least come and meet him."

"All right." Victoria slid across the leather seat and followed Mary out the door. MacKenzie jumped out the opposite door, but instead of helping with the horses, he lurked near the back of the stage.

Flat prairie and short green grass stretched in every direction. Gold replaced the blue of the sky, silhouetting the distant mountain peaks as the sun lowered behind them.

From inside the adobe building, two men emerged. Mary ran straight into the arms of the taller man. Victoria waited, trying not to look toward MacKenzie, even as she wondered why he watched them so intently.

Mary gave a quick peck on the cheek to the older man. They talked for a minute then Mary waved Victoria closer.

"Ruth, I'd like to introduce you to my brother, Mason Parks, but everyone calls him, Bud. And this is my uncle Emmett."

They exchanged greetings and talked while the teams were changed. Emmett retrieved Mary's bags and set them in the back of a two-seater buckboard.

The stationmaster opened the stage door as the driver climbed up top. "Time to go folks. We got a schedule to keep."

Victoria hugged Mary and promised to write, then turned and boarded the coach.

Mr. Puglisi sat in the same forward facing seat, but the rancher moved to sit where Mary had been. Victoria returned to her usual place and once again, at the last moment, MacKenzie swung on board.

A ripple of unease rolled through her body alerting the tiny hairs at the back of her neck. She had thought he was buying a horse from Bud Parks. Had that been a lie he told the stationmaster in order to gain free passage, or was he following her like the man in the buckskin shirt?

Unable to knit in the fading light, she leaned over to put the sock and yarn in her bag. As she did, she noticed that while he appeared to be sleeping, MacKenize had extended the legs of his rangy frame and pinned the hem of her skirt to the floor with the rowels on his spurs. Maybe she was overly cautious, but it appeared as if he was worried she'd try to leave while he slept.

She grabbed a fistful of the black bombazine intending to yank her skirt from beneath his boots then froze. From the way his hat covered his eyes, he couldn't know she'd discovered his little ploy. She released the worsted fabric.

She could do nothing until the stage arrived in Greeley, but at least now she knew MacKenzie was a man to avoid.

****

Though she managed to doze on the stage, Victoria ached to lay her head on a pillow and curl up in a real bed. Shortly after one in the morning, the driver stopped in front of the Greeley Hotel.

She was almost glad MacKenzie had spent his entire trip, shoving the drunken Mr. Puglisi off his shoulder. When the man wasn't sipping from his flask, he coughed and muttered under his breath.

Anxious to escape confines of the stage as well as MacKenzie's presence, she grabbed her heavy carpetbag from the driver's hand before he could set it on the board walk. Hurrying inside, she approached the

A Tarnished Knight

desk.

"Could I please have a room for tonight?"

"Certainly." The young man reached for a room key and set it on the desk. "Number three, ma'am, top of the stairs, second door on the left." He slid the guest ledger and ink well closer to where she stood.

She scrawled the name of a character her grandmother had once played on the stage in London. Glancing toward the front door, she saw nothing in the glass but her reflection.

"Do you know when the next train comes through?"

"Well that depends where you want to go. The number two train comes through from Cheyenne to Denver about eight, eight-thirty in the morning. Then there's the one up from Denver to Cheyenne later in the afternoon."

"Thank you, sir, for your help." She picked up her bag and hastened up the stairs before MacKenzie came inside.

Once in her room, she locked the door then shoved a chair under the door knob. She checked the window lock, and certain it was secure, she pulled the curtains.

Feeling relatively safe, she stripped out of her heavy black dress and padding. Then with only cold water in the basin, she washed as best she could before turning down the lamp and climbing into bed.

When she opened her eyes, daylight filled the room. Panic fluttered through her chest, and she threw back the covers, afraid she'd slept away the morning. She dug through her carpetbag and removed her grandmother's watch from one of the pockets.

Twenty past seven. She sat back on her heels and

breathed a sigh of relief. Plenty of time to implement her plan to avoid MacKenzie.

After splashing some cold water on her face, she dipped her tiny boar bristle brush in some bicarbonate of soda to freshen her mouth. But instead of donning her widow's weeds, Victoria pulled on a pair of boy's britches and an over-sized jacket. She then twisted and pinned her waist-length hair into a bun and shoved it all under a tweed cap.

Carpetbag in hand, she quietly slipped down the stairs and glanced around the lobby. Less than twenty feet from where she stood clutching the newel post, a small divan and two wing chairs had been positioned around a low table where an assortment of catalogues, newspapers, and periodicals had been spread. But what made her breath freeze in her lungs was the pair of long legs extending from one of the chairs. One foot stretched beneath the table, and the ball of the other rested on the edge. She couldn't see his face, hidden by the wing of the chair, only the top of his head and those scuffed brown boots with the heart shaped spurs.

Was he following her or was she overly suspicious? Maybe he was an early riser, relaxing with the newspaper before the train arrived. But why had he lied about buying the horse? Victoria couldn't take any chances. Nicholas had money and far reaching connections. She had only evaded him this long by using her wits and trusting her instincts.

Squaring her shoulders, she reminded herself that even if he did notice her, he expected a full-figured widow, not a boy.

Grateful the desk clerk this morning was an older man, she handed him her key and dug the coins she needed from her vest pocket.

Without looking at MacKenzie, Victoria walked behind his chair and out the front door. When he made no move to follow, she heaved a sigh of relief, pulled the door closed, and headed to the livery.

Chapter Three

The glass panels in the top half of the door rattled as it was pulled closed. Ryder glanced over but saw only a boy in a cap turning away from the front of the hotel.

His stomach rumbled. It had been two hours since he'd wolfed down eggs and coffee. Ignoring the gnawing in his belly, he switched his attention back to the week-old copy of the Rocky Mountain Star. Unable to afford a room, he'd spent what was left of the night sleeping in the loft at the livery.

Then this morning he'd been forced to sell his saddle. The damn thing had been barely broke in. He'd had it custom made at a little shop on Seventeenth Street in Cheyenne, when he believed his life finally had some value.

He imagined Flint was enjoying a good laugh. The bounty hunter deliberately forgot to mention there were two women dressed in black. Now Ryder was one day closer to losing his cattle for good, and one day further from collecting the five thousand dollars.

And Flint had better be telling the truth about that reward money, because if it was a fabrication of his twisted sense of humor, Ryder would hunt him down and rip the five thousand dollars right out of his sorry hide.

Ryder folded the newspaper and tossed it onto the

table. Where the hell was she? If she was taking the train to Denver as she'd mentioned yesterday, she'd better hurry. Had she walked past and he hadn't heard? No, not possible.

He rose and after taking a deep breath approached the desk clerk. The clerk stared at Ryder's face for several moments, before glancing down to rearrange some papers.

Ryder leaned against the desk. "What room is that widow woman staying in?"

The desk clerk glanced up and stared. "I don't know, sir. Can you tell me her name?"

Ryder reached out and grabbed a fistful of the man's white shirt.

The desk clerk paled. His Adam's apple bobbed up and down above his starched shirt collar. "A-a woman signed the register last n-night," he croaked.

"Room?"

"Room th-three."

Without a word, Ryder released the man, then whirled around and took the stairs two at a time.

Behind him the clerk called, "B-but she checked out. S-sir, she's not there!"

Needing to be certain, Ryder strode down the hall to room three. He knocked. No answer. Damn it, how had she gotten by him?

A train whistle blared in the distance. He tried the knob. Locked. An uneasy suspicion rolled through his stomach. It seemed as though she knew he followed her. He could go downstairs and have the desk clerk come back with the extra key, but he didn't have time. His five thousand dollars might be purchasing her ticket to Denver. Before he raced to the train station, he had to be sure she wasn't hiding under the bed waiting for him to leave.

He stepped back, raised his foot, and kicked the door.

Two doors down, someone yelled, "Quiet!"

Two more kicks and the frame splintered as the door slammed against the wall. Ryder rushed in. His toe caught on the leg of a chair that had been oddly placed by the door. His momentum tumbled him over the seat, and he hit the floor. His sore arm grazed the edge of the chair leg, and he sucked a breath of air through his teeth.

Damn. He rolled to his feet, rubbing his right bicep. His fingers came away wet. The bullet that killed his horse had first plowed a furrow across his arm. Now the newly formed scab had broken open.

He shouldn't be surprised. Fiona was right. He was cursed the day he was born. Sometimes he wondered why he tried so hard to persevere.

The room was neat, the bed made. Aside from the chair, nothing was out of place. Three long strides brought him to the window. He raised the sash and poked his head outside, nothing but the back of the hotel. No trees, no drainpipe, or any other way to climb down from this window without jumping or using a rope. Now how the hell had this overweight widow managed to slip past?

The train whistle shrieked again.

He swung around and yanked open drawers looking for some clue as to her whereabouts. He dropped to his knees and peered under the bed as a commotion of voices and pounding feet burst into the room.

"What are you doing?" The desk clerk demanded as Ryder rolled to his feet. "Are you going to pay for this door?" Two men flanked the clerk on either side, and another peered into the room from the hallway.

Ryder didn't have time for this. He had to get to the train station. If she made it into the congestion of Denver, he'd never find her, and his chance to collect the five thousand dollars would be lost.

He shoved past the two men and stepped into the hall.

Behind him, the desk clerk called, "I'm getting the sheriff!"

Ignoring them, he charged down the stairs and across the lobby. The clerk and his supporters thundered along right behind him.

Ryder strode down the street, putting distance between himself and the small mob that followed. He stopped abruptly at the corner of the depot building. Through puffs of steam, he searched the milling crowd for the widow but couldn't spot her.

He entered the station and marched straight to the teller's cage. The ticket agent, seated behind a small barred window, stared. Ryder glowered until the man began to fidget with his ledgers and pens.

"You sell a ticket to a widow woman going to Denver?"

The man adjusted his black cuff-protectors then pushed his spectacles higher on the bridge of his nose. "I'm afraid, sir, that it is against company policy to—"

"Just tell me before I reach in there and check the ledger myself."

The man closed the book and hugged it against his chest. "This is only a record of ticket sales."

"Then tell me who bought the tickets before I climb in there and choke it out of you."

The ticket agent paled. Beads of sweat popped out across his brow. "I only sold four tickets to Denver. A minister bought two. Some kid bought a ticket for his grandmother, and I sold one to another man in a suit. Now please leave, or I will be forced to summon the sheriff."

Ryder turned away and slowly walked from the building. Now what? Maybe the princess had someone purchase a ticket for her.

"All aboard!"

He searched the crowd and glimpsed a woman in black boarding the passenger car at the end of the train. A minister climbed on after her.

Ryder started toward them.

"Hold up there!" boomed a voice from behind.

Ryder swung around. Marching toward him was the desk clerk from the hotel with the sheriff in tow.

The train whistle blared again. "All aboard!"

"You the fella who busted down the door at the hotel?" The sheriff's chest puffed out, swelling to match the width of his girth, as he made his accusation. Thick mutton chop sideburns stretched out to touch the corners of his mouth.

"That's him," the clerk confirmed, safely ensconced behind the sheriff's bulk. "Kicked the door right in. Broke it off the hinges and refused to pay."

With soft, slow chugs the engine inched toward Denver.

"You got two choices, mister," the sheriff stated. "Pay what you owe for the damages or go to jail 'til the circuit judge comes through."

Well, it wouldn't be the first time Ryder had been in jail. And the thought of some sleep and a few free meals would have been tempting any other time, but the train was gaining speed, and the open tender loaded with wood had just passed them. He'd be damned if he'd let that spoiled, rich princess get the better of him.

Gritting his teeth, he pulled his purse from the inside pocket of his vest and passed over just enough coins to cover the cost of the broken door as the baggage car clattered past.

He whirled around and raced for the train, grabbing the handrail at the end of the passenger car just in time to swing on board.

He opened the door and ducked into the last seat. He slid low, hoping the conductor wouldn't notice him, and scanned the car, half full with passengers.

The widow woman sat on the opposite side, half way down the length of the car, with her back toward him. Beside her sat the minister. Apparently she'd found another ally.

Now he had to figure out a way to separate her from the minister and get her off the train without raising any suspicion.

The train rattled through Evans without stopping. The conductor entered the car and began checking tickets. Ryder slouched lower in the seat, bracing one knee against the back of the seat in front of him.

Wearing a frock coat and dark slouch hat, the conductor zig-zagged from passenger to passenger, punching tickets as he made his way toward the back of the car.

Ryder pulled his hat down over his eyes, hoping the conductor would leave him be.

"Sir, can I see your ticket please?"

So much for luck. He ignored the man, pretending to sleep, hoping he'd go away.

A hand landed on his shoulder and gave him a shake. Ryder lifted his hat off his face and pushed himself higher on the seat.

"Can I see your ticket, please?"

Ryder dug through all the pockets of his vest and checked the front pocket of his shirt. "It's here someplace," he said. He looked on the seat, on the floor and leaned around the conductor to check the aisle. "I must have dropped it somewhere."

The conductor gave him a disapproving frown. "How far are you going?"

"Denver."

"Well at the next stop, I'll send a wire to the stationmaster in Greeley. Do you think he'll remember you?"

"I'm sure of it," he mumbled.

"Good. Otherwise buy a ticket, or I'll put you off the train." He turned and walked back to the other end of the car and out the door.

Ryder slid back down in the seat. Hopefully he could slip unobtrusively from the train at the next stop with the princess in tow. The rhythmic clacking of the wheels against the rails lulled him to sleep, and he dozed until the whistle blew.

Rubbing a hand across his eyes, he straightened and glanced out the window. The train must be reducing speed to pick up passengers. It was now or never. He rose and moved up and over a few seats. One woman gathered her shawl and reticule. The man beside her stood and lifted a small carpetbag from the brass rack overhead.

The train slowed. Up ahead he could make out the gabled roof of the depot. He moved to the next seat. Neither the minister nor the widow beside him made any move to get off the train.

A loud hiss of steam and the train braked to a stop. On the sign above the depot entrance he read, Platteville. The man and woman left their seats and started down the aisle. Ryder approached the minister and the woman beside him.

"Victoria Van Der Beck, I'm here to take you back to New York and to your husband. Would you please come with me?"

The woman gasped and looked up. Crow's feet fanned out from the corners of her eyes and deep lines bracketed her drooping mouth. He hadn't seen the princess much during daylight, and never without her veil, but for some reason, he'd thought she was younger.

"See here!" the minister demanded. Lunging to his feet, he positioned himself between Ryder and the woman.

"She isn't who you think she is," Ryder explained.

"I'm quite sure she is, sir. Now please leave."

Ryder reached around the minister, grabbed the woman's arm, and hauled her to her feet. "You're coming with me."

She screamed.

The minister tried pulling Ryder off. Other passengers swarmed around him. Several hands gripped his shoulders, his sore arm. Tenaciously, he hung on pulling his five thousand dollars with him as he was yanked backward. She hit him and tried scratching his face.

"He's crazy!" the minister cried. "Don't let him hurt my sister."

His sister? Ryder peered closer. Her hand, as she tried to pry his fingers from her wrist, was dry and work worn. The hands he'd watched on the stage as she flipped yarn and clicked needles, were soft and well-manicured. His grip loosened as a fist slammed into his lower back.

He grunted and his arms were grabbed from behind.

"Oh, they remember you in Greeley all right." Announced the conductor from somewhere behind him. "Get him off my train, boys."

Ryder struggled to jerk free, but there were too many hands and the space too confined. He was dragged backward through the door onto the tiny iron platform at the rear of the train then shoved.

He hit the brick cobblestones on his hands and knees and rolled. His aching body screamed at him to stay still, but Ryder pushed past the pain and eased to his feet. He drew a deep breath and waited for the throbbing in his knees to go away. From the intense stinging in his palms, he suspected they were scraped and imbedded with grit.

Above, a window slid open, and his hat sailed out to land at his feet. Resisting the urge to press his hand against the pain in his lower back, he leaned over and picked up his Stetson. Placing it squarely on his head, he turned toward the road and started the long walk back to Greeley.

How the hell many widow women were there west of the Mississippi?

He hadn't gone more than a mile when the blisters he'd acquired on his heels walking to Julesburg broke open. He could feel the inside of his boots rubbing against the raw skin. Another mile and his socks were wet with blood.

He lowered himself to the ground and drew up his knees. Crossing his arms, he rested his forehead and tried to think.

By his reckoning he still had another fourteen miles to go.

Hopefully he could catch a ride with someone, but the princess would be long gone by the time he got back to Greeley. Chasing five thousand dollars had been a waste of time. He needed to get to Ogallala and find his cattle before they were sold.

He pulled off his boots and socks. Both socks were worn through and the wool stained and damp with blood. He grabbed each foot and twisted it so he could check the damage. Each heel had an open sore the size of a five cent piece.

He shoved the socks inside a boot then undid one of his spur straps, looped it through the strap on the other boot and buttoned it back. Rising, he draped his boots over one shoulder and gingerly put one bare foot in front of the other.

****

Victoria dismounted and stretched. After a long day in the saddle, an aching body was a small price to pay for staying ahead of Nicholas' lackey in spurs.

She rubbed the tight muscles of her lower back then led the horse inside the barn. Though her body ached, pride straightened her spine.

Ironically, Nicholas had been the one who insisted

she learn to ride. At the time she'd resented his need to put her on display along the bridle paths of Central Park. Today was the first time she was actually grateful for the groom he'd hired to teach her about horses. She'd used her skills to escape the very man Nicholas had hired to catch her.

She'd seen MacKenzie that morning leaping onto the train bound for Denver and smiled, pleased her ruse to elude him had worked.

Once he realized she wasn't on the train, he'd head back to Greeley, but according to the schedule, the stationmaster gave her, the number one train didn't leave Denver until almost five.

Needing to get ahead of MacKenzie, she rented a horse and arrived in Cheyenne a few minutes ago. If her nemesis took the train, it wasn't destined to arrive until eight-forty tonight. By then she would be asleep in bed.

While MacKenzie spent the next day searching Cheyenne, Victoria planned to catch the first train heading west.

She untied her carpetbag from the pommel of the saddle, and the livery owner led the horse away. After folding the receipt, she shoved it into her vest pocket, left the stable, and started down the dusty street.

For now she needed a respectable, not too expensive, out-of-the-way place to spend the night.

Dyer's Hotel, on the west side of Eddy Street, looked perfect.

"I want to rent a room for me and my sister," Victoria told the desk clerk, keeping the brim of her cap pulled low. "She's down at the bath house right now, but she'll be along later."

The desk clerk, focused on a game of solitaire,

hardly spared her a glance. He passed her the key, and she signed the register. He didn't even look up when she grasped her carpetbag and walked back outside.

****

Steam rose around her face as the matronly woman poured a kettle of hot water into the cooling water of the bathtub. Heat seeped into Victoria's aching muscles. Submerging herself to her chin, she closed her eyes and sighed.

For the first time in days, her scalp no longer itched, and her skin could finally breathe. She longed to remain in the tub until her fingertips wrinkled, but others sat in the waiting room, and the women's side of the bathhouse was only open until seven.

After toweling dry, she rolled up her boy's clothes and stuffed them into her carpetbag then donned an over-sized skirt and blouse. The high neck of her blouse hid the slender length of her throat, and twisting her damp hair into a bun, she shoved it under a wig of reddish brown curls. For the finishing touch, she once again stuffed her cheeks with small strips of rolled linen.

Back at the hotel, she ordered a sandwich and tea to take to her room and settled into bed with her supper and her knitting. Before dousing the lamp, she jotted in her journal—

The evil prince is still out there. Now his minions are chasing me. On days like this I feel strong enough to escape, other days I fear he will catch me. Either way, I will never go back. I'd rather end my own life than be returned to his castle.

Chapter Four

Ryder decided never to walk anywhere again. If he couldn't get there on the back of a horse, he wasn't going.

Easing himself onto a bench in front of Ingersoll Livery Boarding and Rentals, Ryder removed his hat and rested his head against the board and batten wall. His stomach, which quit rumbling hours ago, felt like a hollowed out oak tree. His parched throat ached for a drink of water, but he was too tired to walk to the pump.

A wizened man with a bowed back wandered outside, a manure fork in one hand. His rheumy gaze perused Ryder from the top of his head to the toes of his feet. "You're lookin' a mite tuckered out, MacKenzie. You come to buy back that saddle you sold me this morning?"

"Nope."

"Left the rest a yer gear here. Wondered if ya was comin' back. Seen that the fancy toolin' on yer scabbard matches yer saddle. Got a mighty fine rifle, too. Ya reckon on sellin' 'em?"

God, Ryder hoped it wouldn't come to that. He'd had the scabbard custom made when he bought his saddle. The Winchester was brand new as well. He'd bought them both this spring when he'd actually had some net worth. Now the only way he could stay above broke was to get his cattle back. "You got any horses for sale?"

Ingersoll poked the tines into the ground and stacked his hands on top of the handle. "You come across any more money than what I give ya fer that saddle?"

They both knew the answer, so Ryder said nothing. "Got a horse I can rent? I need to get to Ogallala."

"Sorry, son, rented my last horse this morning to some kid going up to Cheyenne. Seemed in kind of a hurry. Didn't want to wait for the train."

Ryder lifted his head away from the wall. "Then I'll just get my gear and be on my way."

He stood and limped into the barn behind the livery owner who pushed open the door of a large tack room. Using the manure fork for support, Ingersoll leaned down to grab Ryder's gear from where it had been piled in the corner. One at a time, Ryder accepted his bedroll, saddlebags, and rifle.

"If ya don't mind my sayin' so, son, yer feet look a mite raw. I got me some salve over there that should fix ya up right fine." He gestured toward a shelf jammed with bottles and jars.

Just hearing the word *salve* soothed his aching feet, but he winced at the thought of pulling his boots on again.

The old man pointed toward the opposite wall. "Have a seat."

Dropping his gear in the corner, Ryder crossed the space and lowered himself onto a pile of bulging burlap sacks stamped *Oats*.

The livery owner shuffled across the floor. The soles of his boots grated against the tiny stones imbedded in the packed dirt. Grabbing a small nail keg, he rolled it close to Ryder's knees. "Set yer leg on this."

Ryder extended his foot so his calf rested on top of the unopened barrel. Ingersoll moved to the other side of the narrow room and lifted a short, wide jar from the shelf.

"I make this salve myself from balsam pitch, yarrow, and tobacco. Now let me see what ya got here, son."

Turning his foot so the old man could better see, Ryder yawned and leaned against a wall curtained with dangling harness reins, the ends trailing onto the oats.

"Hmmm." The old man's nose nearly touched Ryder's foot as he studied Ryder's heel. "Ya got some hole here, son. I ain't seen too many worse than this."

"Seen that many horses with blisters?"

The old man smacked the bottom of Ryder's foot as he shot him a narrowed glare. "No, you knot head. It was back in forty-seven in the war with Mexico."

Ryder chuckled and closed his eyes.

"I served under General Winfield Scott. We captured Vera Cruz then marched all the way to Mexico City."

The salve stung at first then eased. Roughened fingertips brushed his foot, and a long cloth bandage wound around and around, over his heel, over and under his arch and around his ankle, as the old man droned on and on.

"Cerro Gordo, Contreras, Churubusco… …beside me lost his arm… …Chapultepec… …at the palace in September…

****

Ryder hit the floor with a thump. What the hell? He

hadn't fallen out of bed since he was a boy.

He blinked at the roughhewn beams overhead, and pressing his palms against the dirt floor, he sat up. Turning a bit he rested his back against the same sack of oats on which he'd fallen asleep. Glancing at his feet, he saw they had both been wrapped in nice white bandages. Odd that he didn't remember the old man doctoring his other foot. He rubbed his hand over his face and around the back of his neck. What time was it?

Light shone beneath the door. At least the sun hadn't gone down yet. He rolled to his feet and arched his lower back. Moving across the room, he lifted the latch and padded down the center aisle of the livery to the pump out back.

As he gulped down two dippers of water, a low rumble of voices caught his attention. He replaced the dipper and wandered around the corral to the side of the building. Leaning on his manure fork, Ingersoll stood talking to a big black man.

The two men laughed, and as Ryder joined them, the big man shoved an extra wheel into the wagon bed loaded with the hides of buffalo, deer, wolf, coyote, and even a bear.

"Train whistle wake ya up, son?" The livery owner asked.

Ryder didn't remember a train whistle, but something had startled him from a deep sleep. "What train?"

The old man shook his head and gave Ryder a long look that seemed to question Ryder's intelligence. "The train from Denver to Cheyenne," he said slowly. "Comes through every evening 'bout six."

"Damn," Ryder cursed under his breath.

The livery owner frowned. "Thought ya was headin' to Ogallala?"

"Got a place northwest of Cheyenne, south of Crow Creek. If I can get there, I can pick up a horse."

"George here is headin' to Cheyenne."

The big man dropped a hammer and pry bar into a wooden box mounted on the side of the wagon then closed the lid. He turned and gave Ryder the once over, his dark gaze landing on Ryder's bandaged feet. "Reckon you'll be wantin' a ride."

"If you don't mind, I'd sure be obliged."

"If Henry vouches for you, I'd be glad for the company."

Ryder nodded. "When are you heading out?"

"Now."

"Now? But it will be dark in a couple of hours."

"Yes, sir, it will. But I can get a good price for this load in Cheyenne, an' anyone thinkin' to take it from me won't be expectin' me to travel at night. 'Sides, Billy and Buck are good night horses, and I got lanterns if the moon won't do."

"Let me get my gear." Ryder headed to the tack room and pulled clean socks from his bedroll. Tugging on his boots wasn't as painful as he expected, although the thickness of the bandages under his socks made the boots a bit tight. His heels were sore, but they didn't hurt. He tossed his saddlebags and bedroll over his shoulder and picked up his rifle. He ran his fingers over the basket-weave and floral tooling carved in the dark leather scabbard. Then with a sigh, he pulled his Winchester free, limped to the last saddle on the rack, and placed the scabbard across the seat.

Outside he climbed onto the wagon and gave

Ingersoll a nod as George headed the team north out of town. The man wasn't much for conversation, which was fine by Ryder, he just wished he'd had a chance to grab an apple or something before they headed out.

He braced the ball of his foot against the dash as the stink of the buffalo hides filled his nose and the back of his throat. His empty stomach rolled and he swallowed, wondering why he hadn't waited for the train tomorrow evening.

Maybe deep inside he was still hopeful of finding the princess, despite this morning's debacle. Had her comment on the stage about going to Denver only been a ploy?

Since leaving New York, she'd been heading west. Assuming that was still her intention, she would have gone north to Cheyenne to connect with the Union Pacific not south to Denver. Since the northbound train had just left, she was either on it, still in Greeley, or she'd found another way to Cheyenne.

Earlier, Ingersoll had said he'd rented a horse to a boy who'd been in too much of a hurry to wait for the train. Had that been her rich royal highness in disguise? No, she was a big woman. She could never pass for a boy. Unless… Had her disguise also altered her shape?

He shifted on the wooden seat as the horses plodded along, their way lit by the dim glow of a crescent moon. He must be crazy to think he'd be able to find her in Cheyenne. But he was headed there anyway, and he probably had a better shot at locating her than he had of getting his cattle away from the rustlers, especially without a horse.

After a long night, stopping only to rest the team, they arrived in Cheyenne as the brilliance of pink and orange streaked across the eastern sky beneath the fading window shade of night.

The wagon bounced across three sets of tracks before George pulled his team to a stop in front of the Union Pacific Hotel which stood on the left side of the train depot.

Like an old man, Ryder climbed from the wagon. His aching body protested each tiny movement. George passed him his gear.

"Mighty nice Winchester," he said after a nighttime of virtual silence. "Ought to get yourself a scabbard, so's it don't get scratched up."

Ryder pulled out a dollar and passed it up to the black man. "I'll do that."

George nodded and clucked his team forward.

Ryder hobbled over to the hotel and stepped onto the walk. With an assortment of hotels and rooming houses in this sprawling town, it would be tough to find her, but as long as he was here…

He drew a deep breath, pushed open the front door, and approached the desk.

"I'm looking for someone," Ryder announced to the clerk. "She's a big woman, maybe thirty-five? She might be dressed as a widow. Did she rent a room here today?"

The clerk stared. Ryder realized he looked rough. He hadn't had a bath or shaved in five days, but after twenty-eight years of stares, he knew his unkempt appearance wasn't what drew the clerk's attention.

The clerk pulled the guest ledger closer. "What's her name?"

"Did she rent a room or not?"

"Got a name?" the clerk snapped.

"Look, she's my sister. I rode all day to get here, and I just want to know if she arrived."

"She's your sister; you ought to know her name."

"She never uses her real name."

The thin man arched his brows. "Then no, didn't see anyone like that."

"What about a kid?" Ryder persisted. "My little brother might have rented the room."

"Your brother got a name?"

Ryder glared at him.

The clerk closed the book. "Of course not," he said dryly. "Look, a couple of salesmen and a married couple, that's it for today. You might try the Rollins House. It's a few streets behind us on Sixteenth. Or you could try American House down from them. Your nameless family might be there."

Ryder clenched his teeth, slid his saddlebags higher on his shoulder, and stalked back outside.

After asking the same question at the next two hotels and having no luck, Ryder doubted he'd ever find the woman. Maybe he should just walk to the depot and wait for the next train west. His blisters would certainly appreciate it.

But at the last minute, he turned the corner onto Eddy Street. There was a hotel called Dyer's where he'd stayed a couple of times while waiting for the bounty on some prisoners he'd brought in.

The clock in the lobby chimed seven times as Ryder pushed open the door and walked toward the desk.

The clerk, still in his teen years, slept with his chair tipped against the rows of cubbyhole mailboxes and his feet propped on something beneath the counter.

Using the palm of his hand, Ryder gave the ornately carved, silver bell, a single whack. The sharp clang snapped the young man upright so fast he tumbled to the floor.

The kid blinked wide-eyed at Ryder as he rolled to his feet, making no effort to disguise the fact he gawked at Ryder's face.

"I'm looking for a woman," Ryder snapped. "Can you tell me if you rented a room to any widows?"

Normally he ignored the looks, but this pimple faced kid and his blatant staring pushed Ryder's worn temper over the edge. He lunged across the desk and grabbed the boy by the front of his shirt.

"I asked you a question."

"I d-don't know. S-s-some kid r-rented a room for his sister, b-but that's all I know."

As another ploy it sounded plausible, and it was the best lead he had so far. He released the clerk's shirt, and the boy stumbled backward into the row of mailboxes.

Ryder leaned over the desk. "Give me a key."

"B-but I c-can't d-do that. Sh-she's a woman alone and you're n-not her b-brother."

"I'm her other brother. Now give me a damn key, or I'll break down the door and get in anyway."

Hand shaking, the kid dropped it on the desk. Ryder snatched it, glancing at the number on the oval fob. Carpet muffled his footfalls as he jogged up the stairs and strode down the hall to the door with a brass eight in the center. There wasn't much time. The kid was probably running for Sheriff Jackson right now.

He inserted the key, turned the lock, and pushed.

The door didn't budge. Something heavy on the

other side prevented it from opening. Turning sideways, he slammed his shoulder and hip against the portal, shoving it inward a few inches. He rammed it again. This time the opening was wide enough to squeeze his lean body through.

Absolute silence raised the hairs on the back of his neck. If his sisters had had an intruder enter their room, they would have screamed loud enough for the whole town to hear. The bed was empty and neatly made. Had the princess slipped past him again? Impossible. He shoved aside the small commode that had been pushed against the door. The leg caught on the edge of the carpet, and the white china basin slid across the surface to balance precariously over the edge.

He turned. There was a flash of white, almost like a ghost in his peripheral vision then nothing.

****

Victoria froze, clutching the handle of the white ceramic pitcher. MacKenzie lay unmoving in front of her chair. Was he actually unconscious, merely play acting, or was he dead?

Her gaze followed the line of his body from his boots, up his long legs to his hips, over his back and shoulders, to the light brown hair of his head. A chill rippled through her. Dear Lord, please don't let him be dead.

She hopped off the ladder-back chair she'd been standing on and stepped over his feet to pull the key from the front of the lock. Then using her foot, she shoved his legs away from the door and pushed it closed. After turning the key, she leaned against the door and stared.

She'd awakened earlier to soft pink light seeping

through the lacey curtains then dressed in the same green skirt and red wig she'd worn after her bath the night before. Carpetbag in hand, she'd been on her way downstairs to enjoy an early breakfast when she spotted MacKenzie at the front desk.

Her body froze on the staircase. Her foot hovered over the next descending tread as her fingers clenched the banister. She'd thought he was in Denver. Keeping a wary eye on him as he'd argued with the desk clerk, Victoria eased herself backward up the stairs. The soles of her shoes were silent on the carpet runner as she hurried back to her room.

She'd just positioned herself on the chair behind the door when a key clicked in the lock and the knob turned. Shoving the door open, MacKenzie squeezed his rangy self into the room just as she'd swung the water pitcher.

Rapid knocking against the door vibrated through her back.

"Yes, who is it?"

"I-it's Warren Mathews, ma'am, from the front desk. Are ya all right?"

Here was her chance. If she told him a strange man had broken into her room and tried to attack her, MacKenzie would be hauled off to jail, and she'd be free. But there'd be questions, and the incident might make one or all of the Cheyenne newspapers. There was a chance Nicholas, or one of his hired detectives, would read the article and find her.

"Miss?"

"I'm fine thank you."

"I heard a lot of ruckus."

"My uh…brother tripped over the carpet and fell."

"Well, your brother seemed in a bit of a temper."

"He's always like that when he's been drinking. He'll be fine once he sleeps it off."

"I can fetch Sheriff Jackson if ya want."

"I'm fine, but thank you for your concern."

"All right. Sorry to bother ya, ma'am."

She exhaled a sigh of relief when the floor boards creaked as he moved down the hall.

Pitcher in hand, she stretched out her leg and poked MacKenzie's thigh with the toe of her shoe. His body shifted, but he didn't flinch or groan.

Stepping over his legs, she moved to the bedside table to light the lamp. While daylight pushed its way into the room, shadows still lurked in the corners, and she needed to see his wound.

With her trusty pitcher clenched in one hand and the lamp in the other, she approached MacKenzie.

Guilt gnawed at her conscience as she studied his unmoving form. Aside from Nicholas, she had never physically hurt anyone before, and despite the way MacKenzie forced his way into her room, this was the same man who played with kittens when he thought no one was around.

His complexion had paled beneath his tan, and a short beard shadowed the lower half of his face and throat. MacKenzie was a handsome man in a rugged sort of way, with his high cheekbones, strong jaw and—*Stop it*, she admonished herself. Just because a man looked good didn't mean he was good. Nicholas had proven that beyond any shadow of a doubt.

Setting the lamp on the floor, she leaned over MacKenzie's shoulder and stretched out her hand so her palm barely brushed his nose and chin. Warm breath tickled her skin, and heat burned her cheeks. She snatched her hand away releasing a long breath. He was alive.

Shifting her attention to his head, she combed her fingers through his hair until they brushed over a large, goose-egg sized swelling behind his ear. Something maternal stirred inside her, vying with her reluctance to put down the pitcher. She sat back on her heels and tried to brush the odd feeling aside. It was merely guilt for having injured him, nothing more.

She bit the inside of her mouth. Had she become like Nicholas, so absorbed in her own needs no one else mattered?

Five years ago she thought her husband sincere in his remorse, sincere with his flowers, his jewelry, and his tears. Now she understood, for Nicholas the apology was part of the show, the more eloquent, the more genuine it sounded, the better he looked for doing it. He never asked how much pain she was in, nor did he care to lessen it.

Well, she might have hurt MacKenzie, but she wasn't Nicholas. Rising, she pulled the quilt from the bed and grabbed one of the pillows. She knelt on the floor and slipped the pillow under his head.

He moaned and she froze, but he didn't stir. She relaxed and brushed back his hair. MacKenzie seemed like a nice man. Maybe, if she told him about her husband...

No, she chided herself, snapping her hand back to her lap. He wouldn't believe her. No one ever did. She'd learned that lesson at a dinner party, early in her marriage.

Victoria had been introduced to one of Nicholas'

business associates. Believing Ainsworth Thorndyke to be a gentleman, she'd told him how Nicholas hit her, then begged him to help her get away. She'd been horrified when he not only didn't believe her, but he'd gone to Nicholas and informed him his new wife wanted to run away with him.

Unconsciously, she reached up and rubbed the corner of her left eye, as though she could still feel the impact of Nicholas' fist when it connected with her face that night.

No, she couldn't afford to waste time on fantasies about a man who wore spurs with hearts. A train headed west today, and Victoria planned to be on board.

She picked up his hat, saddlebags, and rifle and set them beside the armoire. From her carpetbag, she grabbed a skein of yarn and her small scissors. He moaned and shifted as she pulled his hands behind his back and wrapped bright red yarn around his wrists numerous times in a figure eight. A moment later she did the same with his ankles then grabbed the quilt and tucked it around him.

The thought of leaving him alone made her uneasy. Though he'd begun to stir, he still wasn't conscious. Even Nicholas had roared to life as she pulled closed the front door that night. What if MacKenzie never woke up? She'd heard things like that happened with head wounds.

She blew out the lamp, picked up her carpetbag, and adjusted her tinted spectacles on her nose. At the door she hesitated, her hand on the knob, and glanced back. His shoulders moved.

Though relieved, she needed to go. Gripping the

cracked leather handles of her bag, she locked the door and headed downstairs. If Mackenzie did wake up in the next few minutes, he would expect her to go to the train station, check the schedules, and get some breakfast, but hopefully he'd be looking for either a widow or a boy.

With her pulse thrumming through her veins, she compelled her feet to move sedately down the street. Gaze lowered, she watched the footwear of each passerby, searching for scuffed brown boots and spurs with hearts.

The back of her neck tingled as though invisible eyes followed her, and she checked the reflection of every window she passed. Nervous, she jumped at shadows, expecting him to leap from every doorway and empty alley. Forcing herself to maintain a façade of calm, when her body was coiled to run, she slowed her steps and stopped to peruse the windows of a dry goods store and dress shop. The depot in sight, she stepped off the board walk to cross the narrow space between two buildings.

"Going somewhere, Mrs. Van Der Beck?"

Chapter Five

A high-pitched squeak escaped Victoria's throat, and she whirled around, swinging her carpetbag. Momentum slammed it against his shoulder with a solid *wump*.

He grunted, but stepping forward, grabbed her wrist. Though he wasn't a broad-shouldered man, he was tall at maybe six-foot-two, and lean, his muscles hard and firm. A blow from him would carry far more impact than any she received from Nicholas. Dread curled her stomach like a dried leaf, and blood pounded against her temples as she waited for his inevitable reaction.

Instead he reached behind himself and withdrew a pair of handcuffs. The iron manacles gleamed in the morning light. If he clamped them around her wrists, she'd have no chance to get away.

Twisting her arm, she leaned back, trying to free herself. Desperate, she kicked his shins, but his high, leather boots made her attempt ineffective. How had he gotten ahead of her? Had he seen her and taken a short cut?

"Hold still," he ordered, trying to attach the handcuffs.

Swinging her palm toward the side of his head, she tried to box his ear, but her hand caught on his hat brim, and she succeeded only in knocking it from his head.

She drew her knee up toward his groin, but he was too tall, and her legs tangled in her oversized skirt and petticoats. Dropping her carpetbag, she made a fist and punched him there instead. His grip on her arm let loose as he staggered back a step, his body folding in half.

Victoria grabbed her bag, snatched her skirts up to her knees, and ran. In that moment it didn't matter where she ran. Her only thought was to run as far from him as possible and find a place to hide.

His boot heels thumped against the planks behind her. With the cumbersome carpetbag banging against her leg, she raced down the wooden sidewalk and darted into a narrow alley.

The pounding of his feet against the ground, blended with her own footfalls to beat a cadence in her mind, *faster, faster, faster.*

An arm snaked around her waist, and she fell forward. The instant before her face would have smashed into the ground, he twisted somehow, and she landed on top of him with her back against his chest.

She needed to move but could do nothing except lie there catching her breath.

Two birds flew across the sky, their silhouettes black against the pale blue expanse.

Beneath her, MacKenzie's chest rose and fell as his breath streamed hot against her ear.

Then he rolled, pinning her beneath him. His complexion grew chalky, as pale as the clouds, making the birthmark along his cheekbone and temple appear more prominent. His hazel eyes had absorbed the browns from the buildings and the dusty ground, muting the green highlighted in their depths. His mouth was wide, his lips full and parted as he breathed.

He shifted. She tensed, expecting his hand to collide with the side of her face as a reminder not to run. She waited for him to yell, to haul her to her feet, and shake her until her head nearly snapped from her neck. Instead he just blinked and breathed.

"I'm sorry," she squeaked. "I'll never hurt you again." Apologies usually made no difference, but she tried anyway.

Then his eyes rolled up into his head, and he collapsed on top of her.

Her breath escaped in a loud, "Ooof!" Oh no, this wasn't good. She pushed at his shoulders. "MacKenzie?"

She shoved him aside, and he groaned as he flopped onto his back. Victoria pushed to her knees. She studied him, wondering if he was all right. As if by their own volition, her fingertips reached out and brushed his hair off his forehead. His eyes opened. Startled, she could only stare back as he gazed into her face. Then he smiled.

Her breath caught. This wasn't an artificial smile like Nicholas and his knickerbocker friends used at parties to flirt with women or cozen future business associates. It bore no resemblance to the sinister grin he flashed just before he dragged her into his bed, nor did it curl into a nauseatingly sweet smile visible only when he apologized.

No, MacKenzie's smile was a simple glimpse of white between his lips. It wasn't broad enough to form brackets on either side of his mouth or spread into the crow's feet at the corners of his eyes. Yet it was winsome and genuine and shy. Then as quickly as it appeared, it vanished. His eyes closed, and he was unconscious again.

Victoria grabbed her wig and hat from the ground where they'd fallen. Keeping a wary eye on MacKenzie, she pulled her carpetbag close and hunted through the clothing for her hand mirror. She twisted her long hair into a bun and pulled the wig over her head. Using her mirror she checked for stray wisps of hair.

MacKenzie groaned as he drew up one knee and touched his fingers to his temple.

Victoria shot to her feet, securing her hat in place with a pearl tipped pin. She shoved her mirror into her pocket, grabbed her carpetbag, and dashed down the alley. Once on the main street, she slowed her pace and stopped to buckle her bag before continuing to the train station.

Several emigrant families milled around on the platform, while their children chased each other through the crowd and around the baggage carts. Inside, other families filled the back-to-back benches in the center of the room as Victoria checked the time tables posted on the wall. With so many trains and towns listed, she wasn't certain which one was which.

She approached the ticket window.

"Can I help you?" The balding man on the other side of the tall counter adjusted his green eyeshade and smiled.

"Yes, what time is the next train west?"

"The west bound, *Overland Limited*, number two train is scheduled to arrive from the east at one ten and depart west at three fifteen railroad time."

She glanced at the watch pinned to her blouse. It was only seven-thirty.

Someone stepped up behind her, and she swung around, every muscle tensed, poised to run. An old man stood holding a black hat against his waist. She exhaled a shaky breath and gave him a weak smile.

Turning back to the ticket agent she asked, "I don't understand, what do you mean, railroad time?"

"See now, noon here in Cheyenne happens at a different time than noon in Omaha, or noon in Ogden. Depending on which way the train is going, you will gain or lose about one minute for every nine miles."

"But what time will the westbound train actually leave?"

He scratched his head then readjusted his eyeshade. "By my recollecting it should depart about two twelve this afternoon, Cheyenne time, if they don't have to make any unscheduled stops before they get here."

She lifted her carpetbag onto the counter. "I'll take a ticket to San Francisco."

"Very good, ma'am. That will be seventy-five dollars."

She withdrew the bills and passed them through the opening. Her purse was nearly empty. At some point she would have to remove a few more bills from the stash of blackmail money she'd hidden in the lining of her carpetbag.

"Unless the signal is out, this train doesn't make any stops, so you might want to go next door to the hotel restaurant. They'll pack you some food for fifty cents."

****

Ryder woke to the heat of the sun beating down on his face. At first he lay with his eyes closed and touched his throbbing head, trying to assimilate the disjointed images which swirled around inside.

A woman had leaned over him, more beautiful than his imagination could conceive. Surrounded by a halo of light, her golden hair had spilled over her white blouse as she watched him with eyes as blue as the sky behind her.

Had she been real or an unwanted effect of the knock on his head? Maybe she'd been a sign his luck had changed for the better.

He pushed himself up to sit and touched the lump behind his left ear. When he had woken on the floor of the hotel room with a pounding headache, he wasn't surprised to realize the princess had bashed him with something hard. What had surprised him were the pillow and blanket. If she hadn't been worth five thousand dollars, he would have taken the lump on his head as an omen, and gone home.

But he'd actually held the illusive woman by her arm. Five thousand dollars in his hand—at least until she had him running a race his body wasn't able to handle.

Now she was nowhere in sight. He picked up his hat and positioned it carefully on his head. Maybe this was a sign he should quit.

He stood. The earth tilted and swayed. His empty stomach rolled like the waves lapping against the dock pilings along the waterfront back in New York. He closed his eyes until the sensation passed.

Every muscle in his body ached to lie down somewhere and sleep, but if he did that, he'd lose the money.

Head down, he searched for his handcuffs in the clumps of tall grass which hugged the foundations of the nearby buildings. They were the only pair he had, and he was certain once he caught the princess, the only way he'd be able to hold on to her would be if he attached himself to her. Sunlight glinted off the metal, and he shoved the handcuffs into the front pocket of his vest.

Taking a breath, he released it slowly then walked to the corner of the building where he'd left his gear.

****

With an ugly shawl wrapped around her shoulders and dark tinted spectacles perched on her nose, Victoria wandered the aisles of the dry goods store. The owner, Mr. Prentiss, had just purchased four pairs of wool socks, a scarf, and the brown cardigan sweater she'd finished this morning while hiding between two baggage carts at the depot. He'd also given her store credit for her black bombazine dress, including the gloves, hat, and veil.

Not wearing the old-style widow's weeds had made her bag hard to close and too heavy. Though the dress had become wrinkled beyond wearing, Mr. Prentiss felt certain his wife could freshen it up and told her to go ahead and browse.

She picked out a bar of soap, tooth powder, a Beadle's dime novel, and three skeins of yarn. As he tallied her purchases, her gaze fell on the row of glass jars filled with peppermint sticks, lemon drops, and licorice whips, which were lined up in front of the cash register.

"Could I also have some lemon drops, please?"

Mr. Prentiss looked up from his receipt pad and peered at her over the tops of his spectacles. He smiled. "Sure thing."

Her mouth watered, anticipating the sweet-sour bite of the candy as the small sugar-coated orb rolled between her palate and tongue. With the memory came the sensation of her grandmother's arms wrapped around her, snuggling her close after a nightmare.

In the months following her parents' death, the scary dreams had come often. Always alone, in the rain, in an alley or abandoned building searching for her mama and papa, but never finding them. Her grandmother would dry her tears and pass her a lemon drop. Then Nanna would fill her head with stories of handsome princes, noble knights, and castles in faraway kingdoms.

"How much would you like?"

Victoria blinked. "A pound." She wasn't sure why she needed so much, but it was a long way to San Francisco. If the train went straight through, she might not have another chance to purchase some.

He carried the jar to the end of the counter and scooped the candy into the bowl of a small scale. "Like lemon drops, do you?" he called back.

"Yes, I love lemon."

He tore a piece of paper from the roll at the end of the counter and fashioned it into a large cone. "I see you picked up some soap. Did you see the lemon scented bars we have?"

"No, I didn't."

He poured the candy into the cone, folded down the top, and set it on counter with her other purchases. "I had all the soaps arranged together, but my wife made this special section over here." He moved toward the back of the store to a small display case.

Victoria followed.

He lifted a bar of soap from the shelf behind and set it on top of the glass case which displayed brushes, mirrors, and hair combs. "She thought it'd be nice having all the ladies toiletries together. We have rose, lemon, lavender, and jasmine soaps. Here's the lemon."

Victoria lifted the bar to her nose and inhaled. Closing her eyes, she was transported back to that day when her grandmother had come to the orphanage to get her. Nanna had hugged her tight to her lemon scented bosom and told Victoria everything would be all right.

"We have rose water and lemon verbena, too."

On the counter, he placed a glass bottle decorated with purple-edged, white blossoms. She set the soap down and wiggled the stopper from the bottle. Yes, she thought as she waved it under her nose. Nanna. And somehow Victoria felt a little bit safer, a little bit less alone.

"I'll take them both."

With her purchases tucked away in her carpetbag, a lemon drop in her mouth and a few more in her pocket, Victoria stepped from the doorway of the dry goods store into the mid-day sunshine and started toward the depot to wait.

Before crossing the entrance of an alley, she stopped. Lifting her dark-tinted spectacles, she peered under them to glance at the front of her blouse, where the gold watch that once belonged to her grandmother, lay pinned.

A shaggy brown puppy raced from the alley to the edge of the street. He snatched up a stick, whirled, and charged back into the alley. A moment later there was a sharp, *yip, yip*.

A familiar chuckle rolled to her ears. "Shut up," MacKenzie murmured affectionately. An instant later the stick flew past and landed in the street, again chased after by the puppy.

Victoria hadn't seen MacKenzie since early this morning, and until this moment believed her disguise had fooled him. She leaned against the wall of the jewelry shop and peered around the corner. She couldn't see all of him. A couple of stacked crates blocked her view. But it didn't matter. Those long legs, crossed at the ankles and extending beyond the crates could only belong to one man. Her gaze went straight to his scuffed boots and the flash of silver where sunshine reflected off the hearts on his spurs.

Victoria pressed her spine against the clapboards then looked up and down the street. Now she understood why she hadn't seen him all morning. This alley was the perfect place for him to watch unobserved, because anyone going to the train station would have to walk past.

The puppy stopped in front of her and dropped the stick. She silently shooed him with her hand, but he merely cocked his head and eyed her quizzically. Fishing a lemon drop from her pocket, she tossed the treat in front of him. After a quick sniff, he gobbled it up then raised his brown eyes expectantly for another. This time she tossed it off the edge of the walk then hurried back the way she'd come before MacKenzie came looking for the puppy.

The soft chink of spurs combined with the hollow thud of footsteps against the boards behind her. Her heart fell. Didn't MacKenzie have something better to do than chase her all over the country? How much was

Nicholas paying him?

The sharp staccato of her heels against the wood distorted her ability to assess how far behind he was. At the mercantile store, she ducked inside.

The bell jingled, but there were so many ladies gossiping around the counter, no one glanced her way. Victoria turned to the left and crouched beside a rack of dresses where she could still see out the front window. She recognized his rangy silhouette as he approached the front of the store and stopped.

He seemed reluctant to enter, staring at the door as though steeling himself for an unpleasant task. His shoulders rose and fell as he drew a deep breath.

He pushed the door inward. The bell jingled. On her knees she bent down and peered through the space between the floor and the hems of the dresses. Scuffed brown boots with hearts on the spurs chinked softly as he walked past. A tiny length of red yarn, caught on his rowel, trailed behind his left boot.

The women near the counter stopped talking.

"Can I help you?" Mr. Prentiss asked.

McKenzie halted. "No."

Annoyance tightened his voice, but Victoria wasn't sure if it was because he couldn't find her or because everyone stared at him.

His footsteps continued past the counter and across the back of the store.

Stooped low and clutching her carpetbag, she waddled like a duck to the front door. As she reached for the knob, someone from outside pushed. The bell jingled. She glanced down the aisle.

MacKenzie looked up.

Their gazes collided. They stared at each other then

he started toward her.

Galvanized by his movement, she scooted past the man who entered. Gathering her skirts in one hand, she ran down the walk and darted into the alley where the puppy had been. Knowing he'd probably seen her, she sprinted to the end and turned left.

She needed to throw him off her trail then board the train without him knowing. Since MacKenzie had seen her wearing this disguise, she hurried to the Union Pacific Hotel and slipped into the ladies retiring room. With one more ruse in her bag, she sped through a costume change that would have done her nanna proud.

With every strand of hair carefully hidden beneath a starched linen wimple, she patted rice powder over her face and returned the dark-tinted spectacles to her nose. Next, from one of the inside pockets of her bag, she withdrew a silver cross which hung from a black cord and slipped it over her head. Last she secured wooden rosary beads to the woven black belt around her waist. Unconcerned with wrinkles, she jammed all her clothes into her carpetbag and tugged the buckle closed.

Certain he would never recognize her, she did as the ticket agent suggested and purchased some sandwiches, apples, and a jar of lemonade.

Back inside the large waiting room, she located a seat on a bench behind a large group of German emigrants. She could see the front door but hoped if MacKenzie entered he wouldn't recognize her.

Though she'd been counting the minutes on the clock, she jumped when the sound of the train whistle blasted through the building.

Moving inside the group of boarding passengers,

Victoria made her way outside. Though her feet ached to race across the open platform and jump on board, she curled her toes and waited, moving sedately toward the passenger cars. The engine sat softly chugging as the crates and trunks were transferred from wide, flat hand carts into the baggage car.

"Alll aboarrrd." The conductor called. Clouds of steam billowed around the big wheels of the engine.

Keeping her gaze focused on the last car, she stepped aside and politely allowed others to board first. Though she desperately wanted to check the crowd for that familiar dark hat, she looked neither to the right nor to the left.

The conductor, who stood at the bottom of the train steps, turned toward her. "Sister, can I take your bag?"

"Yes, thank you." She passed him her carpetbag and sack of food then grabbed the rail with one hand, gathered the hem of her habit with her other, and climbed up the steps. The conductor returned her bags then stepped back to offer his assistance to the woman boarding the train behind her.

Victoria made her way down the aisle, locating a seat at the end of the car across from the necessary. The back of the seat opposite her was locked in the rear facing position, so if she had been part of a family, conversation would have been easy.

Relief weakened her knees, and she sat. She placed her bag and lunch sack on the other seat instead of the overhead rack.

The whistle shrieked again. Chewing the inside of her cheek, she leaned forward and searched for MacKenzie among the people gathered on the platform.

A few minutes passed as other passengers settled

into seats. From outside, the conductor yelled, "All aboard!"

Please hurry. She mentally prodded the engineer to get the train moving.

Then she spotted MacKenzie stepping from the depot. With his hat brim pulled low, she couldn't see his face, but from the way the people on the platform stopped and stared, she knew they could.

With his saddlebags and bedroll tossed over his left shoulder and his rifle in hand, he strode toward the train as though their gawking didn't bother him.

The cars jerked and groaned as the train eased out of the station. Gradually the chugging of the engine increased in tempo. He would never be able to jump on board now. Her anxiety eased, and a flutter of excitement rippled through her body.

Releasing a quick, *Amen*, she glanced out the window as the landscape flew by. The same exhilarating rush she'd felt when she escaped Nicholas, washed over her, whisking away the fear that had weighed her down since she met MacKenzie.

The door at the front of the car opened then closed with a sharp bang. Victoria glanced up, expecting to see the conductor. Instead, MacKenzie stood there, frowning at each face in the car as he moved in her direction.

She lowered her gaze to her lap and her folded hands, praying he wouldn't recognize her.

His spurs chinked softly, and his boot heels thudded on the floor as he moved down the aisle. She raised her head just enough to peer over the tops of her spectacles and watch him come her way.

Though the rocking of the train made it difficult for

anyone to walk a straight line, he seemed to stagger a bit more than the rhythmic motion warranted. When he stopped beside her seat, her stomach lurched like a puddle that had just had a large rock dropped into it. She lifted her gaze to meet his. Evidently he'd seen enough of her face from their early morning tussle that he recognized her.

With a barely perceptible nod, he reached up and placed his rifle, saddlebags, and bedroll in the overhead rack then stood looking down at her, his brow furrowed. His intense gaze studied her from the top of her white wimple and black veil, to the scuffed toes of her shoes which peeked from beneath the skirt of her habit.

"You're not fat," he announced.

Chapter Six

She blinked at him.

His cryptic observation seemed to imply her smaller size was a greater sin than her nun impersonation.

Before she could form a response to his outrageous statement, he reached across, grabbed her left arm, and closed one ring of his handcuffs around her wrist.

"Help!" she screamed, her mouth in line with his ear.

He winced. "Stop it." He latched the other ring around the curve of the armrest.

She jerked her arm, but the manacle held fast. With her free hand, she punched his upper arm and lashed out with her foot, connecting with his shin.

"Here!" yelled a tall, red-headed man in a suit. "What are you doing?"

"Holy Mary, Mother of God," Victoria cried. "This bounder wants to have his way with me!"

Another man, sporting a full beard and built like a blacksmith, strode down the aisle, seized MacKenzie by the back of the collar, and lifted him right off the seat.

"Get off me." MacKenzie reached over his shoulders grasping at the bearded man's arm. "She's my prisoner." But the man dragged him backward up the aisle.

The red head stepped into the aisle and drove his

fist into MacKenzie's stomach as he then snatched MacKenzie's gun from his holster with his other hand.

MacKenzie grunted, drew up his foot, and kicked the man in the center of the chest. The red head staggered back. He hit the armrest of a seat, lost his balance, and fell to the floor. The revolver skidded under the seat.

Victoria pulled at the handcuffs. "Can somebody please get the key?"

The red headed man scrambled to his feet and started forward but stopped short of kicking range.

The bearded man locked one arm around MacKenzie's neck while with his free hand, tried to search through MacKenzie's pockets, Victoria assumed for another weapon.

MacKenzie turned his chin into the crook of the man's elbow, then with one hand at the man's wrist and the other under the elbow, he shoved the man's arm up as he dropped to one knee. Still gripping the big man's wrist, momentum yanked the man down, slamming his face into the back rest of the nearest seat.

With the red head still in the aisle blocking his way, MacKenzie stepped onto the nearest seat, bracing one hand on the overhead compartment. The woman in the seat screamed as she swung her reticule like a club whacking MacKenzie around his waist and thighs.

Ignoring her assault, his long legs marched him over the back of the woman's seat onto the next, then the next, stepping between the startled passengers, toward the back of the train and Victoria.

The big man pushed to his feet. Blood trickled from the corner of his mouth into his beard. Like an angry bull, he shoved the redhead aside and charged.

MacKenzie stopped on the seat where Victoria had placed her things. Then in one smooth motion, he grabbed his rifle from the overhead rack and jumped into the aisle.

Victoria switched her attention to her hand and tried squeezing her pinky and thumb as tight together as possible in order to pull her hand through the circle of metal. A scream of frustration bubbled up in the back of her throat as the first joint of her thumb jammed against the handcuff.

A double click sound brought Victoria's head up. The big man stood with his hands raised, MacKenzie's rifle aimed at his wide chest. The red headed man shrank into his seat as the other passengers ducked low in theirs.

"Back away," MacKenzie's warning rumbled in his throat like a feral snarl.

The man who played with kittens was gone. In his place, stood a man whose aura radiated the same raw danger which encompassed this harsh western land.

Victoria's palms started sweating, and she tugged frantically at the handcuffs. At this moment MacKenzie appeared more evil than Nicholas ever had.

The door burst open at the front of the car, and the conductor strode down the aisle toward the group. The young boy who entered the car right behind him slid into the first seat where a woman holding a baby pulled him close.

"Now see here," the conductor commanded as he peered around the big man still holding his hands in the air. "I'll have no gun play on my train."

Reaching into his vest pocket, MacKenzie withdrew a folded paper and giving a couple of shakes to open it, held it up. "My name is Ryder MacKenzie. I'm a bounty hunter, and this woman is no more a nun than I am. She's a thief, wanted in New York, and I'm taking her back. Now tell these men to leave me alone and let me do my job."

"No," Victoria called watching them move back up the aisle. "He's lying."

The conductor reached out and took the paper. He seemed to read each word twice, then handed it back. "You sure this is the woman?"

MacKenzie nodded toward her. "Check her carpetbag," he said. "It's full of disguises. This nun outfit is just another way to throw me off her trail."

The conductor glanced at the bag.

Victoria feared he would actually search it. Instead he leveled his attention on her. "This true?"

Defeat settled in the pit of her stomach like a lump of cold oatmeal. It didn't matter, truth or a lie, she would still end up with Nicholas. She tried to explain.

"You don't understand. My husband will kill me for leaving him. You can't let this man take me back." Tears filled her eyes. She detested the weak-willed woman Nicholas had turned her into, a woman whose only response to conflict was begging and crying.

As usual, neither had any affect. The conductor wasn't swayed. "It's not my place to come between a husband and wife."

He gave MacKenzie a quick nod. "Now put that rifle up, son. I want no more trouble."

The passengers cast pitying glances over their shoulders and returned to their seats as Ryder shoved the paper back in his pocket.

The conductor pulled open the door at the front of

the car. "Appreciate you folks trying to help," he said. "But it's none of our affair."

Victoria gave the handcuffs one more tug. She drew several deep breaths to stop the tears from spilling.

Shooting her an angry glare, Ryder MacKenzie returned his rifle to the overhead rack then walked back up the aisle. He bent over a couple of times and when he returned, he held his hat in one hand, his revolver in the other.

With a groan Ryder lowered himself beside her and placed his hat on his knee.

"Please, let me go." She hated to beg, but unless she hit him over the head again and stole the key, she saw no way to escape.

He checked the chamber of his gun, then with his shirt tail, he carefully wiped each bit of dust and grit from the barrel.

"You don't understand." She pleaded. "My husband is a terrible man."

Ryder slipped his revolver into his holster and picked up his hat.

"Last month Nicholas paid to have a young man who flirted with me killed."

Using the side of his forearm like a brush, he swiped across the brim and crown of his hat.

"Now he's blackmailing another and is going to have one of the man's sons beaten if he doesn't pay. You can't take me back."

Bracing both feet against the edge of the opposing seat, MacKenzie leaned back then dropped his hat over his face.

"Please, I'll give you whatever Nicholas is paying

you."

From beneath the hat, he mumbled. "You got five thousand dollars?"

Five thousand dollars!

"Didn't think so. Now be quiet and leave me alone. We're getting off at Granite Canyon."

Victoria trembled with the urge to scream, or at least hit him a few times like the woman with the reticule had. A well placed kick might even make her feel better.

There must be some way to remove these handcuffs, some trick she could employ to escape from him.

She could threaten to shoot him with his gun if he didn't set her free, but he'd stashed the rifle in the overhead compartment, and his revolver was on the other side of his body. Maybe she could reach across him and carefully pull it from his holster. No, she'd better be certain he was sound asleep before she tried anything like that.

The chugging of the engine and the clacking of the wheels against the rails grew hypnotic so she was no longer aware of the open grassland which flew past her window. Beside her, one of Ryder's feet slipped off the edge of the opposite seat and landed squarely on the floor with a thump. A few minutes later his second foot followed suit.

She expected the sudden movement to startle him awake, but he slumped lower in the seat. His body swayed with the motion of the train, and his head slid closer and closer until it rested against her shoulder.

Frowning, she pushed at him. His hat fell to the floor, and his head slid onto her lap. She reached out, intending to shove him right on top of his hat, but froze, her hand inches from his shoulder. If she didn't disturb him, maybe he'd sleep right through the next stop and maybe the next. Hope surged through her veins.

The door at the front of the car opened, and the conductor returned. Slowly he moved from seat to seat, checking the tickets of each passenger. Victoria slipped her hand into her pocket beneath the weight of MacKenzie's head. Her fingers brushed the ticket. Slowly she pulled it out and transferred it to her restrained hand.

Afternoon sunlight spilled through the windows, highlighting rich caramel streaks in his brown hair. Time and sun had etched tiny lines in the skin around his eyes, and a short, dark beard coated his gaunt cheeks. With the left side of his face pressed against her thigh, she wondered if he'd hidden that part of himself from the world for so long it had become instinct.

The fierceness which had hardened his features a short time ago was gone. In sleep lingered traces of the little boy Ryder MacKenzie had once been. And she couldn't help but wonder if he'd had a happy childhood.

Telling herself she was merely checking his bump, she slipped her fingers through the hair behind his ear where it hung long over the knot of his blue bandana. She'd suffered a few head injuries herself and recalled the nausea, the fatigue, and the mental confusion.

"Ticket, Sis—er um...ma'am?"

Victoria jerked her hand from MacKenzie's hair. Heat scorched her cheeks as she whisked her ticket from the fingers of her chained hand and passed it to the conductor without meeting his gaze.

If the man had held the slightest inclination toward believing her claim, seeing MacKenzie's head in her lap proved not only that she wasn't a nun, but implied something more between them than kidnapper and victim.

He punched her ticket and passed it back. She shoved it into her pocket.

"Does your…er…um…*friend*…have his ticket?"

This isn't what it looks like, she wanted to explain. She needed this man, with his judgmental glare to understand that while what he saw might appear inappropriate, and though she might not be a nun, she was still a lady.

"Just a moment," she said instead. Placing her hand on Ryder's shoulder poised to give him a quick shake she suddenly questioned the need to wake him.

Instead, she carefully searched all four pockets of his vest. Nothing. Fingers trembling, she slipped her hand beneath to his shirt where the heat of his body lay trapped between the soft, blue cotton and the black wool of his vest. She wondered about the look of his chest, the cut of his muscles, and the dusting of hair which covered them.

The heavy paper she found in his breast pocket was warm, and as she passed it to the conductor, her fingers felt the chill of its loss.

No. You are acting like a fool. Remember where your fantasies landed you and learn from it.

When the conductor held the ticket out, she snatched it back and shoved it inside her pocket along with her own. With a disapproving frown and a snort of disgust, the conductor turned back the way he'd come.

Not knowing where to put her arm, she rested it

across the back of the seat.

Gurgling noises growled in Ryder MacKenzie's stomach. She smiled. She couldn't imagine Nicholas allowing his body to emit such a sound.

The train stopped at Granite Canyon, but it was a small depot in the middle of nowhere. One man got off, but no one boarded.

As the train chugged west, she considered how much longer MacKenzie would sleep. She needed that handcuff key, and the only pockets she hadn't checked were the front of his pants.

Maybe it was the nun's habit, but it suddenly felt as though she were committing a sin to even think of sliding her hand into such an intimate place, especially without his knowledge.

Instead, she forced herself to imagine the alternative. Her stomach twisted like a wet wash rag. In her mind Nicholas' harsh voice demanded an explanation for her escape. She almost winced in response to the pressure of his long fingers digging into her upper arm moments before he tossed her against a wall or piece of furniture.

A quick glance around the car reassured her that no one paid her any mind. Taking a deep breath, she lowered her hand to Ryder's hip, just above the dark walnut grip of his revolver. Before she could change her mind, she slipped off the leather loop, grasped the wood, and inched it from his holster. Unsure where to put it, she passed it over his head to her opposite hand then placed it on the seat between her hip and the outside wall of the train.

His chest maintained its steady rise and fall, and she exhaled a long breath. Returning to her original task, her hand hovered over his pocket. With him being right-handed, she hoped he'd have shoved the key into his right pocket. Her thumb brushed against the button of his suspenders where the hem of his vest had risen above his waistband.

If she thought his shirt pocket warm, this pocket was an oven. Victoria wiggled her hand lower, beneath the weight of his leather gun belt. Just a thin piece of material lay between her fingers and his drawers, between her fingers and the edge of his groin. Her hand inched lower. Her cheeks burned. She tried to focus on her task, afraid if she looked up she would discover someone watching.

Then her finger tips brushed the coin-shaped end of a small key. She bit back her exclamation of triumph and scissored the short length of metal between her index and forefinger.

The shrill blast of the train's whistle shattered the quiet. Brakes screeched metal on metal, and the train jerked to a stop. Ryder tumbled to the floor, and Victoria fell to her knees on top of him. The wrist handcuffed to the armrest, yanked her arm back, while her right hand, still trapped inside his pocket, pulled her forward.

"What the hell…" He groaned as Victoria yanked her hand free, the key squeezed tight inside her fist. "Get off me."

"I'm sorry." She put her hand on the arm rest, her fist on the seat, and levered herself up. "The train stopped so suddenly…"

MacKenzie slowly pushed to his knees.

Victoria inched closer to the armrest and pulled her skirt over the gun.

He rubbed his hand across his face then leaned forward to look out the window. "Damn it," he muttered.

Victoria followed his gaze. In the distance, stretched an endless herd of what looked like large cows with big, wooly heads and shoulders. "Are those buffalo?"

"Yeah." He raised himself off the floor to sit beside her.

"There are so many," she said, awed by what she guessed must have been thousands of the beasts. "I've heard about them, but I've never seen one. They're huge. And look at all the little babies." She turned to look at him, but his attention was focused on reshaping the crown of his flattened hat.

Her gaze swung back to the buffalo. She tightened her fingers around the key. She couldn't feel sorry for Ryder MacKenzie. He was the enemy, and she had to escape. Casually, she slipped the key into her pocket. For now, she'd wait, hoping he wouldn't notice she'd taken his gun.

"Where are we?" He leaned close to look out the window.

"I don't know, exactly." She caught a whiff of his earthy scent.

He grunted and relaxed in the seat, extending one long leg as far as the cramped space allowed, and propped the bottom of his other boot against the edge of the opposite seat.

"How many stops did I sleep through?" He shot her an accusatory glare.

"One."

His gaze lingered on her lap then turned away as

though he were embarrassed to realize where he'd been sleeping. "And if the train hadn't slammed on the brakes, you would have let me sleep all the way to the Pacific Ocean."

Knowing he was right, she said nothing.

The door at the end of the car swung open, and the conductor stepped inside. "Sorry for the sudden stop folks. Hope everyone is all right. We'll get underway as soon as we can, but it looks like we're going to be here a bit."

Several people left the car and stood outside the train watching the buffalo. A few seats away a woman opened a picnic basket and passed food out to her family.

Craving some of the lemonade she'd purchased, Victoria leaned toward her food sack. As her fingertips stretched past the wine-colored carpetbag, a hand clamped around her wrist.

"What are you up to now?"

She yanked her hand back unsure of his mood. "I only wanted to get my food."

He sat back. A pink tinge dusted his cheekbone to the bridge of his nose. "Pardon me, Princess. I wouldn't want to keep you from your meal."

She leaned forward and reached for the sugar sack. "Would you like a piece of chicken or a cheese sandwich?" She told herself it was simply her ingrained sense of decorum which prompted her to offer the food, not concern for his well-being.

His gaze fastened on her hands as she removed the quart jar of lemonade and an apple. She thought he was about to accept, then seemed to change his mind and shook his head.

She wasn't sure if he was being polite or if he really wasn't hungry. From the way his stomach had rumbled earlier, she suspected he was being chivalrous. Regardless, he needed to eat.

She held the lemonade in her manacled hand and set the fruit in her lap while she withdrew a sandwich from the bag. The apple rolled forward and thudded against the floor.

Ryder leaned over and picked it up.

"Thank you," she said as he held it out to her. "But you can have it."

He stilled. "What's the matter, Princess? Don't want it cause it's bruised?"

"I didn't mean—"

"I don't care what you mean. All I care about is the five thousand dollars your rich husband is going to pay me when I bring you home." There was a loud crunch as he chomped off almost a quarter of the apple.

Victoria unwrapped her cheese sandwich.

Many Sunday evenings, when Hester was on her half-day, Victoria and her grandmother would eat cheese sandwiches in the parlor while they played checkers. Sometimes they would fry the sandwiches in butter until the cheese melted into a gooey mess. As time passed and Victoria went off to school, those Sunday evenings faded away. But today, biting into the soft white bread with the blend of yeast and sharp cheese brought all those happy memories to life. Sometimes she wondered if she would ever be that happy again.

From the corner of her eye, she spied Ryder popping the entire core into his mouth. She'd never seen anyone eat an apple so fast. Even horses ate them slower. The poor man must be half- starved.

She sighed and lowered the sandwich to her lap. "I can't eat this."

"What the hell is wrong with it?"

"The bread is dry, and the cheese is too hard."

"What were you expecting, cucumber sandwiches and petit fours?" He snatched the sandwich from her lap. "Tastes fine to me," he mumbled around a giant mouthful.

She smiled. He needed the food more than she, and Victoria doubted whether he would have accepted any if he hadn't believed it wasn't up to her royal standards.

Minutes later he shifted on the seat. Did he ever sit still? She glanced over. He looked pale.

Immediately, he bolted from the seat and charged out the door. Though his retching was quiet, the sound of him being sick caused her own stomach to roll.

A few minutes later, he returned and slid into the seat.

She held out the jar of lemonade, but he shook his head. Setting the jar on the floor, she pulled her carpetbag into her lap. She unbuckled the strap, dug through one of the inside pockets, and withdrew the paper cone of lemon drops. She turned and offered it to him. "Take some. You'll feel better."

He lifted his gaze to meet hers as though judging her sincerity. He really did have the most beautiful eyes…

Reaching his fingers inside, he withdrew two. "Thanks." He popped them in his mouth. As he'd done earlier, Ryder pulled his hat over his eyes and settled back with the bottoms of his boots on the edge of the opposite seat, his bent knees bridging the space between.

Victoria put the candy back, but before she fastened the buckle, she slipped his gun inside and set the bag on the opposite seat.

"Are you feeling better?" she asked, even as she told herself not to care.

"Yeah," came the muted reply. "What'd you hit me with anyway?"

"The water pitcher."

She wasn't sure if the muffled sound which came from beneath the hat was a grunt or a snort. Despite wanting to hate him, there was something very likeable about Ryder MacKenzie.

"Well, don't do it again," he said.

She smiled. Yes, very likeable.

Chapter Seven

The engine sat on the tracks chugging, until the buffalo herd thinned out enough for the train to creep forward. Beside her, Ryder's chest continued to slowly rise and fall.

Certain he slept, she unlocked her handcuffs then inch by inch, stretched across his torso, and snapped one ring around the arm rest. The sharp scent of sweat, the smell of horse, and the sweet aroma of hay filled her senses as she breathed. She stared at the crown of his hat, unnerved by the sensation that through the heavy felt, Ryder MacKenzie watched her. She would have secured his wrist but feared if he moved in his sleep, the jerk on his hand would wake him.

The conductor entered the front of the car. "We got Sherman Tunnel coming up, then next stop, Laramie."

Victoria stiffened, expecting the booming voice to startle Ryder awake. His breathing remained slow and even.

A few minutes later the car grew dark, and suddenly having MacKenzie asleep beside her seemed almost intimate. Strangely she missed the weight of his head in her lap, the softness of his hair beneath her fingers.

Gradually light streamed through the windows, and she shook the foolish notions from her head. Carefully she reached across MacKenzie's lap and lifted his forearm. His hand drooped at the wrist. Guilt held her still, as though leaving him was an act of betrayal. But she had no choice. She couldn't go back to Nicholas.

Her hand trembled as she clamped the manacle around the blue cuff of his shirt sleeve then eased his hand onto his thigh.

As the train pulled alongside the depot, the other passengers rose and collected their belongings. Victoria lifted the skirt of her habit, exposing black stockings all the way to her knees, and climbed over Ryder's legs. Then grabbing her carpetbag, she fled the train.

As her feet touched the platform, she glanced back. No Ryder. Hurrying forward, she blended into the crowd which mingled in front of the depot. Before Ryder freed himself and came after her, she latched onto a family headed to New York House, for a good meal. As they passed a tobacco shop, a man, dressed in a buckskin shirt, emerged from the store. His mustache drooped as had the man's on the train from Ogallala to Julesburg.

Her heart racing, she continued behind the family, maintaining her serene nun-like pace. Before she reached the hotel, she turned down a side street and ducked inside the first store she came to. Hiding behind a barrel stuffed with brooms, she peered through the front window praying she'd lost the man in the buckskin shirt. And if her luck held, Ryder MacKenzie would sleep all the way to San Francisco.

"Can I help you, Sister?"

She gasped and swung around.

A short, balding man watched her through tiny spectacles.

"No, thank you. I'm just looking."

"I also have heavier push-brooms in the back with the pitch forks and other barn tools." He eyed her dubiously.

"Actually, I just arrived on the train, and I'm not familiar with your town. Could you recommend a place to stay?"

"Well there's the New York House, over on Front Street, then there is Worth's Hotel and Mechanics' House."

Knowing MacKenzie would check the hotels, she amended her question. "I'm really looking for someplace quieter and more serene for my prayers and meditation."

"Well, if you don't mind a bit of a walk, Mrs. Proctor has a boarding house less than a quarter mile east of town." He raised his arm and gestured toward the corner. "Just head down that way and keep walking, you'll see it."

"Bless you, sir."

"She don't serve supper 'til half past five, so you can probably get yourself a good meal."

Victoria crossed the street as the door closed behind her. She wondered if Ryder was awake, if he realized she was gone. He'd be furious when he discovered she not only had his gun, but the key to his handcuffs. When she'd slipped it into her pocket, she hadn't given a thought to how he would get free. More than likely he had an extra one in his saddlebags. He'd be fine, besides there were plenty of people around to help.

With her guilt assuaged, she followed the dusty road out of town. The sun against her back combined with the fresh air to clear the train soot from her lungs and bolstered her spirits. In the distance a gray, sun-bleached house stood alone surrounded by prairie, its wide, wrap-around porch inviting her to hurry. Maybe there was a rocking chair. It would be lovely to sit outside after supper with her knitting and watch the sun set.

Behind her came the thudding cadence of hoof beats, and she moved off into the grass expecting the rider to continue past. Instead the hoof beats stopped.

She looked up. Looming over her from atop a dark chestnut horse was the man in the buckskin shirt. Icy tentacles of fear climbed upward from the knot in her stomach to choke out the first bit of joy she'd managed to find in years.

"Going somewhere, *Sister*?" He grinned around the stub of a cigar clamped between his teeth.

Unwilling to surrender so easily, she whipped off her veil and waved it in front of the horse. The animal reared then swung around in a lop-sided circle as the man in the saddle fought to bring him under control.

Victoria dropped to her knees and fumbled to undo the buckle of her carpetbag. Shoving her hand inside, she groped for the pistol. Seizing it, she snatched up her skirts and ran toward the house. "Help!" she screamed. Maybe someone was on the porch and would hear her cries. "Help me!"

The horse pounded up behind her again. She ran faster, even as part of her brain told her she'd never make it to the house.

She darted to the left, but he brought his horse around and cut her off. She whirled and raced back to the road, but he easily blocked her way.

Holding the walnut grip with both hands, Victoria

raised her arms and aimed MacKenzie's gun slightly to the left of the man's chest. She didn't want to kill him, just make him believe she would. Instead, amusement danced around the edges of his mouth.

"Let me go or I'll shoot." Despite shaking hands, she expected the threat of death to be a little more sobering to the man. Maybe it was the nun's habit.

She closed her eyes expecting a loud bang as she squeezed the trigger. Nothing happened. She tried again, this time with her eyes open. Still no bang.

He moved his horse in front of her, reached out, and lifted the weapon from her unresisting fingers. She choked on a scream of frustration. As he shoved the pistol into the waistband of his pants, she snatched up her skirt and ran.

Behind her he chuckled. "There's no point in running Mrs. Vandy Beck."

Drawing a deep breath, she ran faster. The horse's legs swished through the tall grass as he trotted up alongside.

"I sent a telegram to your husband the other day when I spotted you in Julesburg. He seemed mighty eager to get you back."

No! Her pulse pounded through the roots of her hair. She swung away from him and raced toward town. Effortlessly, the horse once again caught up to her.

She stopped and sank to the ground. The earth tilted, and tiny flashes of light danced before her eyes as she fought for breath. Running, while wearing a corset and heavy wool, hadn't been her best idea.

Without a word, the man swung from the saddle, scooped her up and onto the horse, remounted, and settled her in his lap.

"While I'm curious to know how you got away from MacKenzie," his tone lowered. "You try any shit with me an' you'll regret it."

Her blood chilled. The edge in his voice sounded almost like Nicholas.

Then he nudged his horse into a lope, and they rode straight down the road past the boarding house. This man was not Ryder MacKenzie wearing spurs with tiny hearts.

****

"Sir?"

Someone leaned close to his face. "Sir, are you awake?"

Ryder groaned and opened his eyes. Trying to remember where he was, he could only blink at the man whose blue-billed cap loomed inches above Ryder's face. He glanced around. The princess was gone! He lunged to his feet, but a sharp jerk on his wrist yanked him back down. "What the hell…"

Incredulous, he stared at the handcuff which attached him to the armrest. He used his other hand to tug on the manacles. Though logically he knew it was futile, his frustration drove him to try.

The conductor cleared his throat. "Sir, you were supposed to leave the train at Granite Canyon."

Ryder glanced out the window. The summer sun hung low in the sky. "Where are we?"

"Laramie."

"Laramie?" Ryder jumped to his feet, but his wrist was held fast, and a wrenching pain shot straight to his elbow. "Sonofa…" He dropped heavily onto the seat.

The conductor frowned and stepped back.

Ryder stomped his boot heel against the floor. How

had she gotten the handcuffs off herself and around his wrist without him noticing? Damn her and her water pitcher. He must have been really out. Normally, he was a pretty fair bounty hunter, and until three days ago, no one had ever gotten the drop on him.

He pushed his hip close to the arm rest so he could slip his hand into his pocket for his key. His fingers froze. What the—His gun was gone. That goddamn, spoiled little princess had stolen his brand new Colt revolver with the walnut grip and the seven and a half inch blue steel barrel.

A string of curses flew from his mouth. The conductor hurried toward the front of the car.

"Get your skinny ass back here!" Ryder bellowed.

A hush fell over the train. Even the chugging of the engine seemed to quiet. Oddly enough, the conductor returned. He shifted his weight from foot to foot, just beyond Ryder's reach.

Ryder shoved his hand into his pocket. No key. His fingers traced the line of the seam. No goddamn key! The brazen hussy must have put her hand right inside his pocket and stolen it while he slept with his head in her lap.

He could almost feel her small fingers wiggling around in there, so close to his groin. Heat flooded his face. His body stirred as he imagined her palm sliding over his hip and thigh.

He gave his head a shake. He didn't have time to waste on the fantasies of a green youth. He'd experienced the cold hard truth first hand. Spoiled, rich women like her didn't want an ugly, worthless man like him.

Ryder pointed up. "My gear is overhead. Get it."

The conductor approached, keeping a wary eye on Ryder while he handed down the saddlebags, Winchester, and bedroll.

"Did she get off here?" Ryder asked as he dumped the contents of both saddle bag pouches onto the opposite seat.

"I couldn't say."

"Of course you can say." Ryder snapped as he shook out a hand towel and his holey blood stained socks. "Nobody gets on or off this train without you knowing."

Where the hell was his extra key?

"Yes, I believe your umm…companion left a few minutes ago."

Ryder double checked the pockets of his vest, untied his bedroll, shook out his blanket then pawed through the pockets of his extra shirt and pair of pants.

"Sir, you are holding up the train."

Ryder was fanning his thumb through the bristles of a horse brush when he remembered the extra key was inside the small pocket on the front of his chaps, and his chaps were tossed over the back of a chair in his cabin.

Damn it. He dropped back onto the seat. When he'd taken off after the men who'd stolen his cattle, he hadn't thought to be gone more than a few days. Now, almost a week had passed.

"Do you have a sheriff or locksmith in this town, or someone who might have a key that would fit these?"

"Don't know of a locksmith, but I can send someone for the sheriff."

"Fine," Ryder growled, and the conductor hurried from the train.

Ignoring the censure in the angry glares of the

passengers, Ryder rerolled his clothes inside his bedroll then stuffed what remained into his saddlebags, checking for the key one more time. He leaned back in the seat, bracing the ball of his left foot on the edge of the opposite seat, and stared out the window.

Two boys ran by rolling a hoop with a stick. A loaded wagon headed out of town. Someone on horseback rode past. Ryder's stomach rumbled and he sighed.

The door opened at the front of the car. Ryder looked up as the conductor entered. Behind him trailed a big man with long, curly black hair, whose shoulders barely fit through the doorway of the train. In one beefy hand, he clenched both a hammer and a chisel. A half dozen spectators brought up the rear.

Instinctively, Ryder tugged the brim of his hat low, thankful for the gloom of the train.

The deep voice of the blacksmith rang out. "Hey, little man. Kinda' dark in here. Can you light some lamps so's I don't smash my thumb with my hammer?" A burst of laughter filled the car.

Ryder cursed his rotten luck as the conductor checked his pocket watch then hurried to light the small lamps along the walls of the train. It couldn't be much past five. What did the man need lamps lit for anyway? The sun was still shining.

"Right in the middle of my supper," the blacksmith announced as he shuffled sideways down the aisle. "But I heard the story, and I had to see for myself." He laughed. The booming sound seemed to push from lungs as powerful as a set of bellows.

The big man stuck out his hand in greeting, "Name's Percy Ogden."

Ryder could only lift his right hand a few inches, but Percy didn't seem to mind and engulfed Ryder's smaller hand with his massive one. "What happened to your face? Nasty bruise ya got there. The little nun knock you upside the head?"

The walls of Ryder's stomach tightened as echoes of childhood taunts drifted through his mind. *"Hey Spot, what happened to your face? Your mother drop you on your head? Spot has the devil's mark. Spot is cursed by Satan. Where are you going, Spot? Look at him run!"*

"Just get on with it," Ryder snapped.

"Can't wait to tell my wife this one. Haw, haw, haw," Percy Ogden laughed. "A bounty hunter handcuffed to the seat of a train by a nun."

The man might look like a bear, but he brayed like an ass.

The conductor checked his watch again then stood hovering, as the blacksmith inspected the handcuff. Next he pulled a small piece of wood from his pocket and wedged it between the chain and the arm of the seat.

Bang. The hammer hit the chisel. The conductor winced.

Percy Ogden slammed the chisel again. With each subsequent whack, the chisel chipped another sliver of iron from the link. "A nun! Haw, haw, haw!"

Bang.

"Made off with your key ta' boot."

Bang.

Another rumbling round of laughter.

For reasons Ryder couldn't understand, the gawking crowd seemed to find the man's laughter infectious rather than annoying, and their chuckles rippled through the car like the echo in a canyon that went on and on.

"An' she stole yer gun, too."

Bang.

"Haw, haw, haw!"

By the time he severed the chain, Ryder was ready to drive his fist through one of the windows. He jumped up and tossed his bedroll over his shoulder before the blacksmith had put away his chisel.

"Do you run the livery?" Ryder asked as he picked up his rifle and saddlebags.

"Sure do, over on Front Street."

The conductor tugged on the single manacle still clamped around the arm of the seat. "Wait. You can't leave this hanging here."

"Hold yer horses, little man. I'll take care of it in a minute."

Ryder raised his arm, the other half of the manacle and chain dangled from his wrist. "You can't get this off?"

"Not unless ya want yer arm broke." He launched into another round of side-splitting laughter.

Ryder rubbed his hand across the back of his neck. "You finished then?"

"Sure enough, son."

With a sigh, Ryder withdrew some coins from his purse and passed them to the blacksmith. He then took a moment to see how much money he had left before he returned his purse to his pocket.

Percy Ogden burst out in a fresh round of strident laughter. "Haw, haw, haw, that little nun make off with all yer money, too?"

Ryder flinched, but said nothing. Oddly, she hadn't. But he reminded himself, money wasn't a problem for her. She would probably laugh at the pittance he guarded so carefully. More than likely, she spent more for ribbon on a hat. She didn't know what it was like to go days without eating, to sleep in the cold, or… He gave his head a shake. Why did it matter? She was simply a means to an end.

He gathered up his gear, gave a nod to the blacksmith, and turned to move down the aisle. As Ryder squeezed past, the conductor checked his watch and shot Ryder a poisonous glare as though Ryder were to blame for the schedule delay.

Dropping his gaze to the floor, Ryder hurried up the aisle avoiding eye contact with the gawking passengers. Stepping off the train, he drew a deep breath then adjusted the weight of his saddlebags and bed roll.

His stomach rumbled as he headed for the closest place with food. He ordered a large piece of apple pie and a cup of coffee. The pie was gone in a few quick bites, then he downed the coffee before the waiter had time to make change from the two bits Ryder had given him.

Hoisting his saddlebags and bedroll over his shoulder once more, he picked up his Winchester feeling slightly less miserable and strode down the dusty street to the first hotel.

But after checking for her at the New York House, Mechanic's House, and the newly remodeled and enlarged Worth's Hotel, his stomach was grumbling, and the broken blisters on his heels again felt warm and wet.

Chasing down the princess had become tougher than the pursuit of any outlaw. He stood on the boardwalk staring across the dusty street. The windows of the tailor shop and tobacco store gleamed bright white against the reflection of the evening sun.

Maybe it was time to go home. His cattle had likely been sold, and he had no idea where the princess was. At this moment all he longed for was to be back in his cabin where he could take a hot bath, soak his feet, and put on clean clothes.

He still had that small bunch of beeves in the west valley. Most of them should be dropping calves early next spring. He could pick up a bounty or two before winter to get him through. He just needed to find a horse.

The first livery he came to was closed. Now that he'd begun thinking of home, all he wanted was to get there.

Except for the horses milling around in a nearby corral, the next blacksmith shop and livery stable looked empty. If one of the wide front doors hadn't been open, he would have passed on by.

"Hello!" he called into the shadows of the cavernous building.

"I'm closed," bellowed a deep voice from somewhere within.

Ryder stepped inside. Harnesses and head collars hung along the wall, nearly hiding a smaller, partly open door. The hinges creaked as he pushed it inward and stepped into a blacksmith shop.

On the other side of the forge, in front of a long work bench stood the large, broad shouldered silhouette of a man.

"Told ya, I was closed," rumbled the familiar voice. "Just stopped by to put some tools away."

Even before the man turned, Ryder knew who he'd see. The apple pie and coffee churned together in his stomach. Acid rose in a bitter wave up the back of his throat.

"Well, hey there, young feller. Ya catch up with yer little nun yet?" He burst out laughing.

Ryder ran his hand around the back of his neck. "I need a horse."

"Well now, I reckon I got one or two I can let go."

He walked back inside the main barn, and Ryder followed him past a buggy, two wagons, a buckboard, and a carriage to the wide doors at the very back of the building.

Outside, a few horses munched hay from a rack inside a corral, and from the quality of the animals, Ryder doubted ol' Percy would take anything less than a hundred dollars for any of them.

A black horse with a star approached the fence. Ryder reached out and petted its sleek neck.

"Like this one, do ya?" Percy ambled up beside him. "Nice animal, well balanced an' about six years old."

Though Ryder suspected he couldn't afford it, he asked anyway. "How much?"

"One-forty."

Discouraged, he glanced around the corral. "Got anything cheaper?"

"I'll take one-ten for that roan over in back of the bay." Percy Ogden raised his thick arm and pointed across the corral to a horse Ryder could barely make out in the shadows. "He's a little skinny, but he's got good feet."

Ryder said nothing.

Percy must have recalled Ryder's limited funds. "Come on, son." He stepped away from the fence and gestured for Ryder to follow him around the side of the barn to a smaller corral. "I'll let ya have him fer whatever ya got in yer purse."

Ryder stared. He blinked to be sure the shadows weren't playing tricks on him, but when he opened his eyes, the long legged, long-eared animal was still there, staring at him with black fathomless eyes. A mule. A bucking, kicking, biting, braying, damn jackass of a mule!

Chapter Eight

The blacksmith seemed to expect Ryder's reluctance. "Ya could wait fer the train."

Ryder sighed. He could spend the last of his money on this pile of trouble wrapped up in teeth, hide, and hoof, or he could see how far his feet would take him.

Dropping his gear beside the fence, he reached inside his vest and withdrew the small leather purse. Carefully he counted out twenty-five dollars. That left him three dollars and seventeen cents to purchase supplies for the trip home.

Percy accepted the money and disappeared inside the livery. The mule stared at Ryder as though sizing him up, as if he knew what this exchange of money meant. Ryder glared right back. "Damn jackass. You better behave yourself with me or I'll—"

The blacksmith returned, carrying a saddle, bridle, and blanket. "This here's what come with him," he announced. He dropped them beside the corral fence with a thud and clatter of buckles. From beneath the blanket, he pulled a thick coil of rope.

"Here." He passed the rope to Ryder. "I'll give ya this too, jest fer takin' him off my hands. It'd prob'ly be a good idea to work off some a the scruffy 'fore ya try ridin' him." He then pulled a folded paper from his shirt pocket. "Here's yer bill a sale."

Ryder nodded and stuffed the paper into his pocket.

Then he took the rope and ducked through the poles of the corral.

"Ya headin' outta here tonight?"

Ryder ignored the question and instead moved into the center of the corral, lining himself up with the mule's shoulder, outside of kicking range. The mule swung his head toward Ryder, his long ears pricked forward.

"Why isn't he wearing any shoes?"

"Wouldn't let me put 'em on." Percy laughed from the fence.

That wasn't a good sign.

Ryder slapped the catch rope against his pant leg, swung his arm out toward the mule's hind end, then slapped the rope against his leg again. The mule moved to the fence and jogged around the corral.

Every time the mule slowed his pace, Ryder swung his arm out, still holding the coiled rope. The animal was well-balanced and moved nicely in the fading light. So far he hadn't bucked or tried to kick. Maybe this was a rare, even-tempered mule. Even as Ryder completed the thought, he knew it wasn't true. Freighters would pay two hundred dollars for a good pair of mules. Why was this animal alone in his own corral, being sold with all the tack, for twenty-five dollars?

After several minutes, Ryder stepped toward the mule's head and swung up his left hand. The mule stopped.

"Ain't never seen that a'fore," the blacksmith said from the side of the corral.

Ryder left the mule, ducked between the poles, and picked up the saddle. He tossed it onto the top rail and looked it over. "This is no good," he said. "It's made for a horse. Mules have a flat back. I need a saddle with a mule tree."

"Maybe that's the reason that feller who left him here had so much trouble with him." Percy burst into a bout of braying laughter which only inspired the mule to lift his head and join in.

Ryder rubbed the back of his neck and closed his eyes, praying the two of them would stop before his head exploded.

A minute later, the mule quieted and Percy had himself under control. He scratched the top of his head as though digging out his next great idea. "Let me see what I can find."

Ryder eased himself to the ground, resting his back against the bottom rail. He drew one knee toward his chest and draped his arm on top. The mule scuffed up behind him. A moment later hot breath streamed against the back of Ryder's neck blowing his hair.

"I don't want to be your friend you damn mule. Just get me where I need to go."

The blacksmith returned with a different saddle and dropped it over the top rail. "Here, try this one."

With a groan, Ryder pushed to his feet.

"Are ya headin' out tonight?" Percy lifted the first saddle off the fence.

"Yup." Ryder stretched to the right then left, trying to work out the kink between his shoulder blades.

The mule's long, dark ears pricked forward.

Ryder slipped between the corral poles then grabbed the saddle and blanket. At least the wool was thick and the weave tight. It should help prevent sores if the saddle didn't quite fit over the mule's flatter withers.

Buckles clanked as Ryder tossed the saddle onto the mule's back. Surprisingly the mule kept all four feet on the ground while Ryder carefully reached under his belly and threaded the latigo strap through the cinch.

He didn't know what back corner Percy had pulled the saddle from, but while it did lay almost flat on the mule's back, the leather was cracked and covered with gray dust. The seat wasn't as deep or nearly as comfortable-looking as the custom-made saddle Ryder had been forced to sell in Greeley. It looked like both he and the mule were in for a long, miserable ride.

The blacksmith watched as Ryder unbuckled the headstall of the bridle and slipped it behind the mule's long ears.

"Wow, that mule sure does like you." The big man observed with a trace of awe.

Ryder waited until the last moment to tighten the cinch. He hoped the saddle wouldn't slide too far forward once the mule started moving. He didn't relish the idea of getting dumped in middle of nowhere, while gravity flipped the saddle and all his gear beneath the mule's belly the instant before the mule took off bucking and kicking, for parts unknown.

He tied on his saddlebags and rifle then drew a deep breath, braced for the explosion.

Percy seemed to be waiting for a show as well, because he remained beside the fence with his arms crossed over the top rail.

Sure enough, as soon as Ryder settled on the mule's back, his head went down and his hind end went up. Ryder let the mule get away with a few bone jarring bounces before he used the reins to pull the mule's head up and to the inside. Rather than give the mule time to think about it, Ryder pushed him into a slow lope and sent him around the corral several times, before dismounting to tighten the cinch. The mule stood calmly when Ryder swung back into the saddle.

With a wave, Percy pulled the gate wide. "Good luck findin' yer nun. Haw, haw, haw."

Ryder waved half-heartedly as sunlight glinted off the single handcuff still secured around his wrist. He squeezed his legs against the mule's sides and jogged down the center of the street, the echo of the blacksmith's braying laughter still ringing in his ears.

He rode up and down the streets, getting a feel for the mule and hoping to spot an open mercantile or grocery. With everything closed, he decided to head for home and shoot some game on the way. Surprisingly, Percy's mule kept his feet on the ground as they trotted east out of town.

Shadows stretched across the road, but as long as Ryder could see, he wanted to keep going. Ahead, light spilled from the windows of a weathered house, set back from the road.

The mule stopped.

Ryder grabbed the saddle horn.

Ears pricked toward what looked like a large rock near the edge of the road, the mule lowered his head and hopped sideways.

Reining the mule's head around, Ryder first squeezed his legs against the mule's sides then thumped him with his heels, but the mule refused to move past the rock.

Trying to get a better look at the thing, Ryder stood in the stirrups and leaned forward.

The mule bucked.

Ryder was weightless as the mule's head, sky, and grass whirled past. He landed flat on his back with a thump. Staring at the charcoal sky, he tried to remember how to draw air into his lungs. The ground vibrated with each hoof beat as the sonofabitch mule galloped away.

Ryder rolled to his feet, letting loose a string of curses that chased after the mule on the evening breeze.

The animal's shadowy silhouette stopped in the distance, and from what Ryder could tell, the saddle was still in place.

Searching the ground for his hat, he spotted it near the terrifying rock. As he walked over to pick it up, he realized the rock wasn't a rock, but a carpetbag which looked exactly like the one the princess carried around.

Odd to find it sitting in the middle of nowhere, opened. He crouched, scanning the ground for some clue that would explain its presence. Then a few feet away he spied the veil for her nun's habit.

A premonition of dread settled heavy on his shoulders. He hunkered down to study the flattened grass and the tracks from shod hooves near the edge of the road. With his index finger, he traced the partial outline of a small shoe. This looked about the right size for the little nun. The imprints of horse hooves moved up the road. The shoe prints sank deeper here, indicating more weight. He rose and followed them east for a few yards.

Walking back to the carpetbag, he dug through the contents, searching for his gun. His fingers brushed across her lacey undergarments and his face heated like a school boy's. He'd handled a few chemises and drawers in his life, but never anything so light and silky. He could almost imagine his hands gliding over her abdomen and down her thighs.

A soft swishing in the grass behind him had him hastily stuffing everything back into the bag. Cheeks burning he buckled the bag closed.

The mule's hot breath blew against the back of his neck in soft gusts.

"You long-eared sonofabitch," he crooned, grabbing one of the dangling reins. Slowly he rose and patted the mule's shoulder. "What kind of game are you playing?" He stuffed the veil into his saddlebag and looped the cracked leather handles of the carpetbag over the saddle horn. "You better behave now 'cause we got us a princess to rescue."

Grateful for the clear evening and the light of a crescent-moon, he swung into the saddle. He braced, expecting Percy's mule to buck, but the animal seemed content for the moment, waiting patiently for Ryder to urge him forward.

By his calculations, Ryder guessed the princess and her captor weren't more than two hours ahead of him. Hopefully he'd catch up when they made camp.

Except for a few stops to adjust the saddle and double check the tracks, he made good time.

A whiff of coffee drifted to his nose, and his nostrils flared even as his stomach rumbled. He eased back on the reins, and the mule stopped.

"Hope this is them," he murmured as he dismounted. He patted the mule on the neck and led him to a small bush. "Now you stay put, or I swear to God I'll put a bullet right between those two big ears of yours."

He wrapped the reins around the limb of a bush

and gave the leather a hard tug. Satisfied when they didn't pull loose, he patted the mule and pulled his Winchester from his bedroll. Ducking to the left, he crept close to study the campsite.

****

Her shoulders and arms numb, Victoria stood, leaning awkwardly against the narrow trunk of an aspen, her hands tied behind her back. The man wearing the buckskin shirt sat on his haunches fanning a tiny fire. He piled little sticks on top, gradually adding larger ones until the fire burned on its own. From his saddlebags, he withdrew a small pot. He walked to a narrow brook, scooped some water, and set the pot in the fire.

Hobbled not far away his horse grazed. She could hear it snorting and chomping grass in the shadows beyond the firelight.

She shifted in front of the tree wishing she could think of some plan to escape. But once her captor told her about the telegram he'd sent to Nicholas from Julesburg, a sad kind of lethargy had settled over her so she could hardly work up the energy to care.

At the fire the man threw a handful of coffee grounds into the pot then reached over and pulled a cup from his saddlebags.

"You can come sit down, you know. I'll untie you so's you can have a cup of coffee and somethin' to eat."

All sorts of spiders and little bugs probably crawled around in the grass. If she sat beside him, Lord knew what sort of insect would crawl inside her skirt and petticoats. She shivered.

"No thank you, I'll stand."

"Suit yourself." He pulled the pot from the fire and

set it on a rock.

From the trees to the left of the campsite came a loud, dry snap like the crack of a twig. "Hello in the camp!" a deep voice called.

The man in the buckskin shirt whipped MacKenzie's gun from the waistband of his pants.

"Show yourself." He rolled to his feet and away from the firelight.

"Don't go getting trigger happy." The voice moved closer. "I smelled your coffee and hoped you felt obliged to share a cup."

Victoria recognized the rangy frame as soon as he stepped from the shadows. A smile tugged at the corners of her mouth. Despite her attempts to evade him, at this moment the sight of Ryder MacKenzie sent a wave of relief rushing through her.

"Sonofabitch, MacKenzie." Her captor called then slipped the gun back inside the waistband of his pants. "What the hell are you doing here?"

"Flint." Ryder stepped into the orange circle of light. In one hand he carried his rifle. He spared her a glance then looked back at Flint. "What are you doing with my prisoner?"

Flint chuckled. "Looks like she's my prisoner."

"Thought you gave her to me." Ryder approached the fire and sat, laying his rifle across his lap.

"Figured you didn't want her no more. I was comin' out of the tobacco store, when here she comes, walkin' past dressed like a nun."

"How'd you know it was her?"

Flint chuckled and swung his gaze in her direction. "Well, I seen what she looked like before she changed into her widow's weeds." He poured some coffee and passed the pot to Ryder. "When I give her to you, I never figgered you'd take her in the wrong direction."

"You're a real sonofabitch you know that?" Ryder filled his cup and returned the pot to the edge of the fire.

"So'd, you get yourself a new horse?" Flint asked. "I don't reckon you followed me all the way out here on foot."

"I left him out there." Ryder gestured back the way he'd come. "I just came to get my prisoner back."

"Well, MacKenzie, this little lady belongs to me now, seeing how you lost her."

Ryder glared at him over the fire. "I'm not giving up what's mine. That Colt at your waist is mine, and the princess is mine. Give them back, and I'll be on my way."

Flint laughed, but the sound slid across Victoria like a piece of ice over her skin.

"That's what I like about you MacKenzie, you never quit.

At that moment something large crashed through the trees where Ryder had entered the camp.

Victoria hid behind the aspen, expecting to see a charging grizzly bear. Instead, a large brown mule stampeded into their camp bucking and kicking. A leafy tangle of brush hung from his reins and bounced around his front legs.

Flint jumped to his feet and dashed toward the aspens, but the crazed mule followed. Victoria tried to run, but with her hands tied behind her back, her legs tangled in her skirt, she fell.

The bucking caused the saddle on the mule's back to flip beneath his belly, which only intensified his fear.

Flint's horse whinnied and tried to flee, but with his front legs hobbled, he swung his hind end toward the mule and kicked. Victoria struggled to push to her feet.

Her carpetbag, which MacKenzie must have found and tied to his saddle, was now open, scattering her garments around the campsite like a snapped clothes line after a summer storm.

The mule continued his rampage, the bush bouncing around his front legs as the saddle flopped beneath his belly. As he tore around the campsite, his big hooves trampled every piece of clothing she owned. One of her petticoats caught on the mule's back hoof, and as his back legs arched high in another kick, the ruffled undergarment flew into the fire.

Flint yelled obscenities and fired his gun the way she'd heard cowboys do during a cattle stampede. As the mule crow-hopped in her direction, Victoria twisted her shoulders and flopped onto her stomach. The shadowy legs seemed twice as long, and his hooves twice as wide as they barely missed trampling her. Terrified the animal would kill her, she curled into a ball, tucking her chin to her chest.

In that instant something large and heavy landed on top of her sending fresh pain shooting through her shoulders. She screamed, but the sound was muffled against the prickle of wool. The circular pressure of buttons pressed into her cheek.

She winced from the impact of each mule kick that slammed into Ryder's body. Thank the Lord only three dull thumps landed before the wild animal crashed off in a different direction.

When several seconds passed she asked, "Mr.

MacKenzie, are you all right?"

With a groan, he inched himself off her and sat back, his left arm pressed against his side.

"I'm fine." He closed his eyes then in one smooth motion rolled to his feet. He sucked a breath of air through his teeth as he moved.

Then reaching down, he grabbed her upper arm and hauled her upright. He stood for several moments, letting air fill his lungs and flow out again. Keeping his arm tight to his side, he reached into the front pocket of his vest and withdrew a small folding knife. He pulled open the blade then stepped behind her and quickly sawed through the ropes binding her wrists.

She rotated her aching shoulders and rubbed her wrists where the rope had dug into her skin. Looking up she met his gaze. An aura of intensity radiated from him as he stood before her so still. The encroaching darkness hid the nuances of his expression, so she couldn't even guess what he was thinking.

"Thank you for saving me," she said quietly.

He stiffened slightly then and drew a breath. "Just protecting my five thousand dollars. I won't get paid if you're dead."

Chapter Nine

Her mouth hung open, but Ryder swung away before she could say anything. After tearing through the princess's clothes one more time, the mule stood oddly quiet at the south end of the campsite.

On his left, Flint emerged from behind a tree. "MacKenzie, that loco mule belong to you? Ought to just shoot the damn thing and put us out of our misery."

Flint raised his arm, pointing Ryder's brand new Colt .45 at the mule.

Without thinking about how much it would hurt, Ryder charged, catching Flint around his waist. Momentum sent them tumbling to the ground.

His ribs screaming in pain, Ryder lay sprawled on Flint's legs. Drawing shallow breaths of air, he tried to breathe through his pain, hoping he hadn't punctured a lung.

"You are not—going to shoot—my mule," he breathed, pressing his hand tight to his side. He tried to snatch the gun from Flint, but the man tightened his grip on the weapon and pushed, shoving Ryder onto his back.

"The little lady had the gun." Flint sat up. "She tried to shoot me. I took it. Now it's my gun." He rolled to his feet and scanned the area, turning in a full circle as he did. "Where'd she go?"

Ryder laughed, drawing up his knees against the

pain. He closed his eyes, and with his hand pressed to his side, he laughed some more.

"And where'd that horse a mine get to?" Flint muttered as he stomped off toward the east side of the campfire and vanished into the dark.

Let Flint chase her this time. She wouldn't get very far in the dark. He'd be surprise if the princess even knew which way to go. When the pain eased, he pushed to his feet and walked toward the mule, who stood trembling, his sides heaving.

"You goddamn, sonofabitch, long-eared jackass," Ryder crooned.

The mule huffed breaths of air through his nostrils.

Wary of the mule's feet, Ryder grabbed the reins, and with a careful eye on those long ears, he untangled the dragging piece of bush. Keeping up his steady stream of low-toned curse words, Ryder slid his palm down the long mahogany colored neck, edging closer to the cinch. Slipping his right hand beneath the mule's belly, he gritted his teeth against the tearing pain in his side as he struggled to hold the heavy saddle in place. Then with his left hand, he unbuckled the cinch. Once the strap released, he let the saddle drop. Ryder jumped back as the mule's head went down and his hind legs flew out behind him.

With the saddle gone, the mule calmed after a few kicks and stood quietly while Ryder approached then ran his hands over the animal's back and down his legs. He tied the mule once more, this time to a sturdy tree. Satisfied Percy's crazy mule would stay put, Ryder walked back to the area near the pines and aspens.

He'd had his Winchester beside him at the fire. It should still be there, hopefully undamaged. From the way his luck had been running, he wouldn't be surprised to find it in pieces.

He leaned down and lifted a charred, lacy garment off the fire and tossed it aside. The flames hadn't been completely extinguished, and grateful for the fresh air, they stretched up and lapped along the edges of the remaining pieces of firewood.

He scanned the area where he'd been sitting and spotted the Winchester lying in the grass. Holding his breath with his arm tight to his side, he squatted and picked it up. He ran his hand over the stock and along the barrel, brushing away dust and bits of grass as he checked it for mule damage.

A stick snapped off to his right followed by a soft rustling. He stilled.

Leaning the rifle against a tree, he ducked under a pine bough into the dark where he suspected the princess was hiding.

She must have heard him coming, because all pretense of being quiet ceased. He followed the sound of her muttering, to a widened space between the pines, in time to see her swing her leg over the back of Flint's dark chestnut.

Not about to let her escape, Ryder leapt toward her. He grabbed for her arm but missed. Instead his fingers latched onto the skirt of her habit just as she kicked the horse forward. But with the darkness and the closeness of the trees, the horse barely moved beyond a jog.

Maintaining his hold, Ryder ran alongside then pulled, yanking her from the saddle. They tumbled to the ground as the horse trotted away. The princess kicked and scratched and struggled to free herself. But Ryder had wrapped his arms around her, and despite the pain in his side, he absolutely refused to let go.

He breathed a sigh of relief when she ceased her struggles and lay still. Her chest heaved, but she didn't move, for which he was grateful. He sought to ease the pain in his side by drawing short breaths of air. The scent of lemon filled his nose. As his aches eased, he realized the soft mounds of her breasts pillowed the weight of his forearm. The hair she'd worn tucked beneath her wigs and veil now tumbled around them. Silky strands lay across his cheek, snagging in his beard.

"I'm sorry," she whispered.

She shifted in his arms then something intensely sharp pierced his bicep nearly to the bone. "Sonofa!"

He released her and yanked the thing from his arm.

She scrambled away.

In disbelief he stared at a hat pin. It was a good six inches long, with a knob of pearl on one end and a tip so fine, if not for the dark smear which now coated most of its length, the pin would have been invisible.

Cursing, he threw it aside and rolled to his feet.

Ahead, she dodged bushes and leapt over rocks, the black skirt of her habit raised to her knees.

Pressing his arm against his sore ribs, he followed. Each jarring step caused pain, but he lengthened his stride.

She poured on an extra burst of speed. Ducking a limb, she became a blur of shadow vanishing into the trees.

He ran after her, damned if he'd let her get away. Coming up behind her, he slammed his shoulder into her back, propelling them forward. As they fell, his arm wrapped around her waist, and he twisted his body to absorb the impact of the ground. They rolled until the momentum was gone, and she lay beneath him.

Their labored breaths collided in the space between their faces, mixing together and blowing back on one another. Her breasts rose and fell beneath him. The color of her eyes was lost to the night and the dilated blackness of her pupils. She squirmed and bucked against his hips; her small fists pummeled his back and arms. One fist hit his tender ribs, and pain sliced through his body.

"Shit!" He clamped his hand to his side.

Her arms flew up to cover her face. "I'm sorry," she cried.

A frown tugged his brow low. He was a little rough around the edges, and most women couldn't bear to look at him, but did she really believe he would hit her?

He wrapped his fingers around one wrist and pulled her hand from her face. "Don't worry, Princess, if I haven't hit that damn mule yet. I'm sure as hell not going to hit you."

She twisted against his grip, but he held her fast. "Please," she cried. "Just let me go."

"No."

"I'll only run away again."

"I'll only catch you again."

"Don't you ever quit?" Tears shimmered in the whites of her eyes.

"No."

"Please, why can't you let me go? Why?" Her voice quavered.

Keeping his fingers locked around one narrow wrist, Ryder rolled off her. Lying on his back, he tried not to think about how much he hurt. Unbidden, the words rolled off his tongue with an exhausted sigh. "Because if I lose you I'll always be worthless."

From the corner of his eye, he saw her head turn toward him, but he couldn't read her expression.

Shifting his gaze to the patches of stars through the tree tops, a vivid memory surged to the front of his mind, like a wave against the docks during a storm. He tried to shove the image away, break it up, and let it drift through the sky, but it closed in on him like a gathering thundercloud, rolling his stomach and chilling his blood with a shudder, just as it had on that day.

****

Seething with rage, Ainsworth Thorndyke stepped around his desk and waved his arm toward the door of his study. "Get out of my house!" He roared.

Ryder longed to scurry away and hide as he'd done so many times before, but today on his fourteenth birthday, he knew the truth. Though his knees shook, he lifted his chin and squared his shoulders. "No. I belong in this house. I am your son."

Thorndyke strode across the room and stopped before Ryder. Mere inches spanned the distance between their noses. Then with a contempt reserved for a piece of horse dung stuck to the bottom of his nicely polished shoe, Thorndyke inspected Ryder. As his dark gaze settled on the left side of Ryder's face, Thorndyke's lip pulled up in a sneer. "You can go to hell for all I care. You're as worthless today as the day you were born. Now get out."

****

Shoving aside a memory that hurt worse than his ribs, Ryder rolled to his feet, yanking the beautiful society princess with him. She grasped his shoulder as she stumbled against him. Her breath escaped in an airy whisper against his neck.

Her lips parted, and the tip of her tongue flicked out to moisten her lower lip.

What would she do if he kissed her? The desire to press his mouth against the lips of this perfect, beautiful woman warred with his fear of the rejection he knew would come. He leaned close.

She stiffened and pulled back.

Hee-hawing erupted from the campsite. He swung around. That sonofabitch Flint damn well better not be hurting Percy. Ryder barged through the trees toward the clearing, his fingers still wrapped around her wrist. "Hurry up, Princess," he grumbled, as she tripped along behind him.

He entered the campsite, his long legs taking him straight toward Flint who stood with his gun aimed at the raised head of the braying mule.

"Leave him alone."

"This what you gonna use to punch cows?" Flint laughed. "All right, I won't kill the worthless sonofabitch." He lowered the gun. "But the little lady is mine."

Damn it. After all the trouble Ryder had been through, he refused to give her up. There had to be a way.

"I'll play you for her," he said suddenly. "One hand. Winner gets the princess."

She gasped.

Though he couldn't see her expression, he could feel her penetrating eyes.

"Why the hell not?" Flint said after a long minute. "I always enjoy a good game of poker. Besides, the way

126

your luck runs, I'll be keepin' her anyway."

"Do you have a deck, or do you want to use mine?"

"My deck, your deal."

Ryder nodded, but Flint was already walking toward the fire where his saddlebags and sack of supplies were piled.

Ryder blew out a breath, wondering what the hell he was doing. He should just climb on Percy and ride out of here. They couldn't be more than thirty-five miles from his place. His cattle had likely been sold by now anyway.

Ryder walked toward the blanket Flint had spread over the ground. The princess pulled against his grip. He searched her face. Her long blonde hair hung over her shoulders in tangles. White lines striped her face where tears had trailed through the dirt.

"I only want to get my things." Exhaustion edged her soft voice.

He let go.

She stepped away, then bent over and gingerly lifted some shadowy item of white from the grass. Holding it away from her body, she shook it furiously for several seconds then draped it over her opposite forearm. Moving on, she did the same with what looked like a pair of drawers.

The corner of his mouth tugged back, and he chuckled to himself.

Flint looked up as Ryder eased himself down. A wide grin spread beneath his drooping moustache. "Now I see how it is, MacKenzie." He tossed Ryder his deck of cards and lit a cigar. "I hope you recollect, MacKenzie, you're supposed to bring her back *untouched*." He chuckled to himself.

"Shut up, Flint." Ryder shuffled the deck, trying to ignore him.

"Hell, I plum forgot, one good look at that plug ugly face a yours an' *untouched* ain't gonna be a problem." He burst out laughing as he gathered his cards.

Ryder set the deck on the blanket and picked up his hand. Ace, jack, seven, two and a four, all from different suits.

Keeping his expression neutral, Ryder looked up.

Flint pulled his cigar from his mouth. "Are we goin' to bet and make this even more interesting?"

"I don't have much cash."

"Let's throw in other things to sweeten the pot. How 'bout I bet my sack of supplies over there. You're lookin' a mite hungry, MacKenzie."

"Fine, I've got about three dollars. That ought to cover them." He pulled his purse from his vest pocket and tossed it in the center of the blanket. "Now how many cards you want?"

"One."

"And dealer takes three." Ryder pulled out the seven, the two and the four. Adding the new cards he studied his hand. Not too bad, two pair, aces over eights. Maybe he had a chance this time. However, Flint taking only one card meant he either had a very good hand, or he was bluffing.

"I'm gonna make this even more interestin'. I'll tell you where to find your herd."

Ryder frowned. "How would you know anything about it?"

Flint shrugged. "I hear things."

Ryder glanced at the princess, a little unnerved by

the way she stood silently watching from beside her carpetbag, her hands clasped neatly in front of her.

He looked back at his cards. He didn't trust Flint. The man always had an angle, but if Ryder won, he'd have the princess and the chance to get his cattle back. Once he had his beef, he could give her what she wanted—her freedom. If he folded, he and the princess would both lose. But he had nothing to bet of equal value except...

"I'll bet my Winchester, but you'll have to give me back my Colt."

"That ain't fair, I already have it."

"It's fair. How do I know your information is good?"

Flint chuckled. "I trust the fellow who give it to me."

"All right, then I call. What have you got?"

Flint fanned out his cards and placed them on the blanket. Three, four, five, six, seven. A straight. Ryder stared at the cards. The hollow cavern inside him ached worse than it had after their last card game. He told himself it was because he would never see the five thousand dollars. Losing the princess meant nothing.

Wordlessly, Ryder tossed his cards on the blanket. Slowly he pushed to his feet and walked across the clearing to the tree where he'd left his rifle. When he returned, Flint was rolling up his bedroll. Ryder passed him the Winchester. Flint tossed the blankets over his shoulder and pulled the Colt from his waist.

"Here you go, MacKenzie. Reckon a man's got to have some kind of weapon."

Ryder nodded and took the gun, the walnut grip still warm from Flint's body. He slid it into his empty holster. Having his Colt .45 back, the weight of it pulling on his hip, solid against his thigh, made him feel a little lighter, a little less down on himself—until he glanced at the princess.

As still as stone, she watched him. Shadows obscured all but the whites of her eyes. She stared at him like one of his dogs whenever he rode out and left them gazing after him from the porch of his cabin silently begging him not to leave. Odd coming from someone who constantly tried to escape him.

Uneasy, he turned away and strode toward the tree where he'd tied Percy. Worse than losing, he felt like he'd let her down, almost as if he'd betrayed her. He gave the mule a pat then looked around for his saddle blanket.

"Aw hell, MacKenzie." Flint called out striding toward him. "I can't do it. You can have her. She looks like she's goin' to start cryin' if you leave. An' I can't abide a weepy woman."

Ryder frowned. Was this twist another one of his jokes? "Why?"

"I done told ya. 'Sides I got plans an' I don't reckon I got time to haul a rich society lady clean across the country. Keep the food, too. You look like you ain't had nothin' to eat in a week.

"But I'm keepin' this Winchester. An' when you get that five thousand dollars, I expect you to look me up for a few hands of poker. The way you play, it'll be easier for me just to win the money back."

Night shadows hid Flint's expression making it difficult to determine his motives. "Why?" Ryder asked again.

Flint cursed under his breath. "Just help me find

my horse."

After all these years, Ryder still couldn't figure the man out. "Come on, he's not hobbled, so he might have wandered some."

Flint picked up his catch rope and joined Ryder on the other side of the fire.

The princess stood quietly watching as they approached. Ryder couldn't figure her out either. He half expected her to be gone. Maybe she understood the futility of escaping in the dark. Or maybe she figured that between Flint and him, he was the lesser of two evils. Better the devil you know and all that.

"Why don't you fix us something to eat? And don't even think of running off, or I'll tie you tighter than a Christmas goose."

Then turning away, he and Flint headed into the trees where he'd last seen the horse. The chestnut hadn't gone far and didn't try to evade them when they approached.

"When I was in Julesburg," Flint began as they led the horse back to the campsite. "I heard some cattleman by the name of Searcy got the contract to sell beef to the Red Cloud Agency up on White River."

"You think he's got my beeves?"

White teeth flashed as Flint grinned then shrugged. They entered the clearing and headed toward Flint's saddle and bedroll. "I hear Searcy's buyin' up cattle an' grazin' 'em on the east side a Blue Creek, north of the North Platte." He smoothed his saddle blanket over the back of the dark horse, then with a clank of buckles, he swung the saddle onto the animal's back.

Ryder pondered the mischievousness which laced Flint's words as he'd told him about Searcy.

He glanced at the princess who continued to stare at him. "Start cooking," he snapped with a wave of his hand. "You can't ring for a servant out here."

Beside him Flint chuckled as he tightened the cinch and tied on his bedroll "You know, MacKenzie, I think you should just forget about them cattle."

He swung into the saddle, then leaned forward, resting his forearms on his saddle horn. "When I spotted your princess in Julesburg, I sent a telegram to that Vandy Beck feller sayin' I had her. Next morning I get a wire from him saying to meet him in Cheyenne. Go to Cheyenne. Take the money. If Searcy's got your herd, he already paid for it, an' he don't seem like the kind a feller to just give it back."

****

Ryder McKenzie confused her. He was surly, abrupt, and rude, the complete opposite of Nicholas' flamboyant charm. Despite all she'd done to Ryder, she'd yet to feel the impact of his fist against her face. Did he even have a temper?

He carried a loaded weapon at his fingertips, which strangely, she sometimes forgot was even there. If Nicholas had held a gun during one of his rages—she shivered—she would be dead.

Odd that while Ryder's tone could be as harsh and demanding as Nicholas, there was something missing, that element which chilled her blood and made her go stiff inside.

Part of her wished she knew what would enrage Ryder, for her nerves were as frayed as old yarn as she waited for an explosion that never seemed to come.

Focused on her cooking task, she noticed blackened bacon still lay burned in the bottom of the skillet. An S-hook suspended a pot of beans from a spit over the flames which surprisingly had not been knocked over by the mule. The pot Flint had used to brew the coffee lay tipped against the rocks which ringed the fire.

What should she do first? She'd watched Flint earlier when he sliced a rasher of bacon and made coffee. How hard could it be? Folding a small towel around the handle of the frying pan, she lifted it from the coals and set it on the ground beside her. Using a knife, she picked the pieces of burnt bacon from the pan and flipped them into the fire.

Next she approached the white canvas food sack. She nudged it with the toe of her shoe. Nothing moved. Bending over, she cautiously lifted the edge. Nothing jumped out. Carefully, she reached inside and pulled out the slab of bacon.

She turned back the cheesecloth and sliced off several strips. Her pieces seemed thicker than those Flint had cut, but she placed the fatty meat in the skillet and set it in the middle of the glowing coals.

Next, she turned her attention to the small pot. She reached out to set it upright, but the metal handle burned her fingers. She jerked her hand back; the pot fell over again. The remaining coffee hissed against the coals. The sudden cloud of steam blew straight into her face.

Coughing and fanning the air, she searched for the small towel. Odd, she'd had it a moment ago when she set the pan in the fire. She gasped. There, still wrapped around the handle was the towel, except now a tiny yellow flame licked along the bottom edge. She reached out and plucked the cloth from the handle, but it slipped from her fingertips and dropped into the coals. The flame flared, engulfing the whole towel.

With a sigh she sat back on her heels. She had a small hand towel in her carpetbag. Glancing over her shoulder, she saw Ryder talking to Flint as they returned leading the chestnut.

Flint mounted his horse. "Don't forget MacKenzie, east is that way." He burst out laughing then turned his horse away and faded into the darkness.

Nearby the mule nosed through the grass, and she wondered why Ryder hadn't tied the animal, especially after he'd torn through the camp. Keeping a wary eye on the mule, she unbuckled the leather strap of her bag and dug through the clothes she'd shoved inside a few minutes ago.

The mule stepped closer.

Victoria froze and watched him, hoping he wouldn't repeat his earlier antics. Instead he continued nuzzling through the grass. Then he paused and began crunching. When the crunching stopped, he sniffed through the grass once more, moving a bit closer. Then he stopped to crunch on something again. Puzzled, she peered into the grass and spotted something small, dark and round. She poked it with her toe. It rolled off the blade of grass and fell closer to the ground. It wasn't a bug.

She bent over and picked through the grass until she found...a lemon drop. They must have spilled when her carpetbag was open.

The mule stepped closer and crunched on something again.

No! This stupid mule was *not* going to eat all her lemon drops. Crouching, she pushed aside the tall blades and found two pieces. Another few inches and her fingers brushed over the paper cone. She picked it up and found half the candy still wrapped inside. Shoving the cone in her pocket she resumed her search. The mule inched closer, still happily crunching away. She crawled forward and touched another piece. Continuing on, she snatched up several more.

Intent on locating every bit of candy, she ignored the scuffling through the grass assuming the mule was nosing for more. She crawled forward, and pushing aside the tall grass, she found herself staring at a pair of scuffed boots, and spurs with small, heart shaped buttons. She lifted her head, her gaze rising up the length of his legs to the waist of his pants, following the line of his vest buttons to his Adam's apple, chin, nose, and narrowed glare.

Ryder McKenzie loomed over her, his thumbs hooked over his wide leather gun belt. Beneath the brim of his black hat, two vertical creases had formed above the bridge of his nose. "What the hell are you doing?" His tone more baffled than angry.

"I'm sorry." Victoria scrambled to her feet, brushing off her skirt with her empty hand. "I was looking for lemon drops. They must have spilled when—I wanted them back—I—I'm sorry."

"And you're fighting with a mule over *lemon drops*?" Disbelief laced each slowly enunciated word.

How could she explain, when she didn't really understand herself? Instead, she held out her fisted hand like a guilty schoolgirl before the headmistress.

Automatically Ryder's hand lifted away from his waist and opened to accept her offering.

She dropped her fist full of the yellow, sugar-coated orbs into his hand. "I'll make your supper right now." Without waiting for him to reply, she swung around and hurried back to the fire.

A cloud of smoke rose from the pan of bacon. Darn, she still had nothing to wrap around the handle. Raising the skirt of her habit, she grabbed the hem of her ruffled petticoat, bunched it into her palm and leaned close.

As she lifted the pan from the fire, a strong arm clamped around her waist, lifting her feet right off the ground. Startled, she dropped the pan. Cast iron banged against rock, as she was swung away from the fire and set down again.

"What are you trying to do?" Ryder's voice rumbled in her ear. "Catch yourself on fire?"

Easing back a step, she lifted her gaze to his shadowed face. "Thank you," she whispered.

He stared back for several moments before he broke the connection and shifted his focus to the pan on the ground.

Rubbing the back of his neck, he heaved a sigh that seemed to be drawn from the bottoms of his feet.

She followed his gaze to the bacon. The pan was tipped at an angle on one of the rocks. Some of the bacon had landed in the fire. Tiny flames licked along the edges of fat. What remained in the skillet was black. The center of each strip remained as raw as when she placed it in the pan.

Ryder blew out a long sigh, reverting to his usual gruffness. "Princess, if I liked my bacon black, I would have eaten already."

"I'm sorry. I'll make some more." She bent over the fire and used the edge of her skirt to pull the pan into the grass.

"Forget the bacon. I'll grab some of these beans." He searched the ground for a plate, brushed it off, and leaning close he reached for the wooden spoon resting against the inside of the pot. He stilled then sighed.

Curious, Victoria straightened and peered inside. Blades of grass and bits of ash lay scattered across the top of the beans. "I'm sorry, I can—"

His hand shot up silently cutting off her words. "I don't even care." He scooped the dirty food onto the tin plate.

Knowing he needed a fork, she swung away and rummaged through the sack. Unable to locate one, she passed him a large spoon as he lowered himself to the ground, bracing the arm that held the plate on his up-drawn knee. He shoved two spoonfuls of beans into his mouth and froze. Slowly he set the utensil down, then after shifting his tongue around, reached up and pulled from his mouth a twig about an inch long.

Victoria stiffened, expecting a verbal explosion.

Instead he twirled the tiny stick between his thumb and forefinger as he carefully chewed and swallowed. "Damn it," he muttered as he tossed the twig into the fire. "I haven't had a decent meal since those rustlers stole my herd and—"

Victoria's breath caught on a gasp. "I'm sorry. I'll make some more. It will only take a minute."

"Forget it. I should have known you couldn't cook."

"I'm sorry. I can do it. Just give me a few minutes."

"Will you stop apologizing and sit down. I'll do it."

Unsure of his mood, she searched the ground for a

place to sit. Did that dark spot just move? She shuddered and stepped back a couple of feet.

He rummaged through the sack of supplies.

Withdrawing a small white bag with a yellow label and red letters, he poured a small amount of roasted coffee beans into the small bowl of a coffee grinder and held it up. "Here."

She stepped forward and took the grinder.

"All you have to do is turn the handle." He tossed away what remained of the coffee and grounds in the pot. Then rising he took the pot and disappeared into the dark. A minute later he set the pot in the fire. Hunkering down, he pulled the burlap sack close and dug through its contents.

"Is that why you hate me so much?" she asked as she cranked. "Because I can't cook? Because I grew up with money?"

He pulled out the rest of the bacon, sliced it, and placed it in the pan. Glancing up, he said, "I don't hate you. I don't even know you."

He turned back to the supplies and withdrew some jerky and biscuits. "I hate what you are."

"I don't understand."

"You're beautiful and you're rich." His gaze darted from the sack of supplies, to the other side of the fire, to fix on the mule still hunting for lemon drops in the grass.

"Women like you are just possessions to heighten a man's status. He'll adorn you with clothes and jewels and show you off at restaurants and theaters. Your presence on his arm tells society he has succeeded and deserves respect. And you manipulate that fact, knowing that in order to keep you on his arm, the fool will give you anything you want and do anything you want.

"I don't know you. I don't care to know you. All you are is a mirror, reminding me of what I'll never be. No, thanks. Give me my five thousand dollars, and I'll be on my way."

Chapter Ten

Victoria winced at the disdain in his voice. She drew a breath to defend herself, to explain she wasn't the grasping, manipulative society woman he believed her to be. Instead she lowered her gaze to her hand, watching as it turned the handle of the coffee grinder around and around. Listening to the soft abrasive sound, she wondered why she even cared what Ryder MacKenzie thought.

Beside her, Ryder rested his forearms on his up-drawn knee. Using his teeth, he tore off a hunk of jerky. In the pan bacon sizzled and popped.

When she finished grinding, he waved his hand in an impatient, hurry-up gesture. She pulled the small drawer from the bottom of the grinder box and passed it down to him. The movement wafted the aroma of freshly ground coffee through the air between them.

He dumped the grounds into the small pot of boiling water. While it brewed, he lifted the bacon from the pan and dropped it onto the same plate he'd used for the beans.

She thought the fatty part still too white and raw to eat, but Ryder didn't seem to care and after blowing on each piece, wolfed it all down. He finished the last of the jerky and poured a cup of coffee.

He lowered his mug. Fire highlighted the moisture glossing his lips, and her heart fluttered. She bit down on the inside of her cheek, suppressing her sudden curiosity to press her lips to his. After all she'd done to him since they met, he'd remained protective and polite, a true cavalier. Part of her was afraid to believe the fairy tale. She'd been so very wrong before.

Despite what he evidently believed about himself, he was one of the best looking men she'd ever seen.

He scowled at her from beneath the brim of his hat. "Quit your damn staring," he snapped rolling to his feet. He moved to the opposite side of the fire, presenting her with his right side. He gulped down the rest of his coffee and tossed the cup toward the pot.

"And sit down. You're making me nervous standing there."

She bit back the impulse to say, I'm sorry. Instead she turned in a small circle scanning the ground. With the toe of her shoe, she poked at a few clumps of grass.

She felt his censure, as he judged her by a standard that someone else had set—someone who had hurt him and made him bitter. She was sorry for that but shouldn't allow herself to care.

Side-stepping a few more inches, she poked at the ground again.

With a growl of frustration, Ryder rolled to his feet and stomped off to where he'd dropped his saddle after freeing it from beneath the mule's belly. Buckles clanked as he lugged everything close to the fire and dumped it on the ground. Next he undid his bedroll and spread it over the grass.

Stepping back he made a sweeping gesture with his arm. "Here you go, Princess. Wouldn't want you to soil your fine gown."

She glanced at the skirt of her habit and

unconsciously brushed at some of the dirty spots. Gnawing on her bottom lip, she stepped toward his blankets. If this was the only place to sleep and he'd offered it to her, where was he going to bed down?

She leaned over and peered at a dark spot.

"What the hell is the matter now? My blankets too coarse for you?"

"No, they're fine, thank you. I just thought I saw…I thought that shadow was a spider."

"A spider?" he said incredulously. "You're worried about bugs? You were just picking candy from the grass."

"That was different," she explained. "They were…important."

"They were lemon drops, not gold nuggets."

He lowered himself to the ground and picked up his plate. "You want something to eat?"

She shook her head. "No, thank you."

"Fine," he grumbled. "Just sit down."

With a sigh she studied the blankets for the best place to sit and carefully lowered herself onto his bedroll.

Though he seemed focused on his food, she could feel him watching. She'd never been one of those girls who chased fire flies or went fishing. She hated creepy crawly things. She'd never slept outside in her entire life and hadn't eaten a picnic on the ground since she was a very young girl.

Ryder leaned forward, added more coffee to his cup then sat back. He didn't say another word, and she released a relaxed sigh.

The thought of escape crossed her mind, but she couldn't just run off. There was nowhere to go. She could steal the mule and head west, back to Laramie, but she'd have to saddle the mule, and that would take time. Ryder would have to be a pretty sound sleeper for her to get away with that. Maybe that's why he didn't tie her up or handcuff her. He already knew.

For the first time, she wondered how he'd gotten free of the handcuffs. She glanced at his wrist. Firelight glinted off the bracelet. A bit of chain link dangled at his shirt cuff. She still had his key. She really should give it to him. Despite everything she'd done to him, he'd repaid her with a sort of backhanded kindness.

"*Mouse*!" Ryder yelled pointing toward her feet.

She screamed. Jumping up she kicked her shoes against the blankets and did a hopping dance around to the other side of the fire. Her heart pounding, she furiously shook out her skirts, the fabric snapping like sheets on a line. The roaring in her ears was so loud several moments passed before she realized someone was laughing. She froze then blinked.

Ryder lay on his back, his knees bent and his arm held tight to his side. Full-throated laughter rolled through the air. Every few breaths she heard an, "Owww."

Her spine stiffened. Stomping around the fire, she stopped beside him. If there had been a floor, the sharp click of her heels against the planks would have conveyed her irritation.

Though his laughter had wound down, every time he opened his eyes and looked at her glaring down on him, he began laughing again. She glimpsed the white of his teeth in the shadow of his beard.

His hat had fallen into the grass beside him, and his hair brushed across his forehead to touch his eyebrows with a disarray that had her wishing she had the right to touch. "Ryder MacKenzie!" she sputtered when his laughter wound down to chuckles. "You are such a…*such a boy*!"

Whirling around, she stomped off.

Ryder burst out laughing again. He couldn't help it. She'd been so funny jumping around the fire with her skirts hiked up, kicking her legs like an Irish folk dancer. He almost wished he'd waited until morning so he could have had a better look at her ankles and calves.

He pushed himself up to sit. Oh God, his side hurt. He chuckled again and pressed his arm to his ribs. It had been worth the pain. This was one of those images he could carry around in the back of his mind. A year from now it would still make him laugh.

She stood on the other side of the fire, her back to him, her neck bowed. He wasn't sure, but he thought her shoulders were shaking.

Was she laughing? From all he'd learned of her since they met, he wouldn't have expected such a simple joke could make her cry. But then he had to remind himself that she was a spoiled, rich society wife. He'd seen those kinds of tears before from women who didn't get their way.

He drew a deep breath and rolled to his feet. Walking around the fire, he said, "You're not crying are you?"

She turned and raised her gaze to meet his. Tears shimmered in her eyes, and firelight reflected its glow in the moisture that traced the hollow around her nose.

The anguish etched in the shadows of her face stunned him. "Victoria, I'm sorry."

"Why couldn't it have been you?" she asked in a

choked whisper.

"What?"

Tears spilled freely from the corners of her eyes. "Why couldn't it have been you who smiled at me from across the ballroom floor? Why couldn't you have been the handsome prince who asked me to dance?"

He swallowed against the lump in his throat. Stunned, his hand rubbed at the sudden pressure in the center of his chest.

She swiped her fingers across her cheek bones, then turned and walked back to the bedroll, taking her carpetbag with her.

Gracefully she lowered herself onto the blankets. She daubed at her eyes with a handkerchief. In the dark, it fluttered around her face like a moth. A moment later she pulled a hair brush from her bag and stroked it through her hair.

Did she really wish she had met him first? Did she just call him handsome? The emotion behind her words had been so powerful he couldn't imagine she'd lied. But why had she flinched when he tried to kiss her? Why did she constantly stare at his face?

She divided her hair into sections. Taking one at a time, she brushed the tips then worked her way upward to her scalp. The flicker of firelight danced in the highlights of her hair. Hand over brush, she continued the hypnotic motion.

He imagined the silky tresses slipping through his fingers as he combed them through her hair. He inhaled, imagining the scent of lemon. Heat warmed his blood and his body reacted. He envisioned her naked body sprawled on top of his, that curtain of hair falling down around him. In his mind he looked into her eyes and saw love shining back.

But things were always different in the dark, and he swallowed against the fear of what he'd see in the morning. In daylight he'd be able to see her eyes and know the truth—unless she was very good at pretending.

He rubbed his palms up and down his thighs. "I'm going to get some more firewood." Without waiting for her response, he swung around and headed into the trees.

He wove in and out between the trunks, scuffing his feet as he walked. When his boot bumped against a stick or broken branch, he picked it up. After a few minutes, he had himself under control and walked back to the campsite.

Though she said nothing, she seemed to be waiting for him. He dropped his pile on the ground in front of the fire and lowered himself beside it. He picked up a stick and snapped off little pieces and tossed them into the flames.

"Just lie down and go to sleep, princess," he said. "I'll be right here all night. If anything bothers you, let me know and I'll kill it."

****

...his armor is a little tarnished, but he has the heart of a true paladin.

Victoria returned her journal and pencil to one of the inside pockets of her carpetbag. To the east trees stood silhouetted against the brilliance of pink. Above their bushy tops, night hung like a partially raised window shade, allowing morning to creep in beneath a line of slate gray.

Ryder sat before the fire, his knees up-drawn and

his back bowed, as he slept with his forehead resting on his crossed arms.

She thought about taking the mule and riding back to Laramie. She had to get away before Nicholas came. And he would come. He wouldn't wait for Ryder to bring her to New York. As soon as Mr. Flint sent his telegram, Nicholas likely boarded the first train west.

Rummaging through her bag, she located her boy's britches and shirt. Then she ducked behind a tree for a few minutes of privacy and the opportunity to change her clothes.

Ryder was reheating the beans when she returned carrying her habit and corset. She sensed him watching as she packed her bag and pinned her hair into a bun. She could only guess what he thought of her confession last night. He believed she was spoiled. No doubt he assumed her female nerves had been overset. While she meant every word of that sad realization, she could do nothing to change his opinion.

Pulling on her tweed cap, she joined him at the fire. He wordlessly passed her a plate then poured coffee into cups.

They ate in an awkward silence that continued while Ryder cleaned the dishes, packed up the camp, then saddled the mule and tied on her carpetbag and Flint's sack of supplies.

Then as though bracing himself for an unpleasant task, Ryder tugged his hat low on his head and blowing out a long breath, he eased himself onto the back of the mule. Immediately the obstinate equine lowered his head, arched his back and bucked.

Fortunately he only managed a few wild hops before Ryder had him under control. The muscles along

Ryder's jaw bunched with tension, and he held his arm pressed against his side as he took a moment to catch his breath.

"Mount up, Princess." He extended his arm as he kicked his foot from the stirrup.

She stared at his hand. Pulling her up behind him wouldn't be good for his sore ribs. She wondered if he shouldn't rest before trying to take her back. Would he get mad if she suggested it?

"If you're even thinking of trying to run, I'll toss you over this mule like a dressed out deer."

His gaze narrowed on her face, and she considered whether he would actually make good on such a threat.

She grasped the inside of his forearm. His strong fingers wrapped firmly around hers. His jaw clenched and eyes squeezed tight as he swung her up behind him.

Without a road she had no idea where she was or how he knew where he was going. They headed toward the rising sun, up and down sloping hills, through wide stands of ponderosa pine and aspens.

At first she held onto the wide cantle at the back of the saddle, but it was awkward and not very secure. Eventually her fingers cramped. She rested her palms on her thighs, but quickly grabbed the cantle again so she wouldn't fall.

"Go ahead, Princess, you can hold onto me. I'm not contagious."

Not sure where to put her hands, they fluttered around his waist.

He sighed. "If the thought of touching me bothers you so much, grab onto my gun belt."

She was as nervous as a school girl at her first ball, worried her every move would be judged and criticized.

She was married, for goodness' sake. But Nicholas had always touched her. She had never initiated physical contact with him or any man—until Ryder. Her heartbeat quickened as the memories from the train invaded her mind.

With the solid wall of his back inches away, she longed to wrap her arms around him, lay her cheek between his shoulder blades and never let go. Instead she rested her hands on either side of his waist.

At her touch, his muscles tensed then relaxed beneath her palms.

Around mid-morning, they dismounted at a small stream. Ryder let the mule graze then walked over to a large rock and sat. Victoria followed, checking the surface for ants or beetles. She resolved to stand.

He passed her his canteen, and she gratefully swallowed some water before handing it back. He tipped his head to drink, and she watched fascinated as his Adam's apple bobbed up and down beneath the dark stubble coating his throat.

Not wanting him to catch her staring, she moved away and scooted behind some bushes for privacy. When she returned, he was standing next to the mule. He withdrew something from his pocket and held it out. The mule nuzzled the palm of his hand and as she drew closer, she heard a distinctive crunching sound.

Ryder glanced up and seeing her watching said, "Percy likes your lemon drops."

"Percy?"

"Yeah, I thought the name suited him."

She smiled. "It's a cute name."

He nodded but said nothing more. She'd never seen him so quiet. She'd only been around him when he was snapping at her and calling her Princess.

Was this his normal self or had what she said last night somehow changed something between them?

"It's about time to head out." He pointed toward the rock. "Wait over there."

Victoria walked over as Ryder gathered the reins and checked the cinch. Then tugging the brim of his hat low, he swung into the saddle. Percy seemed less enthusiastic about bucking this time and only delivered a few quick bounces, before he resigned himself to Ryder's seat.

She grabbed the cantle to pull herself up behind him so he wouldn't have to take so much of her weight, but when she started sliding down he grabbed the waistband of her britches and hauled her up anyway.

"Ready?"

"Yes." She slipped her hands all the way around his waist. He stiffened for a moment then relaxed and nudged Percy forward.

"Where are we going?" She'd thought he planned to pick up the train heading east at one of the small towns along the way.

"My place."

"Your place?"

"That surprises you?"

"No." She shrugged. She'd been so busy trying to get away from him she never thought he had a life outside of his mission to return her to Nicholas.

"I overheard you and Mr. Flint discussing cattle. Is that what you have, a ranch?"

"Yeah. I want to stop and pick up a couple of horses, then ride east to Ogallala. Some rustlers took my cattle, and I want them back."

They stopped again, later in the afternoon. "How much farther is it?" She stretched her lower back.

"About four more hours, but it looks like we might be in for some rain."

"Rain?" she squeaked. She looked up. Judging from the bank of slate gray clouds pushing across the sky behind them, she realized it would soon be pouring.

"Sorry, Princess, but with my luck I expect we'll both get very wet."

****

She pulled her grandmother's watch from her pocket and glanced at the time as the mule plodded along. Nearly four hours. She shivered beneath Ryder's poncho. He'd pulled the gum blanket from his bedroll and given it to her when the first raindrops fell. The steady shower quickly soaked through her wool cap and hair. Rain trailed down her neck, dampened her collar, and had drenched the lower half of her legs. Otherwise she was mostly dry. Ryder, however, had gotten soaked. Though he shivered, excessive warmth radiated through his clothing into her palms.

"How much longer 'til we get to your ranch?" Aside from a desire to change into warm clothes, she needed to use the necessary.

He didn't reply, and she hoped he was merely dozing. Raising her voice she asked, "Are we going to stop?"

He cleared his throat and coughed. "Don't call me that," he snapped.

"Stop?"

"My name is *Ryder*."

"I know, but you're not making sense. Do you feel all right?"

He gave his head a quick shake. "Sorry. Guess I fell asleep."

"Where is your ranch? When we crossed that river you said we were almost there."

"We are here." He straightened in the saddle and made a sweeping gesture with his arm. "All this is mine."

Wide, sloping meadows, shaded with copses of pine and aspen, spread in every direction. Misting rain muted the greens and golds of the landscape around her. Gray sky hid the mountains and silhouetted the tree tops of the low hills.

The saddle creaked as Ryder shifted his weight. "Imagine how it looked with cattle."

She tried to envision the hillsides dotted with brown and white cows, their heads down as they munched the thick, short grasses that covered the land.

"I wasn't worthless then," he said. "A little more work and I'd have made something of my life. I could have shown him."

She frowned. "Who?"

He raised his chin then, squaring his shoulders he picked up his reins. "No one." He pushed his mule into a lope.

This odd glimpse into the real Ryder McKenzie had been a surprise. She just wondered who *him* was, because the overwhelming need to give *him* a piece of her mind stiffened her spine. Ryder was somebody. He had value beyond money and cattle. He was not worthless.

Ahead she spotted the main buildings of Ryder McKenzie's ranch. The cabin drew her attention first. The logs looked freshly hewn, lacking the gray weathered look of so many of the buildings she'd seen since coming west. A stone chimney rose above the peak on one end, and a porch spanned the length of the front. On either side of the door was a window, framed with thick wooden shutters, each with a single hole cut in the shape of a diamond.

To the left stood a small sod hut surrounded by corrals made of poles. On a hill behind the soddy a windmill creaked, the wide blades turning slowly in the constant breeze.

Barking and high pitched canine baying erupted from the cabin as three dogs leapt from the porch and bounded through the grass toward them.

Percy stopped. His long ears perked forward, then as the dogs closed the distance, Percy's ears swung back and flattened. He lowered his head and lunged for the first dog. He struck out with his front hoof then started bucking.

Victoria sailed off, landing flat on her back with a soft *wump*. She lay in the wet grass orienting herself to the fact she was no longer on the mule. Nothing hurt so she pushed herself to her feet. The mule trotted off, her carpetbag still tied in front of the empty saddle.

"Ryder?"

He lay a few feet away enveloped in a wriggling pile of dogs. She walked toward him counting three, two of which stepped all over him vying for the chance to lick his face, while the third sat nose in the air and bayed.

She laughed.

His arms came up as he tried to push them off. "Stop it, Charlie. Beau, get off me."

Almost immediately, Victoria noticed the golden-colored dog, Charlie, had only one front leg. The large black dog, who kept stepping on Ryder, had one ear almost torn off. And the hound dog who sat beside him baying incessantly had eyes that were so opaque she doubted the poor animal could see.

Ryder slowly sat, one arm pressed to his side as he shoved dogs aside with his other. "Sally, shut up!" He yelled above the din. He reached for his hat and rolled to his feet. He swayed a bit then set his hat on his head. "Damn mule."

Wading through the dogs, he walked toward the cabin. "Come on, Princess," he called over his shoulder.

The dogs raced back and forth between her and Ryder as they walked the rest of the way to the porch. He stumbled a couple of times, and when she didn't see anything on the ground, wondered if his spurs had caught on the clumps of grass.

At the door he shooed the dogs away and ushered her inside. It took a few moments for her eyes to adjust to the darker interior, but before she had a chance to look around, he'd turned a chair away from the table and gestured for her to sit.

Puzzled, she took the seat and watched him rummage through a wooden crate near the fire place. When he straightened, she spotted a length of rope in his hand.

She bolted from the chair. But he must have expected it, for he had her by the wrist before she could make it to the door, though the exertion further whitened his complexion.

"Why do you need to tie me up?"

He pulled her back to the chair.

"Because I don't trust you."

The prickly fibers of hemp slid against her skin as he wrapped the rope around her wrist a few times then tied it to the back of the chair. "I have to feed the dogs and chase down that damn mule. There are horses in the corral, and I don't want you stealing one to get away while I'm in the smoke house." He tied her other wrist then came around front with additional lengths of rope.

Afraid he would tie her ankles to the chair legs, she kicked him in the shins and tried to shove the chair away. She pushed her feet against the floor, tipping the chair back.

He grabbed her shoulders before the chair flipped. "Stop it. You'll hurt yourself." He squatted in front of her. She intended to push the ball of her foot against his chest and shove him over backward, but as she drew her knee up, he leaned forward. Her knee collided with the underside of his chin. She winced as his teeth clicked together.

"Goddamn." He shoved to his feet and dabbed at the blood oozing from the top of his lower lip.

Victoria stilled. She wasn't sure if he'd bitten his lip or his tongue, but anger tinted both cheeks bright red. He looked furious. Her stomach tightened, and her heart thudded against her breastbone. She twisted her wrists against her bonds.

"Flip your chair," he yelled. "Lay there all night like a turtle on his back. I don't care. All I want is my five thousand dollars. Then I can quit thinking about you every minute of the day, and my life can go back to the way it was." He swung around and stormed out of the cabin, yanking the door closed behind him with a bang.

Several seconds passed before she was able to

breathe again. Gradually her heart beat slowed to normal. Was that it? When he came back would he still be angry? Would he punish her then?

She ceased her struggles against her bonds and looked around the cabin, Ryder's sanctuary, his refuge from the world.

Though her bedroom alone had been twice this size there was a homeliness to this place that Nicholas' four story mansion lacked. Shelves filled with books lined the walls on either side of the stone fireplace. Positioned near the hearth was a rocking chair. She could almost picture him here, his feet propped by the fire, lost in a good book at the end of the day while winter gales blew outside.

On the other side of the cabin, on the wall opposite the fireplace, was Ryder's bed. Made of logs and rope, it was not as big as her bed in New York, but it was still wide enough for two. Her face heated at the thought of lying in it with Ryder. She tried to imagine what kind of lover he would be. Would he make her do things she didn't want? Would he hurt her?

She wanted to believe he would treat her the same way he did the kittens, with low words and soft chuckles.

Though he didn't see himself as handsome, she did. When she gazed at his face the birthmark couldn't detract from his beautiful hazel eyes, his high angular cheekbones, long straight nose, and square chin. He needed a shave, but for some reason the rough stubble coating the lower half of his face, somehow made him even more attractive.

Extra clothes hung from pegs on the wall behind the bed, and a trunk stood at the foot.

A small desk and chair had been positioned in front of the wall opposite the bed. A ledger, papers, pen, and an inkwell covered its surface. The bottom drawer had been left open. Was that what he had been doing, when he learned his cattle had been stolen, working on his ledgers, seeing if he was successful enough to "*show him*?"

Behind Victoria stood a cast iron stove, wall shelves, and a pie safe. No rugs covered the plank floor, and cut in the center was a trap door to what she assumed was a root cellar.

A lamp stood on the small table in front of her, and a pair of leather chaps had been tossed over the back of the opposite chair.

She wished she could stay with Ryder in this cozy cabin he had made into a home, something her opulent mansion had never been. She sighed. It could never be. The only way she could survive was to keep moving, for Nicholas would never stop until he had her.

She struggled against her bonds. Surprisingly, the knots were looser than she expected, and the ropes easily fell away.

She heard him then, the soft chink of his spurs, the hollow footfalls of his boots against the floorboards of the porch. His low voice rumbled, telling the dogs to stay as he pushed the heavy plank door inward then shoved it closed before the dogs could sneak in.

Victoria whisked her hands behind her, hoping he wouldn't notice the rope on the floor.

Without a word, he dropped her carpetbag, his saddlebags, and bedroll on the table. Then he lifted the leather chaps from the back of the chair. Shoving his fingers into a tiny front pocket, he withdrew a small key. With his right arm held across his chest, he inserted the key into the lock of his broken handcuffs and popped open the single steel ring. He tossed them both on the table then turned and hung his hat from a peg on the back of the door. Using the boot jack, he pulled off his boots then stumbled toward his bed.

"I need some sleep." He flopped face down across the blankets. "And don't try to escape. I'll be watching."

Victoria wondered how he would accomplish that when his eyes were closed, but rather than put his skill to the test, she waited until she was certain he slept before she picked up her carpetbag. Tip-toeing across the room, she stopped beside the bed. He slept with his face to the wall, but his unblemished cheek burned bright red. His clothes were as damp as hers, but while she felt fine, Ryder trembled.

She set her bag down and reached for the white wool blanket with bold yellow, red and green stripes, folded at the end of the bed. Good Lord, she thought staring at the dried blood around the heels of Ryder's feet and socks. How had that happened? Easing the blanket over his shoulders, she told herself he would be fine. Ryder had lived alone for a long time. He knew how to take care of himself.

She couldn't stay here. Nicholas would find her. She had to go. Slipping Ryder's rain poncho over her head, she picked up her carpetbag and slipped outside.

The dogs happily followed her to the corral. Percy began to hee-haw. Trying to hush him before he woke Ryder, she dug through her carpetbag for a couple of lemon drops, and after ducking between the poles, hurried toward him with her hand extended. His braying stopped. His long ears pricked forward. She even petted his neck while he crunched the candy.

In a second corral, near a pile of hay stood what should have been a pretty buckskin horse, but the poor animal had so many brands burned into his body he looked like a brand book.

Nearby a small gray horse stood watching her. Deciding to take that one, she walked to the sod barn hoping to find a saddle and bridle. An orange cat with one eye blinked at her from the corner.

No need to feel guilty, she told herself a few minutes later, as she led the horse through the gate and swung into the saddle. Nicholas would kill her if he ever got his hands on her. Ryder could always make more money and buy more cattle. He needed to understand that for her it was a matter of self-preservation.

The dogs followed her for a few minutes then at some invisible boundary line they stopped and sat, refusing to go any farther. When she looked back, they watched her departure with such soulful eyes tears burned behind her own.

Her stomach churned. She rubbed her arm and squeezed the reins, trying to ignore the sense of foreboding by telling herself nothing was wrong. Ryder was fine, though she didn't quite believe it.

Turning away from the ranch, she nudged the horse forward, following two wagon ruts which cut through the grass and wound toward what she assumed would be the nearest town.

Hopefully, she would make it before dark, which judging from the gathering clouds, would probably come soon.

She was not abandoning Ryder. She had to leave if she wanted to stay alive. He knew she'd run that's why he tied her up—except the ropes hadn't been wrapped very tight.

She kicked the horse into a lope as more rain drops fell.

Chapter Eleven

Her hair and trousers were soon soaked through again. The ruts became more and more difficult to see as daylight faded. Even the horse seemed reluctant to continue, walking slower and slower until, even with Victoria kicking his sides, he was barely plodding forward.

She shivered and pulled back on the reins. The horse stopped. Victoria stacked her arms on the saddle horn then rested her forehead.

What was she doing? It was utter foolishness to try and escape at night in the rain. She had no idea where she was going. She couldn't see and she was cold. Had she lost all vestige of common sense?

And what about Ryder? How could she have just ridden away and left him, knowing something was wrong? Even after hitting him with the pitcher, handcuffing him to the train's seat, and stabbing him with her hat pin, all he'd been in return was kind and brave. He hadn't yelled or hurt her in any way.

She recalled his rare, boyish smiles, his soft chuckles when he played with the animals and his laughter when he'd teased her about the mouse.

Before Nicholas, she never would have blatantly disregarded the feelings of another person. She would never have injured someone deliberately, nor abandoned them when they were ill.

Did she even know who she was anymore? Had the self she thought she knew faded into a shadow of the man she despised? Like Nicholas, had she become so driven by her own goals no one else mattered? Nicholas had taken her innocence, her belief in happily-ever-after, but could she let him take her soul?

If she rode back to Ryder, Nicholas would find her. He would probably kill her.

A great, aching emptiness washed through her. She shuddered and choked on a sob. Maybe that had always been her destiny.

She raised her gaze to the bleak grays and blacks of the world around her and swiped at the mingling of tears and raindrops sliding down her cheeks. If five thousand dollars was the price of her life then Ryder MacKenzie deserved to have it.

She swung her horse around.

****

The dogs raced to greet her as she rode up to the barn and dismounted. She hitched the horse in a straight stall, stripped off his saddle and bridle then forked some hay into the manger. Eager to get inside and change out of her wet britches and shirt, she picked up her carpetbag with one hand and holding the lantern in her other, she backed out of the barn, using two fingers to pull the door closed.

As she swung toward the cabin, she spotted the dogs sitting in a line watching something inside the fence. They turned their heads as she approached. Searching the corral she spotted Ryder with a saddle in his arms, barely more than a shadow in the rain and dark.

The mule, Percy, dodged Ryder and the saddle by

jogging along the fence in a wide circle. The hound dog howled.

"Shut up, Sally," Ryder called from the center of the ring.

A chill rippled through her body, and her chest tightened. She stepped up beside the dogs. "Ryder," she called raising the lantern high.

He stopped following the mule around the corral and glanced over his shoulder, but didn't seem to see her.

"Ryder, I came back. I'm very sorry I left."

He coughed and muttered something that sounded like five thousand dollars then tried once more to put the saddle on the elusive mule.

Percy stopped and turned to her with his long ears pricked forward as if to say, do something.

Setting down her bag, she ducked through the corral poles.

He blinked at her as she walked toward him carrying a circle of lamp light. Rain flattened his hair and ran down his face and neck in rivulets. The thin cotton shirt and undershirt molded to his chest and back.

While she found the outline of every muscle intriguing, she wondered what had happened to the wool vest he'd had on when she left.

"'Toria," he said simply then coughed, a deep rasping sound that pulled from the bottom of his lungs.

"Ryder, what are you doing? Come inside," she coaxed and started toward the gate.

"I didn't think I'd be able to catch you this time." He fell in step beside her.

He tossed the saddle over the top rail, as she

opened the gate and closed it behind them.

Studying his face as they walked, she tried to determine if his cheeks were still flushed, but she saw nothing other than shadows and the whites of his eyes. On the porch he stepped back allowing her to enter the cabin first, and as she turned, holding the door open, she realized he wasn't wearing any boots.

Mud coated his socks and splattered his pant legs. Her pulse skipped a beat, and she shuddered as frisson of fear rippled down her spine. She set her bag on the floor and grasped his hand. His wide palm was wet and cold against hers.

He resisted her grip and pulled free. "No." He turned to stand on the edge the porch and watch the rain spill off the roof. "It's too hot."

With a high a fever, she understood why he was drawn to the rain, but he could easily catch a chill. "Why don't you come in and get some dry clothes, then I'll bring your rocking chair out here, and you can sit where it's cool."

He seemed to mull this over then followed her inside. She set the lantern on the table then tossed the poncho and her cap onto a chair.

Pulling out the second chair, he sat while she grabbed a dry shirt and pants from pegs in the wall. Next she rummaged through the trunk at the end of his bed, searching for a dry pair of drawers and socks, but every pair of socks she found had holes worn through the heels.

Her knitting bag contained a couple pair, but it was still on the porch. Closing the lid of the trunk, she tossed the clothes she'd found on his bed and turned.

Ryder was trying to pull off his shirt but had

tangled it up in his suspenders. It would have been comical if his teeth hadn't been chattering.

"Let me help you." She yanked his shirt tail back to his waist then slipped his suspenders off each shoulder. Without the restriction, she easily pulled both the unbuttoned shirt and the top half of his underwear over his head.

Goose flesh covered the pale skin of his torso beneath the tee-shaped pattern of his chest hair and pebbled the centers of his coin-sized nipples. On his left side, a deep purple bruise had formed in the shape of a hoof print. Her fingers stretched out, lightly tracing the shape.

Guilt washed over her, weighing her down like a sack of wet wool. Ryder hadn't once complained, and each time he'd winced or sucked in a breath, she had callously ignored him and not even offered to wrap his ribs.

"Your hair is wet." Ryder mumbled. "You'll get sick if you don't change."

"I'm fine," she replied as she straightened. Stepping away, she reached into the trunk for an extra blanket and draped it around his shoulders.

"If you can manage the rest, I put some dry clothes on your bed."

She started for the door.

"Where are you going, Princess?" He raised his gaze to meet hers.

"Just outside. I won't leave. I promise."

On the porch she opened her bag and dug through the contents until she'd found both pairs of socks. She shivered and thought about how nice it would be to wrap herself up in her flannel nightgown and robe, sit by the fire with a hot cup of tea, and read a book.

When she pushed open the door, Ryder was climbing into bed.

Shivering he pulled the covers up to his chin and coughed. "I feel like shit."

"I know. I'm sorry." She set the bag down and approached the fireplace. Flames licked eagerly along the edges of dried bark on the fresh logs Ryder must have added. Holding out her chilled hands, she sighed and absorbed the fresh wave of heat that washed over her.

She thought about that hot cup of tea or maybe a bowl of soup. Surely they would be easy to make.

"Where is your food?" She turned to warm her back.

He chuckled then coughed beneath the pile of blankets. "Victoria, you can't cook."

"I can try."

He sighed and his voice sounded sleepy when he spoke. "You'll need water. The pump is outside in front of the corral. Smoke house out back and potatoes in root cellar. Careful. Ladder's steep."

"Thank you." She glanced around and spotted two buckets on the floor beside the stove. Ryder must have started a fire in there as well because waves of heat radiated through the cast iron.

Just the thought of going back into the rain sent a shiver of revulsion down her spine. Before lifting the latch, she inhaled a deep, bracing breath of air.

"'Toria," Ryder mumbled. "Don't forget my rain poncho and hat."

She turned and retrieved the rubber coated cloth from the chair. It hung to her knees, engulfing her in shiny black. His hat was too big and sat low on her head, just above the bridge of her nose, but it was oddly intimate to wear something of his that was so personal, and it warmed her more than the rain gear.

At the last moment, she grabbed the lantern. Even in the rain the windmill on the hill behind the barn creaked and groaned. Somehow water must have been fed from the wide, shallow water tank at the bottom of the windmill down the hill to this water trough and pump.

Percy and the buckskin horse watched from the protection of the lean-to at the side of the sod barn as she hooked the first bucket on the spigot. Working the handle up and down, she pumped until fresh water filled the pail. Water splashed onto her pant legs and shoes as she lifted the bucket to the ground then filled the second. More water sloshed over the sides as she lugged both buckets across the yard to the cabin.

While Ryder probably found getting water to be a simple task, for Victoria it was an accomplishment that straightened her shoulders with pride.

Setting the buckets on the porch, she took the lantern and tromped around the cabin to use the necessary. At the smoke house, she unhooked a piece of meat as long as her forearm and half as wide. If she cooked it slowly in a pot of water maybe she could make soup.

Ryder was asleep when she set the meat on the table. He didn't even stir when she clomped across the floor spilling water as she walked. After closing the door, she lit another lamp and found a small towel hanging from a hook on the wall near the stove. She carefully wiped up the water from the puncheon floor then grabbing a lamp she opened the trap door and cautiously descended into the cellar.

Crouching half way down the ladder, she held the lamp high, searching the floor and timbers for spiders. Cobwebs swooped between the logs in the low space. She shuddered. Dirt covered the floor, and she studied every dark shadow for beetles and rats. Onions, potatoes, and what she thought might be carrots and turnips spread out over shelves to the right of the ladder.

She drew several breaths, working up the courage to collect the rest of her ingredients. Maybe the meat would be enough. Quickly she retreated back up the ladder and lowered the door in place.

Locating a pot on the shelf, she set the meat inside and filled it half way with water. Tossing a couple more pieces of wood in the stove, she stared at the pot wondering what to do next.

From the bed Ryder coughed. She bit her lip. He needed those vegetables. She stared at the trap door as though it were an evil dragon. She could do this. Go fast and don't think.

Before she could talk herself out of it, she snatched up her tweed cap and stuffed her long hair underneath, then grabbed the lantern and returned to the abyss.

Don't think about it, she chanted to herself. She reached for a potato then realized she had nowhere to put it. Setting the lantern on the floor, she removed her boy's vest and tied the corners into a make-shift basket. Clenching it with one fist, she tossed in which ever vegetables were the closest.

Something tickled the top of her hand as she reached for a potato. She screamed and raced for the ladder. Potatoes and onions tumbled from the sides of her vest-sack as she went. She'd forgotten the lantern, but she didn't care and dropped the door with a bang.

At the table she loosened the vest and let the remaining vegetables spill across the surface. One onion rolled toward the edge, but Victoria had reached the door before it thudded against the floor. On the porch the dogs, sleeping beside the cabin wall, raised their heads and watched as she threw the vest into the rain, followed by her cap and shirt.

Flipping her hair upside down, she scrubbed furiously at her scalp with her fingers, then combed through the rest of the length shaking it as she worked her way to the ends.

Kicking off her shoes, she pulled off her britches and threw them to the other end of the porch.

"I hate bugs!" she declared as if she had to explain her actions to the dogs. Brushing off her arms and legs, she straightened her shoulders and walked back inside.

Glancing toward the bed, she saw Ryder still slept. She wasn't sure if that was good or bad. Digging through her bag, she found her lemon soap, poured some water into a basin, and scrubbed every inch of her body.

After she changed into her nightgown and robe, she pulled on the second pair of socks she'd made. They were a little big, but her toes were warm, and that was all she cared about as she washed and cut up vegetables.

While everything simmered in the pot, she added more wood to both the stove and fireplace, wiped off the table, then dragged the rocking chair close to Ryder's bed. She pulled her journal from her carpetbag, set the lantern on the table, and turned the wick low. Additional light shone from the fireplace as well as the thin, yellow outline of a square in the center of the floor.

She sat in the rocker and pulled her feet up cross-legged. She tried to close her eyes and sleep, but she was too uncomfortable and keyed up to doze. Instead she opened her journal.

My knight has fallen ill, but he has seen me safely to his castle. The destrier he rides is no less noble than he, and I wonder how many battles my knight has fought for he has long ago earned his spurs.

Her gaze fell to his boots, near the trunk at the end of the bed. One boot stood upright and the other lay on its side. Made of dark brown leather, they were tall, almost as high as his knee, the leather of each one scuffed and worn.

Funny, how they were the first thing about Ryder MacKenzie she'd noticed. Actually it had been his spurs and the tiny heart shaped buttons on the ends of each yoke.

Rising from the chair, she walked over and picked up his boots. Clutching them against her chest, she returned to the rocker overwhelmed by a sense of wrongness. He should be up and moving. These boots with the spurs needed to be on his feet at the ends of those long legs of his. He should be chasing her down, calling her princess, not lying in bed feverish and shaking with chills.

With her forefinger, she touched one of the silver buttons. Why had he chosen these spurs? What had drawn him to the hearts?

There was so much about him she didn't know and

suddenly ached to learn. Tears burned her eyes. Why couldn't she have met Ryder first? How much time would they be able to share before Nicholas came?

"Why are you hugging my boots?"

She flinched, startled by the sound of his voice.

"Because they belong on your feet."

He nodded as if her explanation made perfect sense. He rolled onto his side, sniffed the air and coughed. "Victoria, is something burning?"

She bolted upright and the boots tumbled to the floor. "My soup," she cried, hurrying to the stove.

"Soup?"

She could smell it now, burned meat. Peering into the pot, she realized all the water had evaporated and the piece of beef and most of the vegetables had baked to the bottom of the pot. She grabbed a large wooden spoon and tried to loosen everything, but it had stuck fast.

Ryder came up behind her, clutching a blanket around his shoulders. He peered into the pot. "I thought I dreamed it, you asking me about food."

"I'm sorry. I wanted to make you some soup. And now it's ruined."

Behind her, Ryder pulled out a chair. "It's fine. Just add some water."

She turned around. He sat wrapped in the blanket with his head on the table, his eyes closed. His face was still flushed bright pink, and his hair stuck out at odd angles.

"Ryder, are you all right?"

"I'm fine. Just a touch of the grippe," he said without lifting his head.

"Are you sure you should be out of bed?"

"Tori, the water," he mumbled.

She swung back to the stove. Grabbing one of the buckets, she tried to add water to the pot. It poured out faster than she intended and while most went into the pot, the rest splashed onto the stovetop with a loud hiss.

"I'm sorry." She set the near empty bucket on the floor. "I'll clean it up right now."

"Don't fuss about it. Just move the pot to the back of the stove and put a lid on it."

Grabbing a thick towel, she pushed the pot to the back then rummaged through the lids on the shelf for one that fit the large pot.

"Damn, it's cold in here."

She swung around. He was sitting up straight and shivering.

"Let me build up the fire for you." She hurried to add chunks of wood to the fire from the box at the corner of the fireplace.

The front door latch lifted with a clunk. She swung around.

"Ryder, where are you going?"

"To the privy." The dogs swarmed around his legs, but he didn't seem to notice.

"But you're sick, you can't go outside."

"I'm not using the damn chamber pot."

"But Ryder—"

"Fine, I'll just go to the end of the porch. Privy's too far anyway."

She started to follow him, then stopped short, flustered. Her face burned. She scooted back to the rocker, her socks sliding easily across the wood floor.

The door opened a minute later. Ryder cursed at the dogs then pushed it closed. He climbed back into bed with a groan and pulled the covers up to his chin.

"Are you going to sit there all night?"

"Ummm, well, yes, I suppose…"

"Tory, come to bed."

Her heart rate accelerated; her pulse pounded against the back of her jaw. She tried to think of a reason to stay where she was, but her mouth had gone dry.

She stood and stepped close to the bed. Ryder slid over, closer to the wall.

"It's all right, Princess; there are no bugs."

A muscle twitched at the corner of her cheek, and though she hesitated for another minute, she did pull back the covers and climb in beside him. The ropes creaked beneath the straw mattress as she settled into a spot close to the edge.

"By the way," Ryder murmured, his voice rumbling close to her ear. "Why is there a lamp lit in the root cellar?"

Chapter Twelve

"Spiders."

"Mmmm." He rolled onto his side, pulling the covers over his head.

Victoria lay staring at the ceiling long after Ryder fell asleep and the wicks burned out in the lamps. Her body ached for sleep, but her mind wouldn't relax. Though her heart recognized she was safe beside Ryder, her body remained tense and her pulse pounded in her ears. She dozed on and off throughout the night, but every time Ryder shifted in his sleep or started coughing, she jerked awake.

By the time dawn pushed the darkness into the corners of the cabin, Victoria was awake and checking on her soup. The aroma which wafted through the room when she lifted the lid was wonderful, and the swell of accomplishment chased away the sluggishness of her sleepless night.

Lifting a large wooden spoon from a hook on the wall, she gave the soup a slow stir. Pieces of meat fell apart in long thin strands. Her stomach rumbled.

"Smells good."

The lid dropped from her fingers and clattered against the floor. She swung around clenching the spoon, pointing it toward the voice, poised for defense.

Ryder sat on the edge of the bed, bare-chested, wearing his drawers and the socks she'd made. He seemed unaware of the way she wielded the spoon.

Hastily she tossed the utensil on the table and bent down to pick up the lid. "Sorry." She briefly closed her eyes and drew a deep breath.

He rose and slipped on a pair of pants and a shirt.

She replaced the lid and turned back to see Ryder pull on his boots. Without a word he lifted the door latch and went outside. A few minutes later he returned, a small bundle of clothes in his hand.

"Found these in the yard. Wind must have blown them off the rail." He coughed a few times, and she wondered if he shouldn't be in bed.

"Don't know how clean they are anymore." He set them on the table then stepped to the stove and peered into the pot.

"This looks more like stew than soup." He set aside the lid and scooped a cup of water from the bucket then went to the bin beside the pie safe and spooned some flour into the cup. Beating it with a fork, he returned to the stove and poured it into the soup. "If you let that simmer, you'll have gravy."

"How did you learn to cook?" she asked.

He filled a blue-speckled coffee pot with water. Then set the pot on the stove and tossed more wood into the firebox. "I was raised by the housekeeper in a mansion on Fifth Avenue in New York. I ran errands and helped the cook."

"I had no idea you were from New York." What a small world. Why, he could have grown up next door to her grandmother. They could have talked when they were children.

"Who did your mother work for? Maybe I know the family." But as she watched him close the stove and brush off his hands, the animation vanished from his features.

"I didn't say she was my mother."

"I'm sorry."

He shrugged. "I need to go out back for a minute."

Once he'd gone she opened her carpetbag and dug through the contents. Aside from her nun's habit and the boy's clothes Ryder had brought in, all she had to wear was the over-sized green skirt and blouse. Before he returned, she hurried to wash and change. Reluctantly she donned the green skirt and used several lengths of yarn to cinch the waist.

Having postponed her visit to the necessary as long as possible, she was forced to hurry, with barely enough time to check the seat for bugs.

She hadn't seen Ryder on her way back and found her steps slowing as she searched for his familiar, lanky frame. The dogs were nowhere in sight. The gelding she'd borrowed the night before now shared the corral with Percy and the buckskin.

Taking a guess, she headed into the sod barn. The sudden darkness caused her steps to slow while her eyes adjusted. Then her toe caught on something, and she stumbled forward into a post.

"Owww."

She turned slowly.

Ryder sat on the floor with the dogs, his long legs extended toward the open door, his back resting against a large tin bathtub.

She stepped closer. "Are you all right?"

"Fine."

"Do you need some help?"

"I didn't think so when I came in here."

A smile quirked up the corner of her mouth. She extended her hand down for him to grab.

"I can get up, but I could use some help dragging this tub inside. I need a bath and don't feel like going down to the creek. I thought you might want a bath, too."

With a sigh she closed her eyes and imagined herself in a steaming tub of water. The thought of immersing herself in water Ryder had used brought a flood of heat to warm her cheeks.

Together they dragged the tub past the mule who watched with his ears pricked forward as they passed the corral on their way to the cabin.

While Ryder ate, she heated water and lugged in several buckets to fill the tub. The fire warmed the tin, and while the water wasn't steaming when she checked, it was warmer than the creek would have been.

To give Ryder some privacy, Victoria walked around outside, petted Percy, and threw sticks for the dogs. Without the cloak of rainclouds and darkness, she had a chance to appreciate the sloping hills of green, framed with sweeping stands of ponderosa pines. Beyond the foothills to the west and northeast rose the blue-gray silhouettes of mountains.

The peacefulness of Ryder MacKenzie's home settled into her soul with every breath of air she drew, soothing the restless need to run that had consumed her since she'd hit Nicholas with the whiskey bottle.

When she wandered back to the cabin, she expected Ryder to be in bed, but he was still in the tub, his knees drawn up, pale and knobby, his head resting on the rim.

She grabbed Beau by the scruff of his neck and

shoved him outside closing the door with a sharp bang.

Ryder jerked upright, sloshing water over the sides.

"I'm sorry," she said. "I'll come back."

"No." He leaned back and closed his eyes. "I'm done. I just want to wash my hair."

"I can do it for you." Before the words were out of her mouth, she questioned what part of her brain they'd come from.

Maybe it was because Ryder was safe, and this was a chance to physically connect with a man on her own terms, without fear.

Maybe she needed to satisfy the curiosity that had taunted her all week, urging her to explore the body of this man she desired.

But maybe it was simply because he was Ryder MacKenzie, and in his own determined, unassuming way, he'd touched her heart and become her hero, and there would never again be a man she so ached to know.

He glanced over his shoulder. "That would be—" He coughed, a dry hacking sound that reminded her that he should be in bed, not sitting in a tub of tepid water. "—nice."

She stepped to the side of the tub and reached for the bar of soap in his hand. His other hand slipped below the soapy-gray surface of the water, holding a wash cloth in place between his up-drawn legs.

Her curiosity surprised her. A week ago she would have been happy never to see that part of a man again, now she found herself curling her fingers into her palms fighting the urge to touch him. She forced her gaze to his face.

He had shaved. He looked so different she couldn't

help but stare. His throat and jaw line were smooth, his chin square with just the hint of a dimple. With his long straight nose and bright hazel eyes, she could almost envision him wearing a suit, her hand on his shoulder as they waltzed around a ballroom. A peculiar sensation washed over her as if she had danced with him somewhere, but that couldn't be.

Ryder's expression hardened. "Never mind, Princess. I can do it myself."

Bitterness laced his words, and she realized she'd been staring. She gave her head a quick shake. Though she hadn't been looking at his birthmark, she knew that's what he thought. Would he believe her if she explained that she'd grown so used to seeing it she no longer saw it as a separate thing, but rather a part of who he was?

"I'm sorry. It isn't what you think."

"How do you know what I think?"

"But I wasn't staring. I was merely taken aback by how handsome you are without your beard."

He eyed her skeptically then shrugged. "If it pleases you to lie then fine."

"I'm not lying."

He blew out a long sigh as a shiver rippled through his body. "Victoria, I've been lied to my whole life, so just forget it. I don't even care right now."

She lathered the soap in her hands and knelt behind the tub. Her fingers easily slid through his hair.

He breathed deep as she massaged his scalp, her hands becoming familiar with the texture of his hair and every bump and indent on his head. She fell into a certain rhythm as she worked the lather from his scalp to the ends of his hair.

His eyes closed, and she took the moments to study every pore of his face, the prominent Adam's apple in his throat, the thin scar that started on the left side of his neck and stretched along his collarbone.

Reaching out she lightly traced it with her soapy finger.

"What happened to your neck? It almost looks like someone tried to slit your throat."

Without opening his eyes, he murmured, "They did."

"What?"

"I got jumped from behind in an alley near the docks. I turned as the blade cut through the skin of my throat. We fought, but he got my arm in four places." Ryder held up his right arm and turned it so she could see the scars. The water flattened the hair and dripped from his elbow so the thin white lines were easy to see.

"He got me here, too" He pointed to his ribs. "And back here." He reached his arm over his shoulder and tried to point to another small scar on his back.

"I was trying to get the knife away and somehow I shoved his elbow up and the blade went into his eye. He screamed and ran off. That's the only reason I didn't die. I stumbled out of the alley, and a policeman found me. I was in the hospital for a long time, and when I got out, I went back to the docks, saved my money, and came out here."

"How horrible. You could have been killed."

He yawned then coughed several times. "I'm kind of tired."

His hand came up and rubbed the back of his neck. "Can you get this soap out of my hair? I want to go back to bed."

She poured warm water over his head, sliding her fingers through the short strands, combing the suds toward the ends. She could hardly imagine Ryder fighting off such a violent attack. Seeing his scars and imagining them as open bleeding wounds left her nauseated.

"Do you have any idea why that man attacked you so violently? For him to steal up from behind like that and try to slice your throat—"

"It was a long time ago, Victoria. Right now my bones ache, and I just want to go to bed."

She set some towels on a chair and stepped outside. The dogs surrounded her as soon as she closed the door, and with only two hands to pet the three of them, they shoved each other aside vying for her attention. Lowering herself to the top step of the porch, she threw sticks for Beau. At the corral, the orange cat stretched and sharpened his claws on a fence post. Percy reached his nose between the rails and sniffed the cat. Unafraid, the cat walked into the corral and wove himself around the mule's long legs.

More than a quarter hour passed before she stepped back inside. Ryder was asleep on his side, the covers pulled up to his ears.

Victoria tried to pull the tub to the door, but it was too heavy. Instead she scooped buckets of dirty water and dumped them in the yard. Once the tub was light enough, she dragged it onto the porch then heated and added more water. Grabbing her bar of lemon soap, she stripped off her clothes and sank into the tub.

With the dogs running up to lap at the soapy water and Percy watching from the corral, Victoria lathered up her soap and hurried through a quick bath.

She spent the rest of the morning in the rocking chair on the porch soaking up the sunshine. First she took in the seams and waistband of her over-sized green skirt and put it on with her boy's shirt. Around noon she helped herself to a bowl of the stew simmering on the back of the stove, then she returned to the porch and began another pair of socks for Ryder.

A couple hours later, Ryder stepped outside. The aroma of coffee drifted through the open door as he paused to pull it closed. Barefoot with a blanket wrapped around his bare shoulders and dressed only in his brown canvas pants, he nodded then descended the three steps to the ground. Immediately the dogs surrounded him and trotted in his wake as he headed around to the back of the cabin.

She heard him coughing as he returned, and setting her knitting aside, she stood so he could take the rocking chair. Instead he lowered himself to the top step and leaned against the support post.

"How are you feeling?" She picked up her knitting bag. His eyes were still glassy and his cheeks flushed.

"I'm fine." He rested his head against the post and closed his eyes, absorbing the warmth of a sunbeam as contentedly as one of the dogs sprawled in the grass.

"Are you hungry? Can I get you a bowl of that beef stew?" She set her bag on the rocker and took a step toward the door.

"Venison."

"Pardon?"

"It was a piece of venison you cooked, not beef."

"Oh, I'm sorry."

"Stop apologizing. You did good."

"Oh. Thank you. Can I get you—?"

"Victoria, sit. I'm not hungry."

"I'm sor—" Apologizing had become such a habit, it was difficult not to say the words. She picked up her knitting and sat in the rocker.

After adjusting the four needles and shaking out the snarls, she resumed the steady rhythm of looping the dark gray yarn around each pointed tip, dropping the needle and picking up the next strand.

"Victoria, why are you here?"

She froze. She'd thought he was dozing. Glancing over she met his hazel green gaze.

"You've been running from me since Julesburg. Yesterday you left, and then you came back. Why?"

She gnawed on the inside of her lip, unsure how to explain—not sure she understood the reason herself. "You're sick. I couldn't just leave you."

"I'll be fine in a couple of days, so why are you here?"

"I…" How could she put into words she didn't like the person she'd become? "I had to come back because…" Because he was sick? No, it was more than that. He was right. He was hardly at death's door. She could have, should have, left long ago. Something much deeper compelled her to stay. She struggled to find it. "I came back because…because…I think I'm in love with you."

The words tumbled from her mouth startling her with their truth. Relief and giddiness spun around inside her like leaves in a whirlwind. She loved him.

Ryder's eyes flew open. His spine stiffened then a scowl furrowed his brow. He shoved to his feet and took a single step in her direction. Tension tightened his features, turning his hazel eyes stony brown.

"What the hell kind of bullshit is that?"

Instinctively, she shrank back in her chair. After all the times she wondered what would cause Ryder MacKenzie to lose his temper, she never imagined it would be "I love you."

"I'm sorry. I shouldn't have said it." If he came toward her again, she could dash to her left and jump off the end of the porch.

"You're damn right you shouldn't have said it. I ought to lock you in the root cellar until it's time to collect my five thousand dollars."

"No!" She bolted from the chair as if every spider and beetle from the underground room were in pursuit.

He was behind her before she reached the end of the porch. His long fingers wrapped around her upper arm in a grip so tight she couldn't twist out of it.

As he pulled her to him she shrank away, raising her other arm to protect her face from his fist. Instead he grabbed that wrist with his other hand, struggling to lower it as she fought to keep it raised.

"What is wrong with you?"

"I'm sorry. I'll be good. Please don't lock me in the root cellar!"

Pulling her against him, he wrapped her in a bear hug. The blanket gone, her cheek pressed flat to the heated skin of his chest. Beneath her ear his heart pounded as rapidly as her own. The fine curling hairs beneath her face tickled her nose, and as her breathing calmed, she became conscious of his hand stroking her head.

She sighed and relaxed against him. Savoring the tenderness of his touch, she squeezed her eyes tight to keep the tears which burned beneath her lids from falling.

"I would never hurt you, Victoria," he crooned in the same low tones he used when talking to Percy. "And I would never lock you in the cellar."

It had been so long since she'd been held so tenderly, she'd nearly forgotten how it felt.

Suddenly she was little girl and a strange woman had come to the orphanage. But when that woman wrapped her arms around Victoria, she'd known she was safe. In Nana's hug all the bad vanished, and Victoria had felt only love.

She slid her hands around Ryder's waist, her fingertips resting in the hollow of his spine. In Ryder's embrace nothing could hurt her. She squeezed him tighter. Her heart swelled. Her need to be closer to him suddenly became more vital to her survival than reaching San Francisco.

"You believe me, don't you?" His voice rumbled in her ear.

She nodded against him.

"I shouldn't have said that. I just don't like being lied to."

"It wasn't a lie."

He stiffened.

Oh, God, she'd done it again. But she didn't pull away. If she couldn't believe him, couldn't completely trust him not to hurt her, then he wasn't her knight, her hero. He wasn't her Ryder MacKenzie.

He gently pushed her back, holding her shoulders, his earnest gaze searching her face.

"Damn it, Victoria. You've been playing games and pretending since I met you. Everything you do furthers your purpose. I can understand that. It's straight forward and simple.

"Then you confound things with your tears and 'I wish it was you.' Now this. You don't love me, Victoria. Women like you don't love me. People don't love me."

"But I do," she whispered.

He let go of her then and turned away, rubbing his hand around the back of his neck. "Mirrors don't lie. I know what I look like."

"But I'm not a mirror. I love the way your hair falls over your forehead when you take off your hat. I love the color of your eyes, the way they change from green to brown and sparkle in the sun. I love the angle of your nose, the shape of your jaw and the way your Adam's apple bobs up and down when you don't know what to say."

He swung back around then. His gaze locked on her face. He swallowed.

"I love the way you laugh, the way you treat animals—the way you treat me, even when I hurt you. You've saved me and protected me. You're the kind and noble man I used to dream about. And that's the man I love, the man you don't see when you look in that mirror."

"Tori," he whispered. Two strides brought him inches from her face. His hands gripped her shoulders, his gaze intense and searching. The next moment his mouth descended to touch hers.

The pressure was light and lasted for a moment then lifted away. Though tension radiated from every pore of his body, his gazed searched hers, asking permission to continue.

That he would give her that breath of time caused

her heart to swell. How could she not love this man? Her arms rose and wrapped around his neck as he slid his hands down her arms and around her waist.

He kissed her again on her upper lip, on one corner of her mouth, then the other.

Heat coiled inside her, urging her closer.

He pressed his mouth to hers, firmer this time as he teased the seam of her lips.

With a sigh she closed her eyes and opened for him, savoring the bitterness of coffee, the strength of his tongue as it slid along the length of hers.

He devoured her as a starving man devoured a loaf of bread.

Time ceased for this enchanted kiss that went on and on in the kind of magical connection she'd dreamed about when she was young and didn't know what a kiss was supposed to be. There was only Ryder, the heat of his mouth, and the warmth of his breath against her cheek.

Her right hand lingered at the nape of his neck, her fingers toying with the ends of his hair. Her other hand slid over the plane of his shoulder blade. She sagged against him, longing to be closer.

Through the layers of their clothes, the rigid length of his erection swelled against her.

A cloud must have passed over the sun, for behind her closed lids the orangey brightness dimmed. Goose flesh rippled up her arms. She shuddered, and at that moment she had the sensation she was touching Nicholas, as if she were waking from a nightmare and not sure where she was.

Horrified she jumped back. She gasped as one hand clamped over her mouth and her other pressed tightly against her stomach.

Ryder, not Nicholas, stood before her. Relief washed through her, leaving her knees weak. A moment later, her racing heart calmed, and when she looked at Ryder, really looked, her heart plunged to the bottom of her stomach like a rock tossed into a pond.

He stared at her, his face pale and stricken. Then his eyes glazed over with the same detached, vacant stare she'd seen many times in the glass of her own mirror.

Before she could form a thought, he swung around and in two quick, long-legged strides he was off the porch.

"Ryder, wait. I'm sorry." She started after him, but her feet tangled in the discarded blanket. Falling forward, she grabbed the nearest post. Though her momentum slowed, she still pitched forward and tumbled down the steps.

She pushed herself to sitting. Ryder vanished into the shadows of the barn with two of the dogs. Sally sat beside her, watching her through opaque eyes.

Victoria's palms stung, one from grabbing the post the other from hitting the edge of the steps when she reached out to break her fall. One knee throbbed and her side hurt where she hit the sharp corner of one of the steps.

Sally rested her head on Victoria's thigh. She stroked the dog's long silky ears a few times, then pulled the hound into her lap. Hugging Sally close, Victoria buried her face against the dog's neck and cried.

Chapter Thirteen

He should have gone back for his boots, or at least his shirt. In the coolness of a barn that had been carved into a side hill and faced with sod, he shivered. Grabbing a saddle blanket, he shook it and draped it around his shoulders. Mistake. The dust triggered a bout of coughing, which with his sore ribs made him feel as if he were being torn in half.

Exhausted, he lowered himself to the floor, drew up his knees, and rested his forehead on his crossed arms. Victoria might be good at pretending, but she wasn't good enough to hide her revulsion to his face, not when she'd had to touch it with her own.

As a boy he tried to scrub the mark off, believing if he wore away enough skin, it would grow back in a normal color. Stupid.

Even the whores he'd been with had insisted the lights be out. What had he been thinking to kiss her in broad daylight? He combed his fingers through his hair and rested the back of his head against the wall. He'd been stupid, that's what, stupid to believe for even a moment her words had been true. Love him? No one ever had, no one ever would.

Another bout of coughing consumed him. Fighting the pain, he focused on trying not to cry, as the dogs watched him with anxious eyes.

If he weren't so stubborn, he'd get up right now,

walk across the yard, onto the porch, and into his cabin. He'd crawl back into bed under a pile of blankets, burrow into his pillow, and go to sleep. The princess be damned.

Then, as if he conjured her with a spell, she stood in the doorway, silhouetted by the pink glow of fading daylight.

"Ryder?"

"Get out of here."

Instead she hesitated, see-sawing back and forth with indecision, neither advancing nor retreating. "You've been out here a long time. Shouldn't you come inside?"

"I'm fine. Now get."

She took a step back then stopped. "I'm sorry."

"Damn it, Victoria, I told you to stop apologizing."

"I'm sorry. It's only that I never meant to hurt you, and I'm sorry for that."

"You can't help how you feel. Just stop pretending."

"But I wasn't…"

The cough rose in the back of his throat, a tickle at first and then an ache that swelled inside. He clamped his teeth together, arched his tongue against the pressure, and shoved his mouth tight to his forearm. But it exploded from his lungs anyway, more violent for having been suppressed.

She was beside him in an instant, her arm around his shoulder, holding him while he coughed and hacked.

"Now will you come inside? Please?"

He pushed to his feet, the blanket fell from his shoulders. She pressed against him, one arm around his waist, the mounds of her breasts, soft and yielding against his side. He didn't need help, but he could pretend as well.

He savored her closeness all the way to the cabin. She played her part perfectly, fussing with his feet, slipping on a new pair of socks when he couldn't bend over to do it, and then tucking him into bed. She even went the extra mile in this strange charade, by brushing back his hair where it had fallen over his forehead.

When he closed his eyes, the memory of her sultry voice floated through his mind, *"I love the way your hair falls over your forehead when you take off your hat."*

Pretend, that's all this was. But for now he would take it.

****

The acrid bite of smoke filled his lungs. He awoke coughing. Fire! Gray haze filled the cabin, and he jumped from the bed, wincing against the pain in his side.

"Tori?" He croaked between coughs.

"I'm sorry," she called from across the room.

Now that his initial burst of panic had ebbed, he noticed the front door and windows stood wide open as though welcoming the night. Fortunately he'd hinged the glass for each window in two panels so they could swing out. Piles of burnt flapjacks littered the table in the glow of the lanterns, and a pan heaped with more still smoldering pancakes sat on top of the stove.

A large quantity of flour lay spilled near the cupboard like a snowdrift across the floor. The dogs snuffled around inside, leaving trails of white foot prints everywhere.

He strode toward her, but his socks slid in the flour like he was on ice, sending his feet in opposite directions. He grabbed the edge of the table to keep from landing on his ass.

Towel in hand, Victoria waved the smoke toward the darkness beyond the window as if she were shooing flies from a pie.

With mincing steps, he reached the stove and turned the lever on the pipe at the back. "Why is the damper closed?"

"I'm sorry; I must have turned it the wrong way."

Caught between dismay and amusement, he shook his head. He leaned to check inside the oven; it was empty. "What the hell is all this?" He gestured to the blackened flapjacks.

She turned to face him, twisting the towel with her hands. "I added water to the pot of stew, because it was sticking to the bottom of the pot, but I added too much, so I tried to mix in flour the way you did. I must have done it wrong, because it turned out thicker than paste."

He lifted the lid on the pot and laughed aloud at the spoon sticking straight up from the center of the congealed glob of stew.

"I wanted to make you something else. You haven't eaten."

"Damn, Victoria, I couldn't eat all this in a year."

"But they're burnt!" She heaved a shaky sigh that seemed to border on tears.

"The first ones were too runny, and I couldn't flip them, so I added more flour. Then they came out too thick, and when I cut them open raw dough oozed out. When they kept burning, I made more, and the cabin filled up with smoke so I opened the door, and the dogs came in.

"I tried to chase them out, but they thought it was a game, and they raced around the table and knocked over the flour."

He gazed around the room, amazed he could have slept through all this.

"And I'm sorry." Tears spilled down her cheeks. She turned in a small circle. "I'll clean it up, I promise."

She looked up at him, and he laughed. It hurt his ribs, but he couldn't help himself. His princess stood in the center of this chaos, her blonde hair hanging in disheveled strands around her face, her clothes dusted with flour and spattered with dried batter, and she never looked more beautiful.

As he laughed, she cried. He tried to feel bad, but it was all too funny. Yet what warmed his heart the most was that she had done all this for him. He opened his arms. "Come here, Tori."

She hesitated then with a sob she filled his embrace. Her arms wrapped around his back, her finger tips digging into his skin as though clinging to him for life. Her tears dampened his chest and trailed down his abdomen. He rested his chin in her smoke scented hair and savored the feel of this woman in his arms.

With just her chemise and boy's shirt between them, it was as if her breasts rubbed bare against his abdomen. With one hand at her back, his fingertips curved naturally into the valley of her spine. His other hand slid to her waist where her ribs narrowed just above the flair of her hips.

She wore no corset or bustle, and he caressed the curve of each hipbone. Heat flooded his groin as he imagined the feel of her bare skin against his body.

She tensed for a moment as the length of him swelled against her.

He lifted his chin off her head. She stared at him through watery, red-rimmed eyes but didn't pull away. The tip of her tongue flicked out to swipe her top lip, and he leaned close to capture it with his mouth.

Swiftly it became as it had been before, each equally giving and taking from the other, before she'd opened her eyes and seen his face.

His fingers worked free the buttons of her shirt then slipped beneath her camisole to cup the satiny mound of her breast. He groaned as her nipple hardened against his palm.

Without breaking the kiss, he backed her toward the table and reached for the knob on the lantern to extinguish the light. As if they were dancing, he guided her to the bed by rote and fell backward across it pulling her on top of him. The pain of her weight was insignificant compared to the straining of his erection against the confines of his pants.

She sat back on her heels, and taking her time, she tugged the tails of her white shirt free from the waist band of her skirt. Slowly she eased it over her head and tossed it toward the floor.

A flash of teeth in the dark was the only hint he had of her seductive smile. Reaching behind, she worked some special magic, and her skirt and petticoat slipped from her waist to her knees, the fabric pooling over his thighs and hips.

His body stilled as her fingers fumbled with the buttons of his fly. Even without closing his eyes, he could imagine the brush of her fingertips along his length.

Aching to be free from his clothes, he grabbed her arms and rolled so she lay beneath him as he straddled her hips. With one hand he held her wrists over her head while his free hand tugged at the bow of her chemise.

But as he pulled, the thin ribbons tightened into a knot. Frustrated and needing the garment off, he released her arms to grasp each side of the chemise and yanked. The tearing sound distracted him until the backs of his fingers brushed her bare skin. Lowering his head, he kissed the valley between her breasts. Her skin was as warm and silky as one of Sally's ears.

The weight of Victoria's hands dropped onto his shoulders. Her thumbs brushed back and forth at the base of his neck, then stilled.

Shoving aside the thin cotton, Ryder kissed her breast then encircled her nipple with the tip of his tongue before drawing the hardened nub into his mouth.

He nipped and suckled and tasted her, every inch of skin from her forehead to just above her navel where the tear in the chemise ended.

Consumed with the need to feel all of her right now, he rolled off the bed to shed his clothes, freeing his swollen cock from his drawers. Then reaching out, he tugged off her skirt and petticoats. He fumbled for the string at the waist of her drawers, but her hands shoved his away, and she untied them. Once he tossed them to the floor with the rest of their clothing, he lowered himself on top of her.

Resting her hands on his waist, she shifted her legs apart.

He ran his palm up her thigh, intrigued by the fine downy hairs. Scooping one arm beneath her shoulders, he cherished the weight of her, the salty taste of her skin, and the faint lemon scent as he nuzzled her neck.

A bead of moisture leaked from the tip of his cock, and he groaned as he pressed himself against the coarse curling hairs covering her mound.

As he pushed into her, her hands fell away from him. He wished she'd touch him again, run her hands up his thighs, press her palms against his chest, or run her fingers down his abdomen. He imagined her naked beneath him in a pasture of spring grass with the strength of the sun beating down on his back.

Instead of merely catching a glimpse of the whites of her eyes, he would watch her blue irises widen with passion. She would gaze lovingly into his eyes, not close them in revulsion. He would watch her face as she climaxed and know it wasn't pretend.

Part of him sensed she was no longer with him, that she was too dry, her muscles too rigid. But so many months had passed since he'd been with a woman, the ache to feel his cock inside her, held tight and warm as he rode her faster and faster, overwhelmed all other thoughts. In a few moments, the pressure built, until there was nothing but pulsing spasms of release.

Sweating and breathless, he collapsed on top of her for a few seconds, then he rolled onto his good side and gathered her close.

"Give me a minute to catch my breath," he whispered in her ear as he brushed back a wisp of her hair. "It's just been so long for me, and you're so beautiful, so perfect." His fingertip on her forehead, he traced her hairline. "I'll make it good for you, too. I want you to feel the same pleasure…"

His finger stopped its journey at her temple where

he found her skin damp. Tears? "God, Tori, did I hurt you?" He kissed her cheek.

"It's not your fault." Her hand lightly rubbed his forearm which lay just above her breasts.

"It's me," she whispered. "I wanted it, too. I tried, but I couldn't…" Her words caught, but her tears no longer had the power to move him.

He pulled away and rolled out of bed.

"Ryder, wait. I'm trying to explain."

Pressing his arm against his side, he leaned over and fumbled his way through the scattered clothing until he located his pants and drawers. "No need." He pulled on his clothes. "I guess you're not as good at pretending as you thought."

He found his boots beside his desk where he always left them. His spurs jangled as he stomped his heels against the plank floor.

"Please, Ryder. You don't understand."

A short bark of laughter escaped his throat, an odd expression of pain and rage. "No, Princess, when your own mother throws you out with the trash on the day you were born, you understand real fast."

"I'm trying to tell—*What?*"

His spurs chinked softly as he strode toward the door. Behind him the covers rustled. Her bare feet thudded against the floor.

"Ryder, wait. Your mother threw you in the *trash*?"

He lifted the latch which raised the wooden bar. There was a thump behind him, followed by, "Owww!"

Ignoring her pain, he stepped onto the porch and slammed the door. Striding into the darkness, he heard the clunk of the latch. A moment later her low voice called out. "Ryder, let me explain."

His pace faltered at the sultry quality of her siren's song. If he turned back before he had a chance to wall off his heart, he would surely sail to his death.

"Ryder, please!"

She called to him as though she cared, but he knew better. With clouds shielding the glow of the crescent moon, she would have to dress and light a lantern in order to find him. He wondered how determined she was to maintain her charade.

He continued into the barn, the dogs trotting at his heels.

After lighting a couple of lanterns, he went to work mucking out the stalls. He forked hay into the hayrack between the two corrals. Pumped fresh water into the trough and grained the horses.

Gray illuminated the horizon when he realized she wasn't coming after him. He told himself it was good she finally understood pretending to love him was futile. He was better off alone. He sighed and rubbed his hand around the back of his neck. His thumb brushed the thin line of scar. Sometimes though, he just wished the man with the knife had been successful.

His cough didn't hurt as bad as it had the day before, at least until he'd started forking the hay, and if he still felt overly warm, it was only because he'd been working so hard.

In the corral he ran a curry comb and brush over Percy. As Ryder scrubbed at some dried sweat on Percy's withers, the mule stretched out his neck, cocked his head, and wiggled his upper lip. Ryder chuckled to himself. Percy wasn't bad for a mule, if you didn't mind all his crow-hopping and didn't try to tie him.

When he finished, he sat down beside the barn, rested his head against the log and earthen wall, and closed his eyes. Sally lay down beside him, resting her head on his thigh while he played absently with her ears. He told himself he was only absorbing the warmth of the morning sun while he listened to the chirping birds. He wasn't exhausted. His knees weren't trembling. His muscles weren't shaking.

Nearby, the horses snorted hay dust from their nostrils and stomped their feet at flies. He sighed, wishing his life could stay like this forever.

He dozed and woke with the skin-crawling sensation he was being watched. He lifted his head away from the wall and saw her standing on the porch all prim and proper, with her hair put up and her hands folded in front of her. Funny how he couldn't see her eyes, but he knew they were making eye contact.

He rolled to his feet, walked over to the pump, and filled a bucket with water. Her gaze remained on him as he approached.

"I cleaned your cabin."

He mounted the steps and passed her on his way to the end of the porch where a basin and towel hung on the wall beside a small mirror.

"I salvaged eight of the flapjacks. And I found a crock of honey to go with them. I tried to make a pot of coffee, but I'm not certain if it's the way you like it."

He poured some of the water into the basin and set it on the simple wooden bench which stood against the wall. "I'm sure it's fine."

"I didn't know if you wanted me to throw away all that food, or save it."

He picked up a bar of soap from the end of the

bench and worked it into a lather. "Keep it for the dogs."

He soaped his face and hands, rinsed then scrubbed the dust and chaff from his chest and arms. She hadn't moved since he started washing. He tried to ignore her, but when he raised his elbow to tackle his sweaty arm pit, he heard her soft intake of breath. His gaze swung to her face.

Wide-eyed she stared, as though mesmerized by the stunning vista of a mountaintop view. That tiny bit of pink tongue flicked out again, to moisten her top lip. She swallowed then glanced away, her cheeks tinged with red.

"I'm sorry," she whispered in that low breathy voice.

"Goddamn it, Victoria." He slammed the bar of soap into the water, driving it straight to the bottom of the bucket. "Stop apologizing. And stop looking at me like you want me."

She inched toward the door. Charlie squeezed himself between it and the bottom of her skirt. "But I do."

"Damn it, Victoria, no more lies." He tipped his head back and exhaled. A lady bug wandered along the length of the beam overhead. "You can't help what you feel. Just don't lie about it anymore."

"But, Ryder, you don't understand. All I know of men is Nicholas and to touch the way he likes. In the dark it started to feel like—he was—that you were—I needed last night to be different. I didn't want him to be there."

"Enough!" He lowered his gaze to meet his reflection in the mirror. Last night, in the dark, he'd hoped she wouldn't remember the mark, that she might think him handsome and want to kiss his face. "I don't want to talk about this anymore. Get your things together. We're heading for Ogallala."

She hesitated as though she wanted to say more, but instead opened the door and slipped inside behind the dog.

He blinked at the reflection staring back at him then brought his fist up and smashed the mirror. Jagged lines fanned out to the edge of the glass. The birth mark was still there, distorted now into more red spots by the refection of a dozen triangles of glass.

Chapter Fourteen

My beautiful knight has been deeply wounded. I want to heal his pain, but I no longer feel I can. There is something broken within me. Years of imprisonment in the tower of the prince's castle has left me dirty and damaged inside. My knight deserves a maiden who is pure, and that will never be me.

Victoria swiped at a stray tear and closed her journal. Pulling her carpetbag across the table, she packed the book and pencil. She wiggled her hand to the bottom of the bag, reassuring herself the money she'd taken from Nicholas, the blackmail payment from Ainsworth Thorndyke, remained hidden.

Ryder had gone outside to saddle the horses and load the supplies he'd packed. All that remained was for her to bring her battered carpetbag.

He refused to talk and when he did, he referred to her as *Princess*, saying the word with that note of disdain which implied she thought herself better than him.

He was determined to find his stolen cattle, and if he couldn't, he reminded her he had no qualms about returning her to Nicholas in exchange for the five thousand dollars. It was as if he'd chosen to forget she had come back, that she was still here.

But until she could find a way—if she could find a way to prove to him she did love him—it was easier for both of them to pretend things were as they'd been before.

The sun had climbed nearly to the top of the sky before they had supplies packed and were underway. She rode the horse she'd taken that first night, and Ryder rode Percy. The horse with the brands was too skittish, and evidently the cattle rustlers had killed the only other horse Ryder owned that hadn't been turned out to graze on open range.

Any conversation between them was minimal, and Victoria had no idea how to mend the breach.

They stopped at a neighboring ranch where Ryder hired one of the hands to feed the dogs and horses. And though the men watched her with curious expressions, the horrified looks they gave Percy nearly made her laugh aloud.

Ignoring them, Ryder turned the mule away from the ranch, the smoky gray horse she rode trailing behind. She stared at the straight line of Ryder's spine, who, like a skunk with his tail in the air, warned everyone to stay away.

With every mile they traveled across the wide expanse of prairie and sky, one question burned inside, screaming for an answer. Had his mother really thrown him in the trash?

While Victoria couldn't believe Ryder had lied, the idea that a mother was capable of such a heinous act, seemed beyond truth. How had he gotten from the trash into the arms of the woman who raised him? He'd said she was the housekeeper for a wealthy New York family, and though he hadn't said which family, Victoria was probably acquainted with them. The thought did strange things to her insides.

Of all the homes where she'd eaten dinner, listened to music, or merely chatted, in which one had Ryder the boy, scrubbed pots and run errands.

Her arms ached to slip around his waist and hug him close, but if the past twenty-four hours were any indication, she wouldn't be able to lay a hand on him without her body responding as if he were Nicholas.

Maybe if he was asleep, as he'd been on the train, or ill, as when they'd first arrived at the cabin, then she could touch him without going rigid and her mind shutting down. For there were fleeting moments when Ryder had held her, when the world was perfect, and she felt as if they'd waltzed together in another life time.

They stopped in an open area and made camp just after dusk. Ryder vigorously shook the blankets reassuring her no spiders or beetles lurked between the layers. Then with an exaggerated, somewhat courtly bow, he gestured for her to sit. In her mind, she could almost hear him say, *Milady*.

But he didn't say a thing. Not one word all day. He didn't even ask her to add wood to the fire or stir the pot of beans. He stripped the saddles from Percy and the smoky horse, hobbled them, and turned them loose to graze. His spurs chinked softly as he moved about the camp, the sound soothing and reassuring.

Firelight glinted off the rowels and heart-shaped buttons, and she considered again why he had chosen them.

His coughing had lessened by nightfall, but once he lay down, the deep raspy sounds tore from his chest. He rose several times and paced the perimeter of their camp. She wished she could ease it for him with some sort of mustard plaster, but her skills as a healer were worse than her cooking.

The next day was the same. He spoke more to Percy than he did to her. He seemed focused on the ground as they rode, dismounting occasionally to study things more closely. She pondered the wisdom of heading east with a man who refused to acknowledge her and who had promised to trade her back to her husband.

"This'll do." Ryder halted the mule near a narrow stream that twisted through the short grass.

Grateful, Victoria swung her leg over the horse's rump and stepped to the ground. Her heel caught a clump of grass, and she stumbled. Broad hands came around her waist from behind. His fingertips tightened against her ribs.

She turned in his arms and found herself staring at his square, stubble-coated chin. He leaned close. His full lips, the color of dusty rose, parted slightly, and she glimpsed the white of his teeth. She raised her gaze to his hazel eyes, gleaming with gold from the lowering sun. Abruptly, he pulled back, released her, and swung away.

He may have spent the last two days trying to convince her that he hated her, but she suspected the person he was trying to convince was himself.

"If you need to—to—relieve yourself, go behind that bush." He waved toward a weedy thicket. "And make sure I can see your head, or I'll come back there and watch."

After all the times she could have gotten away, he suddenly decided to treat her like a prisoner? She shot him an angry glare, then stomped off to duck out of sight. "Beast," she muttered.

Now she doubted whether she'd actually seen the longing in his eyes, that smoldering second of time when he'd nearly lowered his lips to hers.

As she stepped out from behind the bush, he turned from his saddle, a coiled rope in his hand. Fashioning a couple of loops he slipped them over the mule's head and nose, then tied the makeshift halter securely to a thin sapling, leaving the extra length to pool in the grass.

He left the sack of supplies tied on the mule along with her carpetbag.

"Are you leaving?"

"I'm going to scout the herd, see if my beeves are here, but these men might be dangerous, so stay here."

A premonition of unease raised the hair on her forearms, the shudder far more chilling than the dread which numbed her when Nicholas walked into a room.

Her gaze fell to her hand, rubbing up and down on her forearm. She lowered them both to her side.

"I don't like this, Ryder. Please don't go."

"Don't follow me," he ordered.

"You can't leave me here." She didn't believe for a second he intended to abandon her, but what if he was wounded or killed. After all, rustlers had shot his horse. "Take me with you or…I'll scream."

"Sorry, Princess." He stepped back. "You can scream all you want, and Percy can bray his heart out. We're far enough from the herd. No one will hear either of you."

"What if you don't come back? I could die all alone out here."

He shrugged. "What do you expect from a beast?"

His last word hung in the air, the way a clap of thunder lingers in the stillness long after the echo fades.

Her gaze shot to his face. She visually traced the irregular outline of the birthmark. She hadn't meant to hurt him. Not the way he believed. She searched his eyes, but there was little to read in their depths. "I didn't mean that the way it sounded. I don't think you're a beast."

"I don't care what you think, Princess." His voice held a dry, flat tone that caused her to wonder if he was thoroughly exhausted or actually didn't care.

She lowered her gaze to the ground, her attention wandering to the toes of his scuffed boots and the heart shaped buttons. She'd hurt him, and though he would hate her for saying it, she knew nothing else to say. "Ryder, I am sorry."

He shoved his hand in his pocket and withdrew what appeared to be lemon drops. He popped one in his mouth and the second he gave to the mule. He scratched Percy's dark forehead, then he rested his own forehead against the mule's mahogany-colored neck.

A long shuddering sigh escaped his lips, and his shoulders sagged, as though he had just conceded defeat in whatever internal battle he'd been waging.

A moment later he reached into his vest, pulled out a small leather purse, and handed it to her. "Take this. If I'm not back in three hours, head south. You'll meet the Union Pacific tracks. Sell Percy at the first town you come to. Adding that money to this should be enough to get you to California."

"Ryder, you're scaring me."

The corner of his mouth quirked up in a half smile. "Don't worry, Princess. I'll be careful." He gazed into her eyes for several moments. A hint of longing glittered in his hazel depths.

Never before had she been the one to initiate a hug or kiss. Never before had she ached to throw herself into the arms of a man, at least not until Ryder MacKenzie walked in from the rain.

"Wait." She swiped her tongue across her top lip then threw her arms around him. "Don't go. These cattle aren't worth your life."

He placed a quick kiss on her forehead then detached her arms from his neck. He searched her face, as though he were trying to gauge her sincerity, before he turned and mounted the smoke colored horse.

"Remember what I said, Victoria. If I don't come back, you get the hell out of here."

Touching his spurs to the sides of the animal, he jogged east.

****

The soft click of a revolver being cocked behind him stiffened every muscle in Ryder's body. He'd been sitting on a low rise, searching the grazing herd for his beeves, watching the men who moved around them, from what he'd thought was a safe distance.

Slowly he raised his hands. He must have miscounted the men who guarded it. He shouldn't have been surprised. Fiona always told him his life had been cursed the day he was born.

At his back, a deep voice rumbled. "State yer business, mister."

Ryder turned his head slightly, searching the shadowy figure on horseback, hoping the man didn't have an itchy trigger finger. "Just looking at your herd, wondering if you might need another hand."

The man nudged his mount forward.

Ryder's brain immediately sorted through hundreds of stored images, trying to recall if he'd seen this stranger's face on a wanted poster. But the brim of the man's tattered, brown hat obscured the top half of his face and a thick, salt and pepper beard hid the bottom half. He had the look of a buffalo hunter, without the smell.

The big man pointed south. "I'll let the boss figger what he wants to do. Camp's 'bout a mile yonder. Get a move on. An' you touch that Colt a yers an' I'll put a bullet in yer back."

The lowering sun cast the red, black, and speckled cattle in a veil of gold and gleamed orange on the massive width of their horns. Some of the cows grazed while others lay chewing their cuds, but they all raised their heads to watch as Ryder and the man behind him wove their horses slowly through the herd.

Ryder spotted several animals grouped together, wearing his MK brand. He was surprised by the audacity of the rustlers, for they hadn't even tried to alter it with a running iron. Surrounding them were cattle wearing various other brands. Aside from a gun at his back, there was a certain relief in seeing with his own eyes, no less than two dozen of his cattle. At least he wasn't chasing a pot of gold at the end of a rainbow.

Ryder and his captor rode toward a line of brush and scraggly trees where an older black man pulled supplies from the back of a chuckwagon while a second cowhand started coffee over a fire.

That man rose and stepped forward. Gray streaked his side burns, and long dark hair brushed his shoulders. He held his right hand loose at his side as if the slightest wrong move would have him whipping his gun from his holster and putting a bullet straight through Ryder's heart. "Who's this?"

"Found him on a rise about a mile northwest a here, watchin' the herd. Said he's lookin' for work."

The man studied him with narrowed eyes, and Ryder did the same, hastily trying to match this face with those of cattle rustlers he'd known through the years.

Ryder rested both hands on the saddle horn and casually arched his lower back. The saddle leather creaked.

"All right then, get down and grab yourself a cup of coffee."

Ryder swung off his horse, grateful the gathering dusk hid the way he favored his sore ribs. He led Smoky past the cook fire to the area where three other saddled horses were staked on picket lines. Dropping the reins, he left his horse ground tied and walked to the fire.

He'd only intended to scout the herd, to see if his cattle were among them. His plan then was to ride back for Victoria and head into Ogallala and talk to the sheriff there. Bradley, if he remembered the name right.

A large shank of meat hung on a spit over the flames while the black man sliced potatoes into a cast-iron spider. Ryder's stomach grumbled.

The long-haired man passed him a cup of coffee and gestured for him to sit.

"Thanks." Ryder wrapped his hand around the tin-ware as he lowered himself cross-legged in the grass.

"Tiny says you're looking for work."

Ironic that someone as big as a buffalo would be

called Tiny. Glancing around, Ryder spotted the silhouette of Tiny and his horse in the distance, returning to the herd.

"I could use a few dollars."

Long hair pulled out a paper and a pouch of tobacco. "So what's your name, friend?" He rolled a smoke.

Ryder sipped his coffee. "MacKenzie. And you?"

"You can call me Deke, and this here is Mose." He gestured toward the black man sprinkling something over the beef. Though Mose said nothing, Ryder didn't miss the well-worn revolver, low on his hip. Deke chuckled and held out his makings.

Ryder shook his head.

Deke stuffed the pouch back inside his vest pocket then stretched his arm out to light his cigarette in the fire. "Now, MacKenzie, you're welcome to coffee and grub, but the man who owns this herd is the one doin' the hiring. You want a job you best go see Frank Searcy up near the mouth of Blue Creek."

Ryder nodded. This was the perfect opportunity to slip away without a fuss. "Obliged. I'll just finish my coffee and be on my way."

He blew on the liquid and took a sip. From behind, he recognized the muted swish of a horse moving through the grass.

There was a creak of saddle leather and the chink of spurs.

"Who the hell is this?" demanded a deep gravelly voice.

The voice was so distinctive, a chill of recognition rippled down Ryder's spine. Casually, he leaned forward and set his cup by the fire.

Deke looked past Ryder. "Now, Jake, the feller's just havin' a cup of coffee 'fore he heads out."

Ryder rolled to his feet and turned, extending his hand, hoping Paul Jacobs wouldn't recognize him. A few years had passed, and Jacobs had grown a thick handlebar moustache, but even in the deepening shadows of dusk, there was no mistake. Their gazes met, and Ryder caught the flash of recall in the other man's eyes.

"Sonofabitch," Jacobs sneered. "This is the same ugly, spot-faced bounty hunter that accused me of cattle rustlin' five years back."

"I didn't accuse you, someone else did. I only brought you in for it." Ryder's pulse thudded against his jaw. The tiny hairs on the back of his neck tickled. Behind him came the muted sounds of Deke rising and stepping closer.

Click. The soft noise of that hammer being pulled back stilled all other movements in camp.

"All right, mister, state your business. And I know you ain't lookin' for work."

"There are two hundred head in that herd, stolen from me twelve days ago. I came to get them back."

"Jake didn't do it. Now take your gun out of your holster," Deke commanded in low, deliberate tones. "Real slow, and hand it over, butt first. Touch that trigger, and I'll blow a hole through the back of your head."

Ryder's gaze swept the area in front of him. "Didn't say Jake took 'em. Didn't even know the sonofabitch was here."

If he threw himself to the ground and rolled as he pulled his Colt then fired, he'd probably be able to hit some part of Jake's body. Deke would likely miss his shot to Ryder's head. But within seconds, Deke and Mose would probably send bullets tearing into him before he had a chance to find cover. Then there was Tiny and the other men with the herd, who would race back as soon as they heard the gun battle.

No, he'd wait. Patience had been his friend in the past.

Grasping the butt of his revolver with three fingers, Ryder slowly lifted his Colt from his holster and passed it to Jake.

"I see how this works. You steal my cattle and sell them to the man who then hires you to watch them. Are these two in it with you?"

Jake strode close and snatched the gun. "You're full of shit, MacKenzie. Likely you're the one sold stolen beef to Searcy, then come ridin' in here bold as brass to demand them back." He stuffed Ryder's Colt behind the waistband of his pants.

"On your knees, mister." Deke ordered.

Ryder's heart thudded against his breastbone, as his rapid breaths grew shallow. He lowered himself to his knees. This wasn't good. He rubbed his damp palms against the worn canvas duck of his pants.

"Untie your neckerchief." Deke stepped in front of Ryder.

Ryder reached behind his neck and worked free the knot. "You have cattle in that herd with notched ears and the MK brand. They're mine." He passed his bandana to Deke.

Another click sounded as Deke released the hammer on his gun. "I known Jake a long time. He might be a little loose on the definition of a maverick, but he ain't never changed another man's brand."

Deke moved out of sight.

A moment later Ryder's left arm was yanked behind him. "It hasn't been changed. I have the brand book in my saddlebags, proving those beeves are mine. I want them back."

Jake burst out laughing. "Oh, do you?"

Mose stood. He shot Jake a narrow-eyed glare and walked toward Ryder. "So whatcha ya doin' out here? Thinkin' to take this herd by yer ownself?"

The cloth was wrapped tight around Ryder's wrist then his other arm was wrenched behind him, the bandana securing both wrists together.

"Stand up," Deke ordered.

Ryder pushed to his feet.

Deke grabbed him by his upper arm and guided him to the chuckwagon.

"Sit." Deke gave him a shove that had him stumbling back a step. The rowel of his spur caught in a clump of short grass and unable to catch himself, he fell, landing on his side.

Pain shot from his ribs like jagged bolts of lightning. He couldn't breathe. Stars sparkled across the backs of his closed eyelids.

"Hey, Mose, ya got something I can tie his feet with?"

"Yeah, they's some rope an' extra hobbles in a sack up front there."

Ryder focused on drawing short, panting breaths through his mouth. He muffled his occasional coughs against his shoulder, hoping they would forget about him, but Deke returned and buckled the leather straps around his ankles. When he finished, he took a piece of rope from where he'd tucked it in the front of his vest. Reaching down, Deke grabbed Ryder's arm, dragged him close to the wagon wheel, and tied him to a spoke.

Fiona was right. He was cursed. He'd lost his cattle, horse, money, saddle, rifle, scabbard, and now his hat lay hidden in the shadowy grass, just about the last thing he had left in this world.

The aroma of roasting beef caused saliva to pool beneath his tongue and his stomach to rumble. Tiny and two other men came into camp to fix themselves a plate.

"Tiny," Deke said as the big man speared a piece of meat with a knife. "First thing tomorrow you and me are goin' to take this feller into Ogallala."

Tiny glanced Ryder's way then nodded. "Sure 'nuff, boss," he mumbled around a mouthful of food.

Deke continued. "Then we'll head on up to Searcy's an' let him know what's going on."

"An' the rest of you boys keep alert for cattle thieves."

The men murmured their agreement.

Apparently Jake and Deke had a later watch. Once the meal ended, they played a few hands of cards, then curled up in their bedrolls.

At least they hadn't decided to kill him. Now he had to wait until they took him to the sheriff. Bradley had only been in office a year, but he knew Ryder. One thing about his damn birthmark was people didn't forget his face.

Whether Jake was involved in the theft of Ryder's cattle or not, he didn't know. But he did know he didn't like the man and wouldn't mind seeing him at least hauled into Ogallala for questioning.

He leaned his head against the wheel and closed his eyes. Moses moved quietly around camp washing the dishes. Soft snores rumbled from the bedrolls.

Victoria's words, *"What if you don't come back?"* echoed in his mind.

He hoped by now she'd high-tailed her little self to the nearest train and headed far away from him, far away from Nicholas. If escaping her husband was really as important as she claimed, she'd have long since been on her way. He wondered if she'd even waited the three hours.

A tiny voice in the back of his mind reminded him that she'd left him once and come back. Because she loved him. Pain pierced the center of his chest. He winced. No one loved him. Her claim was bullshit. She must have had another reason for returning that night and staying with him. He just needed some time to puzzle it out.

From the other side of the creek, the mules grazing with the horse herd abruptly began hee-hawing.

Curses drifted from the bedrolls.

Jake's gravelly voice yelled out, "Mose, get those damn jackasses to shut the hell up."

"I don't know why they's riled. They only does this when they's another…"

The vibration of hoof beats radiated through the ground before their thudding could be heard. Deke and Jake leapt from their bedrolls as if anticipating a stampede, except the herd was a mile away.

The cacophony of braying was rejoined by the hee-haw of a single mule from the west side of camp. A moment later a single rider charged into their midst on a very familiar, gangly, long-legged, long-eared mule.

Ryder closed his eyes and groaned. For on Percy's back, sat a very familiar woman. Her blonde hair tied in a long braid, she clutched the saddle horn with one hand and with the other a tuft of Percy's black mane.

Though touched by her quixotic attempt to rescue him, he clamped his teeth together to keep from yelling at her. What the hell was she doing riding into a camp full of lonesome cowpunchers with her skirts and petticoats hiked nearly to her knees?

Mose dashed forward and took hold of the reins, pulling Percy to a stop.

Deke grabbed Victoria around the waist and lifted her from the saddle.

Laughing she smoothed her skirt. "I thank ya kindly, gentlemen."

Her normally low, sultry voice had suddenly taken on the slow, beguiling drawl of a southern accent. The soothing tones stirred his blood and warmed his insides, enticing him through the darkness, even as his hands itched to ring her pretty little neck.

"Ya'all have surely saved my life. I couldn't get this ornery ol' mule to go anywhere I wanted." She laughed again and looked around the campsite.

Mose led Percy toward the picket line where Smoky was tied with the other horses.

"Why now I see he was just lonely. Don't ya'all think so?"

Ryder's blood chilled. He struggled against his bonds.

Her laughter carried through the night. "Maybe lookin' for a bit of companionship?"

Goddamn, this was not going to be good.

Chapter Fifteen

"My name's Deke. What's your name, darlin'?"

Victoria forced a smile. "Ivy Devine."

As Percy was led away, she spotted Ryder's smoky-gray horse standing with his hip cocked, beside three other horses.

"Devine, like from Heaven?"

"No." She sashayed closer, swinging her hips. "Ivy," she crooned as she placed her hand against the center of his vest. He smelled of dust and cows and sweat, but she pasted on her most captivating smile. "Like a clingin' vine." She slid her hand up to his shoulder and twined her fingers in the edges of his greasy hair. "I like to wrap myself around a nice—thick—trunk."

Then while he gawked with his mouth hanging open, she laughed and twirled away, wiping the invisible crawlies from her hand onto the side of her skirt where Deke couldn't see.

"I don't suppose ya'all might have a little somethin' to steady a girl's nerves? I declare that mule gave me such a fright. Why my little ol' heart is just a racin'."

Deke veered to the left, striding straight to the front of the chuckwagon. Climbing to the seat, he swung his leg over the back and disappeared beneath the canvas.

Her gaze connected with Ryder's. He did not look

happy to see her. Since he usually sat with one knee drawn up, she suspected something wasn't right.

"Where are you headed, sweetheart?" Someone asked from a pile of bedding on the other side of the fire.

"Rosie Mae, Lilly, and I were headin' for Ogallala. Any you boys been there?"

"I been there." Deke jumped from the wagon, a bottle in his hand.

"Me too," added the black man who'd bravely stopped Percy.

Victoria stepped close to Deke. "Then ya'all understand that with the new stock yards, drovers will be coming up from Texas—in droves." She giggled as she traced the length of his arm with her finger and accepted the bottle he held. "Rosie Mae feels there will be a great need in that town for a…um boardin' house, where young, unmarried ladies, lookin' to make a start in this world might have a room. Rosie Mae is goin' name it after her dear mama, Mrs. Caroline Everhart.

"I tried to keep up with my friends, but my mule, why he was either buckin' or refusin' to move, no matter how hard I kicked him."

The black man scrutinized her for several seconds. "Why didn't yer friends wait?"

Had he seen through her ruse. "Well now, they might have if we hadn't argued this afternoon. I believe they are jealous, because I am prettier."

The man with the thick handle-bar moustache wandered close, took the bottle from her hand, popped the cork, and tipped it to his lips. Dropping his arm around her shoulder, he kissed her cheek. "My name's Jake, and I think you're about the prettiest little gal I ever seen."

She forced herself not to shudder as the wet hairs of his moustache pressed against her skin. For five years she'd lived as Nicholas' whore; she could do this. "Why thank ya, sugar." She shrugged her shoulder from beneath his arm and swiped the dampness from her cheek. Jake didn't seem to notice as he raised the bottle for another swig.

Deke snatched it back. "I never heard of no Mrs. Everhard."

"Hart, sugar. You must be thinking of another person. A gentleman perhaps?"

She twirled her finger around the end of Jake's bandana, just below the knot. "Ever-*hart* is the name Rosie is goin' to give her new boardin' house. Ya'all will come an' visit us now, won't ya sugar?"

"I sure will." Jake grinned as he took the bottle from Deke.

He tipped it to his lips then offered it to her. She ignored it and yawned, stretching her back by raising her arms over her head, and shifted away from the fire toward the chuckwagon.

"Sho is strange," the black-skinned cowboy continued, gesturing toward her with his chin. "Her showin' up same time as that cattle thief."

He snatched the bottle from Jake and jammed the cork down tight.

"Cattle thief?" she asked the three men now sitting around the fire.

"That's right, sweetheart," Ryder called from the back wheel of the chuckwagon. "Come over here and give me a kiss."

"Well now, sugar, how about I bring you a drink

instead?"

"Only thing I got me a taste for is your sweet lips."

The familiar tones of his voice soothed her anxiety the way her grandmother's voice soothed her after a nightmare. Her feet itched with the need to run into his arms and never lose sight of him again, but she had to maintain the ruse. She could do this. She was good at pretending.

"Yeah, sho' is strange," the black man continued with a note of suspicion. "Ya comin' on in here, askin' for whiskey an' inchin' your way toward that rustler all casual like, makes me wonder is all, maybe ya ain't quite who ya say ya are."

This time all three men stared at her, waiting for her response, waiting to judge her answer. Her plan to get them drunk on *flagons of ale*, find *the captive knight,* and *flee the castle*, was not coming together the way it had in the story Grandmother told of *The Damsel and the Highland Warrior*.

Jake didn't seem interested in the suspicions of Mose and tugged her toward some blankets spread out on the other side of the fire. "Come on honey, it's getting cold. Let's stay warm together."

She twisted her wrist and turned, freeing herself from his grasp. "Hold on a minute, sugar." She walked toward the back of the wagon. "I want to see this cattle thief."

"Stay away from him, honey; he's dangerous." Jake warned in his low, gritty voice.

She locked her gaze on the moonlit areas of Ryder's nose and cheekbones. "Aren't you the handsome one."

Hiking her skirts, she straddled his extended legs

and lowered herself to sit on his thighs.

"Have you been a baaad boy?" she asked loud enough for the others to hear. "Why he's already tied up. Ain't that nice." She slipped her hand into his vest pocket, closing her fingers around Ryder's pen knife.

"Victoria, what the hell are you doing?" he whispered.

"I like bad boys," she said aloud, prying the knife blade open. Leaning close, with her breasts pressed to his chest, she toyed with the hair above his ear, while the hand no one else could see, slipped around Ryder's waist. Holding the knife in her fingers, she slid her hand down his arm to the cloth knotted around his wrist. Hooking the blade under the twisted cloth she began to cut.

"Get over here, darlin', and sit in my lap," Jake called.

"I'm comin', sugar."

She pressed the knife against Ryder's palm. His fingers curled around it, brushing against the soft underside of her wrist. Goose bumps skittered up her arm.

She unbuttoned the first three buttons of her shirt, exposing the ribbon of her camisole, which outlined the swell of her breasts.

"Don't tease these men, Victoria." Ryder's whisper was nearly a growl. "Stay close to me. They're going to take me to the sheriff in the morning."

"How can you be sure? They stole your cattle and killed your horse."

"Tori, listen—"

"Miss Ivy, I told you to leave that man alone." Deke's voice carried a sharper edge of authority than

Jake's.

She whispered against Ryder's cheek. "Give me a minute to get a gun for you."

"Goddamn it, no." His shoulders shifted rapidly as though he worked frantically to cut through his bonds.

She leaned close one more time. "I'm sorry," she whispered then drew back her hand and slapped Ryder's cheek.

"Liar!" She jumped to her feet. She swung around and stomped toward the fire and men who sat watching her.

"He promised me a dollar if I let him kiss me." She declared with a huff.

The men around the fire laughed. Deke rolled to his feet, grabbed her hand, and held up a coin between his thumb and forefinger. It gleamed silver-gray in the light. "I got me a dollar; can I have the liar's kiss?"

Deke's other hand slid around her waist, and he snapped her tightly against his chest. He lowered his head and was about to swoop in for his kiss, when Victoria stopped him by pressing her hands against his shoulders.

"No, sugar." She smiled despite the tension which suddenly radiated from his stiffened spine.

"He didn't kiss me here." She pressed one fingertip against the corner of her mouth.

"He kissed me…" She drew her finger slowly over her chin, down her throat to the center of her chest, where she see-sawed her finger across the swell of her breasts. "…down here." She caught the length of ribbon and twined it around her finger.

He dove on her bosom with the enthusiasm of a slobbering dog.

She clenched her teeth and allowed him a few moments to suck on her skin then she snatched the coin from his fingers and twirled away.

"Why thank you, sugar."

"I got me two-bits right here." Jake stepped toward her. "Does this mean I get one titty?" He laughed and grabbed her hand.

She giggled, but to her ears, the sound was dry and brittle. "I don't rightly believe that tallies correctly. Maybe I'll let you kiss my hand." She toyed with the button of his shirt, just above the 'v' of his vest. Then stepping back she extended her arm and waggled her fingers like a debutante at a ball waiting for a gentleman to make his bow.

At the fire Mose poured coffee into a tin-ware mug. "Sounds like the whore's gettin' above herself a mite."

The flickering light reflected in the whites of his eyes as he glared at her. She swallowed past the tightness in her throat.

"Relax, Mose." Deke grinned, lowering himself beside the cook. "Have a drink and wait your turn."

"Mister Searcy ain't gonna like it none. Us drinkin' and whorin' whilst cattle thieves move in an' take his herd."

His suspicious gaze followed her as Jake grabbed her hand and yanked her close.

In an instant Jake's mouth was on hers. Without any attempt to woo her, he gave her a squeeze that drove the breath from her lungs in a gasp. Then while her lips were parted, he shoved his tongue inside.

In that moment, it was as if Nicholas were forcing himself on her, and she was as powerless to stop him as she'd always been. His roving hands pulled her blouse free from the waist of her skirt. Then while keeping his mouth locked with hers, he ripped open her blouse without taking the time to undo the buttons. But underlying the repugnant moustache and the taste of whiskey on Jake's tongue was the foulness of rotting teeth, a taste Nicholas had never had. She tried to wrench her mouth away, but Jake grasped the back of her head with one hand while his other hand painfully squeezed her derrière. His fetid breath curled around her tongue, and she gagged.

She pushed at his chest, but not hard enough to get him to stop. In her mind Nicholas taunted her. *Come-on, Victoria, fight me.*

Jake's hand slid lower and hiked up the fabric of her skirt. Cool night air swirled around her legs as his fingers slipped beneath her petticoat and followed the line of her leg to the opening of her drawers.

Her insides tightened as they did when Nicholas touched her, when he drove himself into her hard and fast. She yielded to Nicholas, just as she always had, allowing him to touch her because it was his right.

Fight me, Victoria.

Obeying, she slid one hand to his hip, then brought her other up to the side of his face, curled her fingers, and dragged her nails down to his jaw.

"Bitch!" He brought one hand to his bleeding cheek as his other palm smacked against her face.

The strength of the blow sent her to the ground. Her vision blurred as a humming sound rang in her ear. Pushing to her knees, she kept an eye out for his foot, expecting a solid kick any moment.

"Jake!"

"What the hell?"

Deke shoved himself between her and Jake as Mose knelt beside her asking if she were all right.

She heard his voice but could barely manage a nod in response.

Then from the corner of her vision, a shadow launched itself from nowhere, like a wolf taking down a deer. It slammed into Jake, driving him to the ground. She could only blink, then she gasped when she recognized the lean length of Ryder MacKenzie. She scrambled to her feet as Deke and Mose both tried to pull Ryder off Jake, but the two men were as intertwined as snarled yarn.

The thuds of their fists pounding into each other coincided with every grunt and groan she heard. When Jake lay still on the ground. Ryder stumbled to his feet. He shrugged away from Deke and Mose then turned. The two men froze staring at the gun in his hand. The hammer clicked back.

Jake pushed sluggishly to his knees.

Victoria scurried across the distance, taking a wide detour around Jake to stand beside Ryder.

"I got no quarrel with either of you men, so just keep your hands away from your guns. Victoria, go get Percy and my gray horse."

Eager to leave, she hurried across the camp to grab the reins of both animals. Ryder inched his way toward her, keeping his gun pointed in the general direction of the men. "I don't know if Jacobs here had any part in the thieving of my cattle. But I do know his nature. He is a liar, a convicted rustler, and now I see an abuser of women."

Victoria mounted the gray horse, and while Ryder

kept his gun aimed in Jake's general direction, he mounted the mule.

"I'm going to the sheriff. And you can believe I'll be back. You have my cattle in that herd, and I want them."

He gave her a nod, and they swung their mounts around. "Go!" he yelled, and she kicked the horse into a gallop.

Chapter Sixteen

Ryder caught up to Victoria less than a minute later. Fortunately, she knew better than to run a horse in the dark. He rode up beside her, and though she glanced his way, she said nothing.

He slipped his Colt into his holster then turned to study her face. Though there was moonlight, he couldn't tell if Jake's slap had given her a bruise. "Did he hurt you?"

She shook her head. "I'm fine. I would just feel better if I could freshen up."

"The North Platte runs south of here. We can stop there."

"Thank you." She turned in the direction he indicated.

Nudging the horse into a jog, she was swallowed by the dark in moments. He continued to stare, wondering why it bothered him to see her as composed as the princess he had always accused her of being.

Willows and cotton woods lined the shallow, sandy banks of the river, and moonlight reflected as silver on the pewter surface of the water. Brush-filled sandbars diverted the water into small streams to twine around them like a frayed rope.

They rode east a few miles to a place where they would only have to splash through the water twice.

He left Percy ground tied beside some shrubs

where Victoria had secured the reins of the smoke-colored horse. Giving her a chance for privacy, he hunkered down and leaned against the trunk of a scraggly tree then waited about twenty minutes before he followed.

He walked to the edge of the water and stopped, trying not to look her way, but watching from the corner of his eye as she sat in the grass and slipped her black stockings on over each milky white leg.

"Don't worry, I'm not running away." She didn't look up. "I needed a bath." She took her time tying the pink ribbon of her camisole, making certain the size of each loop in her bow matched the other.

"Are you all right?"

Rising, she slipped on her shirt, drew a deep breath through her nose then released it on a sigh. She pushed each button through its corresponding hole from the hem all the way to the collar. "I was teasing them. I deserved what happened," she said without looking his way. "It didn't bother me."

"Bullshit."

Her chin jerked up. He stared at her. The breeze lifted the edges of her hair where it had loosened from her long braid.

"It bothered me," he snapped. "He had no right."

She tucked her blouse into the waistband of her skirt. Next she evened out the bunched cotton, making certain each little pinch of material was the same size all the way around her waist.

And he considered in that moment if he had remained in the cabin the other night, would he have seen this same behavior? Was that the reason she hadn't followed him to the barn, because she'd been washing?

Scrubbing the scent of him from her body, readjusting her clothes until she was once again the proper, rich princess?

She squared her shoulders then walked up to him and slipped her arms around his waist. As she pressed her cheek to his shirt, just below the top button, he felt the tug at the back of his vest as her fingers clutched fistfuls of the soft wool.

In response, he wrapped his arms around her as though enfolding her in a blanket.

Another shuddering sigh escaped her lips in a long whisper of breath.

The knot of tension that had been twisting inside his chest since she charged into camp, melted like a scoop of lard in a hot skillet. He dropped his chin to the top of her head.

Her fingers twisted tighter at his back and she sniffed.

"Are you crying?" He eased back trying to search her face, but she squeezed him tighter.

He winced under the pressure of her arm against his side. "Not so tight, Tori."

She shifted that hand up to his shoulder and grasped another fistful of wool as though she would lose him if she didn't hold on.

He held her this way for several long minutes. The fresh scent of lemon filled his nose, and he breathed deep, unwilling to release her, afraid if he moved she would pull away. That she clung to him so desperately strengthened his desire to hold her close, to protect her from ever being hurt again and to let the whole world know she was his.

Eventually her fingers released their grip on his

clothing and with a small sniff, she took a step back and swiped her fingertips across her cheekbones.

He searched her face but couldn't read her expression in the dark.

She reached up and brushed the backs of her fingers from his jaw to his cheek bone, then rested her palm against his stubble coated jaw.

"I love you, Ryder MacKenzie," she whispered.

He closed his eyes, savoring the warmth of her touch. Then it was gone.

She took a step back, smoothed her skirt and climbed the slope to the bush where Percy and the horse were tied. Except for the soft chink of his spurs, he followed in silence.

She was already mounting as he checked the cinch and grabbed Percy's trailing reins. "We can camp here if you want to rest. We can ride to Ogallala in the morning."

She replied with a small shake of her head. "If you don't mind, could we keep moving? Once we're out in the open again, it will be bright enough, won't it?"

Though a bit surprised to find she wanted to continue, it had been his hope all along. "If we ride all night, we should make it to Ogallala by morning."

****

Looking down from the sandy bluff where she and Ryder sat on their mounts, there was little more to see of Ogallala than what she'd seen last week from the section house when the train stopped for lunch. A small cluster of buildings stretched between the South Platte River and the railroad tracks. West of town were the unfinished cattle pens and loading chute she heard about on the train.

A pink-yellow glow bathed the town, and to the east mauve and lavender clouds stacked one upon the other in streaks of brilliant color from the top of the sky down to the line where the prairie met the morning sun.

They passed a few scattered homes, some of which looked brand new. Not much was open when they crossed the tracks and rode down the wide dusty street. It looked as if only one place served food, and its front door stood open as two men entered.

Victoria followed Ryder as he halted Percy in front of the hitching rail and dismounted. As she swung her leg over the rump of the horse, Ryder's hands came around her waist. His long fingers gripped her securely, and she stood willing her knees not to go weak. Lord, his touch did funny things to her heart.

She turned in his arms and smiled. His brow furrowed. Though she understood his suspicion, it saddened her to know she'd been the one to cause his hurt.

She shook out her skirt and entered the building. Ryder gestured toward a small table in the corner.

As she moved toward the chair, Ryder stepped behind her and seated her as smoothly as any gentleman of her acquaintance. She glanced back to thank him and was struck again by the sense he'd done this for her before.

He frowned. "What's wrong?"

She gave her head a small shake. "I'm sorry; I suppose I'm just tired."

Though he nodded and moved to his own seat, she read the doubt in his face. She wished she could fix things between them but didn't know how.

Ryder ordered enough steak, eggs, and biscuits to

satisfy three men and consumed it all in silence, while she sipped her coffee and slowly ate two eggs and a piece of toast. She was glad his appetite had returned and realized his cough had almost disappeared.

He must have retrieved some money before they'd left the ranch, for he had his wallet out and paid the waiter before she could get to her purse.

Ryder paused at the door allowing her go first, but as soon as she stepped into the morning light she froze. The gray horse she called, Smoky stood in front of her, still tied to a hitching rail that looked like a giant letter 'M,' and Percy was nowhere in sight.

Ryder bumped against her as he stepped past.

"Goddamn, sonofabitch, long-legged jackass of a mule."

Two men, walking toward the eating house, burst out laughing. One of them pointed west. He said something, but he was laughing too hard for Victoria to understand him.

Ryder stomped off, his long legged stride taking him quickly in the direction the men had indicated.

Not wanting to stand here awkwardly in front of the door, she wandered down the street and stopped to look in the wide front window of Drover's Store. It looked like the owner had a bit of everything, from canned goods, to shovels and boots, to cigars and various kinds of liquor. But what caught Victoria's attention was the blue calico dress on a hanger in the corner of the crowded window display.

She glanced down at the boy's shirt and green skirt. Too big, torn and dirty, she'd been wearing the outfit for days and days. Suddenly the longing to own that simple cotton dress superseded any desire she ever had to own the most beautiful of Worth's gowns.

"Can I help you, ma'am?" asked a male voice.

She turned to find a short man in a black coat and bowler approaching the store with a key.

"I was looking at that blue dress."

"Come on inside if you like and take a closer look."

He slid the key into the lock and pushed the door inward. Victoria glanced up and down the street but didn't see Ryder. She shrugged. "All right."

The man motioned her inside then hurried past her to lift it from its hook.

Victoria removed the hanger and held the dress pressed against herself as she kicked out one foot to check the length.

"Do you have any others?"

He shook his head. "No, I don't get much call for ladies' things. I got that a year or so ago from a family passing through with a wagon. They were looking to trade for supplies, so I took it." He smiled. "Looks like it will fit you just fine."

She held it at her waist to see if it reached half way around on either side. It did seem as though it would fit, but she wasn't sure about how it would fit over her breasts. She wasn't large, but this bodice didn't seem full enough.

"Do you have a place where I might try it on?" The thought of wearing these clothes for one minute more made her skin crawl.

"Sure, you can go straight through to the back storage room. I got some things to do up front here anyway."

"Thank you." She smiled and hurried away eager

to put on something new.

She wished there was a mirror. Used to having gowns and dresses made for her, she'd never worn something made for another person, until she ran from Nicholas.

Whoever had sewn the dress had done an excellent job. The seams were straight and held with tiny stitches. The lace around the collar was finely tatted, and the pleats down the front of the blouse were each exactly the same width. Only the hem hung a couple of inches too short, which surprised her since she wasn't all that tall, and the bust was a bit snug. Looking down at herself she couldn't see any gaping between the buttons, so it would work just fine until she could adjust the seams a bit and take down the hem.

From the other side of the door, came the sound of raised voices, followed by the thumps of boot heels and jangle of spurs.

The door to the backroom burst open, and Ryder charged in as though he were chasing someone. He was moving so fast that when he saw her and stopped short, it looked as if he'd slammed into an invisible wall.

Victoria clamped her hand over her mouth to keep from laughing.

"What are you doing?" he asked as if it were an accusation rather than a question.

Since the answer was obvious, she spun around in front of him, holding the skirt out on each side. "What do you think? Do you like it?"

His eyes widened as he gave the dress a quick perusal. "Looks fine."

In that moment, the flash of desire in Ryder's eyes meant more to her than the insincere flattery she usually received when she walked into a room wearing the newest most expensive gown.

Realizing Ryder had never seen her dressed in anything that actually fit her, it became unexpectedly important that she look nice for him, that he was proud to be seen with her.

"Did you find Percy?"

"Yeah, I got him. Are you ready to see the sheriff? He's probably in by now."

Her mouth quirked up at the corner. He continued to stare at her.

"I just have to pay for this."

She gathered her old clothes and started for the door. He held it open.

"I'll pay for it," he said.

As they started down the aisle, she realized it might be inappropriate to accept such a gift from a man who wasn't her father or husband. "It's all right. I have enough in my pocket."

"What's the matter, Princess? My money not good enough for you?"

"No. I never meant—"

"I'll pay for the damn dress."

The heels of her shoes clicked against the wood floor as she hurried to keep up with him. Maybe once the issue with his cattle was resolved and he had a chance to sleep, he'd be in a better mood.

Percy stood calmly outside, his long reins trailing in the dirt. Ryder grabbed them and stood scowling until she caught up to him, and they could walk back to the broken hitching rail where her horse was tied.

She unhooked the handles of her carpetbag from the saddle horn, set the bag on the ground, and lowered herself in front of it to stuff her old clothes inside. Ryder's spurs chinked softly as he stepped up beside her blocking the sun. Something about his scuffed boots and those spurs with the tiny hearts drew her, and she almost reached out to touch.

"Got anymore of those candies?" Ryder asked from above.

"Ummm… sure."

She shoved aside her clothes to reach into one of the side pockets and withdraw the paper cone. Ryder leaned close, his shadow falling over her, and held out his hand. She shook a few into his palm and watched as he popped two into his mouth.

She also picked one to suck on as she buckled the strap.

Ryder took her carpetbag and looped the handles over the saddle horn then passed her the reins to the horse.

Leading Percy and Smoky, they walked less than half a city block to a small frame building with a sign that read Keith County Courthouse. Victoria led her horse to the hitching post beside Percy and looped the reins around the cross rail.

Instead of tying Percy, Ryder let the reins drop then held his palm under the mule's nose. "Here you go, you long-eared sonofabitch," he crooned in that low sultry voice of his that melted her insides like a summer night in August.

She watched, captivated by the movement of his arm as he ran his hand down Percy's dappled brown neck and patted the mule's shoulder.

"Stay put, 'cause if you head for the Platte I'll put a bullet right between your two big eyes."

He turned and walked to the front door.

Mesmerized, her gaze roamed from the width of his shoulders down the line of his spine to his hips, where his gun belt hung low, then down his long legs to the heels of his boots and the glint of the tiny hearts. Her finger tips tingled as they recalled the ridges of his scars and the warmth of skin as they'd roamed his body in the night.

"Are you coming?" he snapped.

Heat flooded her cheeks, and she hurried forward, avoiding his gaze as she stepped through the doorway.

Inside the small front room, a desk sat in the corner near the window. A row of wooden file cabinets flanked the wall behind it. A man stood before a small black stove pouring coffee into a cup. He looked up as they entered.

Taking a guess, Victoria thought he might be in his early forties, touches of gray at his temples and the wisdom of a few lines in his face.

Ryder stepped forward extending his hand. "Bradley."

Recognition warmed the other man's brown eyes as he engulfed Ryder's hand with his own. "MacKenzie. How you been? Want some coffee?"

Ryder shrugged. "Thanks."

Sheriff Bradley turned to Victoria. His shrewd gaze locked briefly on her face. He held out coffee he'd just poured. "Ma'am?"

She smiled and accepted the white ceramic mug. "Thank you." She took a sip and tried not to shudder, suddenly wishing for sugar and cream.

The sheriff poured a cup for Ryder. "Now don't tell me you're here to collect a bounty on this little gal.

I don't recall seeing any posters for women lately."

"No, this is Victoria. She's uh, she's uh…"

"I'm his wife," she blurted, looping her free hand around Ryder's arm and leaning close. She wasn't sure why she said it, maybe so the sheriff wouldn't think her less than a lady, maybe so the man wouldn't judge Ryder for consorting with a married woman, or maybe she just wanted to pretend, if only for a little while that she was his, that this unassuming, gallant, and wonderful man belonged to her.

Beside her, Ryder stiffened. He glared at her, his eyes narrowed with suspicion.

She smiled back sweetly.

"Wife? Congratulations." Bradley smiled. "Can't believe you got this pretty little thing to marry you." The sheriff gestured toward the pair of leather chairs in front of the desk. "Have a seat. Tell me how I can help you."

He set his cup on the desk then lifted the books and stacks of papers from the chairs to an already over-flowing side table.

She and Ryder took a seat as the sheriff lowered himself into the wooden swivel chair behind his desk.

Ryder set his cup on the corner and crossed his ankle over his opposite knee. "About two weeks ago, some cattle were stolen from my place northwest of Granite Canyon. I was trailing the sons of bitches east, but they bushwhacked me north of Julesburg, and I lost them. Then a few days ago, I got word Frank Searcy has been buying beef. So, I came to check the herd he has grazing up east of Blue Creek."

The sheriff's chair creaked as he leaned back. He gave his head a quick shake. "I got to tell ya son, Frank

Searcy ain't the kind of man to steal cattle."

Ryder dropped his foot to the floor and leaned forward. "I'm not saying he did, but Paul Jacobs is working that herd, and there was a bounty on him a few years ago for rustling."

"An' Searcy ain't the kind of man to let go too easy of what he thinks is his."

"I don't care. There's two hundred of my beef in Searcy's herd. I've got a copy of the Wyoming Stock Growers Association Brand Book in my saddlebag. You'll see the MK brand is mine."

"Well, them cattle ain't goin' no where. And I got me some paperwork to get done for the county 'fore the circuit judge comes through. How 'bout we meet back here tomorrow after breakfast. Searcy's place is only a couple hours away. We'll see what he has to say. If that don't resolve things, I'll send a wire for the WSGA brand inspector and let him handle it."

"Tomorrow?" Ryder shot to his feet. "I can't wait 'til tomorrow."

"Now hold up, MacKenzie." The sheriff glared at Ryder. "You want to ride out to Searcy's place, all het up looking like you do, go ahead. He ain't gonna believe a word and will likely have you run off.

"Clean yourself up, get a shave, and some sleep. Then meet me in the morning."

"Just give me his direction." Ryder growled. "I'll handle it myself."

The sheriff shook his head but told Ryder how to get there. "Now you best calm down 'fore you go. I don't want no trouble outta you. Searcy ain't one a your bounties," he warned as Ryder started to the door.

Victoria rose.

The sheriff did too.

"Thank you for your help, sheriff."

"You're welcome, ma'am. Anything else I can do for you folks?"

"There anyplace we can get a room?" Ryder blurted out turning around. "We rode all night and… my…" Ryder shot Victoria a scowl. "…wife is very tired."

"Well, they're putting up a hotel next door, but that won't do ya much good today." The sheriff stepped around his desk and pointed out the window. "But see those houses on the other side of the tracks. See that real big one? Mr. Greene rents rooms to folks sometimes. I'm sure he'll let you and your missus stay and rest while you take care of business."

Outside, Victoria stepped into Smoky's saddle as Ryder swung onto Percy's back. A moment later the mule started bucking. Either Ryder had not been expecting it, or he was too tired to stick, but in the blink of an eye he was sprawled on the ground, flat on his back.

She jumped off the horse and hurried to his side. "Ryder, are you all right?"

He pushed himself to his elbows. "No, Mrs. MacKenzie, I am not all right."

Concerned, she searched him for signs of injury or pain, but only deep fatigue etched his features and underscored his eyes with shadows.

She held out her hand. Surprisingly, he accepted it, his palm warm and rough and gritty against hers as he rolled to his feet.

"Look at me." He brushed at his clothes. "I haven't had a bath in days. My clothes stink, and I ache all over. I ride a goddamn mule, and I don't even have a hat. How am I going to convince one of the most respected men in the county I'm not just feeding him a line of bullshit to con him out of beef he already paid for?"

Victoria mounted the horse and adjusted her skirt around her legs as Ryder swung onto Percy again. This time the mule stood placidly waiting for Ryder to urge him forward. When Ryder didn't move, she turned toward him, searching his face.

He met her gaze. "I have to get them back. Without those cattle I'm worthless."

He nudged Percy into a jog, and they crossed the railroad tracks in silence.

The house was easy to find as it was indeed the largest one in town. Three stories high, with a wide porch that wrapped around the corner of the house and trimmed with lots of gingerbread scroll work, Victoria couldn't wait to step inside and see if the interior was just as beautiful.

Mr. Greene gladly rented them a room on the second floor then informed Ryder there was a bath house back across the tracks between the saloons.

Ryder shot him a scowl as he passed him the money in exchange for the key.

Victoria bit her lip. The man must have smelled Ryder and was reluctant to have the charming room ruined.

Lacey curtains fluttered in the constant breeze that brushed across the plains. A colorful quilt covered the large brass bed, and a white enamel pitcher and basin stood on a dark commode in the corner. A wing chair had been positioned next to a pie-crust table on which lay a doily and a Bible.

Ryder dropped Victoria's carpetbag, his saddlebags, and bedroll in the corner of the room. The owner passed Ryder a key then left.

Heaving a sigh, Ryder rubbed the back of his neck. "I'm going to take care of the animals. Then I'll head to the bath house."

"If you leave me your vest, I can brush it out while you're gone."

He nodded and shrugged out of the dusty garment.

She took it and held it against her chest, the fabric still warm.

Returning to the corner, Ryder unrolled his blankets and pulled out a clean shirt, drawers, and pants.

She swiped the back of the vest, trying to remove most of the dirt from the street. "If I stay here, you won't have to ride Percy."

He stared at her as if trying to gauge her motives. Then turning to the pile of gear, he grabbed his saddlebags and started for the door.

"Do you have a tie?"

He sighed. "No, I don't have a damn tie."

"I'll see what I can find."

"Victoria, why are you doing this?"

She raised her chin and met his gaze. "Because if it takes two hundred cows for you to believe you are not worthless, then I will do whatever I can to make sure you get them."

Chapter Seventeen

"Tori."

His saddlebags and clothes tumbled to the floor, his fingers no longer able to maintain their grip. In two strides he was across the room, his arms around her in a hug so desperate he couldn't let her go.

Through the fabric of his shirt, her fingertips dug deep into the muscles of his back.

His heart thudded erratically against his breastbone as a tumult of raw emotion tumbled through him like thunder clouds churning across a summer sky.

Until this moment he'd never known how it felt to matter. He kissed her ear and the hollow behind it. The soft scent of lemon teased his senses. She cared.

Her head tipped back offering him access.

"Tori," he whispered hungrily as he trailed kisses down the curve of her throat to the top of her collar. His fingers worked free six of the tiny buttons, exposing lace and the bow of pink ribbon.

He kissed the swell of each breast then licked the salty skin between them.

Her one hand clutched the back of his shirt as her other hand sifted through his hair, tugging at the roots. A soft whimper escaped her throat.

He lifted his gaze to her face. She stared back at him with eyes as blue as a mountain lake. Silver highlights reflected the light of the morning sun as it pushed through the curtains, dappling the floor and bed with lacey shadows.

Lost in the depths of blue, he noticed a tiny fleck of brown along the edge of her right eye. It heartened him to see that someone so flawlessly beautiful had an imperfection.

Her lips parted. Whether it was to inhale or to speak, before it could happen he claimed her mouth with his own.

The bitterness of coffee lingered on her tongue, and he lost himself to all but the taste and texture of her mouth. Wisps of her breath tickled his cheek like the brush of a feather.

Slowly, he backed her toward the bed until her legs bumped the side of the mattress, and they tumbled onto the quilt.

Grabbing her wrists, he raised them over her head. His nostrils flared at the sour whiff of his own body odor, and he stilled.

Her expectant gaze focused on his face, but the chill of memory washed over him leaving him feeling inadequate and uncertain of her willingness to continue.

He rolled off the bed.

"Ryder, wait. Where are you going?"

He stepped to the center of the room and picked up his saddlebags and clothes. "To take a bath."

She'd pushed herself up onto her elbows. The pose thrust her breasts higher. He swallowed. The taste of them lingered on his tongue. Did she realize—?

Shifting her weight to one elbow, she grasped one end of ribbon between her thumb and forefinger then slowly pulled. A teasing smile spread across her face. "Hurry back now, Sugar."

He fumbled to maintain his grip on his suddenly slippery clothes and saddlebags. Swallowing a lump that went down his throat as easy as a stone, he pulled open the door and hurried down the stairs.

****

As the last of Ryder's footfalls drifted up the stairwell, Victoria pushed herself to sitting and retied her camisole. She missed him already, but he really did need a bath.

Maybe she should remove her dress and petticoats and wait for him on the bed wearing only her underclothes. It was daring and risqué, but the thought of playing a wanton caused giggles to rise from her belly like bubbles in a flute of champagne. This joyous ache to be with Ryder longing to do things with him that had repulsed her with Nicholas caused her mouth to go dry and her heart beat to quicken.

She tried to think of ways to trail her fingers over the intimate places of Ryder's body that wouldn't remind her of how and where she'd touched Nicholas. She couldn't let him ruin this for her again.

Removing her dress, she draped it over the back of the wing chair then retrieved Ryder's vest from the floor where it had fallen. She dug her clothes brush from her bag and moved to the bed to clean away the dirt and refresh the wool fibers. Maybe she could make Ryder a tie from the black, diamond-shaped sash she'd worn around the waistband of her green skirt. It wouldn't take long to whip-stitch a hem. She should have checked to see if the shirt Ryder had taken with him had a stand-up collar.

Satisfied the vest was as nice as she could make it, she placed it on the chair with her dress. Then after freshening up with the water in the pitcher and her bar of lemon soap, she set to work ripping apart the sash.

A few minutes later, boots thudded against the wooden stair treads, accompanied by the soft chink of spurs.

Weaving her needle through the fabric, she brushed stray threads from her lap and tossed her sewing onto the chair.

The door opened just as she turned. Their gazes locked. With his damp hair combed off his forehead and his face clean of all stubble, she was again overwhelmed by a half-formed image of him in a ballroom, wearing a white waistcoat, shirt, and ascot. He'd been smiling, not frowning as he was now.

She drew a breath to refocus her thoughts as a slow, hopefully sultry smile, spread across her face. She lifted her hands for the combs on either side of her head and pulled them free. Her hair spilled down her back and tickled her shoulders.

"Aren't you the handsome one," she crooned with a southern drawl as she sashayed toward him.

Kicking the door shut, Ryder tossed his balled up clothes in the direction of his saddlebags and strode toward her. One hand delved into her hair, cupping the back of her head, his other reached behind to grip her derrière as his mouth swooped low to claim her neck.

She threw her arms around him as he backed her toward the bed.

"Ryder, why do I have the feeling I know you?" she asked as they tumbled onto the mattress.

"You do," he murmured between kisses as his lips caressed their way to her breasts.

"No." She ran her hands up his back to his

shoulders. "It's so strange, but sometimes I feel as though I've danced with you in a ballroom."

He rolled off the bed, pulling his shirt over his head while he toed off his boots. "It was probably one of my brothers," he said. Then still wearing his pants, he dove on top of her, fumbling to untie the ribbon of her camisole.

"What?" She pushed against his shoulders. "What are you talking about? You have a brother?"

Raising his head, he briefly met her gaze. "Brothers."

He tried to resume kissing, but she pressed her hand to the center of his chest. "Brothers?"

"Victoria…"

Realization dawned. "Oh my goodness. Phillip?" She wiggled from beneath him and scooted further back toward the pillows. "Phillip Thorndyke? I've danced with Phillip. And Spencer. They're your brothers? And Alice and Priscilla?"

"Sisters." He shifted onto his side and propped his head up with his hand.

She swatted his fingers that wiggled their way under the bottom of her corset. "But your name is MacKenzie. Are you Ainsworth Thorndyke's…love child?"

A sharp, bark of laughter escaped his throat. He rolled onto his back.

She poked his shoulder. "I don't understand. You told me you grew up as a pot boy in the kitchen of a wealthy family. You said your mother threw you away, but you were ill. I didn't think you meant it literally."

He sighed. "It's a long story, and none of it matters anymore."

"It matters to me."

He rolled onto his side again and pulled at the opening of her camisole. "Come on, Tori, take this off."

"Ryder, stop it." She pushed his hand away. "Are you Ainsworth Thorndyke's son?"

Leaning closer, he blew a soft stream of breath into her ear, sending goose bumps rippling over her body. She shivered.

He tried to kiss her, but she turned her head as his lips bussed her cheek.

"Ryder, stop."

His brow furrowed, the teasing glint in his hazel eyes gone.

She regretted pushing him away, her body aching to be back in his arms. "Don't try to dissuade me with one of your kisses."

The rigid set of his shoulders eased. "Yes," he said with a sigh. "He's my father, but he will never acknowledge me."

"Because you were…you were born out of wedlock?"

Rolling onto his back, he draped his arm over his eyes. "You're not going to let this go are you?"

"Please?" Maybe she shouldn't pry, push him to reveal secrets he preferred to keep, but she needed to know all of him, every shade, every nuance, every mystery that had evolved into this man beside her.

"Nearly thirty years ago, Mary Thorndyke gave birth to a baby," he began, his voice flat and dispassionate. "She and her husband took one look at it and decided it would be best if the baby were dead. Whoever was chosen to smother it couldn't do it. So they wrapped it up, stuffed it in an old carpetbag, and threw it in the trash."

She gasped, but her chest had tightened so hard, that the tiny intake of breath was almost too painful to endure. She rolled toward him, threw her arm around his chest, and pulled him close.

She didn't like Ainsworth Thorndyke, but she'd been to his home, laughed with Alice and Priscilla, danced with Phillip and Spencer, and talked with Thorndyke himself. She thought of her own battered carpetbag, trying to imagine a shrouded infant inside struggling to breathe.

"Why?" Her voice little more than a choked whisper.

He shrugged.

She kissed his shoulder and squeezed him tighter, as if her hug could make it all go away. The Thorndykes were rich, powerful members of New York's Five Hundred, along with families like the Astors, Rockefellers, and Vanderbilts.

Had the Thorndyke image been so important to them that they would risk murder rather than have that image marred by a child whose birthmark made him less than perfect?

"What did they tell people?"

"I suppose they said the baby died."

"Tell me all of it."

"Do we have to talk about this now? It's a long story."

He slipped his arm under her neck and cupped her shoulder. She snuggled closer waiting.

"The Thorndyke's cook found it in the trash."

"She must have known. What did she do?"

"She heard crying and knew the baby wasn't dead.

So she took it to her sister-in-law. Ruth MacKenzie had just had a new baby, so she nursed it with her own."

Victoria tipped her head to look at him, but his gaze was fixed on the ceiling. "It? You mean you."

His Adam's apple shifted.

She kissed his throat, his skin smooth and warm beneath her lips.

"Yeah." His fingers squeezed her shoulder just a little tighter. "Me."

Warm tears slid down her cheeks and dripped onto his skin.

"These better not be pity tears."

She shook her head. "No, of course not. They're happy tears, happy because they saved you and gave you a real home."

A grunt rumbled through his chest.

"You weren't happy?" She sifted her fingers through his chest hair and drew figure eights around the flat planes of his nipples.

He shrugged then stilled her hand with his own, squeezing her fingers tight. "I went to the cemetery once."

Beneath her hand his heart beat quickened. He drew a shaky breath.

"There was just a tiny stone marker. It said, Thorndyke Infant 1846. They never even gave me a name."

Her chest tightened, squeezing her breath into a lump. The words, "I'm sorry," lodged in her throat. He wouldn't want to hear them, so she said nothing.

His arms wrapped around her then, crushing her against him with a desperation she wasn't even sure he understood. For several minutes he held her. Birds chirped outside the open window. A clock ticked from the small table near the chifforobe.

Gradually the tension in his arms eased. She shifted and reached out with her index finger to lightly trail a path over his cheekbone, across the center of his birthmark.

His intake of breath was slight, but she felt its escape against her chin in a warm puff of air.

When her wandering finger reached his mouth, she pressed it against the dry warmth of his lips.

His Adam's apple bobbed up and down.

She studied the shape of his nose, his hazel eyes, more brown today than green, and his dark lashes, so thick and long she wished hers were as beautiful. The sharp edge of his razor had made his beard nearly invisible, and she leaned close to press her lips against the smooth warmth of his skin, against the smooth warmth of his birthmark.

He flinched, as though her kiss had inflicted pain. After a moment, he pulled her close. His lips traced the shape of her ear, her nose, and each eyelid, almost as if he were using his mouth to imprint a tactile image of her face in his mind.

The fingers of one hand slipped between their bodies and pulled at the ribbon and lace of her camisole.

"Wait," she said, stilling his hand.

He tensed and raised himself up, his elbows locked.

She held his forearm and searched his face, confused by the sudden chill which emanated from his body. At least now she understood why trust was so hard for him, why he'd so misunderstood her reaction to his lovemaking at the cabin. Something warm and maternal swelled her heart, aching to ease his hurt. By comparison her own suffering didn't seem quite so bad.

At least she'd known love.

"Ryder, I find your enthusiasm exciting, but my grandmother made this for me, and I don't want you to tear it."

Doubt tugged his brow together. "You don't have to lie."

Lord, it broke her heart to know how badly his family had hurt him. She reached up to cup his face. "I'm not lying."

"I know it's not dark and…"

"Ryder, I'm glad the sun is shining through the window, and I can look into your beautiful hazel eyes and know you're not him."

Slowly she reached down and slipped free the bow.

His gaze shot to her hands, his pupils dilating as he watched. Taking her time, she pushed each pearl orb through its tiny buttonhole.

Lowering himself to his elbows, he kissed her neck and collar bone, his free hand sliding over her hip and thigh.

An ache grew inside her. Longing to be closer, she hooked her stocking clad foot over his calf and slid her hands up his back, delighting in the silky heat of his skin, marveling at the solid form of his muscles.

His hand slipped around her waist over the pink silk covering the rigid shape of her corset. "Why do you wear this contraption?"

"I need the support." Her fingertips dug into his shoulders, and her lips sought his.

He fumbled to undo the hooks, but the corset was

too snug for him to release them with one hand, so Victoria reluctantly wedged her hands beneath his chest and soon had each hook popped free.

His mouth lowered to her bosom, and she smiled when he stilled, knowing he'd been stymied by her chemise.

"Damn. How many clothes do you have on?"

She giggled as he raised his head and met her gaze. Her own body aching with the same frustration she read in his eyes. She pushed herself up so she could shrug out of her camisole and corset. Then wiggling herself around on the bed, she tugged the length of her chemise up over her hips so she could pull the sweat-dampened garment over her head and toss it to the floor with the rest of her clothes.

With a groan he wrapped her in his arms and rained kisses across her breasts and belly.

She drove her fingers into his hair, wanting more of him, all of him. Clutching his head to her breast, she buried her nose in the fine silk on top of his head.

A moan rose in her throat as his tongue and teeth first caressed then nipped her breasts. Her nipples peaked under the onslaught. She arched her hips against his as his lips surrounded one hardened tip. Her insides softened and melted like a scoop of vanilla ice cream in the summer sun, and she looped her other foot over his leg so the length of him lay nestled between her thighs.

He trailed kisses down her stomach, swirled his tongue around her navel, then raised his head.

Her gaze met his, his eyes sparkling with laughter. Between his teeth he held one end of the drawstring that gathered her drawers at her waist. Pressing his palms into the mattress he raised himself up, tugging loose the bow as he moved.

She slid her hands down his back to the end of his spine, then trailed her fingers around his waist, allowing her nails to lightly graze over his skin.

He shivered and dropped the drawstring. It fell, curling against her stomach.

Brushing the top button of his pants, she paused. She'd never ached like this before, had never known this mindless need to rip away the barriers between bodies and pull him closer to that unexpected throbbing in the core of her being.

He swallowed, his muscles taut, anticipating her next move.

Locked on his heated gaze, she popped each button free. Slipping her hands into the heat between his drawers and his hips, she hooked her thumbs over the top of his pants and slowly eased them down. Her palms slid over the sharp angles of each hip, the muscular globes of his buttocks, and the fine hair covering his thighs. Unable to reach farther, she glided her hands back over the same path to his waist.

Breaking her gaze from his, she looked down, absorbing the sight of him, longing to touch that part of him, as curious and nervous as a virgin. Heat flooded her cheeks as it had on the train when she'd slid her hand inside his pocket, so near the groin she now ached to touch.

He stiffened as her fingers closed around the length of him. She glanced up for a moment. His eyes were closed, his breathing shallow.

Up and down she explored every warm, smooth inch of him, then dipping lower, cupped his sack with her palm. He groaned as she stroked him again, her thumb brushing over his moist tip.

Then with a growl rumbling in his throat, he seemed to collapse on top of her, trapping her hand against him as he devoured her mouth with his.

Her free hand roamed his back, savoring the feel of his muscles beneath his damp skin. Every nerve ending in her body pulsated with need, sensitized by the cotton of the quilt beneath her, the brush of her drawers against her thighs, the light tickle of his furred chest against her abdomen.

Without breaking his kiss, he rolled her enough to shove down both her drawers and his pants, squirming around until they were gone. Grasping her wrist, he pulled her hand away from him and pressed himself against her mound, even as her own need to be closer to him arched her hips against his.

She hooked her legs around his again, her stockings slipped easily over his thighs. He groaned, poised at her entrance. Her fingers squeezed his butt cheek, as every fiber of her being screamed for him to take her.

He glided inside as if he was meant to be there. She felt no pain, no revulsion only a yearning to be consumed by him, and only him.

She breathed deep, absorbing his essence as his musky scent filled her senses, and in that moment as her eyes drifted closed, it no longer mattered, dark or light she would always know him.

The bed squeaked as the tempo of his thrusts increased. Twisting her mouth from his, she moaned and clutched his shoulders as the tension in her body built toward some unknown crescendo. Her hips arched toward his, matching his rhythm, harder and faster, building and building until her toes curled and giant pulsating waves of pleasure crashed through her body. His name escaped her lips, and her nails dug into his back, clinging to him as he stiffened and shouted her name.

He collapsed on top of her, panting and sweaty. But instead of praying he'd leave, she hugged him close, praying he would stay forever. His breathing evened out and as hard as she tried to hold onto him, he slipped from inside her, and a few moments later, he rolled off leaving her bereft.

"C'mere." He pulled her tight against him so she was wrapped in his arms.

With a contented sigh, she snuggled close sifting her fingers through the soft hair of his chest as it rose and fell beneath her palm in slow, even breaths.

When soft snores rumbled in his throat, she raised her head from his shoulder. His eyes were closed; his thick dark lashes lay in half moon shapes against the top of his cheek bones. Snuggling close, she watched him sleep, trying to memorize every bump and shadow of his face, savoring the woodsy scent of him, afraid what they shared was too perfect to last.

"Thank you," she whispered. "For showing me how it's supposed to be. And no matter what happens, know that I will always love you, Ryder MacKenzie. Always."

She swiped a tear from the corner of her eye and reluctantly slipped from his warmth. She folded the quilt over him then gathered the scattered clothing and dressed.

Settling herself in the wing chair by the window, she returned to her tie project. After she stitched together the two lengths cut from her black sash belt, she hemmed the edges all the way around.

When she finished, she took out a skein of fine gray yarn and four needles. Ryder could use another pair of socks.

Chapter Eighteen

"Here." She held out a Coulter shirt in a natural ivory color.

Ryder glanced up from buttoning his suspenders to his pants. "Where'd you get that?"

"I borrowed it from Mr. Greene. I made you a tie, but the shirt you were going to wear doesn't have a collar."

For a moment he seemed poised to argue. Instead he accepted the shirt and pulled it on over his head. "Thanks," he said doing up the buttons. After he tucked it in and hooked his suspenders over his shoulders, she passed him the tie. He fumbled with it for a minute before she stepped in front of him and crossed, and looped, and pulled the black cotton into a perfect bow.

He slipped on his vest, and she reached up to brush dust that wasn't there, from his shoulders.

"Wait a moment." She dashed to her carpetbag. From inside the pocket with the lemon drops, she pulled out a watch and chain. "Here," she said, turning, "the finishing touch."

He accepted it from her outstretched hand and brushed his thumb over the shield-and-leaf design embossed in the gold. He lifted it to his ear then popped open the cover. He indicated the picture inside. "Who's this?"

"My mother." Victoria stepped closer and turned

the watch over. "See, '*Henry, All My Love, Anne.*' She had it taken before they were married then gave my father the watch for a wedding gift."

"She's beautiful. Like you." He glanced up then back at the watch as though embarrassed.

"They died of influenza when I was seven. I don't remember them too well. I know they were happy. And I recall holding onto my father's pinky when we walked along the streets. I wish I could recollect his face. All I have are impressions."

She stepped back as he closed the cover and pushed the timepiece into the pocket of his vest then clipped the chain to his buttonhole. "What happened to you after?"

"I was sent to an orphan home until my grandmother came from England. She used to be an actress in London, and she told me the most wonderful stories." Victoria smiled to herself as she watched Ryder strap on his gun belt. "She passed away about a year after I married. She believed as I once did, that Nicholas was the perfect prince. I'm glad she never knew the truth."

Ryder straightened and looked directly at her. "Are you ever going back?"

Victoria's breath caught. "Lordy," she exhaled. "You look..." She wanted to say perfect, magnificent, wonderful, any or all of those things, because that's what he was. "...handsome," she said instead.

He responded with a quick up turning at the corner of his mouth as though he didn't believe her compliment, but he'd play along anyway. He ran his finger around the inside of his collar, rolled his head, and shrugged his shoulders.

She laughed, captivated by the fleeting image of him as a small boy. "You ought to be glad it isn't a starched collar."

Meeting her gaze, he grinned. "I hate getting dressed up."

"Really?" She feigned surprise. "Well, I think you look like a respectable rancher. Mr. Searcy will have to take your claim seriously."

When he gave a doubtful shrug, she ran her hand up and down his bicep. "You are not worthless, Ryder MacKenzie."

"I wish I had my hat."

"Just think of yourself as the wealthiest cattleman in Wyoming Territory," she encouraged. "If you believe it, he'll believe it."

He turned and reached for the door knob, but instead of giving it a twist, he spoke to the door. "I don't know what your plans are, Tori, after today, but if it works out…with Searcy…would you want to go back…I mean come back…home with me?"

Stunned, she could only stare at his back, wondering if he had actually spoken those words, or if her imagination had conjured them for a fairy tale she desperately wanted to believe.

When she said nothing, he gave the door a brief nod, then pulled it open.

"Wait, Ryder."

He turned.

She stepped close and threw her arms around his neck. "Yes," she whispered then kissed him.

His arms wrapped around her back, pulling her closer.

She returned his kiss, meeting each thrust of his

tongue with a parry then attack of her own. Exploring all the hidden recesses of his mouth, she closed her eyes and surrendered to the pure pleasure of being close to him. Heated breaths mingled in the tight confines between their faces.

He pulled away, his breathing ragged. "I have to go," he said, his lips reddened from the hungry pressure of her own. "Before we end up back in bed."

"Go on then, and get your cattle back."

Flashing a quick grin, he opened the door and headed down the stairs.

She spent the afternoon knitting socks in the chair beside the window. Every so often she'd glance up as a horse or wagon clip-clopped past the house. The clock ticked on the small table, and she wondered if Mr. Searcy had agreed to return Ryder's cattle.

Lack of sleep drew her to the bed, and removing her shoes, she thought she'd lie down for a half hour. Instead she fell sound asleep, and when she opened her eyes, she found Ryder stretched out beside her, his hands stacked behind his head as he stared at the ceiling.

She rolled toward him. He'd removed the tie and borrowed shirt and she rested her hand on the center of his chest, the cotton of his undershirt warm beneath her fingers. "When did you get back?"

He shrugged. "Five, ten minutes ago."

"So what happened?"

For a long minute he said nothing. She wanted to push the issue, but still not used to questioning a man and worried he'd get angry, she waited.

"When was a kid, I used to wish the MacKenzies were my family." His low voice rumbled in his chest below her hand. "That my brothers and sisters were really my brothers and sisters, even though they made sure to tell everyone that I wasn't, and even though Douglas MacKenzie was a drunk. I just wanted to belong somewhere."

While she was curious about his childhood, she didn't understand what this had to do with Searcy and the stolen cattle.

"I thought they hated me because of my face. Douglas called it the mark of Cain. But I was just an extra mouth to feed. When I was about six, Ruth brought me back to Fiona."

"Didn't the Thorndykes recognize you?"

"Not for a long time. Fiona kept me with her in the kitchen, scrubbing pots and peeling potatoes. I don't think the Thorndykes knew where the kitchen was."

"When did they realize you were living in their house?"

"I don't know. When I got older, I started running errands, and the children noticed me first. They used to tease me and send me on wild goose chases. When I got back without the thing they sent me for, they'd laugh and call me stupid."

"How horrible. I never would have imagined Phillip and Spencer could be so cruel."

"They were no worse than any other boys. But Priscilla and Alice… It was constant sometimes." He raised the low tone of his voice to a falsetto. "There's a draft in here, run upstairs and bring my shawl. I left my gloves in the carriage. Run down to the livery and get them. Sp—" He swallowed. "Take my new dresses to my room."

Victoria mulled over the word he'd barely caught

himself from saying. He implied their teasing hadn't mattered, but that stumbling omission indicated at least one of their taunts was still too painful to share.

She toyed with the four buttons of his undershirt. "I didn't know Priscilla or Alice well. They were both married, and I never socialized without Ni—From what I knew of them, they were both a bit shrewish. Is that why you call me princess, because you think I'm spoiled like they are?"

"At first maybe, but now I know you're simply helpless."

She rose up on her elbow and grinned. "I should mention I know exactly where the kitchen is. I've been there many times. I just never cooked in it. Though when I lived with my grandmother, I used to make fried cheese sandwiches."

He withdrew one hand from beneath his head and ran the backs of his fingers down her cheek. "I hope they're better than your pancakes."

She gasped then laughed. When he didn't even crack a smile at his own joke her smile faded. "Ryder, what's wrong?"

He sighed. "Searcy showed me a bill of sale for two hundred MK steers at twelve dollars a head. And it was signed by me."

"What?"

He grabbed a second pillow and shoved it behind his head. "Someone pretending to be me sold Searcy my cattle for twelve dollars each and forged my signature on the bill of sale."

"Can't the sheriff vouch for you to Mr. Searcy that you weren't the man who signed that receipt?"

"He already did. Searcy rode back to town with

me."

Victoria frowned. "I don't understand. Why aren't you happy?"

"Because Searcy offered to give me the same twelve dollars a head he paid to the thief, as long as he gets to keep the cattle."

"And that's bad?"

Ryder gave her a quick, defeated smile. "Victoria, those cattle are worth anywhere from nineteen to twenty-two dollars a head. If that's what Searcy can get for them, he's only lost four hundred dollars, and I'm out twenty-six hundred."

"Why doesn't he just give you your cattle back?"

"Because then he's lost the original twelve dollars a head which is over two thousand dollars. And yeah, I'll have my herd, but I'm broke. It's over two hundred miles to my place. At roughly a penny a mile per head, I couldn't afford it, even if wanted to."

"There must be some way two gentlemen can work this out. Why don't you go back and talk to Mr. Searcy?"

"Because Bradley threw me out of his office. Told me to go somewhere and cool down."

Victoria worried her bottom lip with her teeth. All Ryder had wanted since she'd met him was to get his cattle back or collect his five thousand dollars. "There must be a way. What about the men who stole them in the first place. Why doesn't the sheriff go after them?"

"Because Bradley's jurisdiction is Keith County. The man who sold Searcy my cattle is no longer in the state."

"How do you know?"

Ryder rolled toward her, burying his birth mark in

the pillow. He reached for her hand, lacing his large tanned fingers between her smaller ones. "I came west when I was about fifteen. After my father tried to have me killed, I didn't want any part of New—"

"What?" Victoria's spine stiffened. "Your father, Ainsworth Thorndyke, tried to have you killed?"

His gaze met hers. "I told you someone tried to slit my throat."

"The man you fought with and stabbed in the eye, he was hired by your father?"

"Yeah."

"You didn't mention that part."

He shrugged. "It doesn't matter anymore."

"I still don't understand how it's possible for you to live in the same house without anyone realizing who you were? How?"

"My mother was dead by then, childbirth I heard, after Spencer. Thorndyke knew I was there, but maybe he enjoyed watching me exist as a servant, at the beck-and-call of his four perfect children."

"But as unconscionable as that behavior alone might be, what prompted him to all of a sudden want you dead?"

"On her deathbed Fiona told me the truth. I went to Thorndyke's study and confronted him. I don't know what I was thinking. I knew he would never call me son. I just wanted him to acknowledge that I actually was, so I pointed out how much I looked like Phillip.

"After he told me I was worthless, he threw me out of his house. He must have realized other people would notice the resemblance. I wouldn't have known the man with the knife was sent by Thorndyke except when he grabbed me from behind he delivered a message. I can still hear that deep, rumbling voice in my head. '*Your father wishes it had been done right the first time.*'"

The blood drained from Victoria's face the same way it did when Nicholas insisted she wear her corset laced tighter, right before her skin went cold and she fainted. A man with a deep rumbling voice and an eye patch.

She clamped her hand over her mouth as bits of that long ago conversation echoed in her mind.

"*...tell me exactly what Thorndyke said.*" Nicholas had demanded in his study that night.

"*Thorndyke, he give me the envelope with the blunt an' said 'twas his last payment.*"

Though her carpetbag sat out of sight, she could see the envelope of cash she'd taken from Nicholas' desk, as if it were a ghostly apparition hovering before her eyes.

"*We'll have to send Mr. Ainsworth Thorndyke a little reminder...One of his sons will serve our purpose.*"

"*Yes, sir,*" Mr. Palmer had said. "*If ya want, I can kill the cove for a century.*"

"*A hundred dollars? Is that what you charged Thorndyke all those years ago? I wasn't aware murder could be bought so cheaply. Fortunately for me, Thorndyke didn't think to purchase your silence as well.*"

A wave of nausea sloshed against the walls of her stomach. Oh my God, Palmer! They had been discussing Ryder's murder. If she hadn't been lying down, she would have crashed to the floor from the impact of that realization. Now she understood the hold Nicholas had over Thorndyke—the murder of his son.

They all believed Palmer had succeeded.

The low timbre of his voice penetrated her thoughts. He'd been talking, and she hadn't been paying attention.

"We rode together for nearly five years. He became the big brother I never had. He taught me to how to shoot and hunt and fish. He introduced me to my first whore. I went with him on man-hunts. He'd tell me stories while we played poker in the light of a campfire. He was a little rough around the edges, but..."

"Who?" Victoria asked, afraid she'd missed the name.

"As soon as Searcy told me he smoked a cigar and wore a buckskin jacket, I suspected it was him, but I didn't want to believe it. But when I saw the signature on that bill of sale, I knew. He always spelled MacKenzie M-c."

"Who?"

Ryder pulled her close and rested his chin on top of her head. "Nathaniel Flint. That sonofabitch betrayed me, and I'm going to find out why."

The man from the train, who she'd been avoiding when she met Ryder, the man who'd taken her from Laramie, *he* was the one who'd stolen Ryder's cattle?

Wrapped tight in his arms with her nose pressed to his neck, the wild beat of his pulse thrummed.

"Damn sonofabitch. Now I know why he was in Ogallala, why he was on the train," his low voice rumbled. "He must have made the deal here with Searcy then met the Pinkerton man and followed you to Julesburg. He got into a poker game using my money, then sent me chasing after you, getting me out of the way so he could make sure my cattle were delivered on time."

"But how did he know who I was?"

"Your husband contacted the Pinkerton Agency and sent them your picture. Flint has a friend named Arnold Pratt who is a detective. He was bringing in another prisoner when he saw you. He followed you to Ogalalla, where he spotted Flint and asked him to take you back. The easy money was probably too big a temptation, so he agreed, until I got in the way."

She snuggled closer inhaling the earthy scent of his skin.

"I shouldn't have wasted so much time zig-zagging around the country trying to lose the detective who'd followed me from New York. I could have been in San Francisco by now."

"I should have seen it that night in Julesburg," Ryder continued, following his own train of thought. "He had money, for poker, whiskey, and a woman. He was smoking a cigar, too. Not one of those cheap cheroots he usually smokes, it was a big fat smelly thing." He gave his head a slight shake. "I just can't figure what he was doing in Laramie. Unless it was for one of those private, high stakes games he loves. But then why did he try to take you back? Must be the money from my cattle wasn't enough of a stake."

"What are you going to do?" she murmured against his collar.

His Adam's apple bobbed, and he heaved a shuddering breath.

"I told Searcy I'll take the twenty-four hundred then I'm going after Flint for what's left."

"I'm sorry, Ryder."

"For what?"

"That he was your friend and he would do such a terrible thing."

He loosed his arms and leaned back, meeting her gaze. He offered her a smile, but it didn't reach his eyes. "At least he didn't try to kill me."

"That's not funny."

This time the grin he flashed was genuine. He pulled her close once more and pressed his lips to hers.

She slid her hands around his waist yielding to his feathery touch.

His kiss was gentle and stroking and went on and on until Victoria had no notion of time or place. There was only the solid length of him beside her, the caress of his hands as they glided over her back and arms, and the taste of him against her tongue.

He must have needed her in that moment as desperately as she needed him, for he pulled her across his hips so she straddled him, her skirt bunched over his waist and knees.

His hand burrowed beneath the yards of fabric to the split in her drawers.

A soft mewling sound escaped her lips as he stroked her and she grasped the brass headboard to keep from falling. Her eyes drifted closed, and she tipped her head back riding his hand until he had her throbbing and aching, reaching for the same glorious climax she'd experienced that morning. His fingers altered their tempo, creating tiny circles that pressed against her, harder and faster, until she cried out his name as spiraling waves of pleasure pulsated through her body.

Withdrawing his hand, he unbuttoned his pants and sprang free against her. She lowered herself over the length of him, sliding up and down, matching his rhythm until he groaned and released himself inside her.

She collapsed on top of him for a minute then slid off next to him. He rolled onto his side and draped his arm over her waist.

Content, she lay savoring the warmth of the day and the peaceful lethargy that settled into her limbs.

Ryder yawned. "We'll go grab some supper in a few minutes."

She nodded. "Ummm hmmm."

"I love you, Tori," he murmured against her neck.

His simple declaration brushed over her heart as naturally the breeze that billowed the curtains. Her breath caught in her chest for the briefest moment, uncertain whether she'd actually heard the words or merely longed for them. But as her breathing returned to normal, she listened to the echo of his voice in her head and a smile spread across her face.

Ryder MacKenzie loved her.

And though she wanted to lean from the window and shout it to the town, it was a gift too precious not to guard close to her heart.

Calmly she responded, "I love you, too."

At this moment life couldn't be more perfect. There was just one small thing she needed to do.

Waiting until soft snores rumbled beside her, Victoria carefully eased herself from the weight of Ryder's arm and slipped from the bed. At the washstand, she splashed a bit of water from the pitcher into the basin, and with her bar of lemon soap, she quickly freshened up.

Revived, she grabbed her carpetbag and set it on the small table in front of the clock. Unbuckling the strap, she opened the bag, pulled out her journal, and placed it on the corner of the table. She wanted to write another paragraph about her wonderful knight while his, 'I love you,' was still fresh in her heart.

But unable to locate the pencil, she decided to pick up another one while she was out. Refocusing on her original purpose, she dug through her clothes and lifted the false bottom to retrieve the envelope of money. Quickly she counted out what she had left—eight hundred twenty-seven dollars and sixteen cents.

If anyone deserved this money, it was Ryder. Besides, she no longer needed it. Slipping it into the large pocket of her skirt, she quietly opened the door and headed to the sheriff's office to find Mr. Searcy.

Chapter Nineteen

Ryder came awake slowly. Hunger rumbled through his stomach and he stretched. Blinking, he scanned the room for Victoria, but she wasn't there. He rolled to the edge of the bed and sat up. Her bag of knitting sat in the chair by the window, and her carpetbag stood open on the small table near the chifforobe.

Sliding his fingers through his hair, he crossed the room to the pitcher and basin. After splashing water on his face, he pulled on his shirt and studied himself in the mirror. For the first time, he didn't hide the birthmark with his hand and wonder how he would look without it.

A grin turned up one corner of his mouth. Victoria loved him just as he was.

He checked the time and saw he'd fallen asleep for almost an hour. She'd probably gone out back to use the necessary. He retrieved his toothbrush and tin of powder from his saddlebags then tossed them to the floor.

But they brushed the corner of the table and knocked Victoria's journal onto the carpet where it fell open. He couldn't help but glance at the words which filled the page.

Ryder MacKenzie is a brave and gallant knight. He rescued me this day, from a band of evil ogres.

His grin widened, both amused and touched that she had referred to him as a brave and gallant knight. The ogres, he supposed, were Searcy's men, though he wasn't sure exactly who rescued who that day.

Continuing, he read, *I only wish he could vanquish my evil prince as easily.*

The prince must be her husband. Maybe once they got to Cheyenne he could find a good lawyer and see if there was a way to vanquish the prince with a divorce. He flipped back a several pages.

But my knight insists I return to the prince. I can see he has sworn fealty to his liege lord and his code of chivalry cannot be broken. There must be some way I can gain his favor. I'll do absolutely anything *to sway him.*

A frisson of something sharp and icy cold stabbed through the center of his chest. No, he told himself, it was only a silly diary. His nonsensical sisters each had one. Their girlish journals meant nothing. Still, he found himself flipping further back.

The prince is an evil demon. I entered the library yesterday and found him there with a maid on her knees, in front of him. I wanted to leave, but he made me remove my clothes and pleasure myself while he watched and she pleasured him. So I closed my eyes and pretended, glad was it she who had to feel his thrusts and taste his bitterness. I'm good at pretending. He never knows. In his arrogance he thinks himself a lover. I always pretend.

The door opened, but he couldn't tear his gaze from the words on the page.

I wish he was dead, this prince with whom I thought to live my fairytale. To think of him cold and still is my only solace on days when I don't think I can go on. Is there no one in the kingdom who can help me? Perhaps a knight from a far away land will come. Perhaps he will avenge my honor and slay this evil man I wed.

In disbelief, he read the entry over and over so the words jumbled together in his mind like a scene in some macabre play, except the gruesome death was to his own heart.

I wish he was dead... Perhaps a knight from a far away land...slay this evil man... There must be something I can do to sway him. I'll do absolutely anything. *I'm good at pretending. He thinks himself a lover... He never knows. I always pretend.*

Cold sluiced through his body leaving his skin clammy. As many times as his mind tried to deny the truth, the handwritten words remained, her intentions clear.

The door closed. "Ryder?"

He raised his gaze to study her, the journal and his toothbrush and powder still in his hands.

Her easy smile faded under the intensity of his stare. "What's wrong?"

"Why are you here?" he asked, surprised his voice sounded so calm when it hurt so much to breathe.

The smooth skin of her brow pulled together in a frown. "I don't know what you mean. I only went for a walk."

"Since the day I met you, you've done everything in your power to get away from me, to get away from your husband. Then suddenly everything changed. Why?"

She backed against the door, twisting her fingers

together at her waist. "I'm sorry, I don't understand. I'm here because I love you and—"

He snorted derisively, like a horse blowing dust from his nostrils.

"Why are you looking at me like that?" Her voice trembled. "What did I do?"

"So sweet and innocent. You're good; I'll say that."

"Ryder, what are you talking about? What's wrong?"

"I read your journal. Now it all makes sense." He flung the loathsome book in her direction.

She cringed. It hit the wall and landed on the floor beside her.

"Your game of pretend is over."

Tears filled her eyes. "What game? I don't understand. I love you."

"Playing your role right to the end. Well, you wrote that you were good at pretending. I even saw the costumes, watched you play the widow, the nun, the wanton… I should have known better, but I still fell—" The rest of his words caught in his throat.

He snatched his belongings and stuffed them into his saddlebags. Striding to the bed, he retrieved his gun belt from the bed post and stomped into his boots.

"What are you doing?" Victoria asked through her tears. "Where are you going?"

He yanked off the tie and threw it aside. Then he tossed the pocket watch onto the bed. "Give that to the next naïve bastard you trick into doing your dirty work."

Keeping her gaze locked on him she slid along the wall, away from the door.

He tossed his saddlebags over his shoulder and reached for the door knob. "I knew from the beginning what you were. It's my own fault for believing anything different."

"Please, don't go." Her voice broke on a sob.

He glanced toward the corner where she stood, looking smaller than he remembered. "You can stop crying. I'm not going to fall for your tears."

"What did I do?" Tears spilled down her cheeks. "I don't understand. I love you."

"Stop it!" He slammed the side of his fist against the door. Two long strides brought him directly to her corner.

She shrank into herself, sliding down as her hands came up to cover her face.

"You don't love me!" he shouted. "And I don't want to hear you say it anymore."

He whirled, yanked open the door, and slammed it behind him. Heart wrenching sobs followed him down the staircase, but he ignored them by telling himself they were merely a ploy to get him to return. Instead he focused on how she'd manipulated him, the pain of her duplicity more searing than that of Flint's, Fiona's, or Thorndyke's. Victoria's betrayal ripped at his soul.

From the corral outside the livery, Percy and Smoky watched him with their ears pricked forward, as he strode past and entered the building. Slipping the bridle over his shoulder, he carried one saddle and blanket outside, setting the saddle pommel side down then dropped the blanket on top.

He should have taken his own advice and stayed away from the rich princess.

Smoky accepted the bit, and Ryder eased the

headstall over the horse's ears.

Victoria Van Der Beck was too beautiful and too perfect to ever want a man like him.

Next he tossed the blanket over Smoky's deep gray back then reached for the saddle.

Maybe he'd fallen for her smiles and charming ineptness because he'd wanted to believe he had value, that deep down inside him there was something of worth a woman like her could love.

Tugging the cinch tight, he dropped the stirrup in place and returned to the gloomy building for Percy's saddle.

Cold seeped into his body like fog creeping under a door. He pressed his back against the rough log wall then bent forward, his hands braced against his thighs. His lungs tight, he struggled to breathe, squeezing his eyes against the burning behind his lids.

He wasn't a little boy anymore, crying himself to sleep wishing someone would love him. He was a grown up, goddamn man! Forcing himself to inhale, he drew several deep breaths then exhaled through puffed out cheeks feeling as if he'd just run five miles.

Swiping his eyes with the back of his wrist, he gathered all of Percy's tack. At the entrance another man approached. Ryder stepped back, retreating into the shadows.

"MacKenzie," Frank Searcy said. "Glad I caught you before I headed out." From the inside pocket of his vest he withdrew a thick white envelope. "I thought about what you said, and this is the best I can offer. Here's an additional eight hundred cash. And as I agreed, I'll have my bank wire the twenty-four hundred to your bank in Cheyenne."

Ryder stared at him confused. Searcy had been adamant earlier about the price. And where had he gotten cash? There was no bank. Shifting the weight of the saddle in his arm, he extended his hand and accepted the envelope.

Searcy gave him a quick nod. "Good luck to you, hope you find that man Flint." He turned down the wide aisle past the buggies and wagons to the row of straight stalls at the back.

Somewhat dazed by the encounter, Ryder tucked the money inside his vest, picked up his saddle, and walked around to the corral. Percy stood patiently while Ryder saddled him and tied on the saddlebags.

But as soon as Ryder stepped into the left stirrup, Percy danced to the side, forcing Ryder to hop after the mule the way he'd done when he was a green kid and Flint first taught him to ride.

The memory of his years with Flint snapped what little patience he had left, and with a curse, he threw down the reins and mounted Smoky instead.

As before, when Ryder tried to ride the horse out to Searcy's place, Percy lifted his head and brayed. The hee-hawing had been so loud earlier, it had carried north out of town beyond the tracks. Afraid the whole town would have him run out on a rail, he'd reluctantly gone back and ridden a perfectly quiet mule to Searcy's ranch.

Now Percy's hee-hawing was so loud and abrasive it nearly drowned out the whistle announcing the train was about to depart the station.

Dismounting, Ryder strode to the mahogany colored mule. "If you want me to ride you, you'd damn well better stand still."

Gathering the reins in one hand, he slipped his foot in the stirrup and eased his weight into the saddle. As he did, Searcy trotted out of the livery on his horse, the owner's little brown dog close on the horse's heels. Spotting the mule, the dog raced around the outside of the corral fence yapping. Percy bucked. Ryder hit the ground with a thump. The air in his lungs whooshed from his body. Pain radiated from his back straight through his chest.

He should have been paying attention. Percy, who was usually good for one or two hard bounces before he settled down, hated dogs.

Afraid someone would notice him lying in the middle of the corral, Ryder drew in a short breath then eased himself into a sitting position. After a moment Percy wandered close, the reins trailing in the dust. His long ears pricked forward, he sniffed Ryder's boots.

Able to breathe freely once more, he casually rolled to his knees then before the damn mule took off through the open gate, Ryder snatched up the reins. Slowly he pushed to his feet. "Behave yourself you long-eared sonofabitch. I don't have any more goddamn lemon drops."

****

Victoria sat on the floor until the echo of the slamming door faded and she could no longer hear the thud of his boots on the stairs.

Why was she such a coward? Ryder wasn't Nicholas. But all she could do when he'd shouted and pounded the door was snivel in the corner. Either she trusted him not to hurt her or she didn't.

Several long blasts of a steam whistle announced the impending departure of the train that had arrived earlier.

She pushed to her feet. Kicking aside the leather bound book, she dashed down the stairs and out the front door. She needed to find him, demand an explanation, and make him understand that whatever he may have read, the pages of her journal were merely filled with foolishness. The writing had been her escape for a fairytale gone wrong.

Crossing the tracks, she hurried toward the blacksmith shop, hoping Percy was still there, that Ryder had only gone for a drink at one of the saloons or stopped for supplies at the store. Wind whisked the tears from her cheeks, leaving her skin tight.

The corral was empty. She whirled and headed for the wide open doors at the front of the building. A yapping brown dog burst from the shadowed interior and raced up to her skirt.

Victoria froze unsure if the dog would bite.

Easing back a few steps, she turned and hurried back up the street. It couldn't have been more than twenty minutes since Ryder had stormed out of the room. If he'd been inside the store or the saloons, she would have seen Percy and Smoky tied in front when she ran past.

She raised her hand to shade her eyes against the glare of the sun and spotted his tall silhouette heading west toward the new stock pens.

"Ryder!" she yelled at the top of her voice. The wind blew her strident call over her shoulder, down the street behind her. Snatching up her skirt, she ran past the saloon and shoe store, past the courthouse and the piles of lumber for the new hotel, until the dust beneath her feet faded into tufts of grass and wide open space.

"Ry-der!"

Struggling to draw breath against the restriction of her corset stays, she slowed to a walk. She called again, but he only seemed to grow smaller.

The whistle blared again. She glanced toward the train, sitting on the tracks in front of the water tower, the engine pointed west as it softly chugged puffs of steam from beneath the large iron wheels.

Drawing a deep breath, she whirled around and ran back down the street. There wasn't much time. She had to get back to Mr. Greene's house, grab her carpetbag and her money, then get back to the section house and buy a ticket before the train left. Hopefully, twenty-seven dollars would get her to Cheyenne.

Panting, she halted in the middle of the street. She pressed one hand against the rigid corset beneath her clothes and wiped the sweat from her face with the other.

To her right a couple of men emerged from one of the saloons. As they drew closer, she turned. If they were boarding the train, maybe they could have the conductor hold it for five more minutes.

At the sight of their faces, cold fear washed through her, numbing every nerve in her body. She could no longer move or even think. The blond man in the tailored suit stepped toward her.

"Hello, Victoria.

No! Her brain screamed, denying what her eyes told her was truth.

"How fortuitous to find you here." The smooth tenor of Nicholas' voice drove a spike straight through her heart. "I had expected to travel to Cheyenne, to meet a Mr. Flint."

He stepped closer. His long fingers grazed her elbow, his pretense of gentle solicitousness familiar. The excessive pressure he applied as he directed her toward the train, triggered her submissive compliance.

She stumbled along beside him, trying to think past the paralyzing terror.

A step behind Nicholas followed his lackey, Mr. Palmer. Seeing his eye patch and knowing how he'd lost his eye brought a swell of satisfaction.

Ryder had done that.

Palmer had tried to slit his throat, but Ryder, brave even as a boy, hadn't given up. He'd fought back, turning Palmer's knife against him.

She could do this. She'd escaped Nicholas before, she could escape him again.

The whistle shrieked its third and final time. The conductor's voice rang out with his sing-song, "Alll aboarrrd!"

"My bag. It's at Mr. Greene's house on the other side of the tracks."

"We do not have time."

"But all my clothes, my money—"

"If you are referring to more of these deplorable, servants' clothes, you will no longer need them. As to *my money* I will telegram to have your belongings held until our return.."

She almost blurted out, *I believe that money belonged to Ainsworth Thorndyke*, but she bit back the insolent words just in time.

They reached the end of the train and crossed two sets of tracks to board from the platform in front of the station. The last car was a private one, which she assumed Nicholas had rented. He would never stoop to riding in the passenger cars with ordinary people.

Nicholas shoved her up the steps at the westward end of the car.

She threw open the door and ran down the narrow paneled hallway, past the bedrooms, kitchen and dining room. Bursting into the open lounge, she skirted sofas, chairs, and tables to reach the iron platform at the back of the car.

From behind, Nicholas shouted, "Go around! Catch her at the end of the train!" Nicholas' footsteps thudded against the carpet as he quickly gained the distance between them.

Turning the knob, Victoria yanked open the door and jumped. Her feet hit the wide strip of grass between the dusty street and the tracks. Forward momentum sent her to and knees.

The conductor called out again. The chugging tempo of the engine increased. The train inched forward.

She scrambled to her feet. Behind her loose stone scattered and crunched. Someone was coming. She turned to see Palmer charge around the end of the car.

Snatching up her skirt, she ran toward the buildings on the other side of Railroad Street.

Footsteps pounded behind her. A meaty arm wrapped around her waist lifting her feet right off the ground as a salty tasting hand clamped over her scream.

Sheriff Bradley stepped out of his office. He yelled, but she couldn't make out his words. It didn't matter anyway, Palmer didn't answer to the law.

Whirling around, he carried her back to the slowly moving train. At the platform, he lifted her into Nicholas' waiting arms then grasped the hand rail and swung on board.

Nicholas shoved her through the open door. As she fell to the floor, she whacked her cheek bone against the padded arm of an upholstered chair.

She squeezed her eyes tight against the pain, as crazy fissures of white zig-zagged behind her closed lids.

Pressing her palms against the carpet, she pushed to her knees. Through a sheen of tears, she caught the gleam of a polished black shoe, a mere second before it slammed into her stomach. Though her rigid stays offered some protection, the force of the impact still drove the air from her lungs. Coughing, she crawled into the tiny space behind the two chairs along the wall of the car.

Once again, this was her life, moments of numbing terror followed by moments of peace. A cycle that would never break until the moment he finally killed her.

"You have inconvenienced me enough, Victoria. Palmer, get her up."

The scuffed toes of Palmer's shoes peeked between the fringed dust ruffles as he reached down and grabbed the back of her blouse.

In desperation, her fingers clenched fistfuls of the thick velvet drapery which adorned one of the windows, but the curtain rod gave way. The heavy fabric tumbled down on top of her. Palmer tugged her from beneath their weight and stood her upright before Nicholas.

"Palmer, go and tell the conductor I no longer wish to travel west."

The man bobbed his head, his hair greasy with

pomade. "Yes, sir." Swinging around, he slipped into the shadows of the narrow, paneled hallway which traveled the length of the car.

Her heartbeat accelerated and her stomach trembled. Nicholas always dismissed the servants before he punished her.

"I'm sorry, Nicholas," she whispered as he fixed his narrowed eyes on her. She retreated a half step, inching closer to the door at the back of the car. "I thought I'd killed you." Though it seemed as if an hour had passed, it had only been moments. If she could get onto the platform before the train gathered full steam, she could jump to freedom, hopefully without killing herself.

"And you hold so little regard for your own husband that you hadn't the decency to come to my aid." He stepped closer, inches from her face.

"I'm sorry," she croaked, through a suddenly dry throat. Carefully she eased back another step. "I was afraid."

"Bitch." His hand lashed out like the end of a whip and connected with her face.

Her reflexes out of practice, she wasn't quick enough to dodge the blow, and its force threw her to the floor.

The copper taste of blood filled her mouth. She pressed her tongue against the cut, where the inside of her lip had connected with her teeth. Closer now to the door, she pushed to her hands and knees then reached toward the knob with a trembling hand.

As if by magic, it opened. Sunlight spilled onto the carpet, along with a pair of scuffed brown boots that sported a set of spurs with tiny silver hearts.

Chapter Twenty

Ryder kicked the door shut behind him. From the corner of his eye, he caught sight of Victoria on her hands and knees. He extended his left hand and pulled her up beside him keeping his eye on the man toward whom he aimed his gun.

So this was Nicholas Van Der Beck.

Victoria had been right. He was handsome. Though not as tall as Ryder's own six-foot-two frame, Nicholas was broader through the shoulders and well proportioned. With his blond hair, long straight nose, and high cheekbones, the man was even better looking than the sons Thorndyke prized so highly.

With a scowl on his face, Nicholas declared, "This is a private car. Who are you, and what are you about barging in here like this?"

"Looked like you were trying to skip town without paying me my five thousand dollars."

Victoria gasped.

"Are you Flint?" Nicholas demanded.

Ryder shrugged. "Sure."

"I thought I instructed you to bring her to Cheyenne."

"So now we're meeting here."

Nicholas glanced at the Colt Ryder held and frowned. "No need for hostility." He gestured toward one of the four upholstered chairs. "Make yourself comfortable. Victoria, get Mr. Flint a drink then re-hang those curtains. I cannot have you leave them crumpled on the floor."

Victoria started forward, but Ryder stretched out his left arm, blocking her advance. "She stays with me until I have the money in my hand. But you go ahead and pour me a shot of whiskey."

Nicholas stiffened. His eyes narrowed before his face relaxed into a broad smile, filled with perfect white teeth. "Certainly. Take a seat, and I'll get that for you."

Glasses clinked as Nicholas fumbled through the cupboard of a small sideboard. Ryder nodded for Victoria to take the chair closest to the door. No matter how she'd lied and manipulated him, she didn't deserve the deep red mark around her eye. He wondered if somewhere in this fancy rail car, there was a piece of raw steak.

A moment later, Nicholas poured a small amount of golden liquid into two small glasses and passed one to him. "Here you go. It's a twelve-year-old single malt Scotch. I think you'll like it."

Ryder accepted the drink then waited for Nicholas to move away before he tossed back one large gulp. The potent strength of the whisky caught him by surprise. His nose stung, and his tongue went numb. Tears burned in his eyes, and he swallowed the urge to shake his head and wipe the sweat from his brow. He'd be damned if he'd let on he had never tasted whisky like this.

Nicholas must have known, for a superior gleam of amusement glistened the ice blue of his eyes.

"Have a seat, Mr. Flint. There's no need to hover over my wife like some feral guard dog."

Ryder stepped closer to Victoria and mentally bracing himself swallowed the last of the drink. It still hit his mouth like a punch, leaving behind a bitter, earthy taste. He passed her his empty glass then leaned his hip against the side of her chair. He told himself he did it for stability against the rocking of the train, but if Nicholas interpreted it as a sign of possessiveness that was fine with him.

He fixed his stare on Nicholas. "Merely protecting my five thousand dollars."

"Are you?" Nicholas sat on the small sofa which faced them from the interior wall and crossed his legs. The focus of his attention switched to Victoria, and his gaze traveled over her appreciatively. "My wife is an incredibly beautiful woman."

He gently swirled the amber liquid in the bowl of his glass, tipping it from one side to the other. "I received my first telegram from you eight days ago. Do you mean to tell me in all your time together, your interest in my wife remained purely monetary?" He put his nose to the glass, inhaled deeply, then raised it in a mock salute. "I commend your restraint."

Putting the flared top of the glass to his lips, Nicholas took a sip, held the whiskey in his mouth then swallowed. "Victoria." He brushed a bit of dust from his trouser leg. "Do tell me, and do not forget—" His voice held the veiled undertone of a threat. "I always know if you're lying. What exactly went on between the two of you?"

"Nothing, Nicholas." Her soft voice quavered. "I managed to elude Mr. Ma—Flint with disguises, until today. "So please," she continued hurriedly. "Give him the money. Let him join the other passengers and leave us in peace."

Ryder shot her a quick glance. She seemed anxious for him to be gone. Odd when minutes ago she'd looked so relieved to see him.

Nicholas raised one eye brow. "My dear, I find your abridged version of events highly doubtful, unless this man is a monk, or his proclivities lie in another direction."

Victoria stared at the empty glass clenched in her hands then lifted her head. "I'm sorry, Nicholas. You are right." Her chin came up. "He did make a few untoward advances." Each word she spoke was laced with contempt. "But do you sincerely believe I would allow a man like this to actually touch me? I am a lady. He has absolutely nothing of value to commend him. He is crude and vulgar, and look at his face." She shivered.

"I was forced to bash him over the head with a pitcher and stab him with a hat pin to get his filthy hands off me. So please, give him the money so he can go, for I never want to see him again."

Having read her journal, Ryder knew that at best, she'd merely endured his touch. Yet hearing each of his insecurities voiced aloud with such cruel disdain only twisted the knife in his back. He schooled his features, hoping his poker face was firmly in place so Nicholas couldn't see him flinch. He gave his left shoulder a casual shrug.

"She is beautiful." He stepped forward, closing some of the distance between himself and the cocky millionaire, tamping down an urge to punch the sonofabitch in his pretty face.

"Thanks for the drink, but if you'll just get my

money…" With the barrel of the heavy revolver, he gestured toward some vague location farther inside the car. "I'll leave you and the little missus to do whatever the two of you do."

Nicholas smiled.

The man's over-confident mien raised the tiny hairs at the back of Ryder's neck. His instincts warned him Nicholas was stalling, but why?

"All right." Nicholas rose and moved toward the shadows of the narrow paneled hall.

"Wait," Ryder commanded. "Let your wife get the money."

Victoria stood.

Nicholas turned. "I don't actually have that much cash with me. You understand, bandits and robbers and other vermin."

"I'll take a bank draft."

Nicholas flashed another insincere smile. "All right. Victoria, my billfold is in my other coat. It's hanging in the first room past the kitchen."

She hesitated. Ryder gestured Nicholas to the sofa. "Sit right there next to the window." Then he replied to Victoria's silent question with a quick nod.

Keeping one eye on her husband, she gave him a wide berth, darting past him as though he were a large spider.

If Nicholas had only suspected something had gone on between him and Victoria these past weeks, their silent exchange just now gave it away, and the narrow-eyed stare Nicholas leveled his way, confirmed it.

Ryder lowered himself onto the arm of the nearest chair. Hopefully the train would stop soon. If he timed things right and waited until the train pulled from the station, he and Victoria could jump off. He could give her enough money to see she got someplace safe, then he'd go back to Ogallala, pay Searcy back for the cattle, and hire some men to drive them to his home range.

A feminine squeal and a scuffle in the hall had him on his feet, with his gun raised toward the noise. A man stood behind Victoria, shoving her forward into the room as she tried to jerk her arm free from his hold.

A glance at Nicholas, sitting so casually, with that superior smile in place, told Ryder that whoever this man was, he'd been expected.

"Let. Her. Go." Ryder bit out each word.

But the man who held Victoria stared at Ryder, his eyes wide, as though he was seeing a ghost. The sudden pallor of the man's face contrasted sharply with the black eye patch he wore.

"Palmer!" Nicholas snapped.

"Sorry sir, caught the mort tryin' to buzz your room."

Victoria renewed her struggle, but Palmer held her fast.

Nicholas stood. "And just what were you hoping to find, my dear? The last time we were together you were searching my desk for my gun. Well today, it is right here." He withdrew a small double barrel Derringer from beneath the left side of his coat.

"So put your weapon down, Mr. Flint, or my associate and I will be forced to do away with your lovely whore."

Ryder hoped he'd been able to mask any expression of astonishment. After all the reward money Nicholas had put up and the trouble he'd gone through to get her back, he couldn't seriously be threatening to kill his own wife?

"Sir," Palmer interrupted.

Nicholas ignored him, his attention focused on Ryder. "I see you doubt me? Don't. All the evidence I need is in both your eyes. No one makes me a cuckold. Especially to realize she has sullied what belongs to me with the likes of you."

"You're wrong, Nicholas," Victoria cried. "I never let him touch me."

"Sir," Palmer tried again.

In two strides Nicholas was in front of Victoria, heedless of Ryder's gun. "I am never wrong." He punctuated his statement with a resounding slap across her face.

Ryder pulled the trigger shattering the mirror above the small sideboard.

Flinching, Nicholas ducked away from the sound.

Ryder switched his aim and fired, hoping to wing Palmer, but the man had drawn back into the shadows keeping Victoria framed in the opening. The bullet thudded into the wood panel on the outside wall of the train.

Victoria cringed.

Nicholas straightened and started to turn, as his gun hand came up.

Ryder pulled back the hammer of his Colt while through the haze of gun smoke, Victoria's hand swung toward Nicholas' head, her fingers wrapped around the short neck of the scotch bottle.

"You think to intimidate me with this show of blust—"

The bottle connected with his head. He fell to his hands and knees. The derringer went off. A bullet tore through the back of an upholstered chair.

Palmer's right arm rose from behind Victoria to lie across her chest, a slender, triangular knife pressed to her throat, the tip of the blade against the base of her ear. "Toss over that barkin' iron," Palmer ordered, "or I'll slash her throat a better job than I did yours."

Ryder stared at the man who held Victoria. This couldn't be him. A gust of cool air seemed to blow through the car, chilling his blood so that he shivered. He swallowed beneath his bandana, recalling the thin blade painlessly slicing through the skin at the base of his throat.

Nicholas rose to his feet, using the small sofa to steady himself, his derringer held loosely in his hand. "What are you talking about, Palmer?"

"This here cove ain't named Flint."

Nicholas's eyes narrowed on Ryder. "Who is he then?"

"See that devil's mark? He's the one Thorndyke hired me to kill all them years ago. He must have the devil in him 'cause I know I slit his throat."

Nicholas shook his head and blinked as though trying to focus. "I'll be damned." He rubbed the back of his head, his mouth tugging into a half smile. "Ironic isn't it? Thorndyke paid us all these months to keep quiet about a crime he didn't commit."

Their voices drifted into a droning buzz as Ryder stared at the eye patch, remembering a glimpse of shadow, of twisting away as he'd thrown his arm up to block the slashes from sinking into his body, and finally shoving that elbow up. The wool of the man's sleeve had been coarse beneath his fingers, and as the tip of the blade had sunk into his eye the scream that escaped the man's throat still echoed in Ryder's mind.

Palmer remembered it too. It was there in the stone cold hatred of that single brown eye.

Ryder swallowed. He'd only seen that look a couple of times in his life. And in that moment of silent exchange, he knew—either he or Palmer would die.

In this confined space, an accurate head shot would be the only way to eliminate Palmer without hitting Victoria. If he was a better shot maybe…

That instant of indecision cost him, for Palmer rushed forward shoving Victoria ahead of him like a shield, closing the gap in a few feet.

She slammed into Ryder's chest. Her hands grasped his shoulders as he staggered back a step. The rowel of his spur caught in the carpet, tumbling them into the chair behind him, his gun arm pinned beneath her weight.

The gleam of the knife blade captured his full attention as Palmer drove it downward.

Ryder threw his left arm up, connecting with the underside of Palmer's forearm, stopping the blade from plunging into Victoria's back as she pushed against Ryder's chest and stomach in an effort to get out of the way.

She shrieked as Palmer grabbed her by the hair and lifted her to stand in front of him again. Her arms rose over her head, her fingers clawing at his hand while her feet thrashed around beneath her skirt.

Ryder dove forward out of the chair, slamming his shoulder into Victoria's mid-section shoving her and Palmer backward.

They slammed into the wall, Palmer's back absorbing most of the impact with a deep "oomf."

Ryder stepped back, the barrel of his gun pointed straight at Palmer's head.

Victoria tumbled to the floor in a pile of blue.

"Hold it right there," Nicholas ordered, from Ryder's periphery. "Drop that gun or I will shoot her, and don't think I won't."

A slow smile spread across Palmer's face.

Ryder hesitated, cocking the hammer, unwilling to surrender his gun, as his mind raced to determine the greater threat.

At his feet Victoria grabbed his ankle as she pushed herself back onto her heels.

Suddenly Nicholas screamed and fell backward.

The derringer discharged. The explosion beside Ryder's ear deafened him as the muzzle flash and gun smoke blinded him. Where was Palmer? Something sharp pierced his side, and he reflexively pulled the trigger. Swiping at his eyes, he saw Palmer slide to the floor and lay still.

Near the sofa, Nicholas straddled Victoria his weight pinning her to the floor. Both his hands were wrapped around her neck while she jabbed repeatedly at his face, back, and neck with something sharp. Blood soaked his trouser leg and ran in rivulets down his cheek, neck, and hands.

Ryder drew back his foot and kicked the man in the ribs as Victoria made one more jab.

Nicholas released his hold on her throat as his hand clamped against the side of his neck. Blood welled between his fingers as he rolled off her and scooted himself up against the wall.

Gasping and coughing, Victoria sat up and leaned against the couch, something round and bloody jutting from between the fingers of her clenched right fist.

"Are you all right?" Deep red splotches covered her neck where Nicholas's hands had been. She looked so small and vulnerable sitting there trying to breathe. He should have kicked the sonofabitch harder, he thought as he fought the urge to wrap her in his arms. Instead he slipped his Colt back into his holster.

She nodded, then her blue eyes widened. "You're bleeding," she croaked in a raspy whisper.

Ryder pressed his hand to his left side. It came away wet. He stared at the glistening smear somewhat surprised. The wound stung but didn't really hurt. "I think he just nicked me."

He extended his hand, reassured of her health by the strength in her fingers as she pulled herself up.

His gaze shifted to her other hand, and he couldn't stop the smile that spread across his face as he realized what she held. "Is that my spur?"

She glanced down at her fist, as if she were surprised to find her fingers still wrapped around it, the shank and rowel protruding from between her index and middle fingers. She handed it back to him with the slight shrug of one shoulder.

Wiping the spur against his pant leg to remove most of the blood, a warm swell of pride filled his heart. But, he reminded himself, it didn't matter how he felt about Victoria because he'd never really mattered to her.

She gasped. Her hand came up to clamp over her mouth.

Lifting his head, he followed the direction of her wide-eyed stare. Nicholas sat against the wall, his head cocked to the side, his hand pinned between his shoulder and jaw. Blood soaked his snowy shirt and cravat. His blue eyes stared back, fixed and vacant.

She continued to stare at her husband as if he were an opossum playing dead, waiting for that instant he might jump to life hissing and snapping.

"Nicholas," she whispered from behind her cupped hand. "Is he…"

Ryder stepped closer and hunkered down to check. "Dead? Yeah. Looks like one of the points on the rowel cut into that big vein in the side of his neck."

"I didn't mean to…I just wanted him to stop choking me."

He stood and turned. The rush of energy driving him since he and Percy raced after the train washed out of his body, leaving him feeling like one of those hot air balloons. The wild, crazy ride was over. He was back on earth, left with nothing but an empty basket and a deflated pile of colored cloth.

"There you go, Victoria," his tone indifferent. "You got what you wanted, and you didn't even need your knight in shining armor to get it."

She sucked in a sharp breath. Her gaze shot straight to his, her blue eyes wide with disbelief.

He almost felt guilty for having said it but reminded himself it was true.

She inched away from him as though he'd hurt her as badly as Nicholas. He swallowed against the pain of it and turned, looking from Nicholas to Palmer, wondering what to do with their bodies as the golden landscape whisked past the windows.

"Ryder, I never used you. I love you."

"No more acting, Victoria."

"I'm not acting."

"You're a rich widow now. You can stop pretending you care."

She swung away then, disappearing into the shadowed hallway. When she returned she carried two blankets. Without a word she passed them to him then walked across the car, opened the door, and stepped onto the platform.

He wrapped the bodies and secured them with the gold cord tie backs from the window drapes. After knotting the last tassel, he carried the bodies to the bedroom just past the small kitchen.

Victoria still hadn't come inside, so he thought he'd make sure she was all right.

The shadow of the car stretched out behind them like the tail of a kite. Pink and lavender clouds stacked upon each other in rows of shifting fluff all the way to the top of the sky.

She stood to the left of the door, leaning against the window, her lower lip clamped between her teeth, and her arms crossed tightly over her chest. He thought maybe she'd been crying, but her eyes were clear and dry. She seemed so cool and distant he didn't know what to say.

"I'm fine. Just leave me alone."

He swallowed against the pain of another rejection. His hand on the knob he pushed open the door, gave her a last look then paused. "Ummm, there's a wasp on your shoulder."

She glared at him, no doubt remembering the mouse.

He almost smiled. "No, really. Stay still and I'll get it." He closed the door so it wouldn't fly inside, then removed his bandana.

She must have believed him, for she was away from the wall in an instant. Her head swiveled from side to side trying to locate it. She tensed, poised to run, but there was nowhere to go.

"Get it off, get it off!" she cried, her whole body rigid. Cloth in hand, he gently nudged it from the back of her shoulder. It circled around their heads, and he swatted it away.

"I think it's gone now." He retied his neckerchief

She said nothing, just sagged against the wall of the car.

Uncertain he reached for the door. Hopefully the train would stop at the next station. The sooner his life returned to normal, the happier he'd be. He sure didn't need any more beautiful women messing it up.

She pressed her hands over her eyes as great wrenching sobs shook her whole body. Unsure if she would reject him again, he let her cry then slowly inched closer.

Before he could reach out to her, she turned and threw herself against him, clutching fistfuls of his vest as she sobbed against his chest.

Against his resolve to maintain his distance, his arms encircled her. He rested his chin on her head and let her cry.

"I didn't mean to kill him," she snuffled against his heart. "I wished he was dead. I wanted him dead, but not really. I just wanted to be free. I wanted him gone." She raised her tear-streaked face. "He was alive and then he wasn't."

"I'm sorry, Tori, that you had to do it. But I'm proud of you. If you hadn't stabbed him, you'd be the one who was dead."

She began crying again, but not as hard, only soft weeping and sniffles.

"I can't believe you came for me." She swiped at her eyes and searched his face. "I looked up and there you were. How did you know?"

He grinned, "All I'll say is you owe Percy a bag of lemon drops."

A frown furrowed her brow. "I don't understand."

He leaned down and kissed her forehead. "I was heading out of town when Percy quit walking. Just stopped dead and wouldn't move no matter how much I cursed or how hard I spurred him."

"You didn't..."

"No, I didn't hurt him, just enough so he'd know I meant business. But I heard my name being called, and when I looked back, Sheriff Bradley was riding toward me and yelling, but the train was passing. I couldn't hear him. All I caught was, *"Someone kidnapped your wife,"* and he was pointing at the train. I reckoned it might have been your husband, so I pointed Percy at the back of the train. I never thought a mule could run that fast."

"What do we do now?"

"I think we're still in Nebraska, but I'd just as soon wait 'til we get to Cheyenne. I know the sheriff, and he'll likely agree it was all self-defense, but I'd best go talk to the conductor so he knows what happened."

"I meant us. What happens now?"

He shrugged. "I don't know." His words drifted out on a sigh.

She pushed away from him and met his gaze. "You still don't believe I love you."

He stepped away and braced his hands on the rail

at the back of the platform. He stared at the track mesmerized by the image of railroad ties spewing from a giant mouth beneath his feet.

"Ryder?" she asked from behind him.

"I don't know what to think. I feel like you've been playing games. Maybe you've convinced yourself you love me, I don't know. But a lot's happened today. Now you'll have to sort through all the legal stuff. Maybe when you return to New York, to your rich life, you'll meet other people more like you."

"More like me?"

He could almost hear her shoulders snap back indignantly. He shouldn't know her so well, but he did, and he wished he didn't.

"You mean rich and beautiful?" she asked, though it sounded more like an accusation.

He couldn't bring himself to agree aloud, but he knew she was aware that's what he meant.

She stepped up beside him, and they watched the eastern horizon grow more distant. "I don't know how to convince you that I love you. I can't change how I look, and I don't want to. It doesn't make me like Nicholas, or your brothers and sisters, or your father. I'm still the same person who made love with you this morning."

He swallowed wishing he could simply believe her. He wanted to, but maybe he just needed some time. Maybe they both did.

She turned away. He heard the door open, then the sound of voices. He swung around.

"Where is he?" asked a young male voice. "He had my brother nearly beaten to death, and he's going to pay."

Stepping into the car from outside, Ryder couldn't make out who was talking.

"Spencer, put the gun down," Victoria was saying. Though her voice remained calm and deliberate, he recognized a slight quaver.

The hairs at the back of his neck prickled.

"I'm sorry about Philip," she said soothingly, but Nicholas isn't—"

What the hell?

Victoria's scream blended with the report of another gunshot as a sharp pain slammed into his left shoulder.

Chapter Twenty-One

Victoria glanced at herself to be sure she was still in one piece. To have walked in and seen a young man who looked so much like Ryder, pointing a gun her way, had frozen her down to her toes. And when he pulled the trigger, she'd thought for sure he'd killed her. Not seeing blood or feeling pain, she exhaled a sigh of relief. "Spencer, put that gun away."

White-faced, Spencer Thorndyke stared past her shoulder, the Derringer hanging loose in his lowered hand.

Dear Lord, she'd been so scared, she'd forgotten— For a moment she envisioned Ryder sprawled dead on the floor, like Palmer, like Nicholas. Moving as stiffly as a wooden doll, she turned.

Seeing him upright, nearly buckled her knees.

"Tori, are you hurt?" he asked.

Too relieved to speak, she shook her head. Then she saw it—a spreading shimmer in the brown wool of his vest. "Ryder, you're bleeding!"

He glanced at his shoulder then lifted his gaze to hers. "I'm fine." He brushed past and yanked the small gun from Spencer's lax fingers.

"What is wrong with you?" he challenged the younger man. "Half-wit. You never point a gun at someone, let alone fire it without knowing who you're shooting, or if they even have a weapon. Goddamn fool, you could have killed Victoria."

The youngest Thorndyke mutely stared at Ryder as though he were seeing a ghost.

"Spot?" he croaked incredulously as Ryder moved aside and emptied the second chamber of the Derringer.

Victoria strode forward, causing Spencer to back away until he bumped against the window glass.

"His name is Ryder," she declared inches from the young man's face. "Don't you ever call him by that horrible name again."

His gaze, more green than his brother's, darted back and forth between her and Ryder. "This isn't Spot?" he asked weakly.

Laying the gun beside the whiskey glasses, Ryder shrugged one shoulder, "Victoria, it doesn't matter. He was just a kid."

"Of course it matters." She studied him as he turned around, the rest of her argument forgotten. His complexion had grown paler, and the blood stain wider.

"I think you should sit." She moved to his side and gestured toward the closest chair.

"There's no need to fuss. I'll be fine," He lowered himself to the seat and sagged back against the cushion.

Twisting her fingers together, she shifted her weight from foot to foot. "What can I do?"

"See if you can find something I can use to stop the bleeding."

She whirled around and dashed into the next room yanking open several drawers of the narrow sideboard until her fingers grasped a small stack of white linen dinner napkins. She darted around the table and through the door way, back to Ryder's side, ignoring Spencer who remained as motionless as a statue.

She dropped the napkins in his lap then brushed aside his hand as he worked free the buttons of his vest. "I'll get them," she said gently.

Lifting the edge of his cotton undershirt revealed a small dark hole, a couple of inches below his collar bone. Carefully, she placed several of the napkins over the wound.

Though she tried not to press too hard, he winced.

"I'm sorry." She blinked against the sting in her eyes.

"I told you to stop apologizing." He lifted her hand away and held his own over the napkins. "None of this is your fault."

"But it is." She dropped to her knees beside him. "I knew about it."

He frowned. "Knew about what?"

Sagging back on her heels, she rested her hand on his knee and searched his face.

"I heard them talking, the night I coshed Nicholas with the wine bottle. He was talking to Palmer about blackmailing Ainsworth Thorndyke."

"Your husband was blackmailing Thorndyke? With what?"

"You."

"Me?"

"I'd only heard bits of conversation before I grabbed the packet of blackmail money and ran. I didn't put the pieces together until this morning when you told me who your family was. And so much happened today, I never had a chance to tell you.

"The day you were stabbed, when your father hired Palmer to kill you, they believed you were dead. Nicholas found out and has been using that information to extort a large monthly payment from him."

Ryder stared at her for several seconds. "Sonofabitch."

"Excuse me, ma'am, Sp—sir?" Hesitantly, Spencer inched forward. "Are you saying Ainsworth Thorndyke is your father?"

Victoria looked up. Lanky, and nearly as tall as Ryder, Spencer hovered beside them. "Yes, he's your oldest brother."

"Brother?" he whispered incredulously. "Spot can't be my brother. He was a servant's child."

"Of course he's your brother," Victoria snapped impatiently. "And stop calling him that."

The color leached from Spencer's complexion as he stared at Ryder, his expression shifting from denial to shock.

Ryder rested his head against the back of the chair and closed his eyes. His light brown hair had fallen over his forehead dotted with tiny beads of sweat. "What the hell are you doing here, Spencer?"

"It is as she says, except my father had refused to pay anymore blackmail. Then Philip was beaten within an inch of his life. All he could tell us was that it had been a man with an eye patch. I knew it was a warning from Van Der Beck, so I hired the Greyson Detective Agency to follow him and look into his finances. When I learned he planned to head west, accompanied by a man with an eye patch, I bought a ticket, packed a bag, and jumped on board. I've remained inconspicuous, working up the courage to confront Van Der Beck. I thought I'd finally done it.

"When you stepped into the car, with the light behind you…I thought you were him. I am deeply sorry."

Ryder grunted in reply as Victoria pushed to her feet. Grabbing Spencer's hand, she tugged him behind her into the hall along the side of the car.

"Please, I'll explain everything about Ryder later, but could you find the conductor and see if there is a doctor on board? Tell him there was an incident in the private car and two men are dead."

Spencer's mouth dropped open. "Your husband?"

"Yes."

"And Palmer," Ryder chimed in from behind them.

She heaved an impatient sigh. "You shouldn't be walking around."

He ignored her advice and slid open the pocket door beside him.

Spencer peered inside to study the two forms on the bed. "You killed them?"

"Didn't mean to deprive you of your vengeance." He slid the door closed and leaned against the wall between two windows.

"I still don't understand how Van Der Beck used your existence to blackmail father. Having a bastard child is not that unusual."

Victoria tugged on Spencer's elbow. "He is not a bastard, he looks just like you."

"No, Tori," Ryder's words began to slur. "Philip. I look like Philip. Though I don't think we look alike anymore after Mr. Palmer's fists of persuasion."

"But Mother and Father's first child was born dead. I saw the marker near Mother's grave."

Ryder shook his head, rolling it back and forth against the wood panel behind him.

"Then why would they say you were dead?"

"Not every baby's perfect as you. They threw me away and then had Philip. Hope there are no scars, or Thorndyke will have to make another son disappear."

While Spencer stared dumbly at Ryder, Victoria tugged the young man backward a few more feet. "Please, go."

She slid open the door of the last room inside the car. As she thought, a second, smaller bed folded out from opposite facing sofas. She shoved Spencer toward the door at the end of the car. "I'll explain later."

But he stopped and turned back to Ryder. "You're really my brother?"

Ryder nodded.

"I'm sorry," Spencer said softly. "Father and I don't often see eye to eye, but this…"

The brothers studied each other for a long moment.

Ryder pushed away from the wall. "It wasn't your fault. You were just a kid."

Spencer gave him a slight nod then turned toward the door.

With a sweep of her arm Victoria gestured toward the room. "Now will you please lie down?"

He followed her into the tiny cubicle and waited as she pulled and tugged the sofas into a single bed. Reaching inside the built in cupboard, she pulled out some pillows and blankets.

She punched the pillows and stacked them at the rear-facing end of the bed. "What can I do?"

"Nothing." Exhaling a heavy sigh, he lowered himself to the edge of the cushion. "I'll be fine 'til we get to Cheyenne." He tried to toe off his boots.

Stepping in front of him, she helped pull them off then set them side by side, next to the bed. Scooting back, he leaned against the pillows and stretched out.

"Sit with me," he said.

Grateful for the truce, she smiled, hoping that tomorrow life could just start over. Not wanting to hurt him, she removed her shoes and sat on the opposite end. Adjusting her skirts, she extended her legs so her toes brushed his knee and his, her thigh.

"I wish I had my knitting."

"Your socks are nice. They don't slide down in my boots." He wiggled his foot against her, and she reached down and squeezed it.

The door opened at the end of the car then banged closed. Victoria hopped off the bed and jammed her feet back into her shoes, leaving them untied beneath her skirt.

A moment later, Spencer stood on one side of the doorway, the conductor on the other.

"Sorry folks, there's no doc, 'til Cheyenne. And like I told that feller with the eye patch, we can't detach this car 'til then neither. Need a side track and a switcher engine."

He gave his gold watch a check then slipped it back into his pocket. "So, somebody want to tell me what happened?"

A half hour later, he lit the lamps in the car and left, muttering about allowing guns on trains.

Though Victoria didn't think Ryder had fallen asleep, his eyes were closed. Not wanting to disturb him, Victoria gestured Spencer toward the lounge area of the car.

"Are you going back to New York now?" he asked after she found a seat.

"I don't know. It depends on what the sheriff says,

and I want to be sure Ryder will be all right." She shrugged. "I'll have to go back sometime to settle Nicholas' affairs." She'd rather stay with Ryder, but maybe the time apart would be good. So much had happened it was hard to believe she'd only known him for nine days.

"I don't know if I should tell you this," Spencer began, "but you're bound to find out."

She searched his face and caught a glimpse of Ryder in his eyes.

"The detective I hired, James Greyson, discovered your husband had invested heavily in railroad bonds. The severe weather last year caused cattle and crop exports to fall off considerably. The railroad lost a significant number of shipments which caused them to default on their bonds. Your husband lost everything in The Panic nine months ago. I hate being the one to tell you this, Mrs. Van Der Beck, but your husband is broke and has accumulated some extensive debt."

"What?" The revelation jarred her wandering mind from thoughts of Ryder as a boy. A funny sense of dread weighted her limbs. For Nicholas, keeping up appearances was everything.

Spencer gave his head a slight shake. "I believe you'll be forced to sell the house and its furnishings in order to cover what he owes. I don't even know if that will be enough. Both your house and the vacation home in Newport were mortgaged to the hilt. The investigator's report shows he replaced most of the stones in your jewelry with paste and sold the gems. I'm sorry."

Damn, Nicholas. Anger coursed through her blood, replacing the numbing lethargy with fire. She surged to her feet and paced the car. No wonder he'd been blackmailing Ainsworth Thorndyke. And what about her inheritance from her grandmother? Nicholas shouldn't have been able to touch it, but what if he'd found a way? If her money was gone, how would she live?

"What are you going to do?" Spencer asked as she strode past him again.

At the door, she stopped and turned. "I don't know. I suppose I'll go back and try and salvage what I can." Odd, but except for the fact Nicholas might have spent her money, the thought of being poor didn't bother her as much as it should have. It was as if she'd been drowning in that world of affluence, and its great weight had unexpectedly been cut free.

She smiled, wondering what Ryder would think of his rich princess no longer being rich.

Spencer, who'd been standing next to his chair since she'd started pacing, took a step in her direction. "If there is any way I can be of assistance, please do not hesitate to call upon me. Though I am young, I am well versed in the business of finance. I may be able to help you salvage something."

Grateful for his offer, she reached out and took his hand. "Thank you, Spencer. If I need any help, you will be the first person I call."

She gave him a quick smile. "You know, you are much nicer than the rest of your family."

His eyes widened, and he gave a quick shrug.

They each returned to their chair and fell silent, the only sound the rhythmic clicking of the rail.

"I suppose it is because I was so much younger." Spencer began. "Father had Phillip and the girls. I pretty much fell into my own way."

Spencer glanced at his hands and examined his nail beds. "My whole life, I honestly thought his name was Spot. Phillip would whistle at him, like he was calling a dog. We all used to laugh. Alice and Priscilla would tell him, *go fetch*, a pair of gloves, a hat, or some frippery. When he disappeared, I wondered where he went, but all I was told was that he ran away."

"How old were you?"

He looked up and met her gaze. "Eight maybe. Phillip would have been thirteen or fourteen, the girls a bit younger when Sp…he—Ryder left." He shook his head. "A brother. I can't understand any of it. Why was it such a terrible secret?"

"I don't know. Only your father can answer that."

"I went to your father once for help when I first married. Nicholas used to beat me, and I thought your father a gentleman. But he turned me away and instead told Nicholas."

She looked out the window, but there was only her reflection in the black. The hollows and shadows of her face looked very much like the bruises she'd received from Nicholas that night. And in the glass just below the reflection of her chin was Spencer's face, which in its distortion looked like a younger version of Ryder.

"I'm sorry," Spencer said. "I never knew."

"I know you didn't." She turned her attention back to him. "But when I learned that Nicholas was blackmailing your father, I took one thousand dollars of it, and I had no qualms the cash rightfully belonged to him."

"You may as well keep it. Father will never know."

"I gave the money to Ryder. Ironic isn't it?"

A movement at the entrance to the lounge area drew Victoria to her feet. Spencer popped up from his chair. Ryder leaned against the door jamb.

"What are you doing up? I thought you were asleep." She moved close to slip her arm around his waist. The heat of him radiated through the layers of clothes to warm her skin.

"I can't sleep." He practically fell into the closest chair, even with her help.

"You shouldn't be moving around, you'll start bleeding again."

"I'm fine," he mumbled. "We'll be in Cheyenne soon."

He didn't like it when she hovered, but she couldn't help herself. He didn't look fine. "What can I do?"

"Can you find me something to drink, besides that Scottish stuff?"

Spencer stepped forward. "I'll check the kitchen."

A minute later he returned with a glass of water.

Though Ryder's hand trembled, he refused her help and drank down the whole glass.

Victoria took the tumbler from him and set it on the sideboard beside the whiskey decanter then sat on the arm of his chair and ran her fingers through his damp hair.

He rubbed his stomach and shifted his position.

"What's wrong?"

"Nothing. That water isn't sitting to good in my belly, that's all. I'll be fine."

Victoria exchanged a worried glance with Spencer, and as the train pulled into the station in Cheyenne, Spencer was out the door.

He returned about a half hour later with a doctor in tow.

Doctor Carroll, a short, stooped man, whose head was bald beneath his bowler, pushed up his spectacles and glanced around the car. "All right, son, how about we find you a place where you can lie down, rather than move you to my office."

Spencer helped Ryder back to the bed and removed his shirt. Victoria watched from the doorway, wanting to be the one who helped, but knowing Spencer needed to do it.

Doctor Carroll laid out his instruments and sent Spencer for a basin of water and a bottle of whiskey.

Once he left, Victoria slipped into the room and sat on the end of bed. She gave Ryder her most reassuring smile.

Someone stepped into the open door way. Expecting it to be Spencer, she was surprised to see the conductor, and from the scowl on his face, she assumed he was no happier now with the goings on in this car than he was when he left.

"Just want to let you folks know the switcher engine is coming to move this car to the side track."

"Now, just hold up there." Doctor Carroll turned. "I can't have this car jerking and banging while I'm digging a bullet out of this man."

"How long is it going to take? I've got a schedule to keep."

Spencer returned cradling a basin of water in both hands and stood waiting behind the conductor.

"I won't know how long it will take until *after* I get the bullet out."

"I can't wait. The railroad runs on a schedule."

Bright spots of red tinged the conductor's cheeks. "We can't change it on the whim of every rich man who hooks on a private car."

The doctor tossed his bag to the floor. "You're telling me that your schedule is more important than this man's life?"

Victoria stepped toward them before they began swinging at each other. "Gentlemen, please."

The gazes of both men widened as they had each apparently forgotten her existence.

"Conductor, how long will it take to move this car?"

"Fifteen minutes or so. Soon as the switcher gets here. But you folks can't stay here."

Doctor Carroll's bowed back stiffened. "Why not? It's a private car."

"Because there are rules," the conductor fired back. "One of which states the water closets on trains can't be used while the train is in the station."

Across the tiny space his gaze met Victoria's, and the flush in his cheeks deepened with embarrassment. "'Scuse me ma'am. Forgot my manners."

She offered him a half-smile. "I understand. It's been a stressful day for everyone."

From the bed behind her, Ryder said. "Tori, get my boots. I'll walk over to the hotel." Each word was slowly and deliberately spoken. "Take the bullet out there."

She turned back to study his face. Lamplight glistened in the sheen of sweat that covered his face and throat. "Doctor?"

"I can do it, son, but I don't like it. Don't like it at all."

The glare the doctor shot the conductor would have killed him if it had been a bullet.

Whirling, the conductor slammed into Spencer, upending the basin and cascading water down Spencer's coat and all over the carpet.

Spencer swore under his breath. Behind her Ryder chuckled.

The doctor gestured for her and Spencer to join him someplace more private, and they all moved to the lounge area at the back of the car.

He focused his attention on Spencer. "Are you strong enough to get him to the hotel and up the stairs without jostling that wound?"

Spencer nodded.

"Good, I think that young man in there," he gestured down the hall with his thumb. "Thinks he's stronger than he is, and I don't want that wound bleeding anymore. It's going to be bad enough when I have to start digging for that slug."

Victoria gathered all the extra linens she could carry and dashed past them on her way to the Union Pacific Hotel, a long, two-story frame building beside the depot. Once she got the key and ran upstairs to strip the bed and cover it with extra bedding from the train as the doctor instructed, she was back in the lobby in time to slip her arm around Ryder's waist and assist Spencer in helping him up the stairs.

Doctor Carroll joined them while Victoria tugged off Ryder's boots. Turning to Spencer, he asked, "Could you go down to the kitchen and bring up a kettle of hot water?"

Glancing down at his still wet coat, then over at the instruments as the doctor placed each one on the bed side table, he sighed. "Sure, I'll be right back."

She sat on the edge of the bed and clasped Ryder's hand. The strength in his fingers as he squeezed hers eased some of her fear.

"I'll be fine, Tori," he said, though he didn't open his eyes. "I've been hurt worse than this."

Leaning close, she ended his sentence with a kiss. His eyes opened, dilating slightly. Those gorgeous eyes of his, more brown tonight than green, gleamed with gold in the lamplight. Long, thick, coffee-colored lashes traced the top and bottom of each hazel eye. Even the shadow of his beard along his jaw and around his mouth added to his striking looks.

His hand reached toward her face. "You're so beautiful." The backs of his fingers brushed upward along her cheekbone. "So perfect."

She grasped his wrist and turned her face into his damp palm. Her lips brushed the rough calluses at the base of each finger. The words, *I love you*, hovered around her lips, but she held them back.

Beside her the doctor cleared his throat. She glanced over her shoulder and saw him nodding his head toward the door. Turning her attention back to Ryder, she gave him another kiss. "I'll be right back."

He grabbed her hand and flashed a quick smile. "Really, I'll be fine."

She grinned as she stood. "I know." She turned and followed the doctor into the hall.

Spencer's tread was silent on the carpet as he walked toward them from the top of the staircase. He set the large kettle on the floor and rubbed his palm against his thigh.

"Is everything all right?"

With his gaze focused on Spencer, Doctor Carroll said, "I could use your help to hold your friend down. I'll give him something to bite on, but digging for that slug will hurt like a sonof…" Doctor Carroll's voice trailed off as he shot Victoria an apologetic shrug.

Spencer's face went white. "Brother," he croaked. "He's my brother."

The doctor nodded.

"He'll be all right, won't he?"

Doctor Carroll removed his spectacles and wiped each lens with his handkerchief, held them up to the light and wiped them again. "Hard to say for certain, son."

The doctor hooked his spectacles over his ears. "Your brother seems strong and in good health. But sometimes those slugs like to bounce around in the body. Makes 'em a mite hard to find. Sometimes I can't. Then there's a chance the wound can go septic. Bits of clothing and me poking around inside don't help any."

Victoria's stomach pitched as if she were on a tiny boat in a rolling sea. She lowered herself onto the seat of a ladder-back chair outside their room.

Leaning against the wall papered with red, cabbage roses, Spencer tipped his head back and stared toward the ceiling. "Oh God," he moaned. "What have I done?"

"You're not going to pass out on me in there, are you, son?"

Spencer shook his head without meeting the doctor's searching gaze.

Doctor Carroll turned to Victoria. "How about you, miss? I could use someone to hold another lantern and hand me my instruments."

She nodded, swallowing the lump in her throat. She really didn't want to have to watch.

"Good. I knew I could count on you. I've found women are much stronger than men when it comes to this sort of thing. During the war, I saw women wade right into the thick of it, blood up to their eyeballs, standing by my side, ready to help. Always a gentle hand and a kind word for the boys afterward too, no matter how bad things got."

While the image he painted only added to Victoria's nausea, at least he had experience extracting bullets.

The doctor removed his coat, draped it over one arm and rolled up his sleeves. "All right, let's get this done."

Chapter Twenty-Two

Fortunately Ryder passed out shortly after the doctor worked his forceps deep into wound.

The bullet hadn't been Dr. Carroll's easiest find, nor had it been his worst case. Victoria learned this because he talked the entire time, relating several anecdotes of other bullet extractions. At last, clamped in the forceps, he held the glistening slug to the light and examined it from every angle, as though committing each detail to memory for his next story.

She swallowed and looked away as bullet and forceps hit the basin of water with a soft plop.

Spencer's complexion had turned an unusual shade of gray-green, and she hoped the grip Ryder had on his arm earlier left bruises. For what he'd done to Ryder, he deserved at least a little pain.

She braved a glance at Ryder and bit her lip sickened by the sight of so much blood, which the doctor wiped up as casually as spilled milk.

"I'm going to leave it open. Hopefully most of the dirt washed out with the blood."

He sprinkled a liberal amount of carbolic acid on a thick pad and placed it over the wound. Next with Spencer's help, he wrapped it in place with a snug bandage. "I'll be back tomorrow afternoon to see how things are. Meantime make sure he keeps his arm in that sling. I don't want him moving around and getting things bleeding again."

Spencer gathered the soiled linens and volunteered to take them to the hotel laundry.

After rolling down his sleeves, Doctor Carroll returned his instruments to his black leather bag. "Let him sleep as much as he needs. He lost a bit of blood, so make sure he drinks whatever he can. Same with food. I'm not much for milk toast and broth. If he can hold it down, let him have what he wants."

"Thank you, so much, doctor." Victoria passed him his coat.

He slipped his arms into the sleeves and did up the buttons. Then patting her on the shoulder, he said, "You were a big help, my dear. I believe he'll be fine."

He closed up his bag. "It will be ten dollars for the surgery. If you want, you can pay me when I come back tomorrow."

"No, I'll..." She forgot she had no money. Everything was back in Ogallala. "Wait," she said aloud, though more to herself than to the doctor. "I'll use the money I gave Mr. Searcy."

She lifted Ryder's vest from his pile of clothes and took ten dollars from the envelope in his inner pocket.

"Thank you." He tucked the money away. "I will see you tomorrow." He pulled open the door then turned briefly. "I have office hours in the morning, so it will likely be after dinner."

When he'd gone, Victoria dropped to the edge of the bed and for a few minutes watched Ryder sleep. Voices drawing closer to the room brought her to her feet once more. Spencer stepped through the door followed by a second man, nearly as tall, but broader with a silver star pinned to his lapel.

"Ma'am." He removed his hat. "Name's Jackson."

"How do you do, Sheriff."

"Like I was telling this feller here, Able Wilkins sent word there'd been a shooting on the train." He stepped toward the bed and peered down at Ryder. "He didn't tell me someone shot MacKenzie."

Victoria gestured toward the hallway. "If you don't mind, could we talk in the hall so we don't disturb him?"

The sheriff's eyebrow quirked, and he glanced from her to Ryder. "Sure enough, ma'am."

As gentlemen, they waited for Victoria to take the chair. Spencer resumed his earlier place against the wall.

Returning his hat to his head, the sheriff removed a small notebook and pencil from his pocket. "Now, somebody want to tell me what got me outta bed at this hour of the night?"

Victoria wasn't sure how much of the story the sheriff needed to know, so she began with the night she ran away from Nicholas, glossing over details until she reached the part where Palmer dragged her onto the train.

The sheriff nodded, then licked the tip of his pencil and started writing.

By the time it was Spencer's turn to explain how Ryder came to be shot, the sheriff had to whittle a new tip.

"Well, I'll let you get some shut-eye." He stepped back as Victoria stood. "I'll be back later for MacKenzie's statement."

He tucked away his notebook. "I'll send an undertaker over to the train car in the morning for those bodies, and you can talk to him about burying arrangements. I'll be sending a wire to Sheriff Bradley and see what he thinks of all this, but from what I saw when I poked around in that car…" He gestured in the general direction of the tracks out front, "…you and MacKenzie acted in self-defense."

Victoria moved in front of the door and rested her hand on the knob.

The austere stare the sheriff leveled on Spencer was one he must have perfected over years of facing down outlaws. "Now you, you'll have to come with me. You can't go shootin' someone and not expect me to arrest you."

Spencer glanced at the carpet and ran a hand through his hair. Lifting his gaze to meet the sheriff's, he nodded.

Oddly, Victoria struggled not to laugh. As much as she felt sorry for Spencer, he deserved some comeuppance for causing Ryder so much pain. She half expected him to argue and flaunt the Thorndyke name, but after saying good bye to Victoria, he walked down the hall ahead of the sheriff.

After they'd gone, she slipped into the room and turned down the lamps.

She kicked off her shoes, and bending over, set her footwear beside Ryder's. Unable to resist, she picked up his tall leather boots and held them in her lap as she sat on the bed. Watching him sleep, she finger-combed his hair off his forehead. Stubbornly the silky length fell back again. His skin, where her fingertips had brushed across it, was warm, but not overly so.

She yawned and holding his boots, arched her back and rolled her shoulders. It was hard to tell in the low light if he was all right, so she leaned close and kissed him.

He opened his eyes. The faintest of smiles tugged at the corners of his mouth.

"How do you feel?" she asked softly.

"Hurts."

"I'm sorry."

His brow tugged together in a brief frown.

She sighed and smiled. "I know, 'stop apologizing.' I'm sorry, I can't help it."

"Is there any water?"

"Sure." Holding his boots close to her heart, like a couple of school books, she moved across the room to the pitcher and basin and filled one of the two glasses.

Glancing at the boots, he chuckled and taking the glass from her hand, downed the contents.

When he finished, she set it on the small table the doctor had used for his instruments.

"I'm fine. You don't need to hold my boots all night."

She'd forgotten she was holding them. Carefully she returned them to the floor, side by side, next to her shoes.

"Come here." He scooted over a bit.

"I don't want to hurt you."

"You won't."

She hesitated then carefully stretched out on the side opposite his injury.

"Go to sleep," he murmured, closing his eyes.

For several minutes, she lay content to listen to each soft exhale of his breath, to watch his chest rise and fall. Gently she draped her arm across his waist.

Connecting with the solid warmth of him, even

through the sleeve of her dress, made her feel safe, the way she'd felt safe when her grandmother had held her after a bad dream.

This nightmare of a day had finally ended. Images flipped through her mind like pictures in a stereoscope, from making love with Ryder, to giving Searcy the money, then Ryder finding her journal, Nicholas, Palmer and that horrible confrontation, then Spencer.

That Nicholas was actually gone felt surreal. After all these years, she'd finally been liberated from the clutches of the evil prince. She should be planning a trip, buying a dozen new gowns, dancing in the street, but none of it mattered if she couldn't share it with Ryder MacKenzie.

She stared at his fingertips, resting on his white bandaged chest, and could almost feel them gliding over her skin. As she breathed, her nose filled with the smell of dried blood and carbolic powder, but in her mind she inhaled the earthy scent of his soap, along with traces of mule and leather. Memories flipped through her thoughts like treasured photographs pasted in an album, of kittens and puppies, a rare smile or two, scuffed brown boots, and spurs with hearts.

"Why won't you believe I love you?" Her whispered words blew against his ribs then curled back in a swirl of breath to brush her face.

Content, her eyes drifted closed as her exhausted body finally relaxed.

"I want to," he murmured, his words barely audible.

The simple words sliced straight to her heart. Behind her lids, her eyes stung, but she remained still, pretending she hadn't heard.

She wished she'd never written in that journal, never created the fantasy of a knight riding to her rescue to slay the evil prince. *I want to,* meant that if he trusted her, then he could love her, but he didn't and now maybe he never would.

****

Sunlight filled the room when Victoria woke and eased herself off the bed. After a quick wash in the basin, she slipped out to use the water closet at the end of the hall. Afterward, she bought a breakfast tray from the restaurant downstairs.

While Ryder picked at his scrambled eggs and toast, a young boy knocked on the door with a message that the undertaker had arrived to collect the bodies.

"I'll be right down." Pausing to check her hair, she smiled at Ryder watching in the mirror. An ugly twist turned down the corners of his mouth, and her smile faded. She swung around, believing his harsh reflection to be a trick of the sunlight in the mirror.

"You'll need money to pay the undertaker, won't you, Victoria?"

He'd called her Victoria. A frisson of fear crawled up her spine.

She frowned at his odd tone. "I can't take your money for this."

"Don't you mean *your* money?"

The blood drained from her face and landed in her stomach with a thud. "What?"

"I hoped I'd dreamed it. I can see now I didn't."

"What are you talking about?" she hedged.

He set his breakfast plate on the bedside table and threw back the covers.

"Ryder, what are you doing? You shouldn't be up."

She stepped to the brass footboard and grasped the rail.

"Don't lie to me, Victoria." Anger seemed to give him the strength to stride across the room, wearing nothing but his drawers, the bandage, and sling. He snatched his vest from the top of the clothes piled on the chair and held it up as evidence.

"I should have figured it out sooner. Searcy had to wire the money to my bank because he'd given all the cash he had to Flint."

"I'm sorry I deceived you, but you deserved that money."

"Why? Did you pity me because I was broke? Your kind is all the same." He sneered. "Unless a man has money, you think he's worthless."

"No, that's not it at all." She stepped toward him, moving around the end of the bed. "The money was Thorndyke's blackmail payment to Nicholas. I took it when I ran away. As soon as I understood why Nicholas was blackmailing your father, I didn't want it. It felt like blood money, and I thought you should have it, but I didn't think you'd accept it so I gave it—"

"You were right. I wouldn't have taken it, and I don't want it now. I wouldn't take a penny that belonged to that miserable sonofabitch. Any dollar I have will be made by me alone." He balled up the vest and threw it in her direction. It hit her in the face then fell into her arms.

Too numb to form a reply, she stared at him, and clutching the fabric, tried to think.

He made it back to the bed just as his energy drained from his limbs, and he dropped heavily onto the mattress.

She started toward him but stopped when he shook

his head. "Just go." His voice was flat, deplete of emotion. "Your husband is dead. You're a wealthy woman. You don't need to manipulate me anymore, and I sure as hell don't need you, or your pity."

Tears burning in her eyes, she whirled and hurried from the room. At the top of the stairs, she took a moment to compose herself and realized she was still holding Ryder's vest. She raised it to her face and breathed deep. The sting began again, and all she wanted was to bury her face in the wool and sob her heart out.

But the undertaker was waiting. She swiped at her eyes and removed the envelope filled with money. Slipping it into her skirt pocket, she started down the staircase. At the front desk, she inquired whether the young clerk, whose name was Danny, could hold the vest for her behind the desk then asked him to point out undertaker.

Mr. Quinn stood barely an inch taller than she, with a girth nearly as round as he was high. He had a ready smile and a quick laugh, and Victoria couldn't help but relax in response.

To spare her delicate sensibilities, he'd sent his two assistants over to the train to remove the bodies back to his mortuary.

Outside the hotel, he handed her into his buggy then drove to his funeral home.

The coffin she chose for Nicholas was nice, but not too fancy, though Mr. Quinn tried his best to persuade her to purchase his top-of-the-line model. She then made arrangements to have his body shipped to New York and gave him a few extra dollars for his trouble.

Though she hated to pay for Palmer, she chose an

inexpensive wooden box and asked to have him buried without any services in a small cemetery outside of town.

Next she stopped at the First National Bank of Cheyenne. The head cashier explained that because of her husband's death, she wouldn't yet be able to touch any of his accounts. He would however, send a wire to New York to see if she could access the money from her grandmother.

After the bank she walked to the jail. Sheriff Jackson was out, but one of his deputies let her into the back to see Spencer. Except for two cells with snoring men who appeared to be sleeping off the effects of too much liquor, Spencer was the only prisoner.

He rose from his cot when he saw her. "How is Ryder?"

"He's doing much better." She smiled as she drew close to his cell. At least he cared, despite what he'd done.

He leaned against the bars and slid his hands between them, resting his forearms on the cross piece. He blew out a sigh. "I've been worried. There was so much blood. I've never seen anyone get shot before."

She gave his hand a squeeze. Dark circles underscored his brown eyes, and his unshaved beard shadowed his face. "He's going to be fine."

"I can't believe I nearly killed my brother. I swear to God, I am never touching another gun for the rest of my life."

"Are you doing all right?"

"I'm fine. The sheriff said my arraignment will be Monday or Tuesday."

"Do you have an attorney?"

"No. I sent a wire to Father to let him know what happened. A reply came a little while ago from Phillip saying Father had followed me and left New York on a train, the day after I did."

"Does he know you're in here?"

"Not yet, but I'm sure Phillip will send word down the line."

"Do you think your father could arrive in Cheyenne today?"

Spencer nodded.

Cold prickles rushed over her, the way it did when someone walked on her grave.

"Oh Lord." She sagged against the bars. "What do you think he'll do when he finds you in here?" Then with her gaze fixed on his, she asked the unspoken question with her eyes, *What's he going to do when he finds out Ryder is alive?*

Spencer shook his head. "I don't know, but he won't be happy."

****

She left him a few minutes later and returned to the hotel. Passengers milled around on the platform out front and an east bound train sat on the tracks near the water tower. The lobby was filled with people who'd just arrived or were getting ready to board. She waited at the edge of the crowd for an opening at the desk.

"Hello there, Mrs. Vandy Beck."

She whirled at the sound of the familiar voice, pressing her hands to her stomach.

Flint stood a few feet away, an obnoxious smelling cigar scissored between his fingers. "Last time I seen you, you was dressed up like a nun. You look mighty fetchin' in that pretty blue dress."

"My wardrobe is none of your concern."

He laughed and gave the side of his thigh a quick slap. "Damn, I love your high and mighty ways." He stepped forward.

She inched closer to the desk.

"Where's MacKenzie? You give him the slip again?"

"That, too, is none of your concern."

He raised his cigar to his lips, drew a couple of puffs, and released a gray cloud of smoke into the space between them. "Well, now Princess…"

"Don't call me that." She struggled to suppress a cough.

He grinned.

"I know what you did to Ryder, Mr. Flint." She gripped her fingers to stop them from fanning the gray cloud away from her face.

He shrugged as though nothing she said mattered then arrogantly blew another puff of smoke her way. "Where is MacKenzie? Are you two staying here together?"

"Again, that is none of your concern. But I think you should give him his money." She didn't want to accuse him outright of cattle rustling in the city that was home to the Wyoming Stock Growers Association.

"Now if you will excuse me." She turned away as space opened up at the desk. Once she retrieved the vest, she started for the staircase, afraid to look around incase Flint was watching.

Her hands still shaky from her encounter, she stood in front of the door, drawing several deep breaths. Voices rumbled from within and at one point Ryder's laughter rang out.

Heartened, she gave a brief knock then entered. The sheriff sat beside Ryder's bed.

"You're a good man, MacKenzie." He rose to his feet as Victoria closed the door. "But I don't care if he is your brother."

He lifted his hat from the table and nodded at Victoria. "Ma'am."

She smiled, even as she covertly searched Ryder's expression trying to determine his mood. He seemed relaxed. She shifted her gaze to the sheriff.

"I was just chatting with your deputy."

"You were down at the jail?"

She nodded. "To see Spencer."

"Did he tell you we were beating an' starving him?"

A brief chuckle rose in her throat. She looked past the sheriff, meeting Ryder's gaze as she continued. "He's waiting for his father to arrive this afternoon."

Ryder stiffened. A shadow fell over his face, obscuring the remnants of his earlier laughter.

The sheriff turned back toward the bed. "Like I said, if you press charges it'll give that boy a couple a days to think about what he did. You can always drop 'em. But just do it before his arraignment on Monday."

"Then I think I'll press charges."

"Good enough." He gave Ryder's good shoulder a pat. "Take care of yourself now, son." Then with a quick nod to Victoria and a brief "Ma'am," he left the room.

As she moved toward the bed, Ryder locked his gaze on hers. "Is Thorndyke really coming?"

She nodded, wondering how he felt about seeing his father after all these years. But any trace of emotion was hidden behind an impassive poker face. Stopping beside the bed, she waited for him to shift his legs, so she could sit next to him. When he didn't, her stomach gave a queasy little flutter.

Her shoes felt weighted as she stepped back and gripped the foot rail with both hands. "I'm sorry; I shouldn't have deceived you about the money. I should have told you and—"

"I changed my mind," he said. "I'll take it."

She stared at him. She'd never seen his face so devoid of expression. Her pulse thrummed against the back of her jaw, as her stomach twisted into a knot.

With an impatient sigh, he tossed back the covers. He rose and started toward her.

Uncertain, she stepped back.

He followed her retreat, holding out his hand. "Give me the damn money."

Her knees shook. Her hand trembled as she slid it into her pocket and removed the thick envelope.

Snatching it from her, he turned away, quickly counting the bills that were left, like the miserly Ebenezer Scrooge, in Mr. Dickens book, *A Christmas Carol*.

"We have to find another place to stay," he said. "Dyer's Hotel has a French restaurant, and I hear they have fresh oysters."

"What are you talking about?"

He swung around. "I need to get dressed. Hellman's Clothing Emporium should have some fine quality suits. And I need a new hat." He pulled several bills from the purse and held them out to her. "Here," he said. "Take it."

Reluctantly she stepped toward him and accepted

the money. Glancing at it, she guessed he'd given her at least three hundred dollars.

"Get yourself the fanciest, most expensive dress you can find. I don't know any dress shops, you'll have to ask at the front desk. And get some jewelry. Diamonds or something." He turned away and eased his arm from the sling.

Chilled to the core by this stranger in front of her, she closed her fingers around the bills and fighting the urge to run, stepped closer.

"Why?" she asked in a small voice, though the name Thorndyke sat heavy in the pit of her stomach.

"Don't you want a new dress?"

"Well, yes, but diamonds and French restaurants? I don't understand."

"You're a beautiful woman. I need you on my arm. You said you felt like Nicholas' whore. Thorndyke will never believe I could keep a mistress like you unless I could afford to pay for the ser—"

Of its own volition her hand swung toward his face, but her fingers, still fisted around the money, slammed against his cheekbone.

He staggered back from the impact, grabbing the back of the vacated chair to keep from falling.

Victoria shook out her hand and rubbed her sore knuckles. "Damn you, Ryder MacKenzie!" she cried, then whirling on her heels, she yanked open the door and ran for the staircase.

Chapter Twenty-Three

The impact of her fist rattled through his head like the rumbling echo of a thunder clap. It jarred him back to himself, as if he'd floated away for a few minutes while his body had been possessed by a person he didn't recognize. *Shit!*

"Tori!" He made for the door. Flinging it back on its hinges, he strode into the hall. A flash of blue caught his eye at the top of the staircase. "Tori! Come back! I'm sorry!"

Finally her blonde head dropped below floor level, and he sagged against the wall. Sweat popped out across his forehead, and his clammy hands shook. Exhausted, he let his body slide down, his skin sticking to the cabbage roses printed on the paper. Keeping one knee bent, he extended his other foot and closing his eyes, rested his head against the wall.

She'd be back, all her things were here. No, they were back in Ogallala. Damn, and he'd just given her a wad of money. She could go anywhere. A low groan shuddered in his throat, and he thumped his head against the wall several times. He was a bigger ass than Percy.

The soft tread of shoes against the carpet runner lifted his heart. He didn't know for certain it was her; it was only that at this moment he needed to believe.

The footsteps stopped beside him. Fabric swished,

brushing against his arm as she turned and leaned against the wall. He exhaled his relief with a sigh but kept his eyes closed, afraid of what he might see in her expression. "I'm sorry."

She said nothing.

He didn't blame her for being mad; he was just glad she was here.

"I used to dream about meeting him again," he said. "I'd be wearing an expensive suit, and he'd immediately recognize the quality. He'd come into *my* house, into *my* study. He'd see all I had and know I had worth. But he'd need something from me he couldn't get from anyone else, and this time I'd look down at him like *he* was the piece of shit beneath *my* shoe. I'd make him beg, and he'd know I was somebody. He'd know I'd become more than the worthless piece of trash he decided I was."

Small hands wrapped around his bicep and squeezed tight, latching on to him as if they stood on the edge of a cliff and he was about to fall.

He hadn't even realized she'd lowered herself to sit on the floor beside him.

The weight of her head came to rest against his shoulder. Silky wisps of hair tickled his skin. He leaned his head against hers, savoring her closeness, relieved she'd come back. "I'm sorry, Tori. I don't want to become him. I don't want to be *like* him."

"You're not." Her hand slid down the smooth skin along the inside of his arm until her fingers tangled with his.

He gave them a quick squeeze. "Do you remember when you said you wished it was me who smiled and asked you to dance?"

"Yes."

"I wish it had been me, too."

If a smile could truly radiate warmth, then she was smiling now, for the chill he'd felt since she fled the room was gone.

"What the hell am I going to do? He's coming here, and I'm a Goddamn mess."

"You are bleeding."

He heaved an exhausted sigh. "Thought so."

Heavy footsteps with a slow, short stride approached from the end of the hall.

Victoria scrambled to her feet. "Good afternoon, Doctor."

Ryder opened his eyes and tried to push himself upright, but his bare foot slipped on the carpet as he rose, and he slammed back down on his ass.

"Come on, son, take my arm," the doctor offered.

Reluctantly Ryder reached up to grip the inside of the old man's forearm, and the doctor hauled him to his feet.

Victoria stepped around them and opened the door to the room.

"Where's that sling I wanted you to wear?" the doctor asked. "You've got to wear it, son, if you want that wound to heal."

Ryder sat on the bed, waiting as Victoria stuffed pillows between his back and the headboard. He'd regretted not wearing the sling shortly after he'd taken it off, when his whole arm and shoulder had begun to hurt.

Hovering beside the bed, Victoria said little except in response to the doctor's questions as he checked Ryder's wound and changed the bandage.

With the sling back in place, the doctor repacked his bag. "Now this time keep it on. And stop wandering around the hotel in nothing but your drawers. You have a bit of fever, so stay in bed."

Without making any promises, he thanked the man.

Victoria escorted him to the door. "Thank you, Doctor Carroll."

"You're welcome, ma'am, and I'll be back tomorrow afternoon. Make sure he minds what I said."

Across the room she sighed. "I'll try."

When she approached the bed, he scooted over so she could sit beside him. He draped his arm around her shoulder and pulled her close. "Why'd you come back?"

She drew a soft breath as if she were about to speak, then nothing. Apprehensive, he squeezed her tighter.

"Is Thorndyke downstairs?" He heard the edge in his voice, and though he hated it, he couldn't have stopped it.

She lifted herself away from him, but at least she didn't leave.

"No." She laid her hand on his thigh. "It's your friend, Mr. Flint."

"Flint's here?"

"I saw him downstairs when I returned from seeing Spencer. He was talking to a couple of other men."

Ryder slid his hand around the back of his neck. "Damn it." He swung his feet to the floor.

"Wait." Her hand reached toward him but fell short to rest on the folds of the blankets. "What are you doing?"

He stood and grabbed his clothes from the table,

then tossed them on the bed. "Help me get dressed."

"You heard what the doctor said. You need to rest."

"I also need to get my money back before Flint loses it all playing poker. He's probably here for some damn high stakes game. That's why he needed the money."

Their gazes met, and after a moment-long silent battle of wills, Victoria sighed and scooted across the bed. She grabbed his socks and waved them in his face. "All right, but you're wearing your sling. It won't do you a single bit of good if you faint in front of him."

He snorted and shook out his pants. Then after pulling them on, he waited for Victoria to do up the buttons. "Men don't faint," he muttered to the top of her head.

He thought he heard an unladylike huff as she turned and grabbed Spencer's small valise.

"What are you looking for?"

"He owes you a shirt."

Though she left off forcing him into an undershirt, by the time she threaded his bad arm through the sleeve, pulled the shirt over his head, and fastened his suspenders, he was gritting his teeth against the pain.

Next he stomped into his boots then held his gun belt in place while she buckled it.

From the frown etched across her brow, he knew he looked like hell. "I'm fine," he growled before she could say it.

She opened her mouth to argue, but he glared at her, and she closed it. Instead she dropped to her hands and knees and picked several crumpled bills off the floor. Between the carpet pattern and the shadow from the bed, he hadn't noticed them when he'd charged after her.

He took the money and jammed it into the front pocket of his pants.

"I could use an extra gun. What happened to Spencer's Derringer?"

Her big blue eyes momentarily widened. She opened her mouth but before she could ask why he needed the gun, he dropped a kiss in the center of her forehead. "I like to be prepared."

He followed her to the table where she'd set Spencer's valise.

Digging through the clothes, she muttered, "I know I saw it. He must have picked it up before we all left the train."

Ryder leaned close as she pushed aside a pair of trousers then lifted out the small pistol.

"Here." She passed it to him, and he checked the chambers. Empty.

"Nicholas' gun is in here, too."

He set down the first one and checked the second. "Did you find any ammunition?"

She rummaged through the bag some more. "Is this what you're looking for?" She turned, holding a small white box with the words *.41 Rimfire Short* written in blue letters.

"Thanks."

"Would you like Mr. Palmer's knife, too?"

He glared at her over his shoulder, not sure if she was being sarcastic or serious. Had she always been this feisty, or had he just not noticed?

"I've already been shot." He set the Derringers on the bed and awkwardly loaded them. "I want to make sure it doesn't happen again." He slipped the first gun under his forearm inside his sling. He passed her the second. "Hide this on yourself somewhere."

She took it but held it pinched, away from her body as though she were holding a polecat by its tail. "Why do I need this? I don't even know how to shoot." She gestured toward the Colt in his holster. "I had your gun when Mr. Flint kidnapped me. I tried to shoot him, but when I pulled the trigger nothing happened."

"Sounds like you didn't pull back the hammer." He stepped up beside her and grabbed the wrist of the hand which held the Derringer. "This gun is an over-under. It has two barrels, two shots."

He leaned close and inhaled as he slid his hand along the length of her outstretched arm. Even without the lure of her familiar lemon scent, she drew him close. He longed to brush her hair back, blow softly in her ear, and taste the skin along the side of her neck.

The rumpled bed teased him, enticing him to pull her onto the mattress and stretch out alongside her. Blood pooled in his groin. His body ached for the tangle of musky scented sheets, her golden hair spread over his chest, the feel of her naked in his arms the way it had been—God, had that been just yesterday morning?

"Ryder?"

He blinked and drew a deep breath. "Sorry." He cupped her hand around the grip and placed the side of her thumb on the hammer. With his own thumb resting on top of hers, he pulled the hammer back one click. "This is half-cock." He swallowed, tempted to guide her hand against him, moving it lower and...

He stepped back, jerking his hand back to his side,

clenching his fingertips against his palm. "Leave it in that position," he croaked. "You don't want it to go off—"

She met his gaze with a puzzled look.

He needed to focus. This was his only chance. Spencer was in jail. Thorndyke would seek him out, just as he'd always dreamed. If the train followed the same schedule, it should arrive later tonight. He needed that money.

He massaged the muscles at the back of his neck. "Leave it like that so it doesn't discharge accidently while it's in your pocket. If you want to fire it, pull the hammer all the way back and squeeze the trigger. Remember that shot will move slow. It's not a distance gun, so if you want to kill someone get close."

She paled and held out the gun. "I don't want to kill anyone—ever again. You take it."

"I can't. They'll search me. If they find what they expect, they'll leave you alone. That palm pistol is my insurance."

"Ryder, you're making me nervous. You're already hurt. How dangerous is this going to be?"

He forced a smile he hoped was reassuring. "I didn't mean to scare you. The only way to get a gun in to one of these games is to plant it ahead of time. But the location of the game is usually kept secret, and they do a room search ahead of time. All we'll do is, go in, talk to Flint, get my money, and leave."

He grabbed her hand. She turned into him and lifted her gaze to his. "You'll be careful won't you? That money is not more important than you."

Searching her blue eyes, he found that tiny brown speck in the brilliant blue of her left eye. That tiny imperfection which only he knew about.

After everything, she was still here. Maybe she really did love him. He longed to immerse himself in her love, keep her close, tell her how much he loved her, that he would shrivel and die without her, but Thorndyke was coming. Right now nothing else mattered.

He needed to get his money and spend it around town. When Thorndyke asked after him, people would remember Ryder MacKenzie like he was somebody. They'd tell Thorndyke... *MacKenzie? He was just in here for this or that. He has a room over at the Union Pacific Hotel.* No one would laugh and say, *MacKenzie? Is he broke again?*

Tomorrow he'd have time to step back and see where his life was, if Victoria intended to stay.

He leaned close and kissed her. "For luck," he said. She smiled and his spirits lifted, as though she had somehow changed his luck for the better.

Hand-in-hand they descended the wide staircase. "Do you see him?" He scanned the large room.

"No, but he was right over there." She pointed to a brocade sofa next to a potted plant. "He was talking to two men. They were wearing suits, and I assumed they were business men. One man had on a western style hat, and the other wore a bowler."

"Let me see if the clerk knows anything." Still holding her hand, he gestured for the young man to follow them to the more secluded end of the wide oak desk.

The skinny man adjusted his spectacles, staring wide-eyed at Ryder's face, waiting as Ryder leaned in.

The temptation to pop the man in the nose flared

for just an instant. Instead Ryder pierced him with his fiercest glare. Victoria never fixated on his birthmark like this. He'd been with her for so long now; he'd almost forgotten how he hated to be gawked at.

"I'm supposed to meet some friends for a game of cards, but I might have missed them."

"Didn't see 'em," the clerk replied, focused on his index finger as he traced the nicks in the surface of the desk. "Why don't you try one of the saloons?"

"This gentlemen's game is a little too exclusive for a saloon."

"Nope. Don't know nothin' about it." He shook his head shifting his attention to Victoria.

She smiled back.

"I know you." He lashed a flirtatious grin. "You left that wool vest for me to watch."

"Yes and, Danny was it?"

Skinny's head bobbed up and down like it was mounted on a spring inside his long neck.

Victoria smiled. "It was so kind of you."

Ryder scowled. What the hell was she playing at?

"And do you recall," she continued as she discreetly set a silver dollar on the desk, keeping it in place with the tip of her index finger, "the gentleman I was talking to when I picked up the vest?"

He rubbed his chin. "I reckon I do."

She drew small, lazy circles with the coin.

The man stared longingly at what was probably a day's pay. "He was one of those fellers invited to play in a private game."

Victoria leaned close and propped her elbow on the desk, then she rested her chin on her closed fist and smiled at the dolt. "Do you recall where they were going to play their little game?"

He gave her a goofy nod.

Ryder clenched his fist to keep from punching him.

"In the back room of Queen City Emporium over on Sixteenth Street."

"Thank you so much, Danny. You've been very helpful."

"But you can't just go over there. They'll know I told you."

"Oh, it's all right." She smiled sweetly. "We've been invited."

Surprised, Ryder stared at her wondering when she'd gotten so confident. Then she slipped her hand through the crook of his arm, and they strolled out of the hotel as if they were ambling home after church.

"What the hell was that?" he asked once they were outside.

"Whenever Nicholas and I went out, that's how he got what he wanted."

"By flirting with desk clerks?"

She laughed. "By paying the men and flirting with the women."

"I could have handled it."

"Yes, but I thought you were going to hit him, and an altercation would have damaged your shoulder."

He guided her onto the sidewalk as a six-mule team and freight wagon rattled past. "I wouldn't have hit him that hard."

When he glanced down, she flashed him a smile that said she was truly happy to be with him.

Warmed, he escorted her to the next block, carefully steering her around the worst of the mud in the street.

"Aren't we going to the sheriff's office?"

"I don't want to involve the law if I don't have to."

"Flint isn't going to just give your money back, is he? Is that why you need all these guns?"

Ryder shrugged. "He'll give it to me, unless he wants to go to jail." He funneled her through an alley which led behind the buildings along Sixteenth Street. "And don't worry, Flint might steal from me, but he'd never hurt me."

At the back door of the third shop stood a broad-shouldered man, his thick arms crossed over his chest. He sported a black suit and wore double pistols with the grips pointed out.

"Name?" He gave them both a quick once over.

"MacKenzie."

The man shook his head. "You're not on the list."

Ryder gestured toward the door. "Go tell Flint to get his ass out here."

Without a word, the guard slipped through the door and returned a minute later.

"It seems Flint is unable to meet with you right now. However, Mr. Larsen says you're welcome to come in and wait."

"Who is Larsen?" Victoria whispered as they stepped into a dark corridor.

"He used to be a riverboat gambler, but he found a way to make more money by running private, high-stakes poker games all over the territory."

Another man, shorter, but similar in build to the man outside, stood in front of a second door. Beside him was a table with a large wooden box. As they approached, he slid a key into the lock and flipped open the lid.

"Weapons," he said.

Ryder set his Colt on top of the knives, pistols, and Derringers already collected inside. As he stepped back, the man's large hands patted his back and waist in a quick search for hidden weapons. Ryder clenched his teeth, enduring the pain of his arm being jostled as the guard searched his sling.

The big man stilled as he slid his hand beneath Ryder's arm. "What's this?" he asked as he withdrew the Derringer.

Ryder gave him a negligent shrug.

The man set the small gun in the box then turned to Victoria.

Panic flashed in her eyes. Hopefully the man would attribute it to the natural reaction of a woman about to be searched.

But only a moment passed before her alarm transformed into condescension. Though the sentry stood taller, Victoria, the actress, managed to glare down her nose at the man, looking every inch the society princess Ryder once thought her to be.

He was tempted to laugh as she silently dared the guard to lay a hand on her.

The man's implacable expression grew baffled, and he opened his mouth to say something then snapped it closed. "Wait here." He reached behind him to turn the knob on the door and ducked inside.

She released a long breath then shot Ryder a shaky smile.

He nodded reassuringly, hoping she didn't notice his own heart beat erratically. He'd told her they wouldn't search her, but he hadn't been sure. At the few games he'd been to with Flint, he'd never seen a woman.

A moment later the guard returned looking even more baffled. "I'm to check you for hat pins."

"Well as you can see, I'm not wearing a hat." Victoria huffed.

The guard stammered an apology. "I-I'm sorry, miss, uh, ma'am."

Opening the door, he allowed them to pass. The room was small, no doubt normally used as a store room, but today it was devoid of any clothing racks, hats, or boxes of shoes and boots. In the center of the room, a gray cloud hung over a table around which sat four men, intent on the cards and chips in front of them.

Flint looked up as they entered. Instead of his usual buckskin shirt, he wore a brand new black wool suit, no doubt recently purchased.

"MacKenzie, I heard you was in Cheyenne." He drew on the expensive cigar he held clamped between his thumb and two fingers. Turning back to the game, he placed a few white chips in the center of the table. "Call."

The bet went to the next player.

Across the room, beside a small sideboard of liquor bottles and glasses stood a balding man wearing a black suit with an ivory brocade waistcoat. "MacKenzie." He removed a cigar from his mouth and stepping toward them.

Ryder shook the man's extended hand. "Larsen," he murmured.

"You're looking for Flint?"

Ryder nodded. "We have business."

"You can see he's in the middle of a game."

"I'll wait."

"You do understand this is a private game, and these gentlemen have paid for the privilege of playing without distractions."

Meeting Larsen's steel-gray eyes, Ryder nodded toward Flint. "My money. I stay."

Larsen's thick, gray eyebrows rose. Questions flickered in the steely depths of his gaze, but Ryder didn't owe him an explanation.

The cards were shown, and the pot went to Flint. The man who sat across from him wearing a checkered suit had a significantly smaller pile of chips than anyone else. Ryder swallowed trying to calculate the value of the large stacks in front of Flint.

Victoria's fingers fumbled against his and squeezed. He looked over to find Larsen's appreciative gaze roaming over her breasts. Without a word, he pulled her to his side and slipped his arm around her waist. He shot Larsen his orneriest scowl, and since he wasn't feeling all that wonderful, it wasn't hard.

Amusement flickered in the man's gray eyes as he acquiesced to Ryder's claim with a slight nod.

At the table everyone tossed in their ante, and the man in the checkered suit began his deal.

Flint bet ten dollars, and when his turn came around, he asked for three cards. Was he holding junk? This couldn't be good. How many hands were left in this game?

"Have a seat, MacKenzie," Larsen gestured to the few chairs along the wall. "You look a little peaked."

Ryder frowned and escorted Victoria to a seat near the corner, but remained standing, positioning himself between them. He didn't have to look to know her gaze was on him. He could feel her silently begging him to sit, but he needed to keep his eye on the game. Instead he poured himself a whiskey, hoping it would steady his nerves as the man with the moustache called.

Flint raised the bet another ten dollars.

Damn, Flint almost always raised his bets when he held poor hands.

Ryder swallowed, hoping no one else had discerned that about Flint, and if they saw the sweat beading on Ryder's brow, they would attribute it to his wounded shoulder.

The man in the moustache folded, checked suit called, and the skinny man in the glasses called.

Flint laid down three sixes.

Ryder stifled a groan.

Skinny flipped over three fours, a ten, and a jack. So far so good.

The man in the checkered suit held two pair.

Ryder tossed back the last of his drink. "Let's go, Flint."

Flint grinned but didn't rise. "Always in a hurry, MacKenzie. Look, I've almost doubled my money."

"You mean my money."

"You gonna fuss about a few dollars? I gave you Mrs. Vandy Beck there."

"Look, you bow out now, or I tell Sheriff Jackson how you came by that money."

The man with the moustache scowled. "Let's go, Flint, you in or out?"

"Come on, let's play," snapped the checkered suit. "Give me a chance to win back my money."

"He's out." Ryder stepped behind Flint's chair.

Larsen moved forward. "Away from the table, MacKenzie." Ryder backed away, holding up his good hand. "Sorry." Then he added. "We leave after this game, Flint."

The man in the checked suit pushed back his chair and stood. "While you two argue, I'm getting a drink." He walked past on his way to the small table.

When Ryder didn't hear the clink of glass, he glanced over his shoulder. Checkers was saying something to Victoria, but even though she was sitting, she once again managed to look down her nose at him.

Ryder stepped closer.

"Pardon me, madam. So sorry." Checkers bowed and backed away, circling toward the table without getting his drink.

Ryder shifted his gaze to Victoria's.

"I don't like him," she whispered.

He nodded as he added another splash of whiskey to his glass. "What did he do?" he asked softly so no one else could hear.

"He acted as if he dropped something then reached under the cabinet, but he didn't have anything in his hand."

Ryder turned back to the game. Checkers was up to something. Ten minutes and they could get out of here. Flint couldn't possibly lose everything in ten minutes.

The skinny man on Flint's right split the deck and fanned the two parts together, repeating the process several times. "Come on, ante up."

Everyone's chip hit the table with four soft clinks, and Skinny dealt Flint's first card. He continued around the table passing one card at a time until each man had five cards.

Ryder stepped closer to Flint's chair, trying to look nonchalant as he peered over Flint's shoulder for a glimpse of his cards when he briefly tipped them up.

An ace of spades, a seven, and a three was all he saw before Flint put them down and set two chips in the center of the table. "I'll open with twenty."

Moustache added his twenty, as did checkered suit and the skinny dealer.

"Cards?"

"Two," Flint said, too good a poker player to give away any tells.

"Two," added Moustache.

Checkers stared across the table at Flint. "I'll stand pat."

On the dealer's right, Checkers held a good position. For him to keep his all his cards while staring down an opponent probably meant he was trying to show strength and had a bad hand—or he was bluffing. "Dealer takes one."

Flint added more chips to the pot. "I bet twenty."

On his right, Moustache set his chips in the center of the table. "Call."

Checkers continued to stare at Flint. What was the man playing at? What sort of gentleman wore a loud checkered suit? Someone supremely confident or someone full of bluster? Checkers added twenty dollars worth of chips then added more. "I'll raise you thirty."

Gnawing on his lower lip, Skinny studied the pot and his pile of chips. After another look at his cards, he gave his head a shake. "Fold."

Flint puffed on one of his expensive smelly cigars. He probably had a good hand. "I'll raise you forty." He slid two stacks of chips forward.

What the hell, Ryder groaned to himself. Fold or call, no more raising. What was Flint trying to prove?

Victoria moved up on Ryder's good side.

Moustache added his chips and raised it another ten dollars, but Ryder noticed a slight tremor in the man's hand. He'd seen that before, when someone had a very good hand.

Larsen moved up behind Skinny. Checkered pants verified his cards then studied the pot. Taking a deep breath, he slid several piles of chips forward leaving him with only a few. "I'll see your bet and raise it one hundred dollars."

If Flint raised the bet again, Ryder swore he was going to grab him by the back of the neck and drag him out of here with what was left. Checkers could go to hell.

Flint must have known better than to push Ryder anymore, for after a very long, staring duel with Checkers, Flint added his pile of chips and said, "Call."

Moustache sighed and shrugged. "I'll fold." His chair creaked as he leaned back and crossed his arms.

With a smug smile, Checkers flipped over a full house—two fours and three aces.

"What the hell?" Flint turned over the queen of diamonds, two aces and two eights.

Ryder blinked staring at the extra ace of spades as a block of ice slammed into his gut. He shoved Victoria behind him and eased backward away from the table.

Skinny and Moustache scrambled from their chairs.

Don't say it. Don't say it, Ryder chanted to himself. "Come on, Flint, let's go."

"No. This sonofabitch cheated!" He shot to his feet.

His left hand on the table, Checkers toyed with his remaining chips as if he expected the accusation.

Oh shit. He had to get Victoria out of here.

"And what were you up to when Larsen asked your friend to get away from the table? How do I know he didn't pass you that ace?" Checkers demanded.

"Who the hell cheats to get two pair?"

From the corner of his eye, he saw Larsen move toward the door.

"Mitchell!" Larsen yelled.

The shout almost covered up the sound of the gunshot. Flint fell back, tumbling over his chair, onto the floor.

Chapter Twenty-Four

"Flint!" Victoria cried.

Skinny and Moustache dove under the table.

Keeping her behind him, Ryder backed straight to the corner. As they moved, she pressed the rigid planes of the Derringer into his palm.

Checkers lunged for Larsen and yanked the older man in front of himself as the door burst open, slamming against the wall with a bang.

Gun raised, Mitchell froze when he came face to face with Checkers, who stood with the barrel of his Derringer pressed against Larsen's temple.

"I will send a bullet into his brain if you don't put that Colt on the table."

"Tori, get down," Ryder ordered, stuffing the gun into his sling. He turned sideways keeping one eye on Victoria his other on Checkers.

Fear dilated her blue eyes, but there was something else in their depths, that same unruffled composure he'd seen amidst the chaos on the train. He gave her a nod as she crouched behind the chair she'd been sitting in minutes ago.

He stepped toward Flint, shoved aside the tipped-over chair and dropped to his knees.

Flint lay on his back, his hands pressed against stomach as blood seeped between his fingers. His bent, up-drawn knee shifted with each grunt of pain.

Footsteps pounded down the short hallway. Ryder glanced up to see the guard from outside skid to a halt.

"Guns on the table," Checkers ordered. "And both of you, sit on the floor over there." He pointed to a spot near Ryder.

As Larsen's two guards lowered themselves to the floor, Checkers stuffed two of the revolvers from the table into the back of his waistband, the third he smoothly switched out for his own Derringer, which he shoved into his coat pocket.

With his bad hand, Ryder gripped the small gun Victoria had given him and pulled off his sling, keeping the gun close to Flint's body, out of Checker's sight.

After lifting Flint's hand away from the wound, Ryder pulled open Flint's vest and shirt. Dark red blood welled from the small hole in the lower left side of his abdomen, just above his hip. Wadding up the cloth, he pressed it against the wound.

Flint groaned and pressed his hand on top of the pad to hold it tight.

From along the wall, one of the guards said, "You'll never get out of here alive, so let Larsen go."

"Not 'til I cash in my chips."

Flint raised his head off the floor. "Shoot the cheatin' sonofabitch," he groaned between clenched teeth. "That pot's mine." His head fell back against the floor with a thud.

Blood pooled on the wide floorboards. Ryder frowned. "Did the bullet go through?"

"Hell if I know," he bit out.

Using his good hand, Ryder pushed at Flint's hip. Sure enough, there was a second hole.

From under the table came a "Pssst," sound.

Skinny waved a handkerchief at him like a surrender flag. Ryder reached out and accepted it along with a second one that must have come from Moustache.

"Obliged," he whispered and packed them both against the exit wound.

Chair legs scraped against the wood floor as Checkers and Larsen side stepped around the table. "Now we're just going to ease over there, and you're going to open that safe."

"That's my money," Flint declared through gritted teeth.

"I can't open the safe," Larsen argued. "You've got to wait for Bob Franklin to get back from supper. It's his store, his safe."

Ryder peered through the tangle of chair and table legs, past where Moustache and Skinny were hiding, to the two guards sitting on the floor. Couldn't at least one of them find the balls to do something? Maybe Larsen thought their intimidating size was enough to provide security for his games.

Ryder shifted his attention to Victoria, horrified to see Checkers had maneuvered himself into her corner.

"Well now, I'll give you five minutes to go get Franklin. Don't bring the law or do anything stupid, or I'll…" He reached down, and in one smooth motion, shoved Larsen stumbling forward and yanked Victoria in front of him. "I'll kill this beautiful woman."

Every muscle in Ryder's body went taut. He shifted, easing his weight onto the balls of his feet. He searched Victoria's face and saw only calm. *I've been in worse situations*, she seemed to say.

Ryder drew a shaky breath. As long as nothing happened to upset Checkers, Victoria should be fine.

Larsen stepped past on his way to the door. Ryder met his gaze. Regret filled Larsen's gray eyes, a silent apology for not noticing the planted Derringer, for permitting Checkers to play, for allowing Victoria to be taken hostage.

"I'm sorry, MacKenzie," Flint whispered.

Ryder glanced down. Sweat beaded Flint's brow, and he'd grown pale beneath his tan.

"For stealing my beeves? You damn well better be."

"I never meant for them to shoot your horse."

"I know."

Flint lifted a shaking hand toward the inside pocket of his coat.

From the corner, Checkers called out. "Hold it right there. You touch that gun and the lady dies."

"You goddamn sonofabitch," Flint called back. "If I had a gun in my pocket, you'd be dead by now. When I aim for the chest, I don't miss." He grasped his lapel and lifted open his coat. "Take it," he urged.

Ryder reached inside and lifted a tri-folded paper from the inside pocket.

Opening it, he saw a bill of sale in his name, spelled wrong of course, for a dark bay gelding, fifteen-two, with a snip and two rear half pasterns. Sold for two hundred and twenty-five dollars.

Ryder stared at the paper in disbelief. This sounded like a very fine animal. He met Flint's gaze.

"Funny as I thought it was," Flint whispered, "you ridin' a mule, ya need a good horse."

Ryder patted Flint's shoulder. No matter what kind of scrape Flint got into, he always managed to redeem himself.

"I didn't spend all Searcy's money on cigars, red-heads, and poker. I got that horse from Bud Parks, down in Colorado."

Thinking back, Ryder realized that was probably when Victoria had grown suspicious of him. He'd claimed to be riding that stage in order to buy a horse from Parks, and when they met the man at the stage station, he'd never even spoken to him.

Flint coughed and shivered. Ryder glanced around, looking for a blanket. This was a damn clothing store, there must be something…

"Ya can pick him up at Ward's Livery whenever you're ready. And there's a brand new saddle down there, to go with yer new horse." Another shudder rippled through him.

"Damn it, Flint, why'd you do it?"

"A man shouldn't have to sell his saddle."

"That's not what I meant."

"I reckoned it was my turn to have what you have."

"What? I don't have anything."

"Since the day I met ya, I ain't never seen no one live under such a cloud of bad luck. But no matter how hard life knocks ya down, ya never quit."

Ryder glanced around, wishing Larsen would get back so Checkers could get his money, and he could get Flint to a doctor.

"I could a more than doubled that money. I would a gave ya half. I just need a stake. I ain't as strong as you, MacKenzie. I might never have a beautiful woman to love me, but maybe I could get me a nice place a my own."

"Don't get sappy, Flint. The bullet went through, you'll be fine."

Flint met his gaze, both recognizing the silent truth that passed between them. There were no guarantees. "Like I said MacKenzie, ya never quit."

From the corner of his eye, he glimpsed the sway of Victoria's blue skirt as she moved one foot to the side and the other back a step. He shifted and met her gaze as she glanced down. He followed her line of sight to her hand, which peeked for an instant from behind the folds of her skirt. Somehow she had lifted the Derringer from Checkers' pocket.

Though the man still had the advantage, if Ryder could get closer, he'd have the element of surprise.

"This man needs a doctor." He gestured with his bad hand as he rose to his feet, keeping his body turned, the Derringer in his good hand pressed against the outside of his thigh.

Checkers shifted nervously. "He can wait 'til Larsen gets back."

"Larsen isn't coming back."

"He will. He won't want this woman's death on his conscience."

Ryder laughed and inched closer. "He only cares about himself. How do you think he survived on the riverboats?"

Doubt briefly crossed Checkers' face like the shadow from a drifting cloud on a sunny day.

Ryder took another step. "Let the lady go, and give up while you can still get out of here." He slid his foot a few inches closer. But the floor was uneven. His boot heel caught on a single plank, its edge higher than the rest. His spur made a soft chinking sound.

Realization hardened Checkers' expression as his gaze shot to Ryder's feet.

At that moment, Victoria shifted then drove her foot down on Checkers' instep as she simultaneously jammed her elbow into the man's stomach.

He grunted and hunched forward as Victoria twisted away. Ryder brought his gun up, just as Checkers straightened and leveled his at Ryder.

In that momentary stand-off, when silence stilled the room, there was a soft click as a hammer was pulled back to full-cock.

Ryder grinned.

Victoria held the barrel of the Derringer barely two inches from the bottom of Checkers' ear.

"I've already killed one man this week," she said in a slow deliberate tone that would do the most hardened gunfighter proud. "So put down your gun, or I'll add your name to my list."

Slowly he lowered his arm. Ryder stepped forward and snatched the Colt from the man's hand as Victoria removed the other two from the back of Checker's waist.

Shoving Checkers' face into the wall and keeping his hand pressed between the man's shoulder blades, Ryder asked, "Anyone want to tie up this sonofabitch?"

Mitchell stepped forward along with the other guard as Skinny and Moustache crawled from beneath the table.

Ryder stepped past them, and Victoria launched herself into his arms.

He staggered back a step, wincing under the impact with a hiss of breath.

"I'm sorry." She tried to pull back, but he wasn't going to let her go, no matter how much it hurt. A tremble rippled through her. "I don't ever want to touch another gun again."

He chuckled, amazed by the depth of her strength. "God, I love you, Tori." He pressed a kiss to the top of her head.

She squeezed him tighter, and he thought he heard a little sniffle. "I'll always love you, Ryder MacKenzie."

He sighed, warmed by her words, by the scent of her hair, and the pressure of her arms around his waist. Would she be content to stay with him forever?

Unexpectedly she pulled away.

His heart did a little flip.

"Mr. Flint." She swiped at her eyes as she dropped to her knees beside the man.

Ryder released the breath he'd been holding, feeling a bit foolish for letting his fear run away with him again.

The guard from outside and his partner Mitchell shoved Checkers, hands tied behind his back, stumbling toward the door.

Flint smiled at Victoria. "You're feistier than I reckoned you was. You the one shot MacKenzie?"

"No," she said. "His brother did that."

"Brother? That family a yours finally come lookin' for you?"

Ryder shook his head. "We'll talk about it after I get you to a doctor."

"What the hell is going on in here?" the sheriff exclaimed as he stepped through the doorway with Larsen close on his heels. He glanced around the room, and his gaze fell on Ryder.

"MacKenzie, you involved in this little dustup, too?"

Ryder shrugged one shoulder then extended his hand to Victoria, assisting her to her feet. She pressed herself against his side and slipped her arm around his waist as he draped his good arm over her shoulder.

The whistle of the approaching westbound train wailed through the night. Ryder exchanged a quick glance with Victoria. Thorndyke.

The sheriff pointed at Skinny and Moustache, lurking near the door. "You two. Head on over to my office with this one here." He jerked his thumb at Larsen. "I want all your statements—tonight. And you." He waved the biggest guard forward. "Get Flint to a doctor. Then get back here and watch that safe. I'll escort Fancy-checker-pants to jail myself."

The larger of the guards bent down and scooped Flint into his arms as Mitchell positioned himself in front of the wall safe.

"Put me down," Flint sputtered as he was carried from the room. "I can walk. I ain't no damn woman."

The sheriff swung his attention to Ryder. "You look as done in as your pardner. Go get some sleep. I'll come find you in the morning."

They parted ways then as he and Victoria followed Flint to the doc's. Doctor Carroll's office was the closest, and they left Flint in his care.

"I'll let you know how he's doing when I come see you tomorrow afternoon," the old man said as he stabilized Ryder's shoulder with a new sling. "And wear the damn thing this time."

A nearly full moon illuminated the streets with silver light. If he hadn't been feeling so shaky and queasy, it would have been a nice courting moon. The kind he used to imagine when he was young and naïve.

As they headed toward the tracks and the Union Pacific Hotel, the piercing bray of a mule sliced through the peace. *Hee-haw, hee-haw.* The abrasive sound could probably be heard for miles. He glanced at Victoria. She met his gaze, her eyes wide and expectant. "Percy," they said in unison.

Rounding the corner, they hurried down the platform to the commotion in front of the depot where several men surrounded the obstinate silhouette of a mule. One man pulled on the lead rope, extending the mule's nose as far as it would stretch while two other men pushed at the mule's unmoving hind end.

Sheriff Bradley spotted them as they approached. "I don't know what got into him," he yelled over the din. "He unloaded just fine then he quit moving."

The incessant braying echoed through Ryder's now throbbing head. "Damn it, Percy, shut up!"

Then as easily as someone ceasing to push a pump handle, the incessant braying, like the flow of water, ceased. The man with the rope loosed his grip, and Percy turned his head, his long, dark ears pricked toward Ryder.

Victoria's hand slipped from his. "I'll be right back,"

He watched her hurry toward the baggage cart near the corner of the depot. The man passed him the lead rope, as Sheriff Bradley continued in a less strident tone.

"I thought I'd bring you all your gear and the little grullo, too. It was fine 'til I tried to take him to the livery."

"Obliged, but I can take him."

"You sure, son? Sheriff Jackson wired me you ran

into some trouble. Gotta say you're lookin' like you were rode hard and put up wet."

Ryder nodded, as he ran his hand down Percy's neck and patted his shoulder. "That's just how I feel."

Bradley grinned as the crowd drifted away. "Where did that pretty wife of yours disappear to?"

Ryder nodded toward a point past Bradley's shoulder. "Here she comes now."

Victoria hurried forward, her battered carpetbag bumping her knee as she walked. She stopped beside the sheriff and set her bag in the grass beside him. Lowering herself in front of it, she undid the strap and dug through the contents.

A moment later, she popped up and swung around, with something clenched in her fist and a triumphant grin spread across her face. Lord she was beautiful in the moonlight, the way it shone silver in her blonde hair and highlighted her nose and perfect cheekbones.

She put a lemon drop in her right hand and extended it to Percy. He crunched on the candy then nudged her for a second piece.

"There, you got what you wanted, you dumb jackass, now let's go." Ryder tugged on the lead rope, and the mule followed along side.

Victoria caught up to him as Bradley called goodnight. They walked to the livery in companionable silence, and with one last lemon drop, they left Percy in the corral with Smoky.

"I thought we could have supper together, but I don't think I can stay awake long enough."

"I'm exhausted, too," she said. "Couldn't we stop at the hotel restaurant and take our meal upstairs?"

Though the dining room was full of train

passengers coming and going, Ryder and Victoria didn't have to wait long to receive their roast beef dinners. Ryder carried his plate while she looped the handles of her carpetbag over her arm and held her plate in her hand. They wove their way between the tables back to the lobby which was also filled with milling people, despite the late hour.

Once upstairs, he dropped her carpetbag beside Spencer's leather valise, then lowered himself to the edge of the bed, releasing a sigh that sounded more like a groan.

Victoria was beside him in an instant. Concern furrowed her brow, the plates of food forgotten on the bedside table. She lifted his hat from his head, setting it aside. The mattress dipped beneath her weight, bumping their shoulders together. Her hand landed on his thigh. "Are you all right?"

"Yeah, other than I feel like shit."

"You haven't eaten anything since breakfast, and that wasn't much."

"I just need some sleep. I'll feel better in the morning." Better able to face Thorndyke. He wondered if the man had arrived yet. If what Spencer told Victoria was true, then yes, he might even have been a blur in the crowd on the platform, or inside the dining room or lobby. His heart beat quickened. After all these years, he'd finally be able to watch the man grovel.

"Ryder?"

He opened his eyes. Funny he hadn't remembered closing them. Victoria knelt in front of him, holding a piece of bread. "Here, at least eat this. Let me help you get your boots off, then you can lie down and get some sleep."

An image flashed briefly of Victoria in this position for another reason, but his body was too exhausted to even work up a passing interest.

Instead of taking the bread, he slid his hand along her jaw, his fingertips buried in her hair as he brushed his thumb over her perfect cheek. Disquiet filled her blue eyes, and he marveled that her worry was for him. She was still here. That she actually, genuinely loved him was such an extraordinary concept, he had a hard time truly believing it.

Her hand wrapped around his wrist, and she leaned into his palm, briefly closing her eyes as though finding pleasure in his touch. She turned her head slightly and pressed her downy lips to his roughened palm. This time he closed his eyes, savoring a moment he never in his dreams thought to experience.

Then his foot was being lifted, and he opened his eyes to find her struggling to remove his boot.

Giving his head a shake to clear the fog, he pressed the toe of his opposite foot against the heel as she pulled.

"Now that I have my yarn and needles back, I'll start you another pair of socks."

"You make nice socks." He swung his legs onto the bed. Scooting himself toward the headboard, he lowered his head into the comfort of the pillows. She was staying. *Love you*, drifted through his mind, but he wasn't sure if he said the words aloud. The image he carried off to sleep was of her, standing beside the bed, clutching his boots against her chest.

Victoria flipped the other half of the bedspread over Ryder, hoping a good night's sleep would erase the flush that matched both sides of his face.

Concerned his fever would spike, she crossed the room and opened the window. Though the summer air wasn't any cooler, at least a breeze billowed the curtains.

A brisk knock sounded against the door. Afraid the noise would wake him, she hurried to answer it, expecting to see the sheriff or doctor standing there.

Instead, as she swung the portal inward, she came face to face with Ainsworth Thorndyke.

Chapter Twenty-Five

"Good evening, Mrs. Van Der Beck." His polite greeting was held the superior edge of a sneer.

"Mr. Thorndyke," she said stiffly. "It's rather late. What can I do for you?"

While she had no intention of allowing him into the room, he pushed his way past her as though it was his right. He strode straight to the bed and stared down at Ryder.

A flutter of alarm somersaulted through her. She stepped up beside him. "Please leave."

"It *is* him." Disdain curled his lips back as though he'd bitten into a rotted apple. "I recognized you in the restaurant. Then I saw him."

"Yes, you were correct, now please go." She dug her fingernails into the leather uppers of Ryder's boots.

Thorndyke swung toward her, his dark eyes narrowed. "I understand it all now."

Victoria instinctively stepped back.

"This…this *person* went to your husband, and the two of them conspired their plan of extortion. Palmer obviously lied to me all those years ago and accepted payment for a job he never completed. That's why Spencer is in jail. He discovered how I have been wronged and tried to kill your husband."

A small choking sound escaped her throat as her outrage tangled together with more words than she could articulate. *"You have been wronged? You have been wronged?"* The pitch of her voice rose along with her fury, until she was screaming. "You arrogant—" Latching onto one of Ryder's boots, she swung it like a club, hitting him with the heel.

"—self-absorbed—"

Thorndyke raised his arm to ward off the blows as he backed toward the door. He tried to grab the boot, but she beat him with the other boot as well.

"—pompous *ass*!"

Reaching behind him, he fumbled for the knob. As he pulled it open, he said, "Does your husband know you're cuckholding him with that worthless—"

She swung the boot one more time, the rowel of the spur catching him on the cheek as he lowered his arm in order to slip through the door. A spurt of blood ran toward his chin.

Furious she chased him into the hallway. "Ryder MacKenzie is not worthless!" She launched the first boot at the back of his head. It hit him with a thud, knocking his hat to the floor.

"I'll have you brought up on assault charges," he fired back without stopping to retrieve his bowler.

She hurled the second boot with all her might, but it fell harmlessly to the floor. "You're not in New York anymore, Mr. Thorndyke! This is Ryder MacKenzie's town!"

She stood in the middle of the hallway until he was gone, then with shaking hands she retrieved Ryder's boots. Clutching them against her chest, she started back to the room.

Head down, she first noticed his gray-stockinged feet as he leaned against the door jamb. Lifting her gaze up the length of him, she stopped when his mouth quirked up in a smile.

"From the way you're always hugging my boots, I'm beginning to think you like them more than you like me."

"I hate your father.

He chuckled. "I know."

"You heard all that?"

He laughed and she smiled, a trifle embarrassed to have been screaming like a fishwife. The entire hotel probably heard. He held out his arm, and she walked into his embrace, the boots squished between them.

"My brave and valiant little knight." He kissed the top of her head and pulled her into the room.

"I'm sorry." She eased from his embrace, as tears burned in her eyes.

Bemused, he chuckled, guiding her to sit beside him on the bed. "For what? You have vanquished my dragon."

"But you should have been the one to confront him."

"He still needs me, though he doesn't know it yet. Tomorrow will only be that much sweeter." He lifted the boots from her lap, moonlight glinting briefly off his spurs as he set them beside his opposite hip.

"Why did you choose the hearts?"

His brow furrowed. "What?"

"On that first day, when you walked in from the rain, I noticed the hearts on your spurs, and I've wondered ever since why you chose that pair."

He shrugged. "They were the cheapest ones."

The cheapest ones? She stared at him. He didn't seem to be joking. All this time she thought he'd chosen them so carefully, been drawn to them because he secretly longed to be loved.

"The more silver, the more they cost. And I wanted the bigger rowels." He draped his arm over her shoulder and gave her a little hug. "I think you're the one drawn to the hearts."

She smiled back, but there was a little squeeze in the center of her chest as she realized he was right. Maybe she was the one who longed to be loved.

He lifted one boot into his lap. Using his good hand, he popped free the spur strap and pulled the yoke from around the back of the boot heel. Tossing his boot to the floor with a clump, he removed his second spur from his boot. Then he slid from the bed and lowered himself to one knee.

A tiny half-laugh escaped her lips. If she didn't know better she'd think he was… Her breath caught. "Ryder, what are you doing?"

"A knight isn't a knight unless they've earned their spurs."

"Don't be silly, I'm no knight."

"Why not? This is my fairy tale, and from the way you swooped in to protect my honor with Thorndyke, I'd say that makes you my knight. And my knight needs her own set of spurs."

"But what will you wear?"

"I've been wanting a pair with bigger rowels anyway."

Victoria ended up holding the yoke in place behind her shoe while he buttoned the leather strap over the arch of her foot.

They nearly fell off when she stood, but she held up the hem of her skirt as she examined each foot from different angles as if she just put on a new pair of dancing slippers.

He rose and sat on the edge of the bed, then grabbing her hand, pulled her down beside him.

Though she hated wearing her shoes on the bed, especially with spurs attached, the thought of removing them at the moment was inconceivable. She snuggled close to Ryder's side. Draping her arm over his waist, he squeezed her shoulder, and she breathed a deep sigh of contentment, absorbing his warmth, feeling the soft thump of his beating heart.

He turned his head, the weight of his cheek rested against the top of her head.

He kissed her hair. "I think I started to fall in love with you that first day on the train, when you gave me your lunch. But you were so beautiful, I was sure you could never love me."

She lifted her chin and searched those magnificent hazel eyes, darkened with the night shadows to brown. Her chest ached for the lifetime of pain he'd endured because of a mark she hardly noticed. "My love for you is real, Ryder MacKenzie. Don't you ever doubt it."

Somber and intense, with eyes able to see into her very soul, Ryder met her gaze. "Will you marry me Tori, my beautiful knight? My kingdom isn't big, and I'm not the handsome prin—"

She pressed her lips against his, halting his words. With a groan he returned her kiss, twining his tongue with hers as his fingers tangled in her hair. She broke the kiss and sat up, as her fingers popped free the top button of her dress. "Don't ever say you are not handsome. My God, you're all that is perfect in a man. How could I not love you?"

Hiking up her skirt, she swung her leg over his hip straddling him as she worked free her buttons.

"Tori, what are you doing?" He brought his hand to rest on her waist.

"This is our fairy tale, and I want to ride my destrier wearing nothing but my new spurs."

He laughed, "God, Tori, I love you."

She eased off him to slip out of her clothes and wearing nothing but her black stockings, shoes, and spurs, she sat astride him, toying with his shirt buttons. "Don't ever doubt that I love you."

A grin spread over his face as his hands rested on her waist. "I'm still wearing my pants."

Leaning close she dropped another kiss on his mouth. "It's not good to gallop a horse right out of the barn. He needs to warm up first."

In all her years of marriage to Nicholas and with all the things they did together in and out of bed, Victoria had never once desired any bedroom play or teasing. Ryder MacKenzie had awakened a woman inside she'd never known existed. This new woman was confident and happy, and Victoria liked her.

****

They made love again in the early morning hours, and after finally eating their cold supper, they fell asleep until the whistle of the east bound train woke them to a room filled with sunlight.

Victoria took her lemon soap and went down the hall to take a quick bath. Leaving off the spurs, she carried their plates back to the restaurant while Ryder had a wash. She couldn't help but scan the face of each man with Thorndyke's build, hoping she would never have to face him again and wondering what to say when

375

she did. Instead she met Dr. Carroll in the lobby, and they walked upstairs together.

After checking the bullet wound, Dr. Carroll pronounced Ryder on the mend. "But keep wearing that sling, and stay in bed, you still have that bit of fever.

"I hope your friend is a better patient," he added as he packed up his black bag.

"How's he doing?" Ryder asked. "He was bleeding pretty bad last night."

"Well, the bleeding stopped, but the organs are packed together pretty tight inside the human body. I don't know what kind of damage might have been done. Right now he's running a fever, which is to be expected, so we'll have to wait and see. That gambler, Larsen stopped by this morning to give Flint his poker winnings. And Flint said to tell you your half is double what you had." The doctor straightened his coat and set his hat on his head.

Victoria searched Ryder's face from where she stood near the end of the bed. His brow furrowed, and his fingers twitched against the coverlet as though he silently assessed his net worth.

Victoria slipped past Dr. Carroll to sit on the edge of the mattress. "After last night, I'm not sure all the wealth of Mr. Rockefeller himself could impress Mr. Thorndyke."

"Thorndyke?" the doctor repeated. "Some puffed-up, fancy pants feller came into my office last night. Demanded I stitch up some little gash on his cheek. Said his name was Thorndyke, like it was more important that I tend to him rather than Flint."

Ryder chuckled and squeezed her hand. She glared at him, pleading with him not to say anything about what she'd done.

But their silent exchange only captured Dr. Carroll's interest. His sharp gaze shot between the two of them.

"What did you tell him?" Ryder asked, a grin tugging up the corners of his mouth.

"Told him I was busy. That he could go bother someone else. He didn't like it, but he got so demanding I shoved him out of my office and locked the door. Never seen the like, a grown man fussing like that over a cut that won't scar more than an inch. Why I've seen two year olds handle worse cuts with less crying."

He started toward the door, then stopped and turned. "Thorndyke. Isn't that the name of the young feller who shot you?"

Ryder nodded. "Yes."

"Didn't you say he was your brother?"

Again Ryder nodded.

The doctor shook his head. "Wish I had a beer and lots more time. I believe this is a story best not rushed, so I'll save you the telling of it for another day."

After the doctor left, Ryder insisted they go see Spencer and save the sheriff a trip. Reluctantly she helped him dress and put on his boots. As much as she wanted him to rest, he wouldn't until this business with Thorndyke was over.

Food and a good night's rest had done wonders for Ryder's mood, for she'd never seen him so happy.

"I think you deserve a new dress." He stopped in front of a dress shop window. "That's pretty." He pointed to a pink calico.

He flashed her such a winning smile, that as long

as he didn't try to buy her diamonds, she couldn't say no. There was something to be said for having such an ordinary shape, and the ready-made garment fit her perfectly. She had her old dress sent to the hotel, and stepping out of the fitting room, she twirled in front of Ryder the way she'd done when she was a girl showing off a new dress in front of her grandmother.

His eyes widened appreciatively and she smiled back.

Looping her arm through the crook of his elbow, they slowly walked toward the jail. Ryder pointed out original buildings and explained how Cheyenne had looked in 1869, when he'd first come here looking to buy some land.

An easy camaraderie flowed between them as naturally, as if they'd been friends for years rather than a week and a half. Victoria hoped her grandmother was looking down from Heaven, because she was sure Nana would have loved Ryder MacKenzie as much as she did.

Sheriff Jackson rose from behind his desk as they stepped into his office. "Feelin' better, MacKenzie?"

Sheriff Bradley also rose, from the chair beside the desk, a coffee cup in his hand. He gave Victoria a nod. "Morning, Mrs. MacKenzie."

She wondered if she should correct him. Ryder gave her a quick wink, and she let the notion go.

"Can I get you a cup of coffee, ma'am?" Sheriff Bradley gestured for her to sit in his vacated chair.

"No, thank you, we just came to see Spencer."

"I hear you two are brothers, MacKenzie. Now that I met him, I can see the resemblance."

Jackson grabbed his ring of keys and unlocked the

door to the back.

"Are you dropping the charges?" The sheriff pushed open the heavy door.

"Not yet," Ryder replied, his tone a bit abrupt considering his mood a moment ago.

Spencer rolled to his feet and grasped the bars. Seeing Ryder washed the tautness from his features and he smiled. "I'm so glad you're all right."

"Glad you won't be charged with murder?"

Victoria frowned and poked him in the ribs.

Spencer's smile faded. "You don't know how sorry I am. I'll never touch another gun again."

Ryder snorted. "Now you sound like Victoria. I can teach you how to handle a gun and shoot."

Spencer leaned forward. "You will? Really?"

With a shake of his head, Ryder muttered, "Now I know how Flint must have felt."

In the other room a door slammed.

"Where is my son?" Thorndyke's harsh demand traveled into the back room. Ryder stiffened, and Victoria stepped beside him, slipping her hand through his elbow and holding on tight.

"Now which son are you looking for?" Sheriff Jackson loudly asked.

"The one who is being unlawfully detained. My other son is at home in New York."

"Ahhh." Jackson mulled this over. "Well, just to clear up a couple of points, one, your son is not being unlawfully detained. He tried to kill a man. And two, I thought MacKenzie was your son."

"That person is no son of mine. I could never have sired a creature like that."

Victoria had latched on to Ryder to keep him from

doing something he might regret, but when she heard those words from Thorndyke, she whirled away from Spencer's cell and marched toward the front of the building.

Halting in the doorway, she called to Thorndyke's back.

"Of course he's your son."

Thorndyke swung around.

She almost smiled when she saw the plaster he'd had applied to his cheek.

His glare narrowed on her face.

"He looks like Philip." She persisted. "Are you so selfish that you have not one shred of remorse for all you've done?"

Ryder came up behind her and grabbed her hand.

Both sheriffs stepped closer to Thorndyke, flanking him on either side.

"It is beyond human comprehension that you wanted him dead the day he was born, but how in the name of all that is holy, could you look at your son every day and feel no remorse for orchestrating such an unconscionable act? And then to hire someone to murder him? From what I see, that makes you a more despicable a human being than any man I have ever known, including Nicholas."

Thorndyke smiled in that superior way Nicholas did when he had the upper hand. Instead of backing down, it fueled her outrage.

"Any other man would have been proud to call Ryder MacKenzie son. He survived every horrible thing you did to him. He is strong, and he never quits. He's gentle and funny, and more protective than any cavalier I could have ever imagined. So maybe I should thank you, for if you'd done nothing, he might have grown to be as arrogant as Philip, as vain as your daughters, and as reckless as Spencer. Either way, I love this man with all my heart, and if either you or your stupid sons ever do anything to hurt him again, I'll… I'll…"

"You think to threaten me?" His chest swelled with indignation. "I am Ainsworth Sheridan Thorndyke. The world believes my first-born son died during child birth. Van Der Beck, Palmer, and Fiona MacKenzie are dead. You and your threats are nothing to me, *little girl*."

Ryder squeezed her hand then slipped his arm around her waist and pulled her against his side. "I don't know, Thorndyke. What happened to your face? Maybe you should count yourself lucky that I'm wearing my boots."

"You forgot about me, Father." Spencer called from his cell. "I am not dead."

Thorndyke's back stiffened and head jerked as though he'd forgotten Spencer was there and been startled by the sound of his voice.

"Nor am I deaf and blind," Spencer continued. "My brother Ryder looks like a Thorndyke, and you have just admitted he is your son."

"Then you can stay in jail until you come to your senses."

"You don't get to make that decision," Ryder said. "I do."

"I don't know, Bradley, did I just hear this man confess to attempted murder."

"Sounded like it to me."

"Reckon I'd better arrest him 'til we can sort this out."

"Unhand me!" Thorndyke ordered as he was shoved toward an empty cell. "You can't do this."

The sheriff gave Thorndyke a shove that had him stumbling into the cell right before he slammed the door.

"Sure I can. I'm the law, and I got to check on the statute of limitations for attempted murder."

****

He hoped she liked the whitewashing he'd given the cabin's interior. He'd even filled a quart jar with wildflowers and left it in the center of the table. The dogs had watched him like he was a new curiosity when he dashed around the yard this morning from one clump of flowers to the next like some demented bee.

Now he hung back, in the shadow of the depot avoiding the stares from the milling crowds. Without Victoria on his arm, he'd reverted to his old habits and kept the brim of his new hat tugged low.

Passengers stepped from the train. He straightened away from the shadows. Two weeks had passed since she'd gone back to New York to settle her husband's estate. Maybe he should have gone with her, but Spencer had insisted he help, and he was better equipped. Besides, Ryder wanted to make sure Flint would be all right.

With his ornery friend healing, Ryder told Sheriff Jackson to let Thorndyke go. Even after two weeks in jail, the man refused to acknowledge Ryder as his son. What did it matter anyway? With Victoria on his arm, money didn't seem to matter as much. He'd never go back to New York, and Spencer was more than eager to claim him as family.

Ryder spotted his younger brother then. Like him,

Spencer stood a little above the crowd. But while many women stepped from the train, he couldn't find Victoria.

Spencer walked toward him, alone, a grim expression on his face. In that moment every fear Ryder had quelled these past two weeks rushed to the forefront of his mind, like a wave crashing against the shoreline during a storm. It hit him hard, knocking him backward until he had nowhere to go, and his spine pressed against the board and batten wall.

She wasn't coming. A knot twisted behind his breast. What they'd shared in that whirlwind two weeks together hadn't been strong enough to win out over the lure of parties and a big house, clothes and servants, dinner and the theater, and suitors. Good looking men with money, who were respected.

Ryder had been confident when she left, with her teary-eyed, *I love you.* She'd even sent a telegram telling him when she'd return. But then, she was good at pretending.

Now it appeared she had changed her mind. Looking back, he realized she'd never actually said yes when he'd asked her to marry him. After all, what did he have to offer beside an isolated life of hard work on a broken down ranch with a man like him.

"I don't understand her at all." Spencer stepped onto the platform. "She made me get off the train in Kearney to buy a pound of lemon drops. I had to go to four different mercantiles before I found them."

Ryder stared at him confused. Lemon drops? He glanced around but couldn't find her. Had something happened? Was Spencer easing him into bad news?

Removing his bowler, Spencer dabbed at his

forehead with his handkerchief and dropped wearily onto a crate.

"You know all the times I danced with her, Victoria Van Der Beck was a timid woman, who never smiled and clung to her husband wherever she went. I don't recognize this Victoria at all."

Ryder wanted to shake the fool. "What the hell are you talking about? Where is Victoria?"

Spencer raised his arm and pointed toward the freight car behind the tender. "I told her it was no place for a lady to ride, but she insisted."

Ryder started forward feeling a bit dazed. A loud bang radiated from the car. The wide wooden door slid open. Tagging along beside him, Spencer kept talking.

"Every place we stopped, she bought another cookbook. I hope you have room for all the trunks she brought. And she's been knitting socks since we left New York."

Ryder stopped in his tracks and whirled on Spencer, barely able to keep from driving his fist into to the kid's mouth. "Will you shut up and tell me where Victoria is."

He pointed again as two men attached a wooden ramp. "She's been riding in there since she made me buy the damn—"

Hee-haw, hee-haw. Ryder swung around. The piercing sound reverberated in the wooden car.

Percy? No. Percy was at home in the corral. Then what the—

"Ryder!" Victoria appeared in the doorway, waving her arm, a broad smile radiating from her face. She was a burst of sunshine, standing there, a beautiful vision in a yellow dress with lace and green trim, and a tiny hat perched perfectly on top of her head.

The knot of tension in his chest melted under her radiance. He started forward, his long legs eating up the distance. He reached the bottom of the ramp the same time she did.

"I missed you so much." She threw her arms around his neck.

Like a magnet, his mouth sought hers as he wrapped his arms around her and lifted her right off the walk. He couldn't get enough of her, the weight of her in his arms, the faint lemon scent of her skin, the whisper of her breath on his cheek and the taste of her as their tongues twined. He sucked in her very essence unable to let her go.

Beside them, Spencer coughed discreetly.

She pushed at his shoulders and he set down. She staggered back a step, one hand on her tiny hat, which for some reason looked quite crumpled. Where there once must have been flowers there were now only stems.

"Tori, what happened to your hat? And why are you riding—"

Hee-haw, hee-haw.

"Oh, I hope you don't mind, but this horrid man in Omaha was beating her with a board."

Ryder lifted his gaze to the cavernous opening. There was another sharp bang.

"I'm afraid she has a tendency to kick, but wouldn't you if someone hit you with a board?"

He blinked. Another mule. A kicking, braying, long-eared goddamn mule.

"Do you mind?" She lifted her gaze to his. Her big blue eyes wide and earnest.

And suddenly he didn't mind. Nothing mattered except that she was here. She had come back. "No," he said.

"Oh thank you." She threw her arms around him. "I love you so much!"

From the way she smiled at him, he could have just laid the fortune of a kingdom at her feet.

"Let me get her, so we can go home." She turned and started up the ramp.

He heard it then, a familiar soft chinking sound.

Beside him Spencer heaved a weighted sigh. "I can't believe she wore them under her dress," he muttered. "She even insisted on buying a pair of boots. I mean, what kind of woman wears spurs with hearts?"

A word about the author...

Kathy Otten began making up stories as soon as she learned to write. Growing up on TV westerns and John Wayne movies, Kathy naturally began to read then write westerns. Fascinated by the historical detail and accuracy of Louis L'Amour's books, she delved into the world of research and discovered what a fun treasure hunt it could be.

A Tarnished Knight is Kathy's third full-length novel and she has already started researching her fourth.

She loves hearing from readers, and you may contact her through her website

www.kathyotten.com

on Facebook at

facebook.com/kathyottenauthor

or follow her on

Twitter.com/kathyotten

Thank you for purchasing
this publication of The Wild Rose Press, Inc.
For other wonderful stories of romance,
please visit our on-line bookstore at
www.thewildrosepress.com.

For questions or more information
contact us at
info@thewildrosepress.com.

The Wild Rose Press, Inc.
www.thewildrosepress.com

To visit with authors of
The Wild Rose Press, Inc.
join our yahoo loop at
http://groups.yahoo.com/group/thewildrosepress/